**Praise for Daryl Wood Gerber's .**

"Plenty of suspects, gardening tips, and fairy lore combine for a sweet treat."
—***Kirkus Reviews***

"*A Glimmer of a Clue* is an enchanting and delightful combination of the whimsical and the cozy mystery genre itself."
—**Fresh Fiction**

"Enchanting series launch from Agatha Award–winner Gerber. . . . Cozy fans will wish upon a star for more."
—***Publishers Weekly***

"Likable characters, including several who should continue to play roles in future investigations, and an entertaining but not-too-intrusive fairy connection make this a winner. There is a useful list of characters and recipes. Fans of Laura Childs' work will enjoy Gerber's new series."
—***Booklist***

"Daryl Wood Gerber's new fantasy cozy series debut is full of fun, whimsy, and a baffling whodunit. . . . After finishing the book fans might want to try their hand at making their own fairy garden, or test the delectable recipes in the back of the book. And of course, readers will already impatiently be waiting for book number two. Fans of fantasy cozy series and this author will absolutely love this bestseller-bound tale."
—***Mystery Scene***

**Kensington books by Daryl Wood Gerber**

The Aroma Wellness Mystery series

*Essence of Foul Play*

The Literary Dining Mystery series

*Murder on the Page*

The Fairy Garden Mystery series

*A Sprinkling of Murder*

*A Glimmer of a Clue*

*A Hint of Mischief*

*A Flicker of a Doubt*

*A Twinkle of Trouble*

# Essence of Foul Play

Daryl Wood Gerber

Kensington Publishing Corp.
kensingtonbooks.com

KENSINGTON BOOKS are published by

Kensington Publishing Corp.
900 Third Avenue
New York, NY 10022



ISBN: 978-1-4967-5151-5 (ebook)

ISBN: 978-1-4967-5150-8

First Kensington Trade Paperback Printing: April 2025

10 9 8 7 6 5 4 3 2 1

Printed in the United States of America

*To Hannah Xiomara Charlotte Gerber-Klein,*
*the newest young lady in my life,*
*for bringing joy and delight.*
*I treasure your sweet smile.*

*The energy of the mind is the essence of life.*

—Aristotle

# Cast of Characters

**Humans:**

Ava Daft, shop owner
Brady Cash, café owner
Courtney Kelly, fairy garden shop owner
Dottie, neighbor
Dylan Summers, detective
Emma Brennan, spa owner
Floyd Marblemaw, reporter
Ginnie Sperling, visitor
Hedda Hopewell, bank lender
Hugh Ashbluff, real estate investor
Indy Hendriks, clothing shop owner
Jason Sampson, spa employee
Kate Brennan, Emma's mother
Lissa Reade, librarian
Mah Kim, Meryl's mother
Meryl Kim, spa employee
Naomi Clutterbuck, language teacher
Olivia Pilsner, daughter of Palmer
Palmer Pilsner, tennis enthusiast
Quinlyn Obermeyer, shop owner
Sierra Reade, Emma's cousin
Sophie Reade, Emma's aunt
Teresa Rodriguez, officer
Tish Waterman, owner of A Peaceful Solution Spa
Ursula Josipovic, fortune teller
Violet Vickers, theater patron
Willow Shafer, owner of Mystic Waters Spa

Yoly Acebo, spa employee
Zinnia Walker, wealthy Carmelite

**Fairies and Animals:**

Fiona, a righteous fairy
Merryweather Rose of Song, a guardian fairy
Ulra, a nurturer fairy
Vivi, Emma's cat

# Chapter 1

"Emma, your new place is wonderful!" Nana Lissa exclaimed. I'd just finished giving her a tour of the interior of Aroma Wellness Spa as well as the café and the gift shop. Slowly, she spun in a circle and drank in the exterior courtyard, with its stone wishing well, burbling fountain, and gardenias. "You've done a remarkable job."

"Thank you, Nana," I murmured. "I couldn't have completed it without you." To her patrons at the Harrison Library, my grandmother was Lissa or Ms. Reade, the head librarian with a staff devoted to helping people find the right books.. To me, she'd always been Nana Lissa or Nana, the woman who believed in spirits and fairies and taught me to dream big. I sure hoped, this time, I wasn't dreaming too big.

"I love the slogans you posted around the spa," she went on.

I grinned. I happened to be a positive-sayings freak. I'd written many on notecards as well as at the spa and at home. That way I could draw inspiration from them when I needed to keep myself on track. Nana was referring to the few I'd printed and framed.

"I love *Immerse in Wellness* and *Indulge in You*," she said, "but my favorite is *Experience Wellness and Wonder.*" She placed a hand on her chest. "I'm breathing easier already."

I'd done a deep dive on the internet to find exactly the right catchphrases.

"I've told everyone in Carmel about the grand opening tomorrow," she said. Carmel-by-the-Sea, a gorgeous town on the coast of California, was the perfect location for a spa. It was an intensely spiritual place that radiated good vibes. "And I've reposted all your memes on Instagram."

For weeks, I'd been creating digital art to boost our presence.

"You could do well with a TikTok campaign," she said. "If you haven't put one together, I can help." My grandmother could navigate social media like a pro. She said her patrons at the library were educating her. "Having the opening on a Wednesday is perfect. Everyone looks forward to a midweek break."

That's what I'd thought, too. In the morning, we would serve goodies to entice people to drop in. The therapists would explain their techniques and styles, and I would talk up the meditation sessions. In the afternoon, the first round of treatments would begin.

"Now, give your old grandmother a hug for good luck." Nana extended her arms.

"Old, ha!"

Nana didn't look like a stereotypical grandmother. She was spry and lean and was stylishly dressed. Her short-cropped silver hair was always neat, unlike my tawny shoulder-length hair, which I swept into a clip or ponytail because it was baby fine, and it snarled if the weather was cool, like now in June, when the marine layer blanketed the coastline until midafternoon.

"The travertine tile turned out nicely," she said, "and the wrought-iron tables on the patio are chic but casual. Very in keeping with your go-with-the-flow vibe. Did I tell you that I love the plate-glass windows? A direct view into the reception area is very inviting."

I smiled. Her enthusiasm was infusing me with confidence.

"Are all the bugaboos taken care of?" she asked. "We don't want any snafus."

"All handled." Of course there were a number of little nits that needed addressing. Any new business ran into roadblocks. Like massage oils that hadn't arrived or singing bowls that had been delayed in customs but were due to arrive today. No matter the hiccup, I couldn't let a few of them get me down. I was an upbeat person who saw possibility in a challenge.

Okay, sure, occasionally I floundered.

"Thank you again," I said, my voice thick with emotion. My grandmother was the sole reason I was able to open my business. Not many in town knew it, but my grandfather, may he rest in peace, had amassed quite a fortune over the years, having been a consultant for some bigwig companies. Nana could retire anytime with the sizable portfolio he'd left her, but she intended to work at the library until she dropped. Rather than blow her money on cruises and the like, she'd invested in me and my adorable cousin, Sierra Reade, who was one year older than me. Nana had supported my post-college trip to Tibet to study meditative arts and had covered my classes to obtain my aesthetician and massage therapist licenses. She'd also paid for Sierra to attend the Culinary Institute of America. Throughout our journeys away from Carmel, she'd sent each of us articles from the *Carmel Pine Cone*, the local paper, telling us what our friends were up to, to keep us current and engaged.

I said, "I can't tell you how much I appreciate your support."

"You're my best investment."

In addition to providing funding, she had found this courtyard, prophetically dubbed the Courtyard of Peace—Carmel had a number of unique and beautiful courtyards and secret passageways—and she'd negotiated the lease for all the shop spaces that bordered it. Plus, she'd arranged for the state licenses I'd needed for the spa, café, and gift shop. I'd worked out the business plan. I'd also come up with the blue-and-sea-green color palette and the logo, and I'd hired the photographer for our brochures and designed the spa treatments menu.

"How did those coupons for girls your age work out?" Nana asked.

*Girls my age.* I chuckled. I was twenty-four and way past girlhood. "Great. It was a brilliant suggestion on your part." The spa was offering discounts for anybody under thirty, because many might not have the financial wherewithal to pay for treatments that wealthier people in Carmel did, yet I wanted them to feel beautiful and *heard.* "I've handed out a dozen or so. Word of mouth will help."

"Emma Brennan!" a woman yelled shrilly. "What in the heck do you think you're doing?" Willow Shafer stomped up the steps. In her espadrilles, she was taller than me by four inches, and I was no slouch at five foot six. She pointed at the new signage. "How dare you open a spa!"

Honestly? She knew I was doing so. I'd told her. Multiple times. As recently as a week ago, when we'd met for a glass of wine, I'd outlined the details. I'd also explained how mine was different from hers and how we wouldn't be competing, given our facilities were located on opposite sides of Ocean Avenue.

"Careful on the steps," I cautioned.

Carmel had some crazy citywide rules, like you couldn't wear high heels without a permit, an odd law authored way back in October 1963 by the city attorney to defend the town from lawsuits resulting from the irregular pavement distorted by tree roots—a law Willow apparently didn't abide by or, conceivably, she thought espadrilles didn't qualify as heels. Maybe she'd applied for a permit.

"Don't worry. I'm fine," she said. "They're not cobblestone."

They had been. When we'd negotiated the lease, the steps had matched the sidewalk, but knowing bumpy pavers could be perilous for customers, we'd switched them out for smooth tile.

"Willow," I said gently.

"Don't try to manage me, Emma."

When I met Willow in my freshman year of college at a gathering to support women's rights, the first thing I'd noticed about her were her brown eyes. They tilted downward even when she smiled. I'd also noted her nose was too big for her face, although I'd never told her that, not even after she stole my boyfriend in junior year. Willow did have a gorgeously long neck that she highlighted by pulling her ebony hair into a knot and wearing big gold hoops to draw attention to it.

"What made you possibly think that this . . . this . . ." She tapped her foot trying to come up with a word. Willow hadn't been the best of students. "That this atrocity could be a success?"

Nana Lissa cut in, "Aroma Wellness is far from an atrocity, young lady. The calming ocean tones of the massage and various therapy rooms walls are perfect. The sound bath room, which will also serve as the meditation room, has been soundproofed."

"To the max," I added. For the uninitiated, a sound bath was a meditative experience where attendees were awash in sound waves. It was super relaxing.

"And the white bistro tables and seating in the café look perfect against the sea-green background," Nana added.

"Willow," I said, "you know my grandmother, Lissa Reade."

"I go to the library," Willow snapped. "Of course I know her. And don't squint like that, Emma. You'll get wrinkles."

For someone who claimed she meditated often, Willow sure could be abrupt. A tart comment was never far from her lips. I blinked to release the tension creeping into my temples and forehead.

"Mystic Waters is the destination spa in Carmel," Willow continued, her know-it-all tone grating on my sensibilities.

According to her, her spa, which she'd opened two years ago, had the best treatments in town. In my opinion, what she offered was limited. Massages, scalp treatments, and seaweed wraps alone did not soothe the soul. Sometimes a customer needed alternative cures, like sound baths and aromatherapy. For years, my aunt, who owned a high-end spa in Sedona, had drummed into me that a spa owner had to study her clientele to know which treatment was best for them. We weren't psychotherapists, she said, and the mind didn't necessarily need to be picked apart. However, the body needed to chill. Often.

"Willow, I love your outfit," I said to defuse her ire. I wasn't lying. She deserved this compliment. She'd donned a chic, multicolored sheath that hugged her lean form. "Geometric patterns suit you."

"Oh, can it, Emma. You'd love anything I put on because you have no flair."

Ouch. That stung, but I pushed the slight aside. Willow couldn't help herself. In college, she'd considered herself the foremost expert on good taste and had nagged me repeatedly about style and fashion. I didn't wear trendy clothes. My bangs weren't the right length. Nevertheless, to this day, she considered me one of her best friends. Why, was beyond me. After graduation, I'd tried my darnedest to put distance between us, but she'd followed me to Carmel. She'd tell you otherwise because, when she made the move, I was off in Tibet doing an intensive meditation course. But I was from Carmel and had always planned to settle here. She had not.

"I'm warning you, shut this place down or else," Willow ordered.

"Willow," Nana Lissa began.

I put a hand on her arm. My grandmother didn't have a temper, but she was a wordsmith extraordinaire. I didn't want her to say something she might regret.

"Did you tell Tish Waterman to shut down, Willow?" I asked sweetly. "I heard she wasn't happy that you opened a spa when hers was the premier, go-to place in Carmel." Tish's spa, located a few blocks east of the Courtyard of Peace, not far from Mystic Waters, offered some wonderful treatments, but there was no café, dining patio, or retail shop, and Tish would never offer the New Age–type treatments that Aroma Wellness would. To get in her good graces and, thanks to the counsel of the wise woman who owned a nearby fairy garden shop, I'd met with Tish to show her my business plan. After accepting how different our models were, Tish had been quite supportive, saying she certainly couldn't provide services for everyone in town.

Willow shook a finger at me. "I hope your opening day is a bust."

"I appreciate your good wishes," I said cheerily. In Tibet, I'd learned to counter an attack with a benign response. It wasn't exactly the tried-and-true, "I'm rubber and you're glue" retort, but it worked. As Maya Angelou would say, "It takes courage to be kind." The Dalai Lama went a step further. "Be kind whenever possible. It is always possible."

"And lose these!" Willow pulled an under-thirty coupon from her pocket and hurled it at me. "Discounts belittle the product."

"Willow," Nana said, "a meditation might—"

"Forget meditation!" She scuttled down the steps at such a pace I worried she'd trip, but she didn't.

At the bottom, she ran into an older, hunchbacked man in a rumpled brown suit and fedora. He had a downtrodden demeanor. If he were standing tall, he would have dwarfed her. Scraggly hair poked from beneath his hat. I heard him apologize and heard Willow utter, "You!" but she didn't pause. She hurried away.

The man gazed at me. I didn't recognize him, although he looked sort of familiar. It was his eyes, I decided. He reminded me of my math teacher in high school who also had sad-as-a-hound-dog's eyes.

He climbed the steps and said, "Got a sec for an interview for the *Carmel Pine Cone*, Miss Brennan?" He raised a pocket-size leather notepad holder in one hand and pulled a pen from the attached loop.

Aha. He was a reporter. “Sorry, no,” I said. “I’m on a strict timetable.”

“It’s about women entrepreneurs. I want to get the inside scoop on the rivalry between you and Miss Shafer.”

“There is no rivalry,” Nana Lissa stated.

“She’s right.” Not on my end, anyway.

“Miss Shafer would beg to differ,” he said. Had he already questioned Willow? Was that why she’d been dismissive of him? Had he followed her here in order to take pictures of us arguing? Were images going to go viral?

Even though the adage was *All publicity is good publicity,* I didn’t want bad vibes hovering around my personal space. “How about next week after we open, Mr. . . .”

“Marblemaw. Floyd Marblemaw.” His veiny face pinched with pain. Or was it guilt? Maybe he’d given me a phony name.

“Next week sometime,” I said.

He tipped his pen to the brim of his fedora. “Good day, Emma Brennan, and you”—he gestured to my grandmother—“whoever you are.”

As he shuffled away. I turned to Nana Lissa and attempted a smile.

“*Phew!* That man!” She brushed my shoulders with her fingertips, as she had my entire life, to rid me of any negativity. “And Willow? What a force. She could do with a sprinkling of fairy dust, don’t you think?”

I frowned at her. “You know I haven’t seen a fairy—”

“Don’t say you don’t believe.” She held up a finger. “Do. Not.”

“Oh, I believe in them. I simply haven’t seen one. I would like to.” I’d heard about the fairy inhabitants of Carmel. With its gorgeous rolling hills, lush valleys, and ocean coastline, it was the perfect locale for magical beings to thrive. I was surprised I’d never encountered one, especially since I tuned into all sorts of supercharged energy for my profession.

"Be patient. You'll meet one." She chucked my chin. "By the way, Thursday evening, I'll be having the monthly meeting for my book club. You should attend. Do some networking."

I clicked my tongue. "Will it be a laid-back-but-everything-is-perfect meeting, in keeping with your new coastal granny persona?"

"Get out of here!" She guffawed. "I'm far from perfect."

The view from Nana Lissa's house was of the Pacific Ocean, and I often teased her that after Papa died, she'd become a coastal grandmother, a term first used by a TikTok influencer, one suggesting a comfortable, chic lifestyle as exemplified by women in Nancy Meyers's movies. Light-filled rooms, fresh flowers, tons of books, and neutral hues were Nana's go-to décor.

"FYI, I've comped each of the attendees a session at the spa in the coming weeks," my grandmother continued. "If they love their treatments, word will travel fast."

"Thank you!" Her book club was populated by some of the wealthiest women in town. "What's the book you're discussing?"

"*The Big Sleep,* a mystery I know you've read."

"It's not simply a mystery. It's the first in a series of eight by Raymond Chandler's Philip Marlowe series."

She smiled. "I knew there was a reason I liked you."

I laughed. Thanks to her, I loved to read. I'd bet she kept a running list of every book I'd ever devoured.

"How is Sierra working out?" Nana asked. "I haven't seen her in weeks."

"Great!"

For the past two years, Sierra had been languishing as a sous-chef at a local vegan restaurant, but now, thanks to our grandmother, she was my business partner, and I couldn't wait to show off her gastronomic skills at the spa's café. We were best buds and as close as sisters.

"Is she still wearing that nose ring?" Nana Lissa asked.

"Don't be judgy." I winked at her.

"I'm not. I was asking."

"Yes, she is. It's not permanent. It's a fake clip-on." I wiggled my nose in jest. "Hey, have you checked out her Instagram page?" I trilled, "Awesome!"

"Good to know. Is she, um, calm?"

"Calmer than calm," I said, hoping that was true. Sierra could be frenetic. Working in kitchens ramped up her energy twentyfold because she had to react quickly to dodge staff, hot plates, boiling oil, and more.

I turned to peek in on her through the café windows, but paused when I caught a glimpse of someone standing on the street peering up the stairs at us. It was Palmer Pilsner, a forty-something socialite who regularly held bake sales to help fund Carmel's educational facilities. She played tennis when she wasn't donating her time. She was also an artist. I'd seen her hawking her seascape watercolors at a plein-air festival, but as far as I knew, she had yet to sell one.

"Hello, Palmer!" I yelled. "Come on up and take a peek."

"No, that's all right." She shoved a postcard into her tennis bag. "Have you seen Willow Shafer? The shopkeeper next to her spa said she was coming your way."

"You just missed her," Nana Lissa said. "You must have taken different routes."

Palmer wore her red hair in a blunt style that Raggedy Ann would approve of. Her white-on-blue tennis outfit showed off her toned frame. If I had her legs, I'd consider running marathons. And her arms? They were the kind star athletes dreamed of having. "Why was she here, Emma? Was she miffed about you opening . . . this?" She gesticulated to the signage as Willow had done.

"This beautiful, enticing, good-for-the-soul spa?" I replied.

Palmer didn't respond to my comeback. To be fair, it wasn't a comeback. It was a passive-aggressive taunt. I'd had enough of people giving me guff about opening another spa. Mine was going to be different, and between the residents and tourists, we had plenty of people in Carmel to keep all of the spas humming.

"Coupon," my grandmother said to me under her breath.

"Would you like a coupon for a discounted treatment, Palmer?" I asked. During opening week, for everyone of all ages, I'd designed ten-percent–off coupons. I dug into the side pocket of my leggings and pulled one out. "The prickly pear massage is to die for. The antioxidants and the vitamin K that the prickly pear oil contains rejuvenate the skin while neutralizing free radicals that cause—"

"No, thanks. I don't . . ." She chewed the tip of her tongue. "No."

What a shame. She could use a treatment that would relax those tight shoulders. "Why did you need to see Willow?" I asked. It wasn't like they were friends.

"I wanted to chat."

"What about?" my grandmother asked. She wasn't nosy by nature, but she did like to draw people out.

"It'll wait."

"Coming to the library soon, Palmer?" Nana Lissa asked.

"We'll see."

Palmer pivoted and bumped smack into Yoly Acebo, the delightful Latina woman who was going to run the gift shop. Both women wheezed from the collision. Palmer apologized. So did Yoly. Then Palmer skedaddled. Was she in a hurry to get to a tennis match or was she worried she might get cooties by being in the vicinity of the spa?

I tamped down a giggle.

"Sorry I'm late." Yoly trotted up the stairs while knotting her long brown hair into a messy bun. She used to work at Open Your Imagination, the aforementioned fairy garden shop, tending the sales counter and occasionally serving the shop's Saturday tea events, but now, having given up on botany as a career—she'd toyed with the idea for a nanosecond—she was working toward getting her massage therapist's license and really wanted to be a hands-on person. To entice her to join my team, I'd offered her the gift shop position. When she did become a therapist, I would facilitate a lateral move, and she could bring the new gift shop person up to speed. It would be a win-win for both of us. "*Hola*, Lissa, nice to see you!" Yoly was a patron of the library.

"Hello, sweet girl." Nana gave Yoly a kiss on her cheek. "Did you finish *Maybe Someday*?"

Yoly pressed a hand to her chest. "I couldn't put it down." Her easy smile was infectious, and her caramel-brown eyes sparkled with warmth. She said to me, "Emma, you would love it. It's about this woman whose boyfriend cheats on her, but there's this handsome neighbor who plays guitar. When the two of them get together . . ." She flicked her hands to suggest fireworks.

"Don't give the story away," Lissa chided. "I want my granddaughter to read it."

I studied my grandmother's face. Did she hope that if I read the book I might try to reignite things with my previous boyfriend? She had liked him a lot, and, sure, he was swoon-worthy, but he'd walked out on me. I would not beg. And honestly, I didn't miss him. Not a whit.

"Emma," Yoly said, "you should join the Bookworms. We're young females who read books that help us with the journey we are taking to become our most authentic selves."

"I'll think about it." *Not*. I had a business to run and no time for psychotherapy or book clubs other than the occasional drop-in to Nana's. Whenever I read a book, it was for relaxation and enjoyment.

A delivery truck with no driver's door pulled up to the curb with a screech. The brawny driver set the brake, left the engine running, and hopped out. He pulled a dolly from the rear of the truck. "Aroma Wellness?" he bellowed.

"Up here!" I replied. Our herb-adorned sign was easy to spot, but he was studying a clipboard.

His gaze went from the steps to the courtyard and back to his dolly, and he frowned. With a grunt, he hoisted a square box, which was easily two feet by two feet, and trotted up the steps. "Three more boxes to go," he announced.

He set the box down and returned for the next one. On his second trip, he caught his toe on a stair, and the box went flying.

The sound of shattering glass—*crack, crunch*—sent a chill through me.

*It's not an omen,* I told myself. *It's not. You are not doomed to fail.*

# Chapter 2

My mother's words of caution clanged in my head. *Starting a business like yours is a risk.* Implied was that I'd be unsuccessful. *I only have your best interests at heart,* she'd added. Her constant focus on me, her only child, developed after my father left to live the life of a world-renowned do-gooder. *You'll be better off doing what I do, teaching literature,* she said when I showed her my business plan. *Literature is brain food.* Though I couldn't disagree—my mother and I did love to read—I could never teach English. No way. My resolve strengthened when she'd added, *This spa thing . . . it's a pipe dream.*

"Don't go there, Emma," my grandmother said, cutting into my thoughts. "Do not allow you-know-who's negativity to seep in." For years she'd referred to my mother, her eldest child, as you-know-who. She loved my mother, but they could butt heads. "No one died. A few bowls broke. Big deal. Has your father called to congratulate you yet?" she asked to divert me.

"No. He won't until after tomorrow." He and I were close, though rarely in the same country at the same time. I'd written him emails to keep him in the loop about every step of my enterprise. When we'd spoken a few weeks earlier, he was excited to hear more and made me promise to send pictures.

"Breathe!" my grandmother ordered, and showed me how.

I mimicked her, inhaling and holding the breath for a count of three and releasing it for a count of six while doing my best not to glower at the delivery guy. After all, he was so upset with himself that he looked like he might dissolve into tears.

"What the heck?" Sierra burst from the café and stared at the mess.

"Broom," Nana ordered.

My cousin returned in seconds with a broom and dustpan. I took them from her and began to clean up.

"What happened?" With her slender, narrow face and strawberry-blond straight hair that she wore super long and pulled into a ponytail when in the kitchen, Sierra resembled an elf in *Lord of the Rings*. A way shorter elf. The sea-green-and-white–striped apron she was wearing over her white blouse and trousers reached her knees. It would hit me midthigh.

"He caught his toe on the stair," I said, motioning to the delivery guy.

Sierra said, "Steps can be hazardous. If our patrons—"

"Relax," I said. "Our clients won't be running up them full steam, and most of them will be wearing flats. Plus, we're insured."

*"Phew,"* she rasped.

Of course, we had a deductible to meet regarding property damage, but we'd get some compensation for the singing bowls. They were not cheap.

"I'll be right back with a claim form," the deliveryman said, and darted around the mess to his vehicle.

The remaining boxes of bowls arrived safely, and as I filled out the claim form, Yoly and Sierra carried the boxes into the spa and gift shop. Twenty of the singing bowls would be placed in the sound bath therapy room. The rest would be available for sale at the shop.

"Got the jitters, Emma?" Sierra asked.

"No."

She gave me an all-knowing look.

"Maybe a little bit," I said. "Okay, a lot."

"It's gonna be great." She bumped my hip with hers. "Promise. This is the storm before the calm."

An hour later, as I was eyeing the fitness dice on my desk, contemplating whether I needed to coax myself into a set of sit-ups or straight-leg jackknifes, Sierra bolted into my office.

"Emma, help! The grocery guy couldn't provide strawberries. Something happened to a shipment. I absolutely have to have berries for the strawberry-açai refresher smoothie. It's going to be a fan favorite. But I can't leave the café." She waved her arms this way and that, reminding me of the Scarecrow in *The Wizard of Oz*. "We have other deliveries, and I'm set to interview one of the waitstaff. Can you go to Fruit Farm? Pretty please?"

"Sure," I said, relieved I didn't have to exercise. To be honest, I wasn't an exercise enthusiast. I liked an occasional run on the beach barefoot, but a daily routine wasn't for me. Hence, the dice. "How many do you need?"

I smiled when she gave me a written list. An extensive written list.

I hurried to the public parking lot on 8th Avenue, not far from the Village Shops where I'd parked earlier, and had the keys to my Land Rover in hand when I noticed an altercation outside Mystic Waters.

Willow was yelling at Hugh Ashbluff, a forty-something real estate mogul who at any given time had a dozen houses for sale as well as rental properties and apartment complexes to let. How he juggled it all was amazing. He swiped the air in front of Willow's face and added a few choice words of his own. Given the way they were going at it, I wasn't sure either could hear the other's argument.

Suddenly, Hugh raised a hand. I happened to know that brawny muscles were lurking beneath the sleeves of his shirt. Though he now sported a sad-sack professorial look, complete with raggedy bangs and a cowlick, at one time he'd been quite the baseball player. According to Nana Lissa, he could have made it in the minors, but his father had forbidden it. Why did parents quash their children's dreams?

Willow held her arms up in defense. I wasn't generally nosy, but far be it from me to allow Hugh to strike her. I made a detour in their direction. Willow caught sight of me and waved for me to stay away.

Hugh spotted me, too, and lowered his arm, but he continued his harangue. "You're late on the rent again," he bellowed. "Payment was due last week."

"Business has been slow," she stated.

"Well, I don't care. I'm reclaiming the property. You have three days to vacate."

Yipes. That didn't sound good.

"Now, hold on, Hugh," she said. "You promised me a lease option."

A lease option was a contract in which a landlord and tenant agreed that, at the end of a specified period, the tenant could buy the property at a preset price.

"Which would be valid if you made payments on time," Hugh said, "but you've defaulted."

"You agreed at the start that if I paid within seven days of the due date—"

"Not on every payment. If you don't pay by sundown Thursday, you're out."

"That's not three days!"

I squinted as I processed their exchange. Why was Willow late every month? Was her business suffering? Was that why she'd been crusty to me at Aroma Wellness earlier? Or was she merely a dawdler who couldn't do anything in a timely fashion? One of my best friends in high school never handed in her paperwork by the due date. She claimed she'd inherited a procrastination gene from her father.

"Oh, no!" a woman cried at the sound of coins hitting pavement.

I spun around and saw Ava Daft trying to pick up the coins she'd dropped near a parking meter but failing because she had ultralong nails. They were painted sparkly blue and complemented her navy-blue leggings and crop top. I rushed to help her.

"Thanks, Emma," Ava said. "Am I a klutz or what?" She used a knuckle to push a dime into her palm. "I hate meters. Why can't we do away with them?"

"Not enough parking to go around," I said, dumping two nickels into her palm alongside the dime.

"All ready for the grand opening tomorrow?" Ava was late twenties, a few years older than me, with long brown hair and a toothy smile. She had inherited her grandparents' collectibles shop, Shabby Chic Nook, which was where we'd met. I loved browsing all the shops in Carmel, particularly ones that sold unique Carmel-themed art or jewelry. "Quinlyn and I are looking forward to Friday's avocado facials." Quinlyn was Ava's business partner as well as her life partner. "It'll be my first ever."

Avocados were great for moisturizing the skin. In one of the free do-it-yourself classes I intended to teach—I'd give the classes monthly as a way to drum up new business—I would show students how to make the mask at home.

"Will you be giving us the facials?" she asked. "Quinlyn booked them but didn't say."

"I will." I'd hired a couple of masseuses and a facialist, but I would give occasional treatments to people I knew. "How is Quinlyn?" I asked. Ava and she had been together for about a year.

"As crazy about beach jogging as ever." Ava fed the meter. "I don't understand why she likes to run and sweat."

*Probably to watch her weight,* I mused. Quinlyn was pleasingly zaftig but always complaining about needing to lose a few pounds. "You perspire doing Pilates," I reasoned.

"Barely." Ava was avid about keeping fit. A Barbie doll couldn't have a shapelier figure. She hitched her chin in the direction of Hugh and Willow. "What's the beef?"

"Willow is late on the rent."

At that moment, Hugh raised his voice and said that he was going to sue Willow.

Ava's eyes lit up. "Could her space be coming up for lease? You know I'd hoped to get it, but she outbid me. I want to expand."

Retail property in Carmel was dear. There were always new businesses waiting in the wings to swoop in on a deal. Ava's shop was on Ocean Avenue, in a prime location, but it was teensy, and rumor had it that the lessor wanted to rebuild and was going to end all the leases in the next year, meaning Ava would need to relocate.

"I doubt Willow is going anywhere," I said. "She and Hugh are simply negotiating."

"Rats," she muttered, but quickly had the decency to blanch. "Not that I wish her ill, of course."

*Of course.*

Ava peered at Willow and Hugh for a tad longer before moseying into Yarn Diva, a nearby knitting shop.

By the time I returned to the spa with Sierra's goods, it was close to four. To make sure everything was ready for tomorrow's opening, I fetched my iPad and went through the spa, room by room. Throughout my life, Nana Lissa had drummed into me: *Check a list once. Check it twice.*

The café had turned out as I'd hoped. Tulip-shaped pendant lights were suspended over the sit-down counter. On the sage-green accent wall behind the counter hung a huge chalkboard with the day's specialty drinks, including açai refreshers, kale smoothies, and immune-system shot drinks. There were also meals that would do the body good, like sesame-encrusted seared tuna, turmeric-and-chicken curry, and an iceberg-and-veggies salad with oregano dressing. I checked the undersides of all the chairs and tables making sure there were no telltale tags on them—clear. Then I examined the walk-in refrigerator—neat as a pin. And the small kitchen where Sierra was baking up some delicious, good-for-you sweets made with organic honey—spotless and orderly. She loved a clean kitchen.

I took a few photographs, posted them on the spa's Instagram account, and crossed the courtyard to the gift shop. "Yoly, how's it going?"

"*Excelente*," she said in her native tongue. "The register is filled with cash. The books you ordered have all arrived and are arranged alphabetically. The plants, though few, are gorgeous."

The walls of the shop were a soft mossy green. On the shelves were dozens of books about essential oils and how to find bliss. We sold wind chimes and small gongs and Chinese stress-reducing Baoding balls in velvet boxes. My favorites of those were the ones with the hummingbird design on them. We also carried geodes and crystals in their basic forms and crystal shapes, like crescent moons, stars, and obelisks. In addition, I'd decided to offer a few bonsai trees to those who might want a pretty plant to go with a Zen meditation garden.

"The bowls look beautiful, don't you think?" She gestured like a TV model.

The singing bowls that were for sale were arranged by height—tallest on the left to shorter on the right. We'd decided on glass shelving so that the undersides of the bowls could be seen from below. Elegantly embossed price tags stood beside each one. There would be no confusion as to cost. No bargaining permitted.

Standing in the middle of the shop, drinking in the joy I was feeling while wrangling with the butterflies in my stomach, I latched onto the idea of putting together a peace offering basket for Willow. Sure, she was upset with me right now, worried that I'd steal her clientele, but I truly believed Carmel was big enough for all of us. As my grandmother often reminded me, the town seemed like a small tight-knit community, but it was overflowing with tourists, and tourists craved luxuries of all kinds. I made a mental note that if the spa was successful and for some reason teeming with customers, I would steer some Willow's way.

"Help me assemble a gift basket," I said to Yoly. "Hand me that candlestick."

We'd opted to stock tooled brass candlesticks that would hold three- and six-inch aromatic pillars. My preference was the lavender candle, but Nana's favorite was vanilla, and Sierra couldn't pass up the cinnamon one. Willow, I decided, might enjoy the one that smelled like plumerias. When we were in college, she'd taken up the habit of pinning a silk version of the flower in her hair, saying it was a Hawaiian tradition, and she'd always wanted to visit Hawaii.

I collected the candle and a couple of my handmade sachets, a gardenia bonsai, a pair of exfoliating bath mitts, and a jar of plumeria body scrub and inserted them into a natural basket. I looped a beautiful green bow around the handle and whispered, "Perfect." If I couldn't win her over with this beauty, she was an ice queen.

My cell phone buzzed with a text message. Nana Lissa was inviting Sierra and me to dinner at Hideaway Café at six thirty. To relax. I replied *yes* with a kiss emoji. Sierra bowed out. She had a previous engagement that she couldn't break. Next, I made a tour of the spa, double-checking that the towels were in place and the essential oils aligned. I wasn't a perfectionist, but I didn't want a thing to go wrong tomorrow. Not a thing.

When my inspection was complete, I walked to the reception area and examined it in detail. The skylight provided exactly the right amount of sunlight. The brass-and-hardwood check-in desk was polished to a shine. The beverage cart to the right of the desk held glasses and a pitcher for ice water, an urn for coffee, another for hot water, and a tea caddy with accoutrements. We would fill the beverage containers first thing in the morning. The giant ferns in the soft green ceramic pots that flanked the entry were magnificent. The rack of health-and-wellness–style magazines that customers could browse before their appointments was tidy. The pair of sea-blue-and-sea-green armchairs begged someone to sit in them. A two-minute refresher meditation, eyes closed, was in order before I raced home to change for dinner.

Seconds after I sat down, the soft chime over the entrance pinged. Darn. I thought I'd locked the door. I bolted to my feet and met the judgmental stare of my mother.

"Darling," she said, stepping inside.

I smoothed the front of my draped T-shirt out of habit. I didn't look sloppy, but something about facing my mother made me jittery. Maybe it was because she was a perfectionist. Perhaps it was because she always looked flawless, as she did now in a tailored jacket, silk blouse, and slacks, her fawn-brown hair recently coifed to outline her face. A professor of her standing, she said, needed to exude confidence or her students wouldn't engage, and she eagerly wanted them to be engrossed. She adored her students. She loved me, too, but we were extremely different.

She eyeballed my yoga pants and sandals—the kinds with boat-shaped soles that made my feet rock from heel to toe in one smooth motion—and I cringed. Her shoes weren't as expensive as red-soled Christian Louboutin heels, but close.

"Well, I see you're going through with it." Frowning, she took in the scope of the spa. "You listened to your aunt and your nana instead of your mama."

My mother—Kate Brennan—had never been Mama. Ever. I had gotten away with calling her Mommy when I was younger, but she'd put the kibosh on that when I turned twelve, saying she preferred Mother or Kate.

"How are you?" I asked, and pecked her on the cheek.

"As busy as ever." Kate was forty-eight years old and looked great. She kept herself in shape. Her skin was pristine. She never went outside without donning sunscreen. "Will Sophie be here to cheer you on tomorrow?"

Sophie—my mother's older sister and my charming aunt—was a thorn in my mother's side. Like me, Sophie had always found calm in nature and spirituality. She embraced relaxation and the natural way to heal one's body. She believed in the essence of energy. When I was growing up, she'd worked at one of the local spas and saved her pennies. She'd been set on opening her own spa one day. When she was a teen, she traveled to Sedona, which was hosting one of the largest branches of the Harmonic Convergence, a New Age synchronized meditation where thousands of pilgrims were getting in touch with the universe at a vortex known as Bell Rock Butte. Fifteen years later, she migrated to Sedona with Sierra and never returned. As a girl, in the summer, I'd often wanted to visit them in Sedona. My mother had refused to take me. Luckily, Nana Lissa had escorted me.

"Aunt Sophie can't come," I said.

Kate clucked her tongue. "How like her to set you up with high hopes with this hoodoo and hullabaloo and then let you fall flat on your—"

"Mom, stop!"

She glowered at me.

"Mother," I revised. "I do not need your negative vibes. I would like your blessing and a pat on the back for being a strong independent woman, like you, who knew what she wanted and did everything she could to achieve it. This is my dream. It doesn't have to be yours."

Kate pursed her lips, ran a finger along the soft shawl collar of her jacket, and finally . . . finally . . . said, "Darling, I want you to be a success."

"Do you? Really?"

It took her a long time to say, "Good luck tomorrow."

"Thank you. 'It is very difficult for the prosperous to be humble.' "

She stroked my cheek. "I love when you quote Jane Austen."

"I knew you'd appreciate that one from *Emma.* Here's another. 'Give a girl an education, and introduce her properly into the world, and ten to one but she has the means of settling well, without farther expense to anybody.' "

"Don't be sassy."

"Didn't you just say you liked when I quoted Austen?" Although the line had been uttered by a revolting character in *Mansfield Park,* throughout my life I'd found it inspiring. "Yes, I believe you did," I said cheekily. Appreciating Austen was my mother's and my one common thread. I didn't read a lot of women's fiction. I enjoyed reading mysteries. But to please Kate, I had read Austen. After all, I was named Emma after one of her protagonists. Over the years, Kate had gifted me so many Jane Austen mementos that my home was overflowing with them. Pieces like a two-inch teapot with miniature Jane Austen books balanced on top. Jane Austen jewelry. Jane Austen magnets. And dozens of things with the name *Emma* on them. Yes, it was her way of buying my affection, which, I hated to admit, had sort of worked.

"May I give you the tour?" I asked.

"Another time."

"Got a date?"

"No."

When my father divorced my mother, saying the world needed him more than we did—his expertise was raising money for areas struggling with blight and horrible water conditions—she was devastated. To prove she didn't care, she chose to go out with intellectual stuffed shirts who could rattle off facts and figures. A number of them read the classics, but very few had a heart or soul. None of them had warmed to me. After a while, Kate gave up on dating.

"What's the rush, then?" I asked.

"I have an appointment with . . ." She twirled a hand.

That was all I'd get out of her.

"'You can be as secretive as a nest of nightingales,'" I said, a comparison I knew she'd appreciate since I was pulling the phrase from John Keats's poem, *Sleep and Poetry*.

"Ta!" she said breezily and, as she made her exit, added over her shoulder, "May nothing go wrong tomorrow."

Her parting comment sent a shiver down my spine.

# Chapter 3

Hideaway Café, one of Carmel's most popular dining destinations, was bustling when I entered. Like the other buildings in the Village Shops, the café boasted a striking dark red wood-and-stone facade. There were bowers of flowers and a beautiful fairy garden at the entrance. The interior was equally warm and inviting. Brady Cash, the handsome owner, guided me to the patio, where strands of twinkling lights gave it a fairy-like atmosphere. A pyramid-shaped skylight roof kept out inclement weather but made the sky a part of the dining experience.

"I don't see my grandmother," I said, switching my Tory Burch wristlet purse to the other wrist. It was rubbing my bangles the wrong way.

"She's running late," Brady said. "She had a reader who wanted to check out twenty books. A librarian's work is never done." He winked at me good-naturedly. "Courtney is here. She's joining you."

Courtney Kelly, a pert woman with a winsome personality, was the owner of the fairy garden shop and a good friend of my grandmother.

As I weaved between tables to reach ours, I saw Willow, clad in a serious black sheath dress that made her skin look sallow. She was dining with her accountant, a man with a stellar reputation and lots of local clients. Were they discussing her financial situation? Not far away sat Hugh Ashbluff, the real estate mogul who'd argued with Willow, and the mayor and another man who was attractive in a silver fox kind of way. Hugh wasn't paying attention to either man. He appeared to be staring at an Asian woman in her mid-thirties whose chin-length black hair cupped her face as if designed to enhance her delicate features. She was sitting alone at a table and checking her watch. If I was a guy, I'd be staring at her, too. When she caught Hugh eyeing her, she flushed, averted her gaze, and began studying her cell phone.

"Hi, Emma," Courtney said as I sat at our table. A glass of white wine stood by her right hand. Her cell phone was lying faceup beside it. She flipped it over and sipped her wine. "It's a great place to people-watch, isn't it? Who are you sizing up?"

"No one in particular."

"The one consulting her cell phone is Naomi Clutterbuck, in case you're wondering. She's a language teacher at the college where your mother works, and she loves making fairy gardens featuring artists."

Nana Lissa once told me that Courtney was very astute as to people's personalities based on their relationship to fairies and fairy gardening.

"What about Hugh Ashbluff, the man in the bow tie and plaid shirt who's sitting with the mayor?" I asked casually, eager to learn more about him after his set-to with Willow.

"He's a prominent property owner and real estate investor."

"That I know. Is he nice?"

"A bit egotistical and sort of a know-it-all but nice enough."

"Who's the guy he's sitting with?"

Courtney's mouth turned up at the corners. "That's Detective Dylan Summers."

Uh-oh. Was Hugh asking the police to oust Willow from her property?

"Whatever you do, don't cross him," Courtney added. "Dylan is a nice guy, but he knows his stuff and will not hesitate to throw the book at you if you're guilty."

"Me?" I felt my cheeks warm. "I've never been guilty of anything." I wasn't a stickler for the rules, but if I wanted inner peace, I needed to follow the law.

"Me, either, but, well . . ." She swirled her wine. "Let's just say I was a suspect in a murder a few years ago. I had to do everything I could to clear my name."

"Hello-o-o. Sorry I'm late." Nana Lissa swooped into view and made a beeline for us. She laughed when she saw that she and Courtney had dressed in nearly identical soft blue tops. "Like minds. Don't you look lovely, Emma?"

I'd dressed in a short-cropped black sweater over a double-layered, black-print mesh skirt. It was the nicest outfit in my closet. I wasn't a clothes horse and never would be.

Nana sat down, and our waitress appeared. "I'll have a glass of that wine," Nana told her. "As will my granddaughter."

"None for me," I said. "I need a clear head."

"Nonsense," Nana countered. "You need to relax."

"No, thanks."

"Sweetheart, your forehead is pinched, and you're doing that thing with your tongue." She pulled a wand of lip balm from her purse.

"I'll take the balm but not the wine." Whenever I got stressed, I had a tendency to lick my lips. They would chap within hours. I took the wand from her, swiped on the goo, and handed it back.

"I see Ulra," my grandmother said, crooking a finger and waving.

"Ulra?" I asked.

"The fairy that resides here." Courtney pointed. "She's in the vines."

"She's having tea with Merryweather Rose of Song," Nana Lissa added.

When my grandmother first told me the name of the fairy that inhabited the library, I'd said she was making it up, but the more I heard about Merryweather, the more I wanted to meet her. If she truly was real. Prior to receiving an education from my grandmother, I had no idea that there were classes of fairies. The four classes were intuitive, righteous, guardian, and nurturer. Merryweather was a guardian fairy, which meant she would protect and serve.

I peered in that direction, didn't detect a thing, and huffed.

My grandmother patted my hand. "Don't be frustrated, sweet girl. You'll encounter one soon."

"So you say."

"Emma, tell me about the sound bath you'll be doing at the spa," Courtney said. "I've never heard of such a thing."

"Sound healing traces its roots to ancient Greece and India. Those societies believed in the transformative healing power of sound, using methods such as singing bowls, tuning forks, and chanting."

"Emma will stir the singing bowls with a crystal rod," my grandmother said, gratefully receiving her glass of wine from the waitress and taking a sip.

"The tonal sound promotes a harmonious environment for the body to heal itself," I said. "I'll offer the baths in groups or individually. Fully clothed, you lie in a recliner or sit on the floor and allow your mind to drink in the waves."

"How lovely," Courtney said. "I must schedule one."

"Hogwash!" a woman exclaimed.

I swiveled in my chair and saw Palmer Pilsner and her best friend, Indy Hendriks, a fifty-something woman who sold her own line of clothing, joining Naomi Clutterbuck at her table. Indy, still standing, had made the crack. I would have recognized her husky voice anywhere. I'd run into her at farmers markets and art galleries. She was brittle but had a good sense of style, tonight being no exception. The cranberry-colored silk jumpsuit she was wearing drew attention to her height and not her robust shape.

"Those newfangled techniques don't work, Naomi," Indy said as she sat down. Primly, she fingered her short hair. "Do they, Palmer?"

"Indy," Palmer said in a scolding tone as if to imply, *Cool your jets.*

Naomi reacted negatively to Indy's barb but remained mute. I wondered how she knew them. She appeared to be decades younger.

Nana Lissa swiveled in her seat and addressed them. "You haven't tried a sound bath, ladies."

"Oh, yes I have, Melissa," Indy replied, using my grandmother's full name, which irked Nana no end. She thought the name was fussy. "I tried it and didn't like it one iota. Ask Willow Shafer, the charlatan."

Willow had never offered anything close to sound bath therapy at her spa. Perhaps she'd suggested Palmer and Indy enjoy the experience at another place, and that treatment hadn't been ideal. There was a spa an hour north of Carmel that offered sound baths. I hadn't checked it out.

"As for you and your new business, Emma," Indy continued with a tartness bordering on hostility, "do not expect us to become patrons. We hope your business will go *poof.*" She gestured with her fingertips and cackled.

Palmer mimicked the noxious sound.

*Witches*, I thought, and quickly forced the negative thought from my mind. *Positive vibes, Emma. Positive.* Maya Angelou said in a YouTube chat I watched, *Prepare yourself so that you can be a rainbow in somebody else's cloud.* I forced myself to smile brightly at the women.

"Don't pay them any heed." My grandmother touched my shoulder to redirect my focus to our threesome. "Indy is an angry woman with a bone to pick with everyone."

"How do you know her?" Courtney asked. "Do you patronize her shop?"

"Occasionally. Also she comes to the library. She solely reads nonfiction. No genre of any kind. How limiting is that?"

"And Palmer?" I asked.

"Women's fiction," she answered, like a librarian mistakenly believing I was asking about reading habits. I let it go. "Now, Palmer's daughter Alexandra loved fantasy, until . . ." Her voice drifted off.

"Until what?" I pressed.

"Never mind."

"Did she die?"

"No. Nothing like that. She moved away."

I'd met Palmer's other daughter, Olivia. It was hard to guess how old she was. Possibly seventeen or eighteen. She had an affection for the Goth look that made her appear young and defiant. She'd stopped by the spa last week as we were finalizing construction. She'd wanted to know whether the well in the courtyard was magical. She'd also asked if the gift shop would be selling tarot cards. She collected them.

"Speaking of books"—Nana tapped the table with a fingertip—"I want your opinions about the fundraiser I'm thinking of having for the library. But, first, let's order our meals."

I opted for the poached salmon with citrus sauce and roasted vegetables. Courtney and my grandmother chose the filet of sole, which would be served on a bed of pureed artichoke.

Task complete, I refocused on the matter at hand. "What about a silent auction?" I suggested.

"How about community partnerships?" Courtney chimed. "One shop teams up with another to cross-promote. All sales that day go to the fundraiser."

I detected movement to my right and saw Willow approaching Palmer's table. She was flapping a largish postcard in one hand.

"Palmer, did you slide this under the door of my spa?" Willow demanded. "With the word *die* on it?"

"I don't know what you're talking about," Palmer answered.

*Die?* I swallowed hard. How horrible. I recalled Palmer shoving a postcard into her purse earlier. The front of the one Willow was waving did look like a seascape Palmer could have painted, though nearly every artist in Carmel rendered seascapes. I'd seen plenty of similar postcards on carousels at Shabby Chic Nook.

"Are you threatening me, Palmer?" Willow demanded.

"Willow, darling," Palmer said, "I haven't been near your spa."

"Did you put one under Emma's and Tish's doors, as well, or are you singling out my spa because—"

"Willow, we have nothing to discuss. Ever. Go away." Palmer waved a hand.

Indy muttered, "Loser."

Naomi pressed her lips together so hard they disappeared.

"Listen up, Palmer," Willow said, unwilling to be dismissed. "I believe in relaxation and massage, and I know you do, too. I've seen you coming out of A Peaceful Solution."

"But you, Willow, do meditation." The way Palmer said the word *meditation* made it sound like an evil form of voodoo. "You want to convert everyone to your ideology."

"I have never wanted to convert anyone," Willow said. "I meditate privately."

"It's woo-woo," Palmer said.

"No, it's not, and be assured, I won't do any of the woo-woo stuff at my spa that Emma will do at hers. She's the one who wants to convert you."

I took umbrage and shot to my feet. Under my breath, so everyone in the place wouldn't hear me, I rasped, "Willow, take it back."

She raised her hands.

"I don't convert," I said, still whispering. "I advise. I suggest. I care about people and how they manage stress."

"Don't lash out at me," Willow said, not lowering her voice a whit. She jutted a hand at Palmer and Indy. "They're the ones who don't like anything New Agey." She made air quotes.

"That's not the half of it," a woman at the next table whispered. It was Zinnia Walker, a trim, sixty-something dowager. She was sitting with a similarly aged dining companion, who was clad in lavender-colored, designer-label clothing. Zinnia caught me staring, nodded in greeting to my grandmother—they were friends—and said with an impish grin, "Don't mind us."

I refocused on Palmer and Indy and said in a measured tone, "Honestly, ladies? Do you live in the Dark Ages?"

Neither woman spoke. Naomi plucked at the cuffs of her silk blouse.

"Emma, sit down. This threat"—Willow brandished the postcard—"is not about you. This is about me."

"Indeed it is," Zinnia rasped. Her companion clucked her tongue.

"Mind your own business," Willow said to them. "You, too, Emma."

I would have, except it was my spa that she'd maligned.

"Go." Willow flicked a finger as Palmer had.

The nerve. Between tight teeth, I said, "Willow, you invoked my name in this conversation. You know very well that I won't offer anything at Aroma Wellness that will hurt anyone." To steady myself, I fingered the tiger-eye beaded necklace I'd purchased when I'd traveled to Tibet, which was believed to infuse its owner with power and calm. If it could work its magic when I was seething, it would be a miracle. "Why would you say—"

"For heaven's sakes, Emma, butt out."

"I'll have you know that I've dedicated my life to making people comfortable while introducing them to techniques that will protect and soothe their bodies. I want people to feel refreshed when they leave Aroma Wellness."

Indy coughed derisively into a napkin. Palmer tittered. Naomi continued to look mortified. Willow stood taller and squared her shoulders.

"Fine, Willow," I muttered. "Be that way." She was as dense as a rock, and not a soothing healing rock. Knowing I couldn't win this ridiculous battle, I returned to my seat. I felt eyes on me but didn't glance around the patio.

"Breathe," Nana Lissa whispered. "Don't let anything or anyone spoil tomorrow's opening."

"Was I too loud?"

"You were a model of restraint."

On the way home, I spotted Willow shuffling into Mystic Waters, her shawl draped haphazardly over one arm, the tail dragging on the sidewalk. She was weeping. I hadn't heard Palmer or Indy say more hurtful things. Perhaps her business manager had told her that keeping her lease was impossible at this juncture.

Determined to kiss and make up and, in the process, infuse her with a dash of positivity, I hurried to Aroma Wellness, picked up the peace offering basket I'd fashioned, and raced to Mystic Waters. The lights were on inside. I rapped on the door, then tried the knob. It was unlocked. I entered cautiously. No one was manning the reception desk.

"Hello? Willow?"

The spa was laid out simply. The reception area was done in black and white, with a counter, two chairs, and a baker's rack of products for sale. It was spare but peaceful. Black-and-white paintings of serene retreats hung on the walls. The white sage smudge candle on the counter was lit, the white tulips in a crystal vase were fresh, and soft orchestral music was playing through a speaker. A hall leading to three therapy rooms lay beyond a swinging door.

I heard sniffling. "Willow?"

She emerged from her office, tissue in hand, mascara streaking her face. Her gaze hardened. "What do you want?"

I held up the basket. "I brought you this."

"Why?"

"It's an olive branch." I extended the gift. She took it from me.

"Is everyone gone for the night?" Usually, her spa offered services until ten.

"We closed early. My facialist is having a baby shower. All the therapists wanted to attend."

"Why aren't you there?"

"I don't do anything baby-related. I don't want children. I've never wanted children. As far as I'm concerned . . ." She didn't finish the sentence and set the basket on the desk behind the counter. "Is there something else you wanted to say?"

I'd expected a thank-you, but not everyone was skilled at graciousness.

"How's your family?" I asked. "Your mom? Your stepfather? Your half sister?"

She tilted her head like an inquisitive bird. "Fine, fine, and fine."

After her father walked out when she was two years old, never to be heard from again, Willow's mother raised her. When Willow turned sixteen, her mother remarried. Within a year, Willow's half sister was born. Willow was stunned by the addition to her family but accepted the new arrangement. She told me that during her senior year in high school, she'd worked the reception desk of her stepfather's used-car business and had hated every minute of it. She went to college to become an accountant like her mother but found she didn't have an affinity for it. After graduation and a visit to a wonderful meditative retreat where she'd *found herself*, she'd landed on the idea of opening a spa.

"Is everyone still living in Sacramento?" I asked.

"Yes. What do you care?" She moved to the cash register, popped it open, removed a bank deposit envelope from the left side, and began withdrawing cash from the till. She stacked it in a pile.

"Willow, c'mon. We're friends. I know you're upset with me, but let's chat. Let's catch up. We haven't talked in—"

"Are you doing it?" She banged the register drawer closed.

"Doing what?" I asked, clearly at a loss.

"Are you trying to scare me by playing spooky ghost sounds?"

"What? Of course not." I cocked my head. "Are you hearing ghosts?"

"Not real ghosts, you idiot. I can tell the sounds are taped. The recording crackles. It's been happening off and on for weeks, right before I leave for the night, as if whoever is doing it knows my schedule." She lasered me with her gaze. "Like you, for instance."

"Ha! Everyone in town knows your schedule. You're like a precision Swiss watch. You walk briskly every morning at seven. You arrive at the spa at eight. You take a half hour for lunch."

She counted the cash and stuffed it into the envelope.

"I swear, Willow. It's not me."

"What about the crank calls?" she demanded.

"What crank calls?"

"Heavy breathing and hang-ups."

"Also not me. You're being punked."

She sighed.

"Maybe Palmer is the culprit," I suggested. "Or Indy. They were pretty vicious at the restaurant."

"Indy's a nutcase. Did you know her name is Dutch?"

I didn't. *Trivia for two hundred, Ken,* I thought, and smiled, recalling fond memories sitting beside my father and watching *Jeopardy!* He always got the right answers.

"It means 'independent,'" Willow added. "But it's not short for *independent* or *Indiana* or anything. It's simply Indy. How silly is that?"

I felt the tension in my shoulders ease, like she was warming to me.

"She's in charge of our neighborhood watch," Willow went on.

"She's your neighbor?"

Willow shook her head. "She lives two streets over. Boy, does she know how to make enemies. She leaves notes on everyone's doorstep. 'Your tree is too big.' 'Your sprinkler is spraying water everywhere.' 'Do this.' 'Do that.' The nerve. On the doorstep!

Meaning she pushes open gates if she has to, without being invited."

Carmel didn't have mailboxes. The town's founders didn't like the practice of house-to-house mail delivery and opted in favor of a central post office.

"She's got too much time on her hands," Willow added.

"Doesn't Hendriks Fashions keep her busy?"

"She's got three employees." Willow batted the air. "However, I doubt she's doing the ghost thing. She wouldn't know how to. She can sew but she doesn't have an ounce of technical skill." She pulled the brass candlestick from the basket to admire it.

"What about Palmer?"

"She can bake and play tennis."

"And paint."

"She'd like to think so." Willow twisted the candlestick to inspect it front and back. "This is pretty. Simple yet elegant."

"I'm glad you like it."

"I don't forgive you," she said matter-of-factly. "I'm not sure I can."

"But we're still friends."

"Yes. Of course. Friendly rivalry is a necessary evil. But don't expect me to come to you for a chakra cleansing or a gemstone reading of any kind. It's not my thing anymore."

"Was it ever?"

She didn't reply.

Silence settled between us. I didn't want to leave yet, comfortable with our renewed friendship.

After a long moment, she said, "They got a dog."

"Who?"

"Mom and Dad. I never had a dog, but Sissy . . ." Her mouth quirked up on the right. "She's spoiled rotten."

Sissy was her half sister. "Are you jealous?" I asked.

"I'd be an idiot not to be. Mom would do anything for that girl.

Sissy is adorable. Sissy is perfection personified." Willow propped a hand beneath her chin and grinned in a phony way. "Don't get me wrong. I love her. She is precious. And I adore my mother, but she can drive me crazy with the way she dotes on Sissy." She paused, then said, "*C'est la vie*. Listen, if you find out who's punking me, you have to tell me."

"Promise."

# Chapter 4

Around eight twenty, I arrived home, which was a unit in a fourplex on San Carlos, southeast of 4th Avenue. When I was in college, my grandmother purchased the charming Spanish-style building and rented out the units. When I moved back to town, she eased out a pair of tenants and gave the two lower units to me. Each unit consisted of one bedroom and one bath, with a small kitchen and living room. I'd turned the second unit into my studio. I needed to cover utilities, but that was it.

When Sierra took me up on my offer to run the café at the spa, Nana Lissa vacated one of the upper units and ceded it to her. A fortune teller named Ursula lived and worked out of the remaining upper apartment. She and her clients were quiet and respectful of everyone's privacy. There was a garden in front and a garden, plus a patio in the rear. Daylilies, herbs, and evergreen bushes flourished in front, but there were a number of bare spots in the back. Taking responsibility for the upkeep, I offered to install more plants but not until after the spa was a success. No way did I have time to nurture a couple of gardens into something spectacular now.

Gigantic pots of lilac stood on either side of the front doors to each unit. I'd hung a set of wind chimes on a small shepherd's hook in the pot to my right and had inserted a kinetic dual wind spinner into the left pot. Each item of whimsy brought a smile to my face.

I unlocked the front door, swung it open, and was met with a loud yowl from my cat, Vivi. She was a Birman, which was also known as the Sacred Cat of Burma. Purportedly Birmans originated as companions of temple priests in northern Burma in the Mount of Lug. Long-haired with color-pointed ears—Vivi's were lilac in tone—Birmans had deep blue eyes and contrasting white gloves on each paw. There was a tradition that all Birmans born in the same birth year were to have a name starting with the same letter. I chose the name Vivi because V was the letter designated to her birth year. Vivi meant "full of beans," and, true to her name, she was frisky to the point of exhaustion. She enjoyed playing well into the night.

"Settle down." I scooped her into my arms and tossed my wristlet purse on the side table by the entrance. The Jane Austen china plate that my mother gave me with the quote, *My good opinion once lost is lost forever*, jiggled on its display stand but righted itself. *Phew*. It was one of my favorite treasures. I'd hate to lose it.

"Hungry?" I danced Vivi into the kitchen singing Taylor Swift's sassy "Look What You Made Me Do" a cappella. Vivi liked to cha-cha. She didn't care if I sang off-key.

Nana had redone all the units after purchasing them. Like her house, each of the apartments was decorated in white with a splash of another color for accent. They weren't cookie-cutter. The accents in my primary unit were blue. In the studio, they were sea green. Sierra's were caramel brown, and Ursula's were soft gold. Each of the foyers were tiled with travertine stone reflecting the units' complementary shades. Each unit's kitchen sported polished ceramic tile backsplashes and white quartzite countertops, plus a bistro table for dining. Also, the cabinetry was handle-free and opened with a simple push. In my kitchen, blue-rimmed coffee mugs hung on a white mug tree. A lacy blue-and-white curtain covered the single window that provided a view of the yard. Blue canisters held flour, sugar, and coffee. The white hutch with blue granite desktop—my home office for lack of more space—held my computer, a few beloved books, and many of the Jane Austen knickknacks my mother had bestowed upon me. On the wall hung a sextet of Jane Austen giclée book covers. My favorite was *Persuasion*, where Anne Elliot, the protagonist of the story, was sitting on a pier reading a book. On the refrigerator was a handful of notecards with positive sayings as well as a dozen postcards from my father, held in place by Jane Austen book cover magnets and magnets featuring silhouettes of Austen's protagonist Emma. As described in the book, Emma had a true hazel eye, with an open countenance and a lovely complexion in the bloom of full health. I did have an *open countenance,* and I was blessed with good skin. Other than that, we looked nothing alike.

"You didn't eat your kibble." I set Vivi on the floor and regarded her bowl.

She mewed, meaning she was waiting for me to dish up her dinner. She brushed my leg as if she thought I needed extra encouragement to do her bidding. I didn't. I adored her.

I browsed the contents of the refrigerator, pulled out a half-full tin of tuna, and spooned it into a fresh cat bowl. Then, because I was too wound up to sleep, I decided to make a few concoctions in my studio. I carried Vivi and her bowl out the back door, veered right, unlocked the studio's rear door, and propped it open to let in the cool night air, making sure to close the screen door after we entered. Vivi couldn't go outside alone. She needed to be supervised.

After setting the cat's food on the floor in the corner in the kitchen where she wouldn't be underfoot and after filling a drinking glass with water for her—heaven forbid she drink water from a bowl!—I clicked on a Taylor Swift playlist on my cell phone and connected the phone to the Bluetooth speaker. The strains of her cover song "Out of the Woods" blasted. I turned down the volume and found myself pulsing to the lyrical beat as I worked.

My setup wasn't fancy. The kitchen served as the laboratory. I'd moved the bistro dining table and had added a freestanding basin, metal tables, and storage racks. The living room was the staging ground, complete with amber-colored glass bottles, containers for creams, packing boxes, gift boxes, and a copper essential oils still. My one creature comfort was an AirCandy inflatable chair for times when I simply needed to crash. I'd converted the bedroom into a storage area. Freestanding bookshelves holding vials of essential oils lined each of the walls. The lighting was dim because the oils needed to be stored in low light. I also installed a refrigerator to hold the items that needed to be kept cool.

The still was perfect for a small-scale operation like mine. I recalled winter breaks spent with Aunt Sophie in Sedona when she lovingly filled my head with facts while showing me how to do the extractions. The oils helped balance hormones, she told me. Some fought harmful bacteria in the body. Some, like rose hips and tea tree oil, rejuvenated the skin, and certain oils, like lavender and peppermint, could add a dash of spice to a dish. Sierra had joined in the fun, but she'd never taken to the art. Whenever I came home from these excursions, I was brimming with enthusiasm, which my mother, to my dismay, loved to dampen.

Tonight I would concentrate on making lavender oil. The aroma itself might make it easier for me to sleep. Next week, once all the hoopla from the grand opening subsided, I would focus on creating some of the creams and masks we were selling in the spa and in the shop. The homemade exfoliant I made with coconut oil, granulated sugar, and drops from a variety of essential oils would be a big seller, not only with women of a certain age but with women in their twenties and thirties who were eager to continue looking young.

I put enough dried lavender buds into the still and covered it with water. Next, I adjusted the setting and brought the water to its highest heat, then switched it to low. For three hours, it would do its magic before automatically turning off. The mixture could cool until I woke up. In the morning, I would remove the thin film, i.e., the essential oil, that lurked at the top after the extraction. I'd pour it into the vials and refrigerate it.

An hour into my efforts, Vivi brushed my leg. I bent to give the top of her head a good scratch.

"Not too much longer," I cooed. "A half hour. Tops."

Grumpy, she nestled into the cat bed in the nook of the end table that I'd placed in the far corner of the living room, which served as the still room, and settled in for a snooze.

I changed the playlist to classics, and as the strains of Mozart's Piano Concerto No. 21 started playing, my mind drifted to memories of my ex-boyfriend, a dishy man who could play anything on the piano. With feeling. Without a single error. No, he wasn't a musician by trade. The last I'd heard, he, like my father, was now traveling the world to save something, but I wasn't sure what. Forests? Coffee trees?

The one gift of his I hadn't discarded, a painting by Emma Brennan, an Irishwoman with my name and a unique style, hung on the far wall. He knew I'd been obsessed with Brennan's work, and though I loved it, I'd stored it in my studio so I wouldn't have to look at it every night before going to bed. I didn't want to remember his kisses or his bedroomy eyes. That would have been too much to bear.

Something stirred in the pit of my stomach. *Uh-uh. Don't go there, Emma.* I would not reach out to him, and I wouldn't look at his social media profiles. I had a business to launch. "That's it, Vivi, we're done here." I switched off the music and, humming, locked up the studio. I carried Vivi and her empty dinner dish back to our place.

In the bedroom, like always, she leaped onto the blue-and-white floral comforter of my bed, ready to play. Even in the summer, nights in Carmel could get chilly.

"No," I said forcefully. She mewed. "All right, one round of rumble-tumble." I rubbed her tummy and flipped her over. She batted me with her paws. I repeated the rub-flip move.

When she was satisfied that we'd played enough, she swished her tail and nestled onto the human pillow on the right side of the bed. I slept on the left. She was snoozing by the time I'd brushed my teeth and slipped into my PJs.

My dreams were filled with successful outcomes for tomorrow. The kudos. The happy faces. The attendees who would become repeat customers. I awoke with a smile on my face.

Wednesday morning, after finalizing the essential oil extraction and sealing all the bottles, I craved a double dose of caffeine, but when I discovered I was out of pods for my Keurig, I decided to go to Percolate, a fun and happening coffee shop. I didn't want to grab a cup at Aroma Café. Sierra would give me the evil eye. Sure, our café served espressos and lattes and the like, but my cousin believed no one needed caffeine—in particular, me. Starting the morning with a soothing cup of herbal tea was her mantra. Most often I complied, but today? Not a chance. I was euphoric, but if my excitement wore off, I would need an artificial buzz to sustain me.

By the time I arrived at the spa, I'd polished off my drink and the protein bar I'd packed for breakfast and felt raring to go. The masseuses and facialist were already there, waiting in the courtyard. My grandmother had arrived. So had her friends, Zinnia Walker, the wealthy dowager, and Hedda Hopewell, the loan officer who'd helped Nana Lissa negotiate the funding for the spa. Hedda was dressed for work in a prim blouse and pencil skirt. She and Zinnia each threw a coin into the well. Were they making wishes?

"Good luck," Hedda said to me as I drew near.

"Yes, may all good things come to you," Zinnia added.

"Sweet girl." My grandmother pulled me aside. "We're all wishing you the very best."

"Thank you."

"The grand-opening sign is marvelous," she added.

It had magically appeared overnight as had a dozen sea-green balloons and a dozen blue ones. Yoly was in charge of the celebratory decor and didn't want to put out anything prematurely.

"Emma, girlfriend!" Meryl Kim trotted into view, the sleeveless, loose-fitting silk sheath she was wearing wafting with each stride. She was our manicurist and one of the funniest people I'd ever met. I swear she had a rubber face, and there wasn't a person or accent she couldn't imitate. "Yeet!" she squealed. "I'm so excited for you."

On weekends, Meryl did a stand-up routine at a comedy club. A couple of weeks ago, Sierra and I went to the club to catch her act. She did a bit about the difference between male and female dating styles, saying women read into everything. They overanalyzed. Especially words in a text. She suggested that if a man was smart, he would pick up the darned phone, if he remembered how to dial one, and skip texting altogether. I wasn't the only person in the audience who could relate. We were all in hysterics.

"Congratulations!" Meryl raised her hand for a high five, but when I moved to reciprocate, she quickly withdrew her hand and ran it along her blue ombré, mostly black hair. "Psych."

"Ha-ha," I said, stepping in for a hug, knowing she'd recoil in horror. She was emotionally warm but not a hugger. Her reserve had something to do with her ex-husband, but she had yet to divulge details. We had only known each other a few short months. We met when I'd begun the process of hiring staff.

"You like?" Meryl held up her forearm to reveal a tattoo of what I presumed was the tree of life on the underside. Both of her arms were rife with ink. "I'm on fleek, don't you think?"

I didn't use the current cultural slang, like Meryl did, but I understood the terms. *On fleek* meant "fashionable." "*Très chic*," I said, teasing.

The most prominent tattoo on her left biceps was the face of Buddha. Why him? I'd asked at our first meeting. She said it was because Korean Buddhists differentiated themselves from Mahayana Buddhists—they wanted to resolve what early practitioners saw as inconsistencies in traditions—therefore, they developed a holistic-approach religion called Tongbulgyo.

"Why the tree?" I asked today.

"It's a reminder that everything goes in cycles—birth, life, death, rebirth. It's in honor of my son." The eighteen-year-old had announced last week that he wanted to move in with his father, a musician in Monterey. The pronouncement had rattled Meryl. She'd done everything she could to nurture him. Her ex hadn't lifted a finger. "I can roll with the punches, right?"

"We all have to," I said. "That's how life operates."

"Emma, it's time to rock and roll." Nana leaned in and added, "You look lovely today. Very pretty."

I'd thrown on my nicest pair of yoga pants, an ocean-themed tank top with shirred straps, and dangly silver earrings featuring otters. The adorable creatures were a big tourist draw in Carmel.

"Ladies!" My grandmother turned to face her eager companions. "Help us get this place up and running. Yoly! Sierra!"

Yoly rushed out of the gift shop and Sierra from the café.

"Ladies, hop to it," Nana said. "One hour. Let's make Emma proud."

"Aye, aye, Captain." Sierra saluted.

I was so *beyond* proud I could barely breathe, but I beckoned them into a group hug, and when we broke, I said, "Thank you, each and every one of you. My dream—our dream—is becoming a reality." I unlocked the main entrance to the spa, propped the doors open, and we all got to work.

I queued up *Secret Garden* on Spotify, which instantly began playing through the spa's audio system. The music was serene. A person had to work hard not to relax when listening to it. Next, I polished the reception desk. I'd buffed it last night before leaving for dinner, but I didn't want a speck of dust on it. Then I filled the pitcher of water on the beverage cart with cucumber water and ice, switched on the urns for coffee and hot water, after which I removed any brown fronds from the oversized ferns. All done with my assigned chores, I took a moment to gaze upward through the skylight. The sun was shining. There wasn't a cloud in the sky.

*Good vibes, Emma*, I mused. *No, not just good. Great.*

At 9:00 a.m. on the dot, after we'd set out platters of fresh fruit kebabs and honey banana mini-muffins that Sierra had baked, the therapists positioned themselves in the reception area, ready to chat up our guests, Yoly returned to the gift shop, Sierra went to the café, and I opened the doors for real. Minutes later, when I peeked out the plate-glass window, I was thrilled to see a line of customers entering the gift shop. Sierra and her barista must have been equally busy because I spied customers already seated at the tables in the courtyard with treats they'd purchased from the café.

Meryl sashayed to me and rested an elbow on the reception counter. "Emma, the spa is going to slay." She meant it was going to be a hit. She waggled a laminated card in front of my face. "These treatment menu cards you made are the bomb. Every client knows exactly what to expect and what to pay." She read one: "Mani-pedi Bella includes a deep foot massage, scrub, and hot rocks." She wrinkled her nose at the latter.

"You don't like hot rocks?"

"Uh, no. They're hot," she said. "Duh. But the customer appreciates them, so I'll be a big girl and make the sacrifice . . . for a good tip."

"Here's a tip. Don't bet on the horses," I wisecracked.

"Tipping . . . it's the way of the Jedi. May the *funds* be with you."

She guffawed and strolled deeper into the spa, where I'd set up a nail salon specifically for manis and pedis. The two recliner chairs with multifunction electronic shiatsu massage features had cost a pretty penny but would be worth it, if for no other reason than I and my coworkers could sit in them at the end of the day to relax.

For the remainder of the morning, people came to check out the spa. The mayor paid his respects. An alderman and a pastor of one of the town's churches did, too. They were followed by a few shop owners in the area. One, an art gallery owner, wished me *Buena suerte, mucho éxito,* which meant "good luck and much success," if my high school Spanish was up to snuff. I thanked her.

By noon, we were well on our way to a fully booked schedule for week one, and I was riding a high I couldn't have gotten from caffeine.

I went to the café, picked up a veggie wrap, and headed to the courtyard to take a quick lunch break when I saw my mother rushing up the stairs. Understand, Kate never rushed anywhere. Hastiness lacked decorum. Therefore, seeing her jogging, her jacket flapping like a sail in a rough wind, made me weak at the knees.

I gulped. Hard. "Mother? What's wrong?"

"Willow," she exclaimed. "Willow's dead!"

# Chapter 5

"Oh, no! What happened?" I asked. "Did she have a heart attack? No, of course not. She was too young. Did she eat something that she was allergic to?"

"No!" popped out of Kate.

"How did you find out?"

"I was . . ." My mother tried to catch her breath. "I was . . ." She pointed toward the street. "I was passing by Mystic Waters and saw patrol cars."

"Patrol cars?"

"She was murdered."

My heart wrenched. "Murdered?"

"Murdered," Kate repeated.

I caught sight of a woman racing into the café. Another tore into the gift shop. Clearly, both intended to convey the news. People who'd remained on the patio murmured to one another. Many had their cell phones out and were aiming them at my mother. Within seconds, if I didn't nip rumormongering in the bud, social media would be buzzing.

"No cameras," I shouted. "No one record anything. Please." The last thing I needed was for someone to think Willow had been killed at Aroma Wellness.

It was then that I realized my mother looked a mess. Her silk blouse was buttoned, but it was off by one button. The front tail of the blouse jutted from the waistband of her skirt. She would hate it if I pointed out she was disheveled, so I kept mum.

Sierra bustled out of the café and Yoly from the shop.

"Aunt Kate," Sierra said, "I heard the news."

"Me, too," Yoly said. "Tell us what happened."

The hubbub of the crowd grew as people yelled for her to tell them everything.

Sierra raised both arms. "Hush, people!" she shouted, using her executive chef voice.

"Kate"—I guided my mother into a chair by the nearest table—"be as specific as you can be. Did you get any information from the police?"

"Willow was bludgeoned. With a brass candlestick."

"In the ballroom," someone at the rear of the crowd quipped.

"Not funny," Sierra snapped.

She was right. Now was not the time for levity, but I didn't agree out loud because my mind was already reeling with the possibility that the candlestick—the very one I'd put in Willow's peace offering basket—might be the murder weapon.

"She was struck five times," Kate went on.

Five? Heavens! That indicated fierce rage. Who hated Willow that much?

"Indy Hendriks found her and contacted the police," Kate added.

"Found her or killed her?" I asked, flashing on the exchange between Indy, Palmer, and Willow at the café last night. There had been no love lost between them.

"She was passing by on her way to work," Kate said. "Hendriks Fashions isn't far from Mystic Spa. You know Indy lives on Dolores, south of Tenth, don't you?"

I didn't, but I also didn't see the need to know where everyone I knew lived. That would take up too much mental shelf space. Why my mother knew stymied me. True, she'd always been good at deciphering maps. Me? Not so much. But she didn't live in Carmel any longer. She'd moved to Carmel Valley years ago.

"She said she saw her through the window. Lying on the floor." My mother mimed a flat surface.

"Hold on!" I bleated. "You spoke to Indy?"

"She was standing outside the building telling everyone what went down."

"Except she didn't know the specifics unless she was in the room where it happened."

Meryl, who had made her way to the patio, crooned the opening lyrics from "The Room Where It Happens," a catchy tune from the hit musical *Hamilton*. I threw her the stink eye. She twisted an imaginary key in front of her lips.

"An officer questioned her," Kate continued. "She said he gave her some of the details. It was . . ." She wrapped her arms around her chest. "It was gory."

Nana Lissa emerged through the spa's main entrance and weaved through the throng to my mother. "Kate," she said, "Yoly texted me. How are you doing?"

Kate unfolded her arms and fanned the air. "I'm fine." Never in a million years would she let Nana mother her.

"Are you shaken?"

"I didn't see the body, for heaven's sakes. I came here at once because Willow was Emma's friend."

Someone in the crowd said, "Were they really friends? I heard they quarreled yesterday."

I balked. Was the person who was chiding me—I couldn't put the voice to a face—suggesting that I killed Willow? "It was an inane little spat," I said to my mother. "Nana, you were there."

"It wasn't even a spat," my grandmother told the crowd. "It was an exchange of words. Willow could be crisp."

*To say the least*, I mused.

"She and I made up last night," I said. "I went to Mystic Waters to take her—" I stopped short. What if the killer saw me delivering the basket? What if he or she saw the candlestick and thought, *Aha, the perfect weapon*, and sneaked inside after I left? My stomach twisted into a knot. My head began to ache. I recalled Willow mentioning the ghostly sounds she'd been hearing and the hang-up phone calls she'd been receiving. She'd wanted me to alert her if I found out who was taunting her. Was that person responsible for her death?

A police siren blared. The screech of tires followed. Within seconds Detective Summers, the handsome older man I'd seen at Hideaway Café last night, came into view at the top of the stairs. His outfit of a white shirt and khaki slacks made him look approachable, but his grim face said otherwise. An attractive female officer not much older than me followed him. She had flawless caramel-colored skin and lustrous black hair, which she'd tied at the nape of her neck.

"Emma Brennan?" Summers said, drawing near with long strides.

"Yes, sir." I stepped forward to identify myself and noticed my mother quickly pivoting, arms and elbows moving as if she'd suddenly realized she was a mess and was righting her appearance.

"I'm Detective Summers. This is Officer Rodriguez. We'd like a word."

I said, "I heard Willow Shafer was killed."

"Yes, ma'am."

"How horrible."

Summers held an old-fashioned spiral notepad in one hand, a pen in the other. "A witness saw you entering Mystic Waters last evening. Is that correct?"

My mouth went bone dry. I managed to squeak out, "Yes, I went inside."

Summers jotted something on his notepad. "What time did you enter the establishment?"

"Around eight. I had dinner with my grandmother at Hideaway Café. Afterward, I fetched a gift basket I'd made for Willow and walked over."

"The witness didn't see you leave."

"Well, I did. About fifteen minutes later." My bare arms prickled with goose bumps. From fear, I imagined. I glanced at Officer Rodriguez, who was studying everyone in the courtyard. She didn't make eye contact with me.

"The witness claims you and Miss Shafer were at odds at the café last evening," Summers said.

"No, we—" *Hold on.* The witness saw me at Mystic Waters and at the café? I licked my teeth trying to moisten my mouth. Why did I feel parched? "No."

"Did the witness lie?"

I swallowed hard. "Willow wasn't happy about me opening a competitive business. She said some contrary things."

Summers didn't acknowledge that he'd dined at the café or heard the exchange.

"I thought taking her a peace offering would ease the tension," I went on, instantly wishing I'd come up with a term other than *peace offering*.

"Things were tense between you?"

"Not *tense* tense. *Friendly* tense." That sounded lame, too. Quickly, I added, "When I left, we were laughing like old times. See, we went to college together, and she and I—"

"You were laughing?"

"Yes. We were catching up, and she told me her parents gave her half sister a dog, and Willow admitted to being jealous . . ." I was blathering and paused. "You probably don't need me to rehash the conversation."

"Where did you go when you left?" Summers asked.

"Home."

Nana drew alongside me. "Hello, Dylan."

"Lissa," Summers said. "This is my newest officer, Teresa Rodriguez."

"You're Renee's sister," my grandmother said.

"Yes, ma'am, I am." Rodriguez didn't elaborate.

Nana refocused on Summers. "I've put a hold on those books you asked for."

"Thanks."

"Now, who murdered Willow?"

"That's what I'm trying to determine."

"She had lots of clients, business associates, and friends," Nana said. "Your list will be long."

"Your granddaughter was seen entering Mystic Waters around eight," Summers said. "The coroner has determined the time of death to be between eight and ten."

He *did* think I'd killed her. Dang it! Didn't he realize that it would be stupid of me to murder her using the very item I'd brought as a gift? After all, my fingerprints would be—

"Ms. Brennan, why did you gasp?" Summers regarded me. "Did you remember something?"

"I . . . I touched the murder weapon, sir, but Willow held it after me. Her prints—"

"How do you know what weapon was used?" he demanded.

Kate raised her hand. "I told her, Dylan."

Oy! She was on a first-name basis with him, too? Was I the only one in town who didn't know this guy personally? He and my mother might have mutual friends, I supposed. They were about the same age.

"People on the street were talking," she added.

*Indy Hendriks, to be precise,* I mused. Would I get brownie points with the detective if I told him she'd spilled the beans?

Summers scribbled down another note. "You say you went home, Ms. Brennan. Did anyone see you?"

"My cat."

Someone nearby stifled a snicker.

Oh, geez! I hadn't meant to give such a sassy reply. I felt my cheeks warm. "Sorry, sir, I meant I'm not sure about anyone—a person—seeing me. My cousin Sierra"—I gestured to her; she had an arm around our grandmother's waist—"was on a date, and the other tenant . . ." I quickly explained how the three of us lived in a fourplex Nana owned and rented out, and that I had two of the units, one of which was my studio. "I think Ursula, the other tenant—she's a fortune teller—is traveling."

"What's Ursula's last name?" Summers asked.

"She says her Serbian name is difficult to pronounce. Therefore, she goes by J," I said. "Ursula J."

"Ursula Josipovic," Rodriguez stated.

"Really?" I asked, surprised. "Josipovic? That's not so hard to say."

"I've consulted her," Rodriguez added. "She's quite talented."

Summers arched an eyebrow. "Thank you, Officer."

Rodriguez blinked and lowered her gaze, sufficiently chastised.

I said, "I can provide you with her cell phone number."

Summers nodded. "That would be great."

I recited it, then racked my brain trying to remember if I'd seen a neighbor when I walked from my car to the apartment, but I hadn't. I knew a lot of them by sight but not by name. There was Brick House Dude and New Mom. I recognized Sunflower Lady, too, and often waved. She had the most beautiful garden. I planned to consult her when and if I got around to sprucing up ours. Dottie No Last Name was another neighbor. She was as sweet as sugar and owned an adorable Yorkie. Recently I'd made a bergamot oil concoction to help the dog's coat.

"I had nothing to do with Willow's death," I said.

"I'll make that determination."

"Dylan," Nana Lissa said, "my granddaughter is innocent. Why, she even takes spiders and ants outside to rehabilitate them with the environment."

*Spiders, yes. Ants, on occasion.*

Summers pressed his lips together as if trying not to smile.

"May I inquire who saw me go into the spa?" I asked, anxiety roiling inside me. When Summers didn't respond, I said, "The witness's identity isn't a secret, is it?"

"It was Indy Hendriks," he admitted.

"Excuse me? Are you saying Indy happened to be the one to call the police this morning, and she was also the witness who saw me entering the spa last night and saw me argue with Willow at the café? Gee, what a coincidence."

"You're not a fan?" Summers's eyes glinted.

"Vice versa. She's not a fan of me or anyone else, for that matter." Other than Palmer and Naomi. "My grandmother says she has a bone to pick with everyone." But why with me? I'd never done anything to her . . . other than open a business that Willow described as New Agey. "What was she doing in the area?"

"She was on her way to bridge club," Summers said.

My grandmother frowned. "Indy is not a reliable witness. She's a bitter woman. Why, she's accused many people of wrongdoing and is always mistaken, but she never apologizes."

"Thank you, Lissa. Ms. Brennan"—Summers readdressed me while folding up his notepad and pocketing it along with the pen—"please do not leave town."

*With a new business to attend to? As if!*

"Yes, sir," I said meekly.

"And if you have anything you think might be of interest, contact me." He handed me his business card and left.

Officer Rodriguez trailed him while still observing the crowd that had gathered.

Needless to say, the possibility that I was a person of interest in Willow's murder put a damper on the day's fun. Every person who came in to check out the spa was keen on learning details of the crime—details that we were not privy to. Around one, my mother left. My grandmother departed, as well, after giving me a huge hug and saying she'd put out feelers to find out what happened. Library patrons or fairies might have a clue.

*Fairies. Yeah, right.*

At around three, Yoly appeared in the reception area, hitching her tote higher on her shoulder. "I locked up the shop and flipped over the *Back in a Few* sign. I'm taking a short break."

"You deserve it. I've seen the activity." I abandoned the appointment calendar on the computer that I'd been reviewing and crossed to her.

"We're selling out of lots of things. We'll need to order more wind chimes, and the books about aromatherapy are quite popular. Oh, and the Brazilian amethyst cathedral"—she spread her hands wide to demonstrate its size—"sold."

"You're kidding." Seventeen inches tall and over fifty pounds in weight, it was quite rare. I'd priced it at twenty-five hundred dollars. "Who bought it?"

"Zinnia Walker. She loves pretty things."

"Did you tell her the crystal has healing properties?"

"She didn't care."

Amethyst was a natural tranquilizer. It relieved stress and dispelled anxiety. Right about now, I could use a one-on-one session with that rock.

"Um, Emma . . ." Yoly ran a hand along the side of her tote. Her face blazed red.

"What's up?"

"I didn't want to show you this earlier." She reached into her bag and pulled out a giant postcard. I held out a hand, but she didn't give it to me. Instead, she pressed it to her chest. The front was an avant-garde type of painting, all swirls and splatters. "It's . . . it's a threat."

"A threat?"

*"Mm-hmm.* I found it shoved under the door of the spa when I went looking for the grand opening banner last night. It says—"

"Give it to me."

She relinquished it.

I read the word on the flip side of the card, *Die,* and jolted. I flashed on the interaction between Willow and Palmer at Hideaway Café. Willow asked Palmer if she'd put an offensive postcard with that word under her door. Palmer denied doing anything of the sort.

"I didn't want to call you last night and spook you. I was worried you'd see it as an omen, and I wanted today to be a success, but now with the police and the murder and . . ." Yoly trailed off.

"Go on," I said. Yoly was rarely quiet. She loved to chat. Loved to laugh.

"Detective Summers said Indy Hendriks was the person who saw you go into Mystic Waters."

"That's right."

"I was wondering"—she reclaimed the postcard—"whether she put this under your door."

"She's not an artist."

"No, but she's friends with Palmer. For all you know, Palmer made these postcards for promotional purposes and gave one to Indy."

"Avant-garde and abstract expressionism aren't the kind of art Palmer does. She paints watercolors. Seascape watercolors, to be specific. Besides, if Indy put one of Palmer's postcards under our door and it's similar to the one Willow received, that might implicate her friend in Willow's murder."

"True, but . . ." Yoly lowered her voice. "I saw Indy yesterday.

She was loitering across the street, looking at her cell phone and sniggering."

"She'd probably paused to watch a TikTok reel she'd posted about her clothing line." Indy had quite a large TikTok following.

Yoly hummed. "Why was she in the vicinity of Mystic Waters this morning?"

If she lived south of 10th, as my mother stated, she could have legitimately been walking to work. Hendriks Fashions was north of Mystic Waters.

Sierra bustled into the spa and came to a skidding halt. *"Phew,* I finally have time to focus." She swooped me into a hug. "How are you holding up?"

"I didn't kill her." Saying the words rattled me to my core. Willow was dead. *Murdered.* I shuddered.

"We know you didn't."

Yoly cleared her throat. "Emma, do you think Indy is deliberately trying to make the police suspect you?"

I broke free from my cousin and gawked at Yoly. "To throw suspicion off herself because she killed Willow? You could be right. She and Palmer locked horns with Willow yesterday about what her spa did and didn't offer. They were pretty contentious about it." I had to admit that seemed like a weak motive for murder. Even so, I continued. "Who knows if Indy paid her a visit later on? She told Detective Summers that she'd been on her way to bridge club when she'd seen me last night. Did he corroborate that? Not to mention, if she did kill Willow and got blood on her outfit, she could have easily disposed of it at Hendriks Fashions, donned new clothing, and continued on in a matter of minutes."

"Good point. Who else might have killed Willow?" Sierra moved to the beverage cart and poured herself a glass of cucumber water.

"I saw Hugh and Willow arguing yesterday," I said. "Outside Mystic Waters. Hugh accused Willow of being late on rent."

Yoly said, "But if he killed her, he wouldn't get paid."

"True, but if he wanted to void the contract in order to raise the rent and lease the site to someone else," I countered, "death would be a great way to accomplish that." I thought of Hugh's athletic prowess. Without a doubt, he could have wielded a candlestick like a baseball bat and killed Willow. "Incidentally, Ava Daft wanted to take over the lease."

# Chapter 6

"Omigosh!" Meryl rounded the corner into reception, her spa coat unbuttoned. "Ava Daft is wackier than Daffy Duck. 'Look at me. Look, look, look.'" She altered her voice to sound like Ava's and wiggled her fingers. "'Yoo-hoo, are you paying attention? I have the longest, most gorgeous nails in the world. I'm *so-o-o-o* feminine.'" She huffed. "If you ask me, Ava is a verifiable nutcase. Totally thirsty."

"Doesn't that mean horny?" I asked.

"Thirsty doesn't always have a sexual connotation. It can also mean needy." She mimed quotation marks around the word. "Like thirsty for compliments."

"I stand corrected."

"I mean, c'mon, how in the heck does she open anything with those nails? No soda cans for her. Uh-uh." She mimed struggling with a flip-top. "And fastening a button? Forget about it. Practicality sailed out the window with that one." She cocked a hip. "Why are you talking about her?"

"She wants to take over the Mystic Waters lease. I was wondering whether she might have—"

"Killed Willow?" Meryl looked from Sierra to Yoly. "By bashing her with a candlestick?"

"Emma, what's your take?" Sierra asked. "Do you want Ava to be guilty?"

"I want someone other than me to be the police's number one person of interest."

"Ava, a killer. In-ter-est-ing." Meryl tapped the ash off an imaginary cigarette like a comical international spy and flicked the fake cigarette away. "Here's something to consider. I saw her the other night wearing noise-canceling headphones."

"She does a podcast about curios," Yoly said. "She could have been broadcasting."

"I've listened to it," I said. "She's chatty and charming and shares lots of details about her business."

Meryl sniffed. "Podcasts are usually done in a quiet room, preferably with lots of furniture, curtains, and rugs to dampen ambient noise. Plus, she would need a good microphone. Believe me, I know. I tried to launch a podcast a year ago."

"I'll bet you were a hoot," Sierra said.

"Nope. I sucked eggs. I was a failure with a capital F. I need a live audience to be funny."

I said, "Ava seemed pretty annoyed that Willow got the lease instead of her. Maybe she was calling a friend and airing her resentment."

"With headphones on?" Meryl asked.

"She could have been getting ready to do a podcast but needed a quick walk to get some fresh air," Yoly said diplomatically. "Mystic Waters is a block and a half from her shop, or . . ." Her eyes widened. "What if she was slinking around town putting the postcards under your and Willow's doors?"

"What postcards?" Sierra asked.

Yoly reached into her tote and pulled out the one we'd received. Sierra peeked at it. Meryl, too.

"Oh, man, not good," my cousin said. "Emma, you have to give that to the police."

"And tell them what?" I shrugged a shoulder. "It's a passive-aggressive threat. It's not like anybody—"

"Willow is dead!" Sierra's pitch was frantic. "You could be in danger."

"She's right," Meryl said.

My stomach did a flip-flop. I hadn't thought of that. Could Willow's killer have it in for all spa owners?

"Better safe than sorry," Sierra pressed.

*No, no, no. This cannot be happening. Not on the first day of the grand opening. Or any day whatsoever.*

I summoned the radiant words that were often attributed to the famous meditation guru, Chögyam Trungpa Rinpoche: *The bad news is, you're falling through the air, nothing to hang on to, no parachute. The good news is, there is no ground.* I recalled how my meditation teacher had explained the meaning and felt my spirit lighten. The ground, which represented the hard basic facts of existence, were the greatest source of a person's anxiety, and though that reality should be respected, it should not rule us. However, he reminded us, we should not ignore or deny that we are falling, either. We needed to be present. We needed to take control.

I eyed the inspirational plaque I'd hung beside the fountain—*Embrace the Moment Fully*—and did my best to obey. "No more talk about murder."

"Don't you want to solve it?" Meryl asked.

"Me? No. I want answers, sure, but I have to trust that the police will figure it out."

Meryl snickered.

"Why are you laughing?" I asked.

"Trust the cops? Get real. Where I come from . . ." She blanched.

"Sorry. I keep forgetting Carmel is a sweet, gentle town. It's nothing like where I come from. You keep on trusting, Emma. Trusting is good."

"Everyone, back to work." I forced a brave smile. "Let's make sure each of our customers has a great time today. Good treatments. Positive vibes. We will not let this news bring us down, do you hear me?"

*Do you hear yourself?* my inner voice shouted. *You're not sad. You're devastated.*

How was it possible? My friend, albeit a thorny friend, had been murdered, and I was a suspect. No, I would not sink into despair. Somehow I would convince the police I was innocent. I would clear my name and rise above the fray.

Pushing my concern to the side, I said to Meryl, "If you have time at the end of the day, I could use a manicure."

"Sure thing." She saluted.

I turned to Sierra. "And I'll need a kale-banana-protein smoothie—stat." The gnawing in my gut about the murder had depleted any energy my morning power bar had possibly supplied.

"Ooh, watch out. She's hangry," Meryl said.

"I'm not hangry, and I'm not angry. I'm just hungry."

"Your wish is my command." Sierra hurried away.

Yoly stood there, postcard in hand. Softly, she said, "Sierra's right, Emma. We need to give this to the police. It could be evidence. If they have the postcard Willow found, they could compare the handwriting and determine if the sender is the same person. At the very least, it might make Detective Summers suspect you less. Is it all right if I take it to him?"

"Sure. Do it."

She nearly clicked her heels with glee.

After downing my drink, I returned to reception and allowed the gentle spa music to calm me. The aroma of jasmine incense—a scent that was helpful in reducing depression, which I was definitely suffering from, what with the worry about Willow's murder as well as from the postcard's warning—reminded me not to be complacent. I needed to be alert.

For the next two hours, I toured the courtyard and spa, asking customers how they were enjoying themselves. A pair of women were sitting in soft blue robes outside two treatment rooms, sipping healthful, nonalcoholic mimosas while awaiting their brightening facials—treatments that would include masks and enzyme peels. A man was reading a spa treatment brochure until his pedicure appointment. He'd already enjoyed a lymphatic massage.

Tish Waterman, a whip-thin woman who owned A Peaceful Solution, emerged from one of the rooms, finger-combing her hair. She was dressed in a robe loosely tied at the waist. "Hello, Emma." A scar ran the length of her right cheek, and I recalled how, the first time I'd met her, she'd fearlessly confided that she'd been drunk when she'd suffered the injury. For years afterward, she'd been ashamed, but now that she was clean and sober, she considered the scar a reminder of the inner battle she'd fought and won. "Your spa is lovely."

"I didn't know you were having a treatment," I said, walking ahead of her to reception.

"I visited the café and the shop and made an appointment for a massage."

"Rival research?"

She tittered. "Heavens no. I heard one of your masseuses gave shiatsu massages, and I've never had one. It was fabulous."

"Don't steal my staff," I said over my shoulder, in jest.

"I won't, but you can bet all my therapists are going to learn how to do it. As for the rest? The shop? The café? Don't worry. I won't copycat your enterprise. I wish I'd thought of it, but I have plenty to keep me busy." At the beverage cart, she poured herself a mug of hot water and didn't add anything to it. She sipped it and cupped it in both hands. "I'm sorry to hear you're a suspect in Willow Shafer's murder."

"I'm innocent."

"Even so, it's a headache. People look at you differently," she said. "They don't mean to, but they do. I know, because my daughter was a person of interest in a murder. It has taken people a long time to embrace her." She took another sip of hot water.

"Tish, was a threatening postcard ever slipped under the door of your spa?"

"No." Her forehead pinched. "Threatening how?"

"It doesn't matter." The killer might not have been the one who'd left the cards under Willow's and my doors.

"By the way," Tish went on, "I heard you do essential oils for dogs."

"Not on a regular basis."

"Well, Dottie—she's a dear friend and regular client of mine—swears by your magic. I have two shih tzus. May I bring them in?"

"I would be happy to consult your pets at my home." I pulled a business card from the holder on the reception desk and jotted down my cell phone number. "Call me."

She tucked the card into the pocket of her robe and headed for the changing rooms.

At around three, realizing the smoothie hadn't filled me up, I went to the café. Sierra was serving up plates of something that smelled ultra-savory. "What's on the menu?" I sidled to the front of the line.

"Turmeric curry," Sierra said. "If you didn't know, curcumin, which is the most active ingredient in turmeric, is a strong antioxidant and has powerful anti-inflammatory effects." She said this without guile. She took food and health seriously.

"Perfect. I'm feeling inflamed by blame," I joked.

"Don't make light," she cautioned.

"Aw, c'mon. Be glad my sense of humor is intact. Serve me up some of that deliciousness."

She took a bowl from beneath the counter, filled it with rice, and topped it with the curry. She handed it to me, and I took a bite.

"Yum. Don't forget, the sound bath is at six for you, Nana, and Yoly."

"Feel free to cancel. We'll understand. You're preoccupied with—"

"No canceling," I said. "We continue with our schedule. If we act like everything is fine, it will be."

Sierra set the ladle down with a clack and said, sotto voce, "I've been thinking about who might have killed Willow."

I'd been trying not to.

"It's all about motive." My cousin wasn't a mystery reader, but she was a devotee of *CSI*-type television shows.

"I'm sure the police are investigating all angles."

"That doesn't mean we can't bat around ideas. You said Hugh Ashbluff came to mind."

"Yes."

"And Ava."

"Right."

"Who else? Give it some thought," she advised.

I polished off my curry and headed to the spa. The manicure with Meryl was everything I'd hoped it would be. I wasn't fussy and didn't wear polish or fake nails, but with all the treatments I concocted, I could mess up my nails royally. While she buffed and filed and the spa chair did its rolling magic on my back, she gave me a rundown of her comedy club schedule.

"You sound busy," I said.

"Never a dull moment."

"Has your son ever seen you perform?"

"No." She wasn't the type to cry, but her eyes grew moist.

"That's a shame."

"His father throws shade on me every chance he gets."

I didn't know how to respond.

"He's a jerk to the max," she said. "Now close your eyes."

She began rubbing a delicious smelling orange scrub on my forearms, after which she rinsed it off and massaged my arms. To her credit, despite her aversion to hot rocks, she went all out with them. As she slid them up and down my arms, I felt the tension in my body melt away.

"I got to thinking about Ava again," Meryl said.

I opened my eyes, relaxing moment snafued. "What about her?"

"Like I said, she's sort of kooky."

*Daffy* was the word she'd used. "Big deal. So what if she has long fingernails? Lots of people do."

"No, that's not it. I go to her store at least once a month. My mother loves jewelry, and the earrings they sell at Shabby Chic Nook are cheap but adorable." She dragged out the word. "Anyway, you know me. I can be chatty."

I bit back a smile.

"I'm always looking for a new bit. Something to joke about. So I was there last week, and Ava was talking to her girlfriend, Quinlyn—"

"She's a life partner, not a girlfriend."

"Life partner. Excuse me for not being politically correct," she said dramatically.

I threw her the stink eye.

"They were discussing their living arrangements, and Ava was telling Quinlyn to write her a check and said she'd deposit it and pay the rent, but Quinlyn protested, asking why everything was in Ava's name. Well, Ava made a face"—Meryl screwed up her nose and mouth—"and Quinlyn started crying and ran out, and, get this, Ava smirked at me. That's not the proper response, you know? It's sus."

"Suspect," I said.

"Yeah. It's like"—she wriggled her fingers—"kooky and controlling."

*Or at the very least insensitive*, I thought.

"Emma!" My mother burst into the treatment room.

Startled by the intrusion, Meryl dropped a rock on the floor and quickly apologized. "Oh, geez, Emma, sorry!"

"It's all right. We're done. Thank you." I twisted in the massage

# Chapter 7

I was vibrating like a tuning fork after she left. How dare she. How *dare* she. All my life, she'd wanted to control me. It stopped now. Actually, it had stopped years ago, but she hadn't caught on, which made me giggle. Not just giggle. I began to laugh. Hard. But then I wanted to scream because she'd made me lose my cool. One of the main reasons I'd studied meditation and subsequently massage and other therapies was to prove to myself that I was better than my mother. I was calm. In control. I was in touch with my inner self. I didn't need to impose my will on others. I didn't need to be hard-headed. At the tender age of thirteen, I'd promised myself I would embrace life and treasure whoever and whatever an individual was or might hope to be.

When the laughing—it was more jagged, nervous sniggering now—subsided, I slogged to the meditation room to prepare the singing bowls. I wanted to regain my calm. I wanted to feel fortified and powerful.

The meditation room was my favorite space in the spa. Six recliner chairs sat in a cluster at the far end of the room. In the center was a large square of rubber flooring. I'd painted the room a soft green and had lined the walls with glass shelving upon which sat the variety of singing bowls. An array of ethically sourced crystals also adorned the room to add to the positive energy. Crystals were like galaxies, each one a unique system of energies creating vibrations that coincided with the place where they were created, and they emitted energy to those who interacted with them.

I dimmed the lights and sat on the floor mat, cross-legged, and placed a hand on my chest. Raising my rib cage, I inhaled and exhaled. With each breath, I remained aware of how my upper chest and abdomen were moving. The point was to lessen the movement of those two body parts and allow the diaphragm to work more efficiently. After three minutes, thoughts of my flare-up with my mother vanished. I rose, slipped on a spa coat, and prepared the room for the sound bath session.

Sierra and Yoly arrived promptly at six, both crowing about the successful day they'd had. I didn't tell either about the run-in with my mother and opted not to bring up Willow's murder. Heaven forbid I disturb the positive vibrations oozing out of them.

Nana Lissa arrived in a flurry. Her cheeks were rosy. The sleeves of her white silk blouse were smudged, as if she'd been tugging on them. "I've been thinking about the murder," she said.

"Nana, let's debrief afterward, over a cup of soothing tea."

"All I wanted to say was Dylan Summers will sort this out. He's highly intelligent and, above all, fair."

*"Shh,"* I instructed. "Clear your mind."

"Emma—"

"Nana, breathe."

Obediently, she inhaled, and her shoulders rose and fell. After a long moment, she said, "Do we change our clothes? How does this work? I've never—"

"Relax." I embraced her, amused that she, who was typically as cool as a cucumber and interacted with fairies no less, seemed nervous. "You keep your clothes on. You'll sit in one of those recliners or you may choose the mat. Lie down or sit up or even curl into a ball. It's up to you. All I want you to do is immerse yourself in the experience as the sound and vibrations encourage your body to relax. Consider it a journey of self-discovery through meditation."

Her skin tone returned to normal, and I guided her to one of the chairs.

"Sierra, Yoly, choose a spot. I've explained everything to you before. Remember to be aware of your thought process and try to avoid distractions. That's the best way to fully benefit from the therapy. And remember to let your feelings come and go. Ebb and flow. There's no right or wrong."

I dimmed the lights, leaving on the recessed lighting that encircled the room, and began to walk around the space, stirring the crystal singing bowls one by one with a resonant rod. The sound was intended to communicate with the participants' chakras. The bowls, each a singular size, emitted a unique sound energy. The square shape of the meditation room allowed the tones to fill and expand in the air, and I found myself breathing deeply.

Softly, I said, "Let the sounds wash over you. Let them guide you to a place of deep relaxation."

I continued swirling the rod in the bowls. "Focus on the sensations you're feeling. Don't let your mind wander. Stay attentive to the sounds." I moved past the chairs. "You might notice deep emotions surfacing. Observe them and let them wash over you. Do not judge a thing." I stopped talking then and simply allowed the sound to work its magic.

When forty-five minutes had passed, I said in barely a whisper, "Start to rouse yourselves. Wiggle your toes. Your fingers. When you're ready, open your eyes."

Slowly, I brought the lighting up in the room—not to full illumination; that would be too bright and could shock their systems—

but to a moderate level so that the trio would become aware that the session was officially over.

"All right. Come to a sitting position. If you feel dizzy, don't rise to your feet until you're balanced."

Sierra opened her eyes and stretched.

"How do you feel?" I asked.

"Incredible," she murmured.

Nana yawned and said, "I've never felt more at peace."

"And you?" I asked Yoly as all of us made our way into the hall and veered in the direction of reception.

She smiled. "I forgot all about what I learned at the police station."

I gripped her shoulder. "Hold on. You've got news?"

"Sure do."

"Tea for four," I said to Sierra. "Outside."

"Yes, ma'am."

Within minutes, we seated ourselves at a wrought-iron table in the courtyard. Sierra brought the tea and accoutrements on a lacquered sea-blue tray. Nana, Yoly, and I couldn't sip ours yet. It was too hot. Sierra was the only one who seemed inured to the temperature.

*"Mmm,"* she hummed. "Perfection. Rooibos tea or red tea is a caffeine-free and flavorful alternative to black or green tea." She sipped her brew again. "Add cream or sugar if you like."

I turned to Yoly. "Fill us in. Did the police find the postcard Willow accused Palmer of leaving?"

"They didn't."

"Meaning they had nothing to compare with the one we received? No handwriting? No fingerprints?"

She shook her head.

Nana quirked an eyebrow. "What do you mean the one you received?"

Yoly produced a snapshot of our postcard on her cell phone and explained where she'd found it.

"The card Willow was waving had a seascape on the front, Nana, not splatter art, like on mine."

Yoly said, "The police don't expect to get any evidence from yours."

"Hey," Sierra said, "do you think Indy swiped Willow's?"

"Indy?" Nana Lissa asked.

I told her my suspicion about how Indy had conveniently been in the vicinity of Mystic Waters last night as well as this morning and how she could have killed Willow, disposed of her soiled outfit at Hendriks Fashions, and continued on to bridge club.

Sierra bobbed her head, agreeing.

Nana said, "She's quite good at bridge. A master of some sort. I'm not clear on all that. However, if she was in a game, I know someone who could corroborate it."

"If she's telling the truth, I'll be at the top of the police's suspect list," I said with a sigh. "But find out. We need answers."

Yoly rose and stepped behind me. "You look tense, Emma. I'm afraid you're going to split in two. May I massage your shoulders?"

"Yes, please."

Using both hands, she kneaded my neck. Her thumbs were remarkably strong.

"You're good," I said.

"I'll get better with practice. I've learned Swedish massage and shiatsu. I'd like to learn tuina."

"What's that?" Sierra asked.

"It's one of the four main branches of traditional Chinese medicine."

"The other three are acupuncture, qigong, and herbal medicine," I said.

Yoly nodded. "Tuina is based on the imbalance of one's life force, or qi. Its intent is to stimulate the flow of qi to knock out imbalances and such." She went on to explain how, in the Chinese culture, qi was a vital part of every living being, like vapor or air or breath. "The practice of balancing qi is called qigong."

I allowed Yoly to work the muscles of my neck for another couple of minutes before saying, "Thank you. That was great." I yawned and covered my mouth with my hand. "I think I'll call it a night." I went to lock up the spa.

My grandmother followed. "Emma." She brushed my shoulder with her fingertips. "A little birdie told me you had a fight with your mother."

"A birdie or a fairy?"

Nana grinned. "Yes, it was Merryweather Rose of Song. After the news about Willow, I asked her to keep watch over you. When your mother lit into you, Merryweather couldn't wait to inform me. She was quite concerned."

"*Aha.* That's why you were tense when you arrived earlier."

"Are you all right? Your mother can be brash."

"We lock horns, but I'm used to it," I said lightly. Was I? The words that had flowed from Kate's mouth had been beyond brazen. They'd been cruel. Today of all days, right as I was opening the spa. I heaved a sigh. "Her timing stinks."

"Merryweather said your mother challenged you again about the business."

"She doesn't believe I can succeed as an entrepreneur. She said I'm not equipped to be a boss. She'll never stop wanting me to become a teacher."

"Bah! You, my sweet girl, are exceptional in the art of mindful meditation. You know exactly what a person needs to balance his or her spirit. It's a gift and one you cannot and should not squander." She gently cupped my cheek. "I'll talk with your mother."

"Don't."

She assessed me for a long moment. "All right. I'll let the two of you sort it out. But if you need my help, or if you need to consult Merryweather . . ."

"If only I could see her."

"She's petting your hair as we speak."

I had felt a light touch above my right ear and thought it was an insect. I peered in that direction but didn't see a thing. Not even a glimmer.

"Soon," Nana assured me. "You'll see her soon. Your heart is open. It's a matter of time."

When I arrived home, Vivi was waiting at the door. Had she spent the day in the foyer anticipating my arrival or did she hear my key in the lock and bolt off the cat pillow in the kitchen to greet me? I tossed my purse on the side table and lifted her for a kiss. "Do you know how gorgeous you are?"

She purred that she did.

"Did you know that your breed was nearly eradicated during World War Two? Only a couple of cats were alive at the end of the war. They belonged to Monsieur Baudoin-Crevoisier and became known as the foundation cats for Birmans. How's that for trivia?"

She complained with a yowl, but I was now a cat nerd, so she was going to have to tolerate me every time I mentioned her origin story. When I was a girl, I hadn't had any pets. My mother claimed she was allergic, but I was pretty certain she didn't want the hassle. When I moved into the fourplex, I wanted a cat so badly I could taste it. However, because I'd be working long hours, I needed to ensure that I picked the kind of cat that could be independent yet lovable. Sierra had suggested a stray because they showered their owners with devotion, but I really wanted a cat with history. I read up on cats—the library had loads of books about them—and I discovered Birmans. Was I ever thrilled that I had. Vivi was very affectionate and extremely intelligent. She was now ten months old and as happy as any cat I'd ever met. I set her on the floor, gave her rump a pat, and she scampered to the kitchen. I followed.

While I dished up some tuna for her and made myself a modest dinner of poached salmon and asparagus, I mulled over the events of the last twelve hours. The police suspected me of Willow's murder. I didn't do it. Who did? Would I need a lawyer? Would I have to investigate, as Sierra suggested, in order to exonerate myself?

I knew many of the people Willow did. One must have had a motive. I didn't think it was a random killing. On the other hand, using the candlestick in the gift basket I'd given her did seem like a spur-of-the-moment act. Had a thief seen Willow inside the building tallying her receipts when I was with her? Did that person sneak in after I left and kill and rob her?

I made a mental note to discuss the possibility with Detective Summers. I wasn't naive enough to believe he'd reveal any of his investigation to me, but helping him could make him trust me more. Yoly believed the police were taking the postcard she'd found seriously since they had appropriated it. If only they could find the postcard Willow had received and do a comparison.

Vivi sidled over to me and swatted my leg with her tail.

"Yes, food. Here you go, princess." I set her dish on the mat and took my dinner to the bistro table.

Cutting off a corner of my salmon with a fork, I continued to mull over the murder. If Indy Hendriks had a verifiable alibi, who else might have killed Willow? I'd told Yoly and Sierra about Hugh arguing with Willow. Yoly had countered that if he'd killed Willow, she wouldn't have been able to make good on the rent. Did he, as I'd suggested, hope to regain possession of the retail space and lease it at a higher rate? Surely, murder wasn't his sole option. After all, he could have found something in the contract to boot Willow out. What other motive might he have? Were there other retailers who'd coveted the space? Could that add to the suspect list exponentially?

Vivi hopped onto the second bistro chair where I'd set a faux fur, navy-blue cat pillow, and let rip with a rumble. She wanted to play.

Obliging, I grabbed a teaser wand fitted with a catnip-filled bird and held it over her head. She rose on her rear legs to paw at it. I dangled it to the right and lowered it. She bounded to the floor to follow.

As we continued our game of hunt and chase, I thought about last night's dinner at Hideaway Café and how Indy, with Palmer as reinforcement, had lashed out at Willow and, by association, me.

Was Palmer the one who'd slid the offensive postcards under Willow's and my doors? Could she possibly be that incensed with spa owners? She didn't have a problem with massage therapy, not if she was a patron of A Peaceful Solution. However, Willow had accused her of despising meditation and New Agey therapy. Was that true?

*No, Emma. That's not a good enough reason to threaten someone.*

Another thought occurred to me. Was Palmer spiteful enough to have been the one scaring Willow with ghost recordings and hang-up calls, hoping Willow would give up the business? Would she start doing the same to me?

Mentally exhausted and realizing that if I wanted to sleep tonight, I needed to quiet my mind, I said to Vivi, "Bed."

After doing my ablutions, I slipped into my pajamas and crawled under the comforter. Vivi curled into a ball on her pillow. Closing my eyes, I began my deep breathing process. Ten minutes later I was still alert. The routine was not doing the trick. I was too wound up. I picked up the Agatha Christie mystery I'd been reading for the past week—I wasn't a fast reader; I couldn't skim—and opened to the bookmarked page. The story was great and compelling, but two chapters later, reading had done the trick. My eyes closed for the night.

First thing Thursday morning, roused by Vivi kneading my stomach with merry abandon, I decided to take a brisk walk. Drinking in fresh air seemed like the best way for me to waken fully as I found my calm. A short loop down Ocean, past the library, and up 4th would be the ideal route.

The sun was shining, and birds were singing cheerily while flitting between the cypress and Monterey pines. By the time I neared the Harrison Library, I was feeling nearly as lighthearted as I had yesterday morning at the grand opening . . . until we received news of Willow's death.

As I thought of her, my blithe attitude faded. Needing a moment to regroup, I trod up the library's stone path and sat on a bench in the drought-resistant garden. It was a lovely place to meditate. The plants were beautiful, and the chitter of insects distinct. Even from this distance, I could hear the sound of the ocean lapping against the beach and I breathed easier.

As my mind once again drifted to aspects of Willow's murder, I felt something touch my shoulder. I moved to brush it off and heard what sounded like laughter.

No way. Was it a fairy? Was it Merryweather Rose of Song? Her name really was a mouthful. I peered at the tree by the main entrance but didn't see movement. "Merryweather?"

Nothing responded. Had I imagined the laughter? Perhaps it was the tinkle of nearby wind chimes. I rose to my feet and spun in a circle, inspecting each tree. Oh, how I could use a fairy sighting right about now, but it was not to be.

Disheartened, I slogged home. Vivi met me at the door and peeked past me. Did she sense I'd come across a fairy? Had she been hoping one would follow me home?

I stroked her under the chin. "Sorry. No visitors this time. I'm riding solo."

She warbled her regret.

"Yes, I understand. You're alone, but you're a cat, and cats like to be alone." I glanced at my watch. "Wow! I'm late. I've got to get cracking if I'm going to open the spa on time." We had appointments scheduled all day. I prayed that would be the standard going forward, and that the novelty of a spa with alternative therapies wouldn't be a flash in the pan. I also hoped my being a person of interest in a murder wouldn't scare off customers.

I plucked a Ping-Pong ball from the drawer of the foyer table and threw it into the living room. Vivi tore after it but was unable to trap it as it caromed from one wall to another.

"Have fun," I told her, and headed to the bathroom.

I loved showers. I didn't even mind that the stall in the cottage was tiny, in keeping with the limited space. Nothing could take away the comfort I felt as warm water sluiced over my skin. I particularly enjoyed the after-shower routine of donning lotion. I clasped my wispy hair in a clip, curled a few loose ringlets with a curling iron, dabbed on lip gloss, and slipped into a pair of leggings and a peach T-shirt with the words *Just Breathe* on the front.

Ready to face the day, I started for the kitchen when a loud bang rang out.

# Chapter 8

Alarmed, I grabbed the handle of the curling iron—not the heated rod, thank heaven—and I raced into the living room, weapon raised.

Vivi slinked sheepishly toward me, her haunches low, her chin even lower. She wasn't scared. She was embarrassed.

My breathing settled down when I saw why. The Jane Austen plate was intact on the table in the foyer, but the metal display stand it had been perched on was on the floor. "Phew," I murmured. I wasn't under attack. I set the curling iron on the coffee table, squatted, and held out my arms. Vivi crept into them. "No worries, little one," I cooed. "Your pouncing maneuver did not break my favorite thing. But no more leaping helter-skelter." I tapped her nose and set her on the floor. "I'll be home soon."

I wasn't lying. Time was relative to a cat, wasn't it? Knowing I could get something to eat at the café, I filled the cat's bowl, passed on breakfast, and hurried out the front door.

Smack into my grandmother.

"Morning, Sunshine," Nana Lissa said, a to-go cup in hand. She offered it to me. "I brought coffee for you."

"Bless you. Thank you. I know Sierra doesn't want me to drink caffeine, but this morning I really could use it."

"All things in moderation," she said. "At least I didn't add sugar."

*Rats.*

"What're you doing here?" I asked.

"I thought I'd walk you to work."

A frisson of panic pinched my gut. "You're not worried about my safety, are you?"

"No. Of course not." She said the words too quickly, meaning she was, indeed, concerned. "I thought we could talk and work through any ideas that might have occurred to you overnight about who killed Willow."

"Emma!" Sierra raced down the stairs, her white T-shirt loose over leggings. "Are you okay? I heard a loud noise."

"What kind of loud noise?" my grandmother asked.

"Like a bang," Sierra said.

"Relax. Vivi thinks she's an acrobat." I explained how she'd knocked over the display holder.

"Ha!" Sierra said. "Remember Inky? He used to swing from the chandelier. Literally." Inky had been the first of many cats in my cousin's life. My aunt loved furry critters. However, when Sierra moved to Carmel, she opted not to burden herself. She did a lot of experimental cooking at home and didn't want to find a stray hair in anything.

We started along the street.

Seconds later, Sierra bleated, "Stop!"

We did and regarded her. She was fiddling with her T-shirt, which she'd managed to tuck half in and half out of her leggings.

*"Ooh,"* she muttered, exasperated. "I can never figure out the right way to do this look. Models in magazines manage it with such ease."

"I'm with you," I said. "Tuck in the right side or the left? Or only the middle six inches?" I scrutinized what she'd done. "It looks fine to me, but then fashion has never been my strong suit."

"Girls," Nana said, "you both look adorable."

"You're biased," I replied.

"Bah!"

I sipped from my to-go coffee as we once again headed in the direction of the spa. Passing Devendorf Park at the northwest block of Ocean Avenue and Junipero Street, I peered at the gorgeous oak at the far end and recalled my peaceful moment in the Harrison Library garden. "Sierra, do you believe in fairies?"

She sighed. "Nana Lissa swears they're real, but I've never seen one. Why do you ask?"

I told them about my morning encounter and the laughter I was certain I'd heard.

Nana Lissa grinned. "One can always believe without seeing."

"True," I murmured.

"Uh-uh. I need to see one," Sierra said. "I need cold, hard facts!"

Nana clucked her tongue. "You sound like Detective Summers."

Hearing his name gave me the willies.

We turned down 7th Avenue, and Sierra said, "Emma, what do you think about doing a Zoom crystal reading with my mom today? Let's cloak you in good vibes."

"I could use all the good vibes in the world." We weren't equipped to do crystal readings at the spa yet. I hoped to hire someone along the way who was adept at providing them. There were plenty of crystal readers online, but to have a reading in person was much more personal and intimate. "Especially since the police consider me a suspect."

"They don't," Nana said.

"Yes, they do."

My grandmother pressed her lips together.

Sierra said, "Have you given more thought as to who might've wanted to kill Willow other than Ava or Hugh or Indy?"

"Palmer comes to mind," I said. "There might be others that Willow tangled with, too."

"She wasn't the gentlest of souls," Nana Lissa said.

Sierra shook her head. "I can't see Palmer doing it. She's got goodness written all over her."

*She didn't the other night,* I mused.

"I agree," Nana said. "Palmer donates her time to worthy causes, and she dotes on that daughter of hers."

"Olivia?" I asked.

"Her eldest, Alexandra."

"The other day you said she moved away."

"Yes, she left and hasn't returned, but that doesn't keep Palmer from talking about her all the time."

"Why'd she leave?"

"She and Palmer clashed like you and your mother do." Nana Lissa smiled softly. "Like your mother and I used to."

"I still think we should consider her a suspect." I recapped the conflict Nana and I had witnessed at the café between Palmer, Indy, and Willow. "Yes, Indy was the aggressor, but Palmer didn't tell Indy to stop."

As we were climbing the stairs to the Courtyard of Peace, Sierra said, "Who else do you think has a motive?"

"Other retailers in Ava's complex who could lose their leases might have coveted the Mystic Waters location," I said. "Prime property is hard to get in Carmel."

Nana Lissa said, "That's an astute observation."

I wondered if I should ask Ava about the other retailers. In the course of the conversation, I could find out what her alibi was for Tuesday night.

"Did Willow have a boyfriend or significant other?" Sierra asked, pausing by one of the tables. No customers were dining yet. None were peering through the gift shop's windows, either.

I said, "Lots of guys were interested in her over the years, including the one she stole from me in college, but lately she'd been keeping info about her love life close to the vest. I'm not even sure she was dating."

"Hold on. She stole your boyfriend?" Sierra whistled.

"Don't tell the police that," our grandmother cautioned.

"Nana, you of all people know I didn't mind." I'd called her the night it happened. Within an hour, she'd made me see the light. "I was well rid of him," I said to Sierra. "Bonzo was a drummer in a band."

"His name was Bonzo? For real?" Sierra snickered.

"Bonzo, aka Bruno Bonzini." I grinned. "FYI, Bonzo happens to be the alternative form of *bonze*, meaning a Buddhist monk or priest in East Asia."

"Really?" Nana asked.

"Trivia for four hundred, Ken. It also means 'self-important person.' However, in this case, Bonzo was the only person who thought he was important."

"Go on," Sierra said.

"He hated any kind of music that was sedate or calming, and he made fun of all the meditative practices I was into. He'd dubbed it woo-woo." Come to think of it, that was what Palmer had called it the other night. Willow had labeled it New Agey. Why had she been dismissive? Had she hoped, by belittling me, she'd win over Indy and Palmer as future customers?

"Emma?" Sierra touched my arm.

"Sorry." I fanned the air. "He and I were complete opposites."

"What attracted you to him in the first place?"

"His eyes. He had soulful eyes. And he was a great kisser." My grandmother didn't seem embarrassed by my candor, so I continued. "The first time he and I connected was at a pizza party. I apologized for having onion breath. He said he didn't give a whit. He'd been wanting to kiss me for months. We were in the same English class. A few weeks later, though, at a frat party, things changed. Willow and I had gone together. Bonzo met her and, wham! He was head over heels."

"Why?"

"Because she couldn't stop raving about John Bonham, the drummer for Led Zeppelin, also nicknamed Bonzo, and how he had it all going—the power, the groove. She spoke Bonzo's language. I didn't stand a chance. I'll admit I was surprised how easily I bowed out, but that had to account for something, right? I obviously wasn't that invested. A couple of months later, Willow hooked up with a professor—a much older professor in his late forties. Bonzo took it hard for about a New York minute, and then he fell for a girl who loved heavy metal."

"Where is he now?" Sierra asked.

"On the East Coast, I think." I hadn't followed his career. Had he stuck with music or wound up as a history teacher, which he said was his fallback plan?

Sierra said, "Who else did Willow date?"

"Are you wondering whether an ex-lover might have killed her?"

"It's not out of the question."

"I don't have a list," I said, "but I could probably come up with a few names."

Were the police looking into her prior boyfriends' whereabouts at the time of the murder? Was it possible one of them had held a grudge? She'd always been the one to end a relationship. "You know, as much as Willow enjoyed being adored—she dated at least ten men that I knew of—rarely did a relationship last longer than a couple of months. I'm not sure why. Friends teased her, saying she had daddy issues. Not that she was in love with him but because he'd abandoned her and bruised her heart."

"Poor Willow," Nana Lissa said, and regarded Sierra and me. "As for you girls and dating—"

"I'm doing fine." I raised both hands. "I don't need a relationship. Certainly not now."

"Me, either!" Sierra exclaimed.

Nana Lissa chuckled. "I didn't say a thing." She glanced at her watch. "I must dash. Don't forget. Tonight. Book club at my place." She bussed Sierra on the cheek and hugged me goodbye. Softly, she told me to keep thinking outside the box. I promised I would.

Sierra hurried into the café right behind her sous-chef.

I toured the spa and therapy rooms, checking out each area to make sure nothing untoward had occurred overnight, all the while wondering about Willow's love life. When I returned to reception, Meryl was there, studying the appointment calendar on the computer screen.

"Busy day ahead, boss," Meryl said, a broad smile on her face. She'd donned her spa coat over a paisley peasant blouse and jeans. "You excited?"

"I am." I nudged her out from behind the desk.

She moved to the front and propped her elbows on it, gazing at me in a goofy way. "Why did the man with bipolar disorder go to the nail salon?"

"I don't know. Why?"

"Because they offered manic cures. Get it?"

I ogled her. "Don't put that one in your act."

"A real groaner, huh?" She sniggered. "How about this? What's the hardest part about being a manicurist?" She waited. Tilted her head. "You really have to nail it."

I laughed.

Pleased with my response, she appraised her fingers, curling them into her palm before spreading them wide and flipping over her hand. She'd painted each nail a different color.

"Your nails look pretty," I said. "Summery and festive."

"Speaking of that, last night I got to thinking about Ava and her super-long nails and how I should talk her into shortening them, and that got me thinking about her partner, Quinlyn."

"What about her?"

"What if she acted on behalf of her beloved? You know, got rid of Willow to pave the way for Ava to secure the lease?"

The notion that Quinlyn could be a murderer hadn't occurred to me. "In-ter-est-ing," I said in the same silly spy way Meryl had yesterday.

At eleven, Sierra summoned me. She'd started a Zoom meeting in the spa's office, which was located behind reception. I hadn't done much to decorate the office. I'd painted it white to make the space seem larger. A window allowed in light from the alleyway between our courtyard and the neighboring building. The white desk near the window held a laptop computer, pencils, pens, and whatnot. A feng shui ceramic water fountain sat on the corner of the desk and emitted a soothing burble. Aunt Sophie said the deep aspects of water connected us to wisdom and intuition, but the flow of water helped interpret how we interacted with the world around us. She also claimed that the constant movement of water stirred up one's life force. I'd wanted to add a fountain at the cottage, too, but hadn't because I feared Vivi would have too much fun playing in it. She wasn't afraid of water.

On the wall next to the window I'd hung a corkboard. Affixed to it were pastel-colored, three-by-five cards, each one containing a task for the spa opening that had needed to be completed. Blue for the spa, green for the gift shop, purple for the café, and yellow for the patio. On them I'd jotted things to buy and itemized chores and sketched layouts. My mother had drummed the color-coded technique into me when I was in high school. She had been intent on teaching me how to write a thesis, and she swore color coding helped organize thoughts. As much as I didn't like the way she'd browbeaten the method into me, it had stuck.

"Hello, I'm here," my aunt said.

"Hi, Mom." Sierra rounded the desk and sat in the chair.

I followed and peered over my cousin's shoulder at the computer screen. "Aunt Sophie," I squealed. "It's good to see you. It's been way too long."

"I feel the same, love. Congratulations on opening the spa." My aunt had fawn-brown hair like my mother, but hers hung in loose curls on her shoulders, and whereas Kate's eyes were hazel and intense, Sophie's eyes were an otherworldly translucent blue. Her clothing style was the polar opposite of my mother's, too. She preferred wearing harem pants in bright colors and kimonos over white tank tops, like the orange print one she was wearing now.

"I heard about your friend Willow," she said, fingering the shattuckite necklace I'd often seen her wearing, a piece that helped her focus her intuitive powers. "How are you doing?"

"I'm fine. Coping." I didn't add *trying to come up with other suspects*, worried she'd think I was being negative.

"Let's do a reading and get your qi in order." Sophie was older than my mother by two years. She had never married, shunning the very idea, though she did think it was right for other people. However, she'd always wanted a child, so she went to a sperm bank to conceive Sierra. She didn't know the donor and didn't want to. She hoped Sierra wouldn't want to, either, but with today's DNA kits, it was inevitable she'd find out. "Ready?"

"Am I ever."

Crystal readings were similar to other forms of readings. They were a spiritual and empowering way to provide self-discovery.

Sophie said, "As you know, my readings are designed to help you gain deep insight into your intuitive powers. I work with twenty crystals."

"Aunt Sophie, stop, you don't need to do the whole spiel. I know each stone has a significance and could have different meanings when bundled with other stones."

She smiled indulgently. "I thought you might have forgotten. We haven't done one of these for two years."

Wow, really? Two years had passed in the blink of an eye.

Sierra said to me, "Mom's been aching to do one ever since you decided to open the spa."

Sophie mock-glowered. "I heard that."

"Well, you have!" Sierra air-kissed her mother, who duplicated the gesture. They had a bond that I craved with my mother but knew I would never have.

"Here are the crystals we'll be using." She held up a velvet-lined octagonal box in which lay twenty tumbled crystals, each about an inch in diameter. Using a finger, she named a few. "Azurite, amethyst, celestite, garnet, tiger's eye."

Sierra said, "Now she's going to tell you that this works like tarot, each crystal having its own meaning."

"Bitty, please don't interrupt," Sophie said.

Sierra moaned. "Mother, when will you stop calling me that?"

"Never. You will always be my bitty girl. When you were born, you barely weighed six pounds, and look at you now. I doubt you weigh sixty pounds."

"Ha!" Sierra stuck her tongue out. "One hundred and fourteen."

"In your chef's outfit." Sophie laughed, the sound like a silky waterfall. "Let's get started. Emma, I need you to have a question in mind. Don't say what it is."

Oh, I knew the question. I had two, in fact. Who'd killed Willow, and how could I get the police to take me off their suspect list?

"I want you to pick nine crystals. If you don't remember the name of one, describe it to me. It's the law of attraction that matters. What you need to hear will manifest in the stones you select."

My insides began to whirr with excitement, and it took me about a minute to choose them. As I did, I imagined my mother's scornful opinion of this *hoodoo* but did my best to tune it out. Nana Lissa would approve. That was all that mattered.

"Now I'll shake them in my hands," Sophie said, "and drop them from about three inches onto this mat."

At my last reading, which had been in person, I'd touched the mat. I imagined its soft nap beneath my fingertips.

Sophie closed her eyes and shook the stones. When she released them, one rolled to the forefront, closest to her. Three others clustered to the left. Four others bunched to the right, but farther away. A single stone rolled to the rear of the mat. I knew, from a previous reading, that that stone didn't have a lot of importance. It was like Pluto in the planetary hierarchy.

"The first is amethyst," she said. "Always a good stone. It's associated with strengthening your intuition and giving you the ability to envision the truth. It's also good for peace, balance, and detoxification. If you don't have an amethyst necklace, consider buying one to help you tap into your intuition."

I needed intuition to help clear myself of Willow's murder.

"These three are intriguing," Sophie said, gesturing to the trio of clustered stones. "The fluorite is an underrated crystal. I consider it the dharma stone, showing you the reason you are here on earth. It, too, is associated with intuition and having the ability to relate to higher planes of consciousness."

*Let's hear it for intuition,* I cheered inwardly. "Go on."

"Beside it is the tiger's eye, the yellow stone that's reminiscent of a tiger's golden eyes. It helps you connect to your confidence and courage."

I might need courage if I had to face Detective Summers again.

"You see how it slightly touches the fluorite? The combination suggests that you have something to learn."

Yes, I did. The identity of a killer.

"Close by is celestite. That's the muted blue-gray crystal, another of my favorites. It's linked to your spirit guides and should bring calm and balance to your life."

I'd feel much calmer once Willow's murder was solved. She deserved justice. I hoped I could be instrumental in bringing that about.

"Now, these others." Aunt Sophie spent the next few minutes explaining the four that were clustered. "The best of the bunch is the smoky quartz. It's the dusky brown translucent one. It cleanses negative energies around you. I'll send you this stone and the fluorite, and you should keep them in your pocket."

"Pocket? I wear yoga pants."

"Don't be sassy. Put them in the inside pocket, the one that's big enough for a room key or credit card. Now, did you feel you received answers to your questions?"

"I didn't get specific ones, but I certainly am filled with hope that I'll have some very soon."

Sierra slung an arm around me and squeezed. "Thanks, Mom, for helping. Emma was a mess this morning."

"Was not."

"Was, too. Ask Nana Lissa."

She was right. When the Jane Austen plate holder crashed, it rattled me, but now, thanks to the crystal reading, I felt focused and ready to go to battle if necessary.

*Charge!*

# Chapter 9

The morning's appointments went off without a hitch. Yes, a few customers asked about Willow's and my friendship, but I dodged the questions by offering discount coupons for additional appointments. A facial here, a massage there. I raved about the sound baths and tried to encourage everyone to come in for one, saying I'd hold them twice weekly, Wednesdays at noon and Saturdays at four, adding that a client could call on the morning of the bath to see if there was space available. Easy-peasy.

At around eleven, Courtney Kelly wandered in, her gaze taking in the various aspects of the reception area. The whimsical nature of her outfit—tangerine-colored T-shirt over capris adorned with flowers and fairies—made me smile.

"It's lovely, Emma!" she crooned. "Exactly what I imagined. I was out taking a walk to stretch my legs, thought I'd grab a snack, and decided to see the spa in person and make an appointment. I'm sorry I couldn't attend the grand opening."

"No worries." I gave her a tour, showing her the entrance to the café and gift shop and telling her how my grandmother had landed the purchase of the site.

"Some outcomes are meant to be," she said.

We returned to reception, and I provided her with the spa treatments menu.

"A mindful meditation sounds wonderful." She read from the brochure. "'The goal of mindful meditation is to awaken the inner workings of our mental, emotion, and physical spirit.' I could use an awakening. I feel sapped of energy lately."

I set the appointment and handed her a reminder card. "Don't miss the excellent selection of foods at the café and feel free to roam the gift shop. Yoly is doing a marvelous job."

She smiled. "I'm glad you could give her a full-time job."

"Me, too."

"Um . . ." She hesitated.

"What?"

"How are you? I heard the police are considering you . . ." She reached out but didn't touch me. "I've been a suspect. It's not easy. If you need anything . . . advice . . . a welcome ear."

"Care to share your fairy with me?" I asked. Nana Lissa told me that Courtney's fairy, who happened to be the niece of Merryweather Rose of Song, was a righteous fairy. "I hear she's a marvel at helping humans solve crime."

"I wish I could, but she's a one-human fairy."

I felt Courtney was withholding something. A one-human fairy? What did that even mean? I said, "Well, if she gives you a tip that can help me clear my name, clue me in."

"Count on it."

At 1:00 p.m., I decided to take a midday stroll. I wanted to stop in at Shabby Chic Nook. I put Meryl in charge of reception. She was on break until her next appointment. Before I left for my walk, I decided to check in on Sierra and Yoly.

My cousin was beaming as I entered the café. Sales had been

through the roof. Word was getting out that the healthy place to sip and dine was Aroma Wellness café.

I gazed at the menu. Each day there would be two daily specials in addition to the regular fare. "Tell me about the sprout sandwich."

"*Mmm.* So good. I have a special seasoning that you will adore. It tastes like what's on an everything bagel without the bread. Then you choose the bread."

"There's bread in the sandwich?"

"Of course there's bread, you goon. The kinds with crunch are good, like rye or sesame. Or you can go with brioche bread. I make it on site. I add homemade aioli sauce, avocado, and tomato, and voilà." She was so exuberant, it was hard not to grin along with her. "Plus, you get a choice of sprouts."

"There's more than one kind?"

"Alfalfa sprouts are the norm, but broccoli sprouts are earthy and have a kick, and mustard sprouts taste like mustard crossed with horseradish. I prefer radish sprouts. They have a real zing. A combo is what I like best."

"Make me your favorite."

With the bento box that held my to-go sandwich in hand, I started for the gift shop when I spied Floyd Marblemaw standing beside the well, staring into it as if it could provide him with the answers to the world's weightiest problems. His white hair poked out from beneath his fedora. He caught sight of me and did his best to stand up tall, but his hunched back made it impossible. I wondered what had caused it? The bad habit of walking with his shoulders slumped forward? Lack of calcium? Kyphosis, the medical term for the rounding of the upper back, happened often in older people due to weakened spinal bones. A massage would do him good.

"Hello, sir," I said. "Making a wish?"

He adjusted the knot of his tie. "I was hoping for that interview."

"I'm sorry. I told you I can't chat until next week. I've opened a new business, and it's taking all of my concentration."

"Please. A few minutes of your time. I want to talk about what happened to Willow . . ." He licked his chapped lips. "To Ms. Shafer."

"Sir, you'd do best to consult with the police."

"You were her friend."

"Next week."

I couldn't talk to a reporter about the murder. No way. I hurried into the gift shop and closed the door forcefully. There weren't any customers. I didn't need to apologize for being rude to him.

"You're here. Yay!" Yoly clasped me in a bear hug and released me. "What a day! The essential oils are the biggest hit, although almost everyone who has ventured in has been asking if you are truly a suspect in Willow's murder. Our quaint village's rumor mill is in full force. I'm proud to say I haven't succumbed to one ounce of gossip, and I adamantly told them no."

"But I am."

"Yes, but they don't need to know that. If it's not on the news, it's not real, right?"

Why wasn't it on the news? Was Detective Summers intent on keeping a lid on his findings? As for Mr. Marblemaw, would a scoop bolster his career?

"Yoly, have you learned anything new from the police?" I asked.

"Ha! They won't confide in me."

"You gave them a lead."

"Yes, but that's all I'm good for. It is not a tit-for-tat relationship." She eyed the bento box containing my sandwich. "Where are you off to?"

"A walkabout and a visit to Shabby Chic Nook."

"After that," Yoly said, "why don't you go to the police department? You must have other suspects in mind by now."

I told her I'd added Quinlyn and Palmer to the list and gave my reasons. Furthermore, I hadn't ruled out Indy Hendriks.

"That's good info. Tell Detective Summers."

"He won't listen to me. I hinted to him that Indy has it in for me because I was friends with Willow and, like her, I own a spa. He wasn't swayed. Although he had given me his business card." I recalled what Zinnia Walker had murmured at the restaurant. "That's not the half of it," she'd said, implying Palmer and Indy had a different gripe with Willow. What was it?

Yoly sighed. "Maybe there was someone who saw you in your studio after you got home. Why don't you canvass your neighbors? Leave messages on their doors."

"Good idea." I amended my mental to-do list, thanked her, and proceeded on my walk.

Though the worry of being charged with murder hung over me like a rain cloud, I didn't let it ruin my appetite. A few minutes later, delectable sandwich devoured and appetite placated, I arrived at Shabby Chic Nook. I tossed my garbage in a nearby trash receptacle and took a moment to admire the shop's display window, which was teeming with collectibles like magnets, ornaments, small pieces of art, a pillow with the town's map stitched on it, a pair of wineglasses with etchings of the bay, and numerous pairs of earrings.

The shop's door was ajar. Wondering how I could coax an alibi out of Ava, I stepped inside and began to browse the greeting cards on a tall rotating rack. Ava had a knack for finding the wittiest cards I'd ever seen. A perfect example was the one at the top of a column. *The more people I meet, the more I like my cat.* I knew lots of people to whom I could send it.

To my right, a man and woman were perusing the Christmas ornaments, which the shop sold year round. To my left, a single woman was scrutinizing earrings in a Plexiglas holder. She lifted a pair of silver jellyfish studs, held them to her lobes, and studied herself in the gold filigree wall mirror.

Ava, dressed in a navy-blue silk jumpsuit that hugged her curves, her hair snared in a royal-blue claw, was at the register taking cash from a middle-aged woman. After Ava made change, her long nails fumbling with the coins as she had Tuesday, she handed the customer an aqua gift bag tied with sea-green raffia and thanked her for coming in.

The woman scurried past me, smiling as if she'd won the lottery.

I plucked the cat card from its slot and moseyed to the sales counter. Beneath the glass lay a variety of necklaces and rings, each unique. "Hi, Ava. What gem did that woman buy? She was ecstatic."

"A small print of the Carmel River at sunset. She grew up near there and hadn't ever seen a painting of it, saying artists always preferred to capture the bay or the cypress trees."

"Lucky her." To delay buying the greeting card so I'd have enough time to wheedle an alibi out of Ava, I plucked a key chain from a display stand near the register. "These are fun."

"They're kitschy but novel."

"And these seascape postcards are nice," I said, touching the face of one on a carousel. Many looked similar to the one Willow had received. "Do you sell lots of these?"

"Tons."

"Do you have any abstract art postcards?"

"No." She smiled. "There's little demand for those." Her smile suddenly vanished. "Oh, my, Emma, I can't believe it. I heard Indy Hendriks accused you of murdering Willow."

I grimaced.

"The nerve of that woman," Ava went on. "I mean, a rumor is going around that you and Willow exchanged a few words, but honestly, you? A killer? Not in a million years. She must be loony tunes."

The loony tunes comment made me recall Meryl saying Ava was wackier than Daffy Duck, given the way she fussed over her gorgeous nails. I suppressed the urge to giggle.

"There's not a chance you did it." She fetched a feather duster from beneath the counter, whisked it across the antique cash register's keys, and returned it to its spot. "You're the most serene person on the planet."

Lately, serenity had been difficult to achieve.

"Tell me the police aren't going to arrest you," she said.

"Not yet. But for the record, you're correct. I didn't do it. However, I was thinking . . ." I leaned forward and whispered, "You know how Willow was late on her rent, and you were hoping to snare the lease?"

"I didn't kill her!" Ava blurted.

"No. Of course you didn't." I waved my hands. "I didn't mean to imply—"

"I couldn't have. I was doing inventory that night. We'd received a new shipment of snow globes."

Shabby Chic Nook had a huge collection of ocean-themed snow globes. Dozens sat on a narrow ledge that lined the perimeter of the shop near the ceiling. More were peppered in with the items on the shelves.

"They were dusty beyond belief," Ava went on. "I had to wonder where they'd been stored to accumulate that kind of schmutz. But my polishing paid off. I sold three Wednesday morning."

That sounded reasonable, but it didn't completely vindicate her. I mulled over how to proceed and decided the blunt approach was best. "I raised the subject about Willow's lease because you were interested in snaring it."

"I was interested, but not now, after a murder occurred there. Ugh!" She wrinkled her nose.

"I understand," I said. "But I was wondering who else in your complex might have known about Willow's predicament. After all, the leases here are up next year, and I'm guessing one of the other tenants could have been as eager as you to get their hands on that space. It's a sizable layout—lots of square feet—which would be great for a retailer who wanted to expand."

"Many of them are retired and only keep their shops open on weekends to occupy their time, but you could be right." Ava busied herself with organizing the array of freebie promotional bookmarks stacked on the counter. "Should I ask around?" She swept a loose hair off her cheek with her fingernail and added slyly, "Gossip is my forte."

"Ava." Quinlyn Obermeyer emerged from the stockroom at the rear of the store carrying two pairs of porcelain candle holders. "I'm sorry to interrupt." She was mid-twenties with a curvy figure. The blousy dress she had on did nothing for her. The first time I met her, I decided her eyes were her best feature. There was an impishness behind her gaze, as if she were harboring an inside joke and couldn't possibly reveal the punch line.

"Emma won't mind," Ava said. "She's browsing. What's up? Don't tell me those are chipped."

"No, they're fine. Not like the last batch."

Ava confided to me, "A shop owner's nightmare is when a delivery arrives and the items aren't up to snuff. Porcelain candle holders are fragile."

*Unlike brass ones*, I thought. *They could be lethal.*

"However, the scarves that came in . . ." Quinlyn paused for effect. "The supplier messed up the order. They're not all Carmel imprints. Some are of Monterey." She set the candle holders on the counter, bussed Ava's cheek, leaving no mark since she didn't wear lipstick—or any makeup, for that matter—and whisked her long blond braid over her shoulder. "We don't dislike Monterey, Emma, but there are plenty of places there that sell locally themed items. We don't need to, as well."

Ava frowned at me. "I'd better deal with this. Quinlyn, please ring up Emma when she's ready."

Quinlyn watched Ava go and addressed me. "Retail business is not for the faint of heart. Don't get me started about how much we fret when sales are slow."

"Doesn't Ava's podcast get the word out?" I asked.

"Sort of."

"She's really good on it. Very natural. I'd think you'd be overrun with tourists all year round because of it."

"Thanks. That's nice of you to say."

I thought of how Yoly had seen Ava lurking the other day with headphones on and I'd reasoned that she might have been live-casting her podcast. When I thought back on it, Yoly didn't say where she'd seen her. Was it near us or had Ava been in the vicinity of Mystic

Waters? What if she'd been checking out the spa, trying to figure a way she could kill Willow and get away with it? Eager to ask a few more questions, I said, "Quinlyn, could I see that dolphin necklace?" I pointed to one in the display case. "My cousin Sierra has a thing for dolphins. She's never seen one up close but vows she will one day."

Quinlyn removed the tray and set it on the counter.

I fingered the necklace and checked the price. It was reasonable.

"Just so you know," Quinlyn said casually, "a few customers were saying that you and Willow were at odds, and that you—"

"I didn't kill her."

She blanched. "That's not what I meant. One customer said you went to the spa that night. I thought you might have seen something."

"I didn't. I met with Willow, and I left and went straight home." Out of the corner of my eye, I caught sight of a display of Bluetooth earbuds, and I flashed on what Willow had revealed at the end of our conversation. She'd been worried that she was being punked. "Quinlyn, speaking of Willow, she said she was afraid because someone had been trying to scare her by making ghostly sounds outside the spa for weeks. Usually, when she was closing up."

"Ugh. I hate ghosts."

"Do you know any personally?" I teased.

I felt a flutter over my right shoulder and turned. I didn't see a fairy, but that didn't mean Merryweather Rose of Song wasn't sneaking about. I could imagine my grandmother giving her marching orders to protect me at all costs. She was right to be concerned. Asking questions like these could be putting me in the killer's sights.

"No, I don't know any ghosts"—Quinlyn shivered—"and I don't want to, but my brother swears his house is haunted. I've told him I won't come for a visit until he exorcises them. I'd be freaked out." She started to return the necklaces to the case.

"Wait, I'm going to buy that one as a gift for my cousin for helping me open the spa."

Quinlyn removed it from the tray and inserted it into a pretty gold box fitted with polyester padding. "Would you like me to wrap it or will ribbon do the trick?"

"Ribbon would be nice."

She rang up the keychain, necklace, and gift card.

I said, "I mention the ghost thing because Meryl—she's our manicurist at the spa—said Ava was on the street doing her podcast last week about that time." Meryl hadn't said she'd seen her at night, but a tiny stretch of the truth was warranted. "What if Ava was near Mystic Waters and saw whoever was trying to scare Willow?"

"I doubt she did," she murmured as she pulled the blade of a pair of scissors along the underside of the ribbon. "Ava was busy doing inventory. If she doesn't keep on top of it, she gets swamped. Tap your credit card to the card reader."

I complied. "Huh. Ava said she was doing inventory the night Willow was killed, too."

Quinlyn's hand slipped. The edge of the scissors flew past the end of the ribbon. She nearly cut herself.

"Is keeping up with it a constant battle?" I asked. "I sure hope it isn't. I haven't scheduled that into my time."

"Yes, it is. Endless." Quinlyn peeked at the stockroom and back at me. "And, for the record, Ava's telling the truth. I was with her Tuesday night."

That caught me up short. Ava had said *I was doing inventory.* Not *we.*

# Chapter 10

I thought about what Meryl had asked earlier. Was Quinlyn the murderer? Did she match her alibi to Ava's to protect herself? If only their facials were today, I could press them for more definitive answers while they were relaxed and their guards were down.

When I returned to the spa and was climbing the stairs to the courtyard, a woman hailed me. "Emma!"

My breath snagged at the sight of her standing by the wishing well. With her swanlike neck and her dark hair pulled into a bun, she resembled Willow. She was older. In her fifties, I estimated. I pasted on a smile and greeted a few of our patrons as I passed them to join her. "Yes, ma'am, how may I help you?"

"It's me. Ginnie Sperling."

Her name didn't ring a bell until I remembered Willow's mother's name was Ginnie and that Sperling was Willow's stepfather's last name. I'd met her only once. She didn't look as I remembered her, in tailored, buttoned-down clothing. Today's outfit of a camel-brown camp shirt and khaki slacks was nice but relaxed. "Mrs. Sperling, I'm sorry for your loss."

"Ginnie, dear. Call me Ginnie." Her voice cracked, and she reached for me. "I can't believe it."

I allowed her to embrace me, and she sobbed softly into my shoulder.

She pressed away and dabbed her nose with a wadded tissue. Her brown eyes, the same color as Willow's, were filled with sadness. "Seeing as I'm the executor of Willow's estate, I decided to come and resolve any outstanding business matters in person. I've already spoken with a funeral home near where I live. When the police release her body, she will be transported there and cremated, which was her wish. I imagine I should have a memorial for her here, but I wouldn't know who to invite."

"I could help you with that."

"Bless you. As for settling her finances, that shouldn't be too hard for me. After all, I'm an accountant. Her lawyer . . ." She hesitated. Her chest rose and fell. Tears pooled in her eyes. "He will meet with me in a few days to review her will." She stanched the tears with the used tissue. "Sissy—that's Willow's sister—is beside herself with grief."

"I hope the dog can comfort her."

"Willow told you about the dog?" A soft smile graced Ginnie's lips. "She was mad that we got it."

"She wasn't mad. She was jealous."

"Ah, yes, that would make sense. Jealousy was a go-to reaction for her. She was jealous when I remarried. Jealous when I got pregnant with Sissy." Ginnie's mouth pulled down at the corners. "I met with the police. They don't know who did it. Do you have an inkling?"

They must not have told her I was on their suspect list if she'd come to see me. "I don't," I said, unwilling to reveal my suspicions.

*Motive*, Sierra said. *It all comes down to motive. Whose was the strongest?*

"Was she dating anyone?" Ginnie asked.

"The last I knew about was a forty-year-old computer geek from Silicon Valley, but that ended at least a year ago." He'd never been married, which Willow said had triggered warning bells.

"Yes, he's been out of the picture for a long time. No one else?" Ginnie asked.

"She went on a three-month sabbatical last year. I don't know if she met anyone while she was away. She didn't talk about the experience."

"A sabbatical?"

"She left during the cold season when business from tourists wasn't as plentiful."

"Where did she go?"

"I don't know. It was a secret."

"Willow always had a lot of secrets." Ginnie sighed.

"We all do, if we're honest."

"I suppose." She hummed. "I was wondering . . ." She ran her teeth across her lower lip. "Her house . . . the one she was renting. I'm leery of going in by myself. You were her good friend. Would you go with me to sort through her things?"

"Ginnie, I'm not sure the police—"

"Don't give them a second thought. They've been through it all with a fine-tooth comb. Lord knows how they left it. And don't get me started on that landlord for the spa. He asked how quickly I'd be finished with the forensic accounting because he wants to relet the place as soon as possible. He's a jerk, if you ask me. That's where I intend to go after checking out her house. The spa. I have the keys." She dangled them in front of my face. "You'll assist me with that, too, won't you?"

Oh, wow. How could I say no? If I could nose around, I might learn more about why Willow was killed. But then I thought better of it. The police would want my head on a platter if they found out I was visiting not only the victim's home but also the crime scene. "I'm sorry, Ginnie. It's not a good time. I need to tend to the reception desk."

"I already spoke with your manicurist, Meryl. She's like a breath of fresh air, isn't she? As funny as all get-out. I haven't laughed that hard since . . . well, since the news about Willow, but she tickled my funny bone." Ginnie hitched her purse higher on her shoulder. "She said she could cover for you because a client canceled. Please come with me. Please."

If the police were allowing Ginnie to enter both places, they must believe there was nothing left for them to discover. I agreed to join her, impropriety notwithstanding.

Willow's place was a teensy storybook house with a thatched roof, aqua-blue door, matching shutters, and a thriving English garden. Hummingbirds were having a field day drinking nectar from the honeysuckle that clung to the white picket fence. I imagined there were a few fairies in the garden as well—it seemed like the perfect spot—but, alas, I couldn't see any.

Out of the corner of my eye, I spied a man clad in brown at the end of the street. Probably a UPS delivery guy. He disappeared from view.

Ginnie led the way up the cobblestone path and paused. Her shoulders heaved. "Willow and I hadn't talked in such a long time. I felt like we'd drifted apart."

I put a hand on her shoulder. "She loved you."

"Did she?"

"She said so."

"She had a rough couple of years after her father walked out. I wasn't the best mother. I was too orderly. Too rigid. I set rules, and she didn't like them." She glanced at me. "I'm much more lenient with Sissy."

Perhaps Ginnie's rigidity was another reason Willow had gone into business to help people relax.

Ginnie inserted the key into the lock and opened the door, and we stepped inside. The aroma of vanilla and lavender was heady. The foyer table held numerous candles and a half dozen incense bowls with joss sticks poking from them. A grayscale painting of the Grand

Canyon in Arizona hung above the table. To either side of that painting were black-and-white images of reflective retreats similar to the ones I'd seen in Mystic Waters. There was no ambient sound other than the hum of the refrigerator coming from the kitchen.

Ginnie ran a finger along the picture frame of one of the retreats. "I never liked all the meditation stuff Willow did. It didn't appeal to me. Going to the Grand Canyon to find oneself and become one with God?" She made a derisive sound. "Church was good enough."

Reverently, we toured the space, with Ginnie taking photographs with her cell phone.

"I'm amazed it's so neat," she murmured. "It's as if the police were never here."

All the furniture in the place was white or black or a combination. There was nothing unnecessary, like throw pillows or fake flowers. The bedroom was sparse. Only a bed and dresser. An army barracks inspector would be pleased with how tightly Willow had made her bed. You could've dropped a coin on the white blanket, and it would've bounced. The bathroom counters were spotless. All personal items were stowed in the cabinet. There was no medicine of any kind.

"It's stark," Ginnie murmured.

Almost monastic, I thought, until I opened her bedroom closet. Within hung colorful dresses, blouses, slacks, and shoes.

"She did have a sense of style," Ginnie said. "She taught me a lot about what looked good on me and what didn't."

That sounded like Willow, always offering her two cents.

We moved on to the kitchen. The cupboards had glass fronts. There were very few plates or glassware. The refrigerator was nearly empty. The pantry held only healthful, natural foods. Nothing was in a can, and there was absolutely nothing containing sugar, although I did see organic honey.

"Oh, my," Ginnie said, covering her mouth to stifle a moan. "She was vibrant all her life. How could she live like this? Is this my fault? She didn't inherit this . . . this . . . frugal lifestyle from me." She wagged her head. "I decorate my house. I eat foods that are bad for me. This . . ." Her voice trailed off.

I agreed that this lean existence looked like some force had altered Willow's lifestyle, though I couldn't put my finger on what. I tried to dredge up conversations with her that might reveal the motivation for it but came up empty. Was a lack of personal finances the reason she'd been late on the rent for the spa? Why had she put all her effort into dressing to the nines while every other aspect of her life was monklike? Simply so she could look the part of a successful businesswoman?

"I'm done here," Ginnie said while creating a text message and sending it. "I asked my husband to find a mover for tomorrow. Let's go to the spa."

I texted Meryl and told her that if she needed to tend to a client, she could ask Yoly to close the gift shop and take over at reception. Then I messaged Yoly and begged her to create an ad for a full-time receptionist position. To be filled immediately. I couldn't have her and Meryl manning the desk every time I needed to step away. Sure, with a light appointment book we could juggle things, but if we got really busy, no way.

The insides of the windows of Mystic Waters were covered with dark paper, but there was no police tape prohibiting us from entering. I followed Ginnie in and switched on the lights. Without sunlight spilling through the windows, the place was gloomy. The police must have cleaned the site—it smelled of potent cleansers—but bloodstains were still visible in the grout of the black-and-white tile floor, and the chalk outline indicating where Willow's body had lain hadn't washed away entirely. A specialized crew would be required to make the place pristine again. Was that Ginnie's responsibility or Hugh's?

"Oh, heavens." Ginnie stumbled. Her knees started to buckle.

I clutched her elbow and held on tight.

"I'm all right," she said when she was steadier. "I can't believe . . . My poor baby. The police said she was struck five times."

I swallowed hard, aching for Willow. I hoped the first hit was the deathblow and she hadn't felt the other strikes. Eager to leave the area, I said, "The office is that way."

Like reception, the office was primarily unadorned. There were more black-and-white photos of retreats hanging on the wall, and there was a framed article about Willow heading up a forum for businesswomen to mentor high school students—the same article my grandmother had sent me when I was in Tibet.

Aligned along the front edge of the black lacquer desk sat an incense burner, a bonsai tree in a ceramic container, a pencil holder, a business stamp, a Zen garden with rake, and a black-framed photograph of Willow with another woman, both dressed in beekeeper's outfits. They were holding jars of honey in their hands. Next to the picture was a stack of business postcards announcing a twenty-percent-off deal for the month of July. The slogan, *Become Your Best Self,* was emblazoned at the top of the card. I recalled Willow chiding me for offering discount coupons, saying they belittled the product.

*What a hypocrite,* I thought, and instantly chastised myself for the notion. *She is dead. Cut her some slack.*

In the middle of the desk lay a white blotter. A closed laptop computer sat on it. The ergonomic desk chair looked comfortable in contrast to the uninviting wooden chair positioned against the wall. A two-drawer filing cabinet stood to the right.

Ginnie perched on the desk chair, opened the computer's lid, and frowned. "I don't have a clue what her password would be."

"Try Sissy," I said. "She adored her."

"She did?"

"She said she was precious."

Ginnie typed. The password didn't work.

"Try the word *massage,*" I suggested.

That didn't open it, either.

"How about *meditation*?"

She attempted that, as well, but it failed. She closed the computer, saying, "I'll take it with the other things and get an expert to access it. In the meantime . . ." She rose to her feet, crossed to the filing cabinet, and opened the top drawer. She muttered, "A to M," as she fingered through files. She landed on something and pulled it out. It appeared to be a ledger. She brought it to the desk, sat on the chair, and flipped through it. "You must understand GL coding, Emma," she said, "given your business."

"I do." General ledger coding was a standard practice. From my vantage point and reading upside down, I could see the leftmost column held what appeared to be numeric codes. I used the same kind of coding for the spa accounts, but I did it using a computer program, not by hand: 1000 for revenue, 2000 for building expenses, 3000 for shipping and handling. Next, I divided the thousands into increments of a hundred, so I used 2100 for building expenses, 2200 for plumbing, 2300 for heating and air, et cetera. In Willow's ledger, I noticed a lot of codes assigned with a 7000 number.

Ginnie flipped a page and hummed.

"Is something puzzling you?" I asked.

"I can see what most of the codes apply to. The two thousands are for décor, three thousands for payroll. The five thousand code seems to apply to her lease. It's a large and steady number month to month. But the amounts of the entries coded with seven thousand don't make any sense. There's only the one code. No breakout groupings, like seventy-one or seventy-two hundred. I can't figure out who is the recipient of these sums, but the amounts are extremely varied, although they appear to be monthly."

I perused the list. Some of the expenses were in the tens of thousands. "Maybe they're donations," I suggested.

In college, Willow and I lent our time to a variety of causes—like women's shelters, feeding the homeless, and rescuing animals. Once she'd started her own business, she'd probably decided on giving cash donations instead of offering a helping hand. I'd done the same. Free time was hard to come by.

"Donations are typically the same amounts," Ginnie said.

"Not necessarily." I explained that I gave much more to my primary causes than I did to, say, saving forests or butterflies.

"Why not be specific about them?" she asked. "Why be secretive and code them but not detail them? Surely the IRS would question her if she were to be audited."

"She might have kept a receipts file."

"If she did, it would be in the lower file drawer, marked N to Z," she said. "Would you check?"

I crossed to the cabinet, squatted to open the drawer, and sifted through the files. They were in alphabetical order. None started with the letters N or O. The first was *Pay Stubs*, then *Pension Info*, *Plumbing*, *Purchases*, *Real Estate*, *Sales*. There wasn't any with the tab *Receipts*.

"Nix." I started to close the drawer and paused when I saw a file dubbed *Self* wedged in before *Tax Dox*.

I pulled out the manila folder. Within, I found mementos. A couple of birthday cards from Sissy. A few from Ginnie and her husband. Some thank-you notes from clients. An envelope bearing a stamp of the Grand Canyon was empty. A simple ecru card conveyed an unsigned scrawled message: *When can we meet?* And on a sheer piece of onion paper was a note to Willow from her grandmother welcoming her to the world.

"What did you find?" Ginnie abandoned the ledger and joined me.

"Keepsakes." I rose to my feet and showed her the items.

She clutched the note from Willow's grandmother to her chest.

I pointed to the ecru card. "Do you recognize this handwriting?"

"No. The ink is peacock blue, though."

"How could you possibly know that?"

She smiled. "I preferred fountain pens as a girl, and the nuns got after me for using an ink that wasn't the standard blue."

I recalled Willow telling me she'd been raised Catholic, but she'd abandoned her faith after Communion, saying she intended to research all religions before she subscribed to one. I flipped the card over. The reverse side was blank. For all I knew, the card was from a lover who'd wanted to remain anonymous.

"No receipts file?" she asked.

"No. You know, Willow had an accountant." That gave me pause. He was one of the last people to have seen her alive. Had the police questioned him? Did he have any reason to want her dead?

Ginnie was waiting for me to continue.

"He should know more about her books. His name would be in her contacts. The police gave you her cell phone, right?"

"Yes, but it also has a password, and I can't access it."

I'd seen Willow open her phone plenty of times. "Try one, two, three, four."

"Ha!" The laugh burst from Ginnie's lips. She covered her mouth. "Sorry. That was rude. But honestly? She used the default code?" Mumbling that people needed to be more careful when it came to privacy, she typed in the digits. The phone opened. She pulled up the accountant's contact page. "I'll reach out." She clasped me in a fierce hug. When she released me, she said, "Emma, I couldn't have done this without you. Thank you."

"You're welcome."

"And, for the record, Willow adored and admired you. That's why I know the police are wrong about you. You didn't kill her."

# Chapter 11

The fact that Ginnie had known I was a person of interest yet trusted me enough to ask me to help her buoyed me beyond words. Similar testaments as to my character could go a long way toward convincing Detective Summers of my innocence, but drumming those up would have to wait.

After returning to the spa and finalizing business, I headed home to change for my grandmother's book club event. As I was crossing Ocean Avenue, I noticed Palmer Pilsner and her daughter Olivia affixing a poster to the window of a restaurant. I'd bet it was a poster announcing another of Palmer's cookie drives. Olivia looked somewhat surly. It wasn't her Goth clothes or the way she'd sloppily clipped her hair with a claw. It was her pinched facial expression.

*Poor thing,* I mused. Her mother must have ordered her to assist her on her mission . . . or Olivia hated cookies. As a girl, whenever I'd helped Nana Lissa and her cronies whip up treats for benefits, I'd enjoyed the enterprise. Not only was it fun to bake but it pleased me that the proceeds of the sale would go to the library. I remember asking once about the myriad bake sales in town, and my grandmother replied that Carmelites never tired of buying goodies for a worthy cause. She didn't care if they ate them or gave them to someone else as long as they pitched in.

Palmer and Olivia moved on to the next shop, with Olivia scuffing the cobblestones with the heels of her Doc Martens, and I continued toward home.

Vivi was waiting for me in the foyer when I arrived. For ten minutes, we played her favorite game—chase the laser beam—then I fed her and, knowing I had an hour before I needed to dress for the book club, decided to surprise my grandmother with a batch of her favorite cookies.

Nana Lissa had taught me how to make them in her kitchen. Heaven forbid I learn at home. My mother hated messes.

Lemon butter cookies were a snap to make. They required six basic ingredients—butter, confectioner's sugar, lemon zest, lemon juice, flour, and salt—and, if desired, a glaze. I'd forgo the glaze because the cookies needed to be entirely cool before applying it.

Humming while baking soothed me. It always had. After setting the first batch in the preheated oven, I swapped out my work clothes for black leggings, a red-striped boyfriend shirt, a Regency-era cameo necklace my grandmother had given me when I was ten, and cute red sandals. I spruced up my lip gloss, pinned my hair up with a silver hairclip, made sure I didn't have flour on my cheeks, and returned to the kitchen. After the second batch baked and cooled enough for me to pack them, I kissed my sweet cat on her nose, assured her I'd be home soon, grabbed a bottle of chardonnay, and drove to Nana's.

Her front door was unlocked. I stepped inside with the wine and cookies and made a beeline for the living room. The savory aromas emanating from the dining room to my left made me salivate. I'd attended only a few of Nana Lissa's book clubs. Each time I'd been amazed by the array of foods. Given her baking prowess, she always made the desserts. I peeked in and spied her specialty, chocolate mousse cake, and for the non-chocolate lovers, caramel cupcakes. I knew I wouldn't be able to pass up either of them.

The living room was expansive and handsomely decked out with white furniture and lots of soft blue throw pillows imprinted with white patterns or stitched with white cypress silhouettes. The hardwood floors were a light oak. The coffee table and end tables were crafted from mango wood, with no hard edges. A round rope mirror hung above the marble fireplace, and there were silver-framed pictures of family everywhere. Large plate-glass windows sprawled from one end of the room to the other and provided a spectacular view of the ocean. The set designer for Nancy Meyers's movies would be envious.

The sun was low in the sky. The few clouds were tinged soft peach and gray. Yoly was standing by the windows chatting with my grandmother and Courtney Kelly. There were a few others in the room whom I recognized as well as a couple of unfamiliar faces. Many were holding glasses of wine or flutes of prosecco. If I didn't know better, I'd have thought my grandmother had sent out a wardrobe memo to the attendees. Nearly everyone was wearing an off-white toned outfit with a splash of blue. Yoly and I were the exceptions. She'd donned a hot-pink, bat-winged blouse over skinny jeans.

My grandmother crossed to me, took the wine, and kissed my cheek. She inhaled the aroma of the cookies. "Lemon?"

"Your favorite."

"I'm glad you're here." Her ecru silk blouse and trousers were exquisite, as were her sapphire earrings. Papa had given them to her on their thirty-fifth wedding anniversary. I recalled the tears of joy that bloomed in her eyes when she opened the gift box. Their devoted relationship was the kind of love I wanted but, due to a few relationship hiccups, doubted I'd ever find. "Would you like a glass?"

"Yes, please. The fresh flowers are incredible," I said, admiring the various vases filled with white roses.

"I went to Daphne's Flower Farm on the way home."

"You are such a coastal granny," I teased.

"I am, aren't I?" She offered a wicked grin.

"Is the faux fur throw over the chaise longue in the corner new?" I asked. The chaise was my grandmother's favorite spot to read.

"It is. Like it?"

"Love it. I want one but won't get one. Vivi would destroy it." I scanned the other attendees. "Kate isn't coming?"

"She had an appointment."

I arched an eyebrow.

"That's what she said," Nana added, "but I think she's on a date."

"A date? She pooh-poohs dating."

"Malarkey." Nana headed to the kitchen. When she reappeared with a glass of wine for me, she said, "Ladies, let's sit and get started. After our chat, we'll eat."

We congregated on the L-shaped sofa and the additional high-end folding chairs my grandmother had arranged, and she introduced everyone to me briefly. "You know Courtney and Hedda. I think you know Zinnia."

Zinnia wiggled her fingers in hello. I wished I could ask her about Indy's grouse with Willow, but now was not the time.

"Next to her is Violet Vickers, a patron of the theater."

I recognized her. She was Zinnia's dinner companion from the other night.

"And Hattie, who is Hedda's sister," Nana said.

"I'm here!" Sierra said, bursting into the room. "Busy day at the café." She hadn't changed from the morning. The T-shirt, the hem of which had been tucked beneath the waistband of her leggings, was now loose and free-flowing. "Hello, everyone. In case you haven't heard, Emma opened Aroma Wellness Spa. You should give it a try."

I beamed. With my grandmother and Sierra as the spa's promoters, who needed to network?

"I'm serving delicious food at the café," she added. "Good-for-the-body-and-soul kind of food. Drop in. One free smoothie for each of you."

Many replied that they would check it out.

When the hubbub settled down, my grandmother said, "Tonight we're talking about *The Big Sleep*, the iconic first novel by Raymond Chandler, featuring Philip Marlowe."

"The quintessential private eye," Yoly interjected.

I wished I could delve into Willow's murder the way Philip Marlowe would. I wouldn't need to be rough and tough like him, but I would like to be as attentive to detail as he was.

Nana Lissa said, "Who can tell me what the story's about?"

"I can." Courtney cleared her throat. She glanced to her right as if listening to someone. "We can," Courtney revised. "Fiona and I."

Oh, my! The fairy was here?

"The story is about a dying millionaire who hires a private eye to handle the blackmailer of one of the millionaire's two troublesome daughters." Courtney paused and seemed to listen to the invisible-to-me fairy again. "But Marlowe finds himself dealing with a lot more than blackmail."

My grandmother beamed. "Well done, you two."

Hedda raised her hand. "Lissa, if I may add something." She was sitting to Courtney's right. Tonight, she'd dressed as she had the other day, in a cream-colored blouse and beige slacks, but she was wearing perhaps the boldest neon-blue eyeglasses I'd ever seen. "Yes, Fiona," Hedda said to the fairy I couldn't see. "I'll tell them. There's kidnapping and pornography and seduction in the book. It's quite disturbing, if I must say."

Raymond Chandler did have a gritty style.

"Not everyone enjoys a noir mystery," my grandmother said.

"Oh, I enjoyed it," Hedda said, "but it's not my usual fare. I'm more of an Agatha Christie aficionado."

"You like cozy mysteries," I said.

"Yes." Hedda smiled. "Give me Miss Marple any day."

Many in the room bobbed their heads in agreement.

"Courtney can handle darker stories," Hedda went on, "because she's witnessed a few gruesome murder scenes."

"Ha!" Courtney jeered. "That doesn't mean I like reading darker novels."

"But one copes when one must," my grandmother said. "Isn't that so, Courtney? After all, the first time you stumbled upon a dead body, you turned out to be the police's prime suspect, and what did you do? You became proactive and sussed out the killer." My grandmother patted my leg. "Emma, give us your take on the novel."

"All the characters had hidden agendas."

"Good observation."

"And there were red herrings upon red herrings. Too many, actually. I took notes throughout, but that's me. Always the dutiful student." I had over ten spiral notebooks holding my thoughts for opening the spa.

"I also jotted down things," Hedda said.

"Me, too," Sierra admitted. "I like to guess the ending of a mystery. Keeping a list of clues helps."

"Exactly," Yoly said.

Nana Lissa motioned to me. "Continue, Emma."

"When Marlowe goes into the rare book shop—" I halted. "This could be a spoiler."

"Who hasn't finished the book?" my grandmother asked. No one in the group raised a hand. "Emma, you have the floor."

"When he finds the bookshop owner who happens to be the blackmailer dead, that throws the whole story a curve."

"Let's talk about Marlowe's character." Nana rose to her feet and offered everyone another pour of wine or prosecco.

While I listened to the group state a variety of opinions, I gazed at Courtney's right shoulder. I didn't detect an iota of movement, which depressed me. *One day*, I assured myself. *One day I'll see a fairy.*

About forty-five minutes later, we disbanded and gathered around the table in the dining room. Nana Lissa had hired a caterer to assist with the evening. The woman had laid out a beautiful silver filigree runner on the table and had set all the food on Lenox Opal Innocence silver bone china. I loved the way the rims of the plates gleamed and elevated the beauty of the food. There were mini blinis, crab puffs, baked feta bites, sweet potato crostini, and antipasto skewers, plus a green salad and crudités with dill dip. On the buffet abutting the wall beyond the table sat the desserts. I knew Sierra would frown if I started there, but the caramel cupcakes laden with caramel frosting were calling my name. *Backward dinner*, I told myself. My grandmother had come up with that term when I was six. If I ate a sweet now, it meant I couldn't have another after dinner. So be it.

The caterer had set up coffee and tea on a beverage cart she'd wheeled in from the kitchen. I poured myself a cup and snagged a cupcake.

No one chose to sit to eat. Almost everyone was roaming around the living room, plate in hand, while admiring my grandmother's myriad statues, artwork, and books or chatting amongst themselves.

I joined Nana Lissa, who was talking to Courtney, Yoly, and Sierra.

Sierra said, "I heard you went to Willow's house with her mother today, Emma."

"Who told you?"

"Meryl."

Uh-oh. I needed to keep my whereabouts secret, or the police might come after me. On the other hand, this was a group of women I could trust, and perhaps sharing with them would help me sort through some clues. "We also went to Mystic Waters."

Nana Lissa said, "Do tell."

I filled them in on the contrast between the colorful persona Willow presented to the world and the sparseness of her home and the black-and-white sterility of the spa. Next, I mentioned the ledger and Willow's coding system and the puzzling seven thousand category.

Sierra said, "What if she was a gambler, and the code hid the fact that she was paying off debts?"

"That could explain why they were varied amounts, but why were they recorded monthly?" I asked.

"Emma, you said she donated to good causes throughout the years," Nana Lissa said. "If she didn't make the donations anonymously, I bet the organizations would reveal that information to you. Perhaps the amounts will match what you and Ginnie found."

I said I'd look into it and mentioned the file folder filled with mementos. "Ginnie was pleased we'd found the items. They gave her something tangible to hold on to." I told them about the moment we'd first entered Willow's house. "Ginnie was sad. She felt like she'd let Willow down." I explained how Willow's father had walked out when she was two and Ginnie had to bear the burden of raising a child on her own. "I assured her that Willow loved her, but I'm not certain that satisfied her."

"It's hard losing someone you love to murder," Courtney said, her voice catching slightly. Recently she'd lost someone she'd known well. "You're always thinking, what if I'd done things differently, or if only I'd thought to say this or that before they died."

Nana Lissa rested a hand on her shoulder. "Sweet girl, if you ever want to talk—"

"I'm good," Courtney said. She listened to the magical being on her shoulder. "Yes, that's true, Fiona. Those who have gone before are watching from what lies beyond and are understanding how those of us who mourn feel. That in itself is a healing concept."

We all shared a moment of silence.

My grandmother was the first to speak. "Emma, I was able to follow up on Indy Hendriks's alibi. She was, indeed, at her bridge club. Three other women confirmed it. She arrived at a quarter past eight and left at eleven. Much to the women's dismay, Indy and her partner cleaned everyone's clocks."

Drat. Detective Summers said the coroner had determined Willow died between eight and ten. Seeing as I left at eight fifteen, that narrowed the window of opportunity to approximately an hour and forty-five minutes.

I spied Zinnia standing by the door, waving good-bye to Hedda. I didn't see her friend Violet anywhere. She must have left. I hurried to Zinnia. "I'm sorry to intrude, but I've been wondering . . ."

"Yes, dear?"

"The night Willow died, you and Violet were having dinner at Hideaway Café."

*"Mm-hmm."*

"You made a wisecrack when Willow claimed Palmer and Indy weren't into anything New Agey, saying 'That's not the half of it.' And when Willow told me to butt out, claiming the attack was about her, not me, you whispered, 'Indeed it is.' What did you mean?"

Zinnia considered her response. "All I meant was Indy lost her boyfriend and blamed Willow, and Palmer, being Indy's BFF, has held her accountable ever since."

"Are you saying Willow stole Indy's boyfriend?" I asked, remembering how she'd swooped in and won Bonzo's heart.

"It matters not. Water under the bridge."

"But Willow's dead!"

"Emma, I doubt Indy holds a grudge. After all, being suddenly single, she found the true love of her life—her business. All's well in the end." She glanced at her watch. "Must run. This book club was wonderful, don't you think?"

It certainly was enlightening.

# Chapter 12

I awoke Friday morning before sunrise with a start. Vivi had nestled next to my head and was kneading my neck. "Stop, cat," I said, nudging her away.

She rolled onto her back and, fully alert, began batting the air with her paws. She kept at it for a good ten seconds.

"What are you doing?" I asked, able to make out her silhouette in the dim light. Was she juggling an invisible ball? Did cats pretend? "Fine. You're determined to be active until I get out of bed. Got it."

Though it was a quarter to six, I knew I wouldn't be able to sleep any longer, not after dreaming of the brass candlestick, the chalk outline of Willow, the unsigned ecru card in her *Self* file, and the number seven thousand. Were they random clues or even clues at all?

I awakened my cell phone on the bedside table and saw that my father had texted me.

**Dad: Congratulations, honey bun. I hope the opening went as planned.**

*Not exactly, Dad.*

**Dad: I'm out of range and can't be reached for a week. Sorry. Long story. I'll fill you in. Know I'm with you in spirit. Be brilliant.**

I sighed. I would be as brilliant as I could be, given the circumstances. I typed in a quick response of *thanks* and *love you* and *call when you're up for air* and pressed Send. Texting him the news about Willow's murder didn't feel right.

Vivi padded after me as I slipped on athletic shorts, a sunny yellow tank top, a broad-brimmed hat, and sandals. Even though the sun had begun to rise, although its full orb wasn't visible, I didn't take risks with my fair Irish skin. I lathered my face, arms, and legs with sunblock.

"I'm edgy," I said to her. "I'm going to take a quick run on the beach and splash my feet in the water. A little exercise—not a lot—should help me loosen up."

I walked to Carmel Bay. A crisp morning breeze caressed my face. A flock of birds passed overhead, their cacophony cheery. At Ocean Avenue, by which time the sun had completely risen, I veered right. In another nine short blocks, I arrived at the beach. When I reached the iconic cypress at the end of Ocean, I kicked off my sandals and, dangling my shoes from a finger, jogged to the water and turned south. Other runners and walkers were out in abundance. I recognized a few regulars and waved hello. Farther on, a gentle wind tried to knock off my hat. I wedged it tighter onto my head and focused on my breathing, inhaling every four paces and exhaling the next four. A Dalmatian, off leash, tried to play tag with me.

A woman cried, "Polka Dot, no!"

I pivoted and spied Hedda Hopewell running toward me. Her sun hat flew off. She quickly retrieved it. "Emma. Sorry."

"No worries," I said, and skirted around the dog. "Have a good morning."

A few minutes later, I slowed to a walk. In the water, an otter was floating, trying to crack something on its chest. I drew to a stop to watch it. A few other beachgoers did, too. That was when I noticed Hugh Ashbluff. He was strolling alongside a woman who was covered head to toe and carrying a parasol. I guessed she didn't trust sunblock to do the job, even this early in the morning. She was wearing huge sunglasses and a balaclava-style face mask that obscured her features. Hugh pointed at a house on San Antonio Avenue with a view of the ocean. I speculated that the woman was a client until Hugh kissed her on the cheek—well, on the mask—which made me think otherwise. Wife? Lover? Not my business.

Polka Dot reappeared and ran a circle around me.

"No!" Hedda shouted. "Dagnabbit, dog! Stop!"

I bent to pet the dog, and she came willingly. "If I didn't have a kitty, I'd have someone like you, Polka Dot." I scratched her behind the ears. "Not exactly like you. Probably a golden doodle. Don't be jealous."

Hedda hooked on the dog's leash and apologized again.

"Really," I said. "It's not a problem. I love dogs. If I didn't work at the spa all day, I'd probably own one, but dogs need people around."

"And long walks and runs twice daily. After all the tugging and pulling she does, I could use a massage." She rubbed her left shoulder. "I'll be calling soon for an appointment."

"Sounds good."

I returned home physically refreshed but feeling mentally edgy. My mind was filled with concerns about the murder. About my being a suspect. About the fact that I needed caffeine but hadn't had time to replenish the pods for the Keurig. I fed Vivi; changed into yoga pants, a floral T-shirt, and my aqua-blue slides; and hustled to Percolate.

The ocean-themed décor in the café always brought a smile to my face. Tulip-shaped pendant lights etched with seahorses illuminated the dining area. Three hung over the counter. On the white-washed brick wall was a huge chalkboard with the day's specials. A number of free-floating shelves behind the counter held plants, loaves of bread, tins of tea, and lovely conch shells.

On my way to order, I neared a booth where Indy was sitting with Palmer and Olivia. Indy was dressed in a soft Moroccan-style draped top that suited her. Palmer looked ready to hit the clay courts in a lime-green tennis outfit, her hair secured in a scrunchie. Olivia's black tank top hung on her lithe frame. A beverage stood in front of each of them. An egg sandwich sat on a plate in front of Olivia, but she hadn't touched it. She was rubbing her arms, which were quite thin. Did she have an eating disorder?

"Why won't Daddy fix the TV and computer?" Olivia stopped kneading her arms and began to angrily twirl the cell phone that was housed in a gruesome Evil Dead impact case, facedown on the table. She gave her mother a dirty look. Palmer must have told her no browsing electronics at breakfast. "At least then I could escape listening to you two carp at each other during dinner."

Palmer said, "Olivia, I've told you—"

"Morning," I said, knowing if I passed by without saying hello, tongues would wag that I was rude.

"Well, well. Emma Brennan. Aren't you the nosy one?" Indy smirked. "I hear you've been questioning my integrity. For your information, I don't lie. Ever."

I assessed her as I would a future client. Maybe I could offer her a honey cream, full-body scrub to sweeten her up. A gentle exfoliation would leave her body feeling as smooth as silk. She'd thank me. Or would she? Probably not if she related spas to Willow and Willow to losing a boyfriend.

"I was Willow's friend," I said. "I'd like to find out who killed her."

"Well, like I told the police," Indy said, "I was playing bridge. I didn't kill her."

"I didn't, either." Palmer sipped her drink. "I was home watching *Jeopardy!* reruns that night. I'm addicted to that show. I should see a shrink."

"Yes, you should," Olivia sniped, her gray eyes glinting with something bordering on loathing.

Palmer childishly mirrored the expression but quickly snapped out of it.

"You'd be smart to take up bridge, P," Indy said. "It really stimulates the brain cells."

"I could never. Card games are not my thing. I play tennis and paint and bake. End of story."

"You do hold some epic bake sales," I said solicitously.

"Thank you."

"Were you and your daughter hanging posters for one yesterday? I happened to see you near Ocean Avenue."

"Yes. We're raising funds for a summer camp for the needy."

Oliva regarded her mother coolly.

"Hi, Olivia," I said. "Have you heard from your older sister?" I recalled our brief exchange when she'd visited the spa pre-opening.

"No," she said, sadness in her tone.

When we'd chatted, she'd raved about Alexandra. How beautiful and smart she was and how eager she was to take Olivia on nature hikes and rock climbing and bird-watching. Now I had to wonder whether the Goth look Olivia seemed fond of had started before or after her sister left town. She didn't strike me as the type to like any outdoor activities.

"You know, Emma," Palmer said, "if you're determined to find out whodunit, you should look into Hugh Ashbluff. I saw him arguing with Willow the other day. It wasn't pretty."

Indy sat taller. "Say, I saw him lingering outside Mystic Waters a couple of days ago."

"That's not unusual," I said. "He owns the property."

Indy narrowed her gaze. "He was using binoculars."

Whoa! That gave me pause. Was Hugh a pervert and hoping to get a peek of a customer in a state of undress?

"I heard there may have been something tawdry going on inside the place," Indy added.

"Like what?" Palmer asked.

"You know, gambling or animal sacrifices."

Palmer knuckled Indy on the arm. "Get out of here. You're pulling our legs."

Indy cackled.

I wished the women well and proceeded to the counter. I paid for a latte with an extra pump of espresso and a packet of Stevia—at least I could tell Sierra I didn't consume sugar—and went to the end of the counter to wait for my beverage. Detective Summers was there, as well, with the strikingly handsome dark-haired woman who owned a pottery place named Seize the Clay. It was located in the same courtyard as Hideaway Café, and I'd visited it on a few occasions before meeting friends for dinner. The woman laughed at something Summers said and blew him a kiss.

How I wished I was bold enough to approach him. I could relay what Zinnia had told me about Indy and ask whether he was considering Hugh Ashbluff or Ava Daft as suspects, but I was loath to break in on their romantic exchange. Summers was friends with Hugh. Did he know about Hugh's issue with Willow? Was he aware that Ava, at one time, had her sights set on taking over Willow's lease? Was he looking into Willow's disgruntled customers? Was he questioning her business acquaintances, namely her accountant? And what about her other friends? Oh, to be a fly on the wall in his office at the police station. I could glimpse his case notes.

Summers caught sight of me and nodded. I returned the gesture. His companion whispered something to him and slyly hooked a thumb in my direction, no doubt asking him if I was his main suspect. I cringed, instantly remembering a time in high school when I caught my peers gossiping about me because I'd failed an English test. Failed on purpose. To irk my mother. I'd been somewhat passive aggressive in my teens until my grandmother convinced me to strive harder.

Summers's order came up first. He took both to-go cups, handed one to his companion, and escorted her out.

I played a game of Wordle on my cell phone until my coffee order was ready. Walking toward the exit, I noticed Indy leaning forward, as if imparting a secret to Palmer. Olivia, shoulders hunched, looked as dour as ever. As I passed the table, another theory about Willow's murder came to me. I decided to head to the library and run it by my grandmother. She was an early riser and always arrived at work by seven thirty.

I found her in the Barnet Segal Reading Room, an expansive, light-filled space complete with a fireplace, tables, and easy chairs. Book club events and poetry readings often took place there. She was chatting with a fellow employee of the library. Both were clad in summer sweaters over skinny jeans. Nana had on hip-looking striped Skechers. I waited until the other woman climbed the stairs to the stacks before drawing near.

"Nana Lissa," I said softly. I never used a full voice in the library. I'd always considered it a hallowed space.

"Sweet girl," my grandmother said, not abiding the whisper policy. She embraced me fondly, then released me. "What are you doing here?"

"I was hoping to pick your brain. It's such a good brain to pick."

She sat at one of the tables. I perched on a chair opposite her and set down my to-go cup.

"Spa trouble?" she asked.

"No. Things are going well there. It's *me* trouble. I'm really worried that if I don't find Willow's killer, I'll be on the hook for her death."

"Nonsense. Dylan Summers is not a stupid man. He and his team are investigating. They'll dig up the truth."

"I'm not sure." I motioned to my to-go cup. "I saw him at Percolate and ached to tell him my theories."

"Whatever you do, don't do that. He won't appreciate it."

"Why not?"

"He's a proud man."

"All men are proud. That doesn't mean—"

"Dylan has a history."

"Everyone does."

"His . . ." She hesitated. "Suffice it to say, when he lost his college roommate, it set his course. He believes he and he alone can solve crimes."

"But you said Courtney has helped him."

"Courtney is a different story."

"Why? Because she has a fairy to help her?"

Nana Lissa gave me a meaningful look. "Emma, listen, Dylan is a levelheaded, good man. He's smart, but he doesn't believe we civilians play a role in his world. Don't ruffle his feathers." She glanced to her left and held out a finger. "Merryweather Rose of Song has joined us." She tipped her finger to the table, to allow the fairy to step off, I supposed. "I hope you don't mind."

"Not at all." I peered at the table but couldn't see a thing. Not a flutter of a wing. Was my grandmother toying with me? To lighten my spirit?

"Back to the murder," she said.

"Sierra says motive is most important."

"I agree. Who has the most to gain?" my grandmother asked.

"Financially?"

"Or otherwise."

I tried to wrap my head around what *otherwise* could mean. "Does Merryweather want to know?"

"No, I want to." She wagged a finger. "Don't be cheeky."

I started at the top of my list. "Hugh Ashbluff," I said, and explained how Willow was late on rent. "He warned her that he'd kick her out if she didn't pay up."

"Sounds like a reason for Willow to want Hugh dead, not the other way around."

"He might make more money with a new tenant."

"True, but even that seems a feeble reason to want her dead."

"Indy Hendriks saw him outside Mystic Waters with binoculars. What if Willow caught him and said she'd report him for being a Peeping Tom?"

*"Hmm."* She pondered that for a moment. "I doubt he could've seen anything. There aren't any windows in the therapy rooms, are there?"

"No."

An older patron entered the area and began perusing audio books he could borrow. He didn't pay any attention to us.

"What if Hugh was trying to peer into Willow's office to keep tabs on her?" I suggested. "To see if she was squirreling away money or was lying about being hard up for cash?"

"What would he gain from that?"

"Leverage to dun her for payment."

She shook her head.

I circled back to one of the reasons why Willow might have been unable to pay the lease and applied it to him. "What if he's a gambler and needs the money ASAP to pay off a loan? Or . . ." I thought of the underlying theme of *The Big Sleep*. "What if someone is blackmailing him?"

My grandmother leaned forward on both elbows. "Hugh knows his way around money. He graduated from UCLA with a degree in finance and became a banker to please his father, but he hated the buttoned-down aspect of it."

"Funny," I murmured. "That's the way he dresses."

"He took all he'd saved and started buying and renovating houses," Nana said. "Once he became successful at flipping them, he began buying commercial properties and apartment buildings. He's flush. He doesn't need to pressure anyone for payment."

"Is he married?"

"He was once, but it didn't work out."

"Maybe he owes alimony."

"No. They parted amicably after five years of marriage. She declined alimony and moved to Kansas to be with her family." My grandmother sure knew a lot about him, but then she knew a lot about everyone.

"What if he's dating someone who's bleeding him dry because she knows a deep, dark secret about him?" I thought of the woman dressed from head to toe that he'd kissed on the beach.

"Oh, Emma." My grandmother chuckled. "You have such a vivid imagination. Hugh has dated a few women in town, but none have hornswoggled him."

"How well do you know Ava Daft?" I asked, switching gears. I told her Ava's motive to want Willow dead and added that I'd visited Shabby Chic Nook. "We chatted for a bit, and Ava revealed her alibi to me for that night. But I got the feeling she was lying. Quinlyn covered for her, saying she was with her, but something seemed fishy about it."

"Interesting."

"Oh, also, they had postcards for sale like the one Willow received."

"Any that resembled the one left for you to find?"

"No."

She shook her head. "Ava is a sweet woman. She's not much of a reader, but then her parents weren't, either. She put herself through school. Math and marketing were her strong suits. Afterward, her grandfather, who was impressed, gave her the business." Nana folded her hands. "Is there anyone else on your radar?"

"Indy." I told her about my conversation with Zinnia after the book club.

"I knew Indy had split up with her boyfriend. I had no idea Willow was a factor. Go on."

I recapped my exchange with Indy and Palmer at Percolate.

She hummed but didn't comment.

"Can't your fairy"—I glanced at the table where Merryweather was purportedly standing . . . or sitting—"help us find the killer?"

"No. She's a guardian fairy. She can advise and instill the desire for knowledge, but she cannot solve a thing. Her niece Fiona can, but she's Courtney's fairy, and they are bonded."

"A one-human fairy. Yes, Courtney told me."

"You spoke to her?"

"She came in to make an appointment." I leaned forward on my elbows and grunted. "The rules for fairies sure are restrictive."

# Chapter 13

Meryl was filing her nails at the reception desk when I entered. All of the employees had keys to the spa so they could get inside to set up if they arrived early, but only Yoly, Sierra, and I had keys to the café and gift shop. Meryl's hair was drawn into a rectangular clip at the nape of her neck. Her eyes were heavily outlined with blue pencil.

"Morning," she said. "The appointment calendar is booked today. You have a meditative consultation at nine, and today's your day to do facials. You have back-to-back appointments at ten and eleven."

"Want to be the full-time receptionist?" I asked.

"Not on a bet, and there's no need. You'll be meeting interviewees for the job at twelve thirty. Yoly said five applied."

Wow! Was she ever on the ball.

"Hey, did you hear?" Meryl grinned. "Nail salons, hair salons, and tanning places are closing. It's about to get ugly out there."

I moaned. "That's pretty good."

She snorted. "I'm thinking of refashioning my routine around a spa and all the quirky characters—"

"Do. Not." I wagged a finger. "Uh-uh."

"Don't get bent. It'd be fictional, of course," she said quickly, adding a disclaimer like a radio announcer in hyperspeed. "All content, jokes, and references to people or locations is the property of me and is protected by valid copyright and intellectual property laws. Not intended to heal anything but your funny bone."

I studied her to see if she was serious. Her smirk was unreadable.

"Emma." Sierra swept into the spa. "Did I see you in Percolate this morning?"

I remembered that I hadn't given her the dolphin necklace, and said, "Ooh. Perfect timing." I fished the box tied with ribbon from the lowest drawer and handed it to her. "I found this at Shabby Chic Nook. It's for you as a thanks for helping me open the spa."

*That'll deflect her disapproval*, I thought.

"It *was* you." She glowered at me. "I was doing my run, and there you were. How caffeinated are you?"

I indicated a tiny bit with two fingers.

"From now on, I'll make you energy smoothies in the morning," she said, brooking no argument. "With coconut, maqui, and oats. You'll thank me. In fact, I'll make one right now."

"I don't want one every morning," I protested.

But she didn't hear me. She scuttled out of the spa without opening her gift.

"Sheesh. She acts like she's your mother," Meryl said. "Why do you give her that kind of power?"

"I don't know." I rotated my head to loosen the tension knots. "She's always been bossy."

"Like Willow was?"

My heart wrenched. No, my cousin was nothing like Willow. She was cute-bossy, in a caring and kind way. Willow had been condescending. Even cruel, at times. I had tough skin, but she'd hurt my feelings on more than one occasion. Had she hurt someone else's feelings? Did that person kill her?

"Take control of your life, boss, or it will control you." Meryl aimed the nail file at me.

"Thanks for the pep talk. You have been heard."

Smugly, Meryl flounced in the direction of the salon, and I made myself a promise to put the kibosh on daily smoothies.

Minutes later, Courtney entered the spa for her mindful meditation. I asked her to store her personal items in one of the spa's safes in the hallway—the coded kind you'd find in a hotel suite—and led her to the sound bath room. I dimmed the lights, and both of us settled on the mat in the center. I instructed her to sit in the lotus pose. I didn't ask if her fairy had accompanied her. I didn't want to know. It could distract me.

In a gentle, steady tone, I instructed Courtney to close her eyes, rest her hands on her legs, and fill her lungs with fresh air.

"That's it," I said. "Now exhale."

She did.

In a soft voice, I advised her that she was not to speak. She was to listen, adding that this particular kind of meditation asked us to suspend judgment. In the silence, we could unleash the natural curiosity as to how our minds processed life's most precious events.

Once she was breathing calmly and steadily, I said, "You feel your energy is sapped. Let's restore that by first concentrating on your gifts. Your strengths. Your talent." I drew in a breath and released it slowly to the count of three. "What you give others is your power. You help others tune in to their creative spirit."

I could see her eyes moving beneath her eyelids. "Breathe."

She did.

"Be mindful of how much time you give to others. Are you devoting the same amount of time to yourself?"

She moaned softly, indicating she was not.

"Are you sometimes depleted by your thoughts? Do they overwhelm you? Do they take you out of the moment?"

She nodded slightly.

"If you don't take care of your own energy—your qi—you will continue to be depleted."

I explained, as Yoly had the other day, what qi was. As the words spilled out of me, I thought of what Meryl had said moments before I'd started this treatment, and she was right. I needed to focus on my own power. My own strengths. I opened this spa to help others, but if I neglected my own spirituality—if I lost my sense of calm—I would flounder. One of my talents was understanding how to read people. Another was my ability to move a group's demand to second place if I needed to care for myself. That time was now. If I didn't exonerate myself of murder, all the work I'd put into opening Aroma Wellness would be for naught.

When I ended the forty-five-minute session, I took in Courtney, who looked refreshed and confident, her skin rosy and eyes clear, and I felt like I was looking into a mirror because I felt the same.

Minutes later, when I was preparing a treatment room for the upcoming facials, Sierra appeared, drink in hand. "Here."

I took it from her and set it aside.

"Drink," she ordered. "Now."

"Don't boss me around."

"If I don't, who will? She who is older by a year," she intoned, "gets to make the rules."

"You made up that decree when we were girls."

"And it worked." She elbowed me. "C'mon, take a few sips. I promise it will give you energy for the rest of the day."

I obeyed and hummed my approval. It was sweet and flavorful.

Satisfied that she'd dominated me, she turned on her heel and said over her shoulder, "Love the necklace." She exited, cackling like a goose.

Ava showed up at ten on the dot and informed me this would be her first facial ever. I noticed her right cheek was twitching. Was she anxious about having the treatment? I'd been nervous the first time I'd had one. Nana took me. I was a freshman in high school. I didn't have a lot of acne, but I had eczema and feared the facialist would judge me. She didn't. Sensing my anxiety, she gently talked me through each procedure. It was because of her that I'd wanted to learn more about facial masks and essential oils.

"Relax, Ava," I said. "There's nothing to worry about. You'll love the experience."

I led her to the room and told her I'd leave while she removed her top, lay down on the bed, and draped herself with the white sheet. She giggled nervously.

After a minute passed, I reentered the room, swept Ava's hair off her face, and wrapped it with a terry cloth turban. "You have gorgeous hair. It's healthy and shiny."

"I use a mixture of aloe vera gel, honey, and coconut oil," she said. "A tablespoon of each. After you shower, put it on and wait five minutes before rinsing it off."

"Good to know," I said. Maybe it would thicken my baby fine hair.

I switched on the steam machine and, peering through a magnifying lamp, examined her skin, explaining each step as I went.

For a young woman, she had very dry skin. As I applied a cleansing cream, I asked her what products she used. She rattled them off. None would have caused the dryness.

"You wash and lubricate every night?"

*"Mm-hmm."*

"Do you drink enough water?"

"Eight to ten glasses a day. Quinlyn says I should've been a fish."

"Do you exercise in addition to doing Pilates?" I asked.

"Yes. I've been swimming a lot lately."

"In the ocean?"

"Ack. No. *Brr."* She shivered on purpose. "At a gym."

"Chlorine can cause dryness," I said. "I'll recommend a few products that you can apply post-swim." A few, but not all, we sold at the spa. I added, "If money is an issue, over-the-counter coconut cream moisturizer is cheap and great for most types of skin."

For a short time, I tended to any breakouts in silence. Following that, I gave her a ten-minute face massage before applying the avocado mask.

"This will really help with the dryness," I said. "I'll send you home with a sample that you can put on next week."

"Lovely." She should've sounded relaxed, but her voice was tight.

While the mask firmed up, I started a three-minute massage on her right hand. Golly, her nails were long. And real. Not acrylic or gel. I thought of Meryl mimicking Ava trying to open a can of soda and couldn't help wondering how she unpacked boxes of goods at her shop without breaking her nails all the time. I moved to her left hand, massaged it, and followed with her feet. When that portion of the treatment was concluded, I washed up and removed the mask with a warm cloth. I applied a dime-sized amount of vitamin C booster cream to her skin and rubbed it in.

"There you go," I said when I was done.

"Emma." Ava sat up and twisted on the table, the sheet wedged beneath her armpits to keep her body covered. "Quinlyn said you questioned my alibi when you left yesterday."

Aha. Fear of being exposed could explain why her cheek had been twitching at the beginning of the treatment. "I didn't question it. I mentioned it in passing. She corroborated it. She said she was with you."

Ava's eyes widened, but she didn't offer anything more. I fetched a cosmetic jar sample of the avocado face mask, handed it to her, and left the room. Minutes later, she emerged in her street clothes and followed me to reception. Quinlyn was seated in an armchair ready for her treatment.

"I'm paying for both facials." Quinlyn rose to her feet while smoothing the front of her boxy dress. She moved toward Ava, but Ava sidestepped her and said, in a crisp tone, that she'd see Quinlyn at the shop later.

*Odd*, I thought. *What was that about?*

I welcomed Quinlyn and asked her to follow me to the facial room. "You look nice," I said over my shoulder.

"That's sweet of you to say, but I need to lose a few pounds."

Once we were in the room, I instructed her as I had Ava, and when she was nestled beneath the sheet, I began. Throughout the steaming and cleaning process, I couldn't shake the feeling that Ava had been disturbed by Quinlyn's claim to have been doing inventory that night. Had Quinlyn lied to me to protect Ava? Or had she lied to give herself an alibi?

I began to massage her right hand.

"Ava told me Hugh Ashbluff is in arrears," Quinlyn said. "He's desperate not to lose everything he has. Which is a lot. Did you know he owns, like, bunches of properties? All are retail."

"Not all," I replied. "He owns some apartment buildings and homes. Where did Ava hear this? Not from Hugh himself."

"From one of the other shop owners in our complex."

I tipped my head, mulling that over. Had Ava asked Quinlyn to mention this to me to divert suspicion from herself? "Did she say how much he owes and to whom?"

"No."

I moved to her other hand.

"Ava's convinced we'd be a better tenant for him," Quinlyn continued. "She's going to talk to him about taking over Willow's lease."

Interesting. Especially after Ava said to me that she wasn't keen on leasing the site after a murder had occurred there.

When I was massaging her feet, Quinlyn added, "She'll even offer above asking price to sweeten the deal. We're as reliable as they come."

I ambled to the head of the table to remove the mask from her face.

"We never have a slow month," she went on as I used a hot towel to wipe off the goo. "Tourists are plentiful in Carmel."

I bit back a smile. Who knew Quinlyn could be as chatty as a magpie? "Isn't your current location better, though? It's on Ocean, after all. That's the main thoroughfare."

"Ava says bigger is better."

As I rubbed in the vitamin C booster cream, another idea surfaced. Had Quinlyn and Ava teamed up to commit murder? The notion made me shiver.

Facial complete, Quinlyn sat up, sheet wedged beneath her armpits, and accepted the mirror I handed her. She viewed her face. "Wow. I'm glowing. I'm going to tell our customers about this spa. Didn't you say you're going to give a class on how to make this mask?"

"Yes."

"When?"

"Classes will begin in a few weeks. We have flyers with a list of our scheduled events." I led her to reception and pointed to the Plexiglas holder of information on the counter. "We'll be inviting some guests to speak in the next few months, experts who can talk about health and wellness."

"Nice." She took a flyer, paid for both facials, gave me a hefty tip, and waved good-bye. On her way out, she passed my mother, who was on her way in.

I stiffened. The last time Kate had stopped by, it hadn't gone well. "Mother, to what do I owe the pleasure?"

"I have to tell you something." She tugged at the lapels of her emerald-green jacket. The color made her eyes seem brighter. "It's private." She nabbed my elbow and dragged me toward the windowed wall behind the reception desk through which we could see the café, a design feature Sierra and I had landed on, believing spa customers might like to see the activity in the café and vice versa.

Sierra and her barista were at the café counter furiously whipping up concoctions. Two waitstaff were circulating between tables. At least a half dozen customers were in line to order.

I closed the blinds on the window and faced my mother. "You missed book club."

She didn't respond.

"Nana told me you had an appointment."

She remained mute.

"Nana thinks you went on a date. Is that true?"

"Yes. No."

"Which is it?"

"No, I'm . . ." She paused. No customers had entered the spa. No applicants for the receptionist job, either. Even so, she lowered her voice. "I'm no longer going to see him."

"Why tell me about it, then?"

"He's married."

Egads! I never would've guessed she'd date a married man, let alone confess it to me. Was that why she'd been disheveled the other day? Had the wife suddenly appeared, causing Kate to run out of the house half-dressed?

"I knew he was," she went on. "I'm to blame. I believed he would leave her. I'm such a fool."

"Who is he?"

"I won't say, but he's the reason I was worried about you opening this business."

"Huh?"

"See, he's a whiz at statistics and knows all about people unrealistically opening new concerns that will fail. He said . . ." She swallowed hard. "He said you'd crash and burn." She gripped my arm. "You're gifted as a masseuse and such, darling, but as a businesswoman—"

"Mother, in college I took dozens of entrepreneurial classes, like marketing and statistics. I'm prepared." I'd taken even more courses online after I graduated. "Please, I don't want you to worry anymore."

She scrutinized her fingernails. They were chewed down to the nibs, which surprised me. A proper manicure mattered to her. Having an affair had clearly upset her. "I don't want you to think I don't love you. I do."

Did she? Or did she simply think she should?

"I'm pulling for you," she continued.

"You've got a funny way of showing it."

She frowned. "The real reason I came in to tell you the news is because if you heard through the grapevine that I was seeing him, I didn't want you to judge me harshly."

"I won't, but I'm glad you're ending it. You deserve better than some guy who's stepping out on his wife."

She didn't respond.

"Don't you?" I crossed my arms. A woman I knew had fallen in love with a married man and, like my mother, thought he would leave his wife for her. Ten years later, he hadn't budged.

"Yes. Absolutely. But we had a lot in common." Her face reddened. "And such chemistry."

"TMI," I said, using the initials for too much information.

"Don't worry. It's over, and I'm never going to date again. Ever."

*Malarkey*, as my grandmother quipped.

"You decide what's best for you," I said diplomatically. I wouldn't chastise her for choices unless she started harping again about mine. "Does Nana know?"

She wagged her head. "Please don't say a thing. It's done. *Finito.* Nevermore."

"'Quoth the raven,'" I gibed.

She bussed me on the cheek and rushed out of the spa.

The energy she left behind felt melancholy, which could only mean she'd fallen for the guy. I swept a hand over each arm to rid my body of her bad juju, then raised both arms and shook them, allowing my hands to flop around to release the tension.

Mini–cleansing routine complete, I returned to the reception desk at the same instance the first receptionist job applicant entered the building. An hour later, after meeting all five, I had a winner. Jason Sampson, a wiry twenty-one-year-old who'd wrestled in high school, couldn't wait to talk to customers, answer phones, and make appointments. It wasn't that he didn't aspire to higher goals. He did.

He was a true-crime writer and thought a steady desk job would give him the opportunity to read or write when there were ebbs and flows of activity. I liked him. Not simply because he'd be around for longer than a nanosecond—a writing career, he said, could take a long time to launch—but because he had good energy, keen eyes, a winsome smile, and was a tech nerd. Plus, his references from his teachers and wrestling coach were top-notch. Better yet? He could start immediately.

For the next hour, I schooled him on the computer program that managed our appointments, ran him through our contacts list, and gave him a tour of the facility, gift shop, and café. When I was ready to direct him to take the helm so I could enjoy an early-afternoon walk, he asked if there were any perks to the position, like a free spa treatment or smoothies. I told him I'd comp him one treatment a month and one café food and beverage a week, like all employees.

Hiring process done, I decided to window-shop on my stroll. My favorite of Carmel's walkways was known as the Secret Garden passageway, a tiny, bamboo-lined corridor that connected Dolores Street to San Carlos Street. Along the narrow path was Pilgrim's Way Books a go-to stop for me a couple of times a year. I loved the garden with its peaceful fountains, the charming gifts, and of course, the books. While browsing the mystery section, I thought of my mother's startling revelation. Her disclosure stirred a memory in my mind and made me wonder about the secrets that Ava, Quinlyn, and Hugh were harboring. Were there other names I should add to the suspect list?

While viewing the various greeting cards the bookstore had for sale, I pictured the threatening postcard that had been shoved under the door at the spa and wondered again about the one Willow had received. She'd accused Palmer of being the culprit. Palmer flatly denied it. Indy was Palmer's bestie. Was it possible, as Yoly suggested, that she'd delivered the cards? No. That didn't make sense. As I'd conveyed to Yoly at the time, if they proved to be Palmer's artwork, Indy would have been implicating her friend. However, even if she had been cavalierly naive in that regard, she didn't kill Willow. She had a verifiable alibi. Palmer did, too, although watching a television show—a rerun, no less—was not a solid one. And yet I hadn't coaxed the alibi out of her. She'd offered it up of her own accord.

No, neither woman was directly guilty, I decided, but what if, as I'd mused about Ava and Quinlyn, they had conspired to kill Willow? I recalled the way they were whispering as I left Percolate. Had they been gloating over their success? No, they wouldn't have done that in front of Palmer's daughter. On the other hand, what if they had been discussing a third person they'd corralled into their scheme. Perhaps the woman who'd been sitting with them at Hideaway Café.

Namely, Naomi Clutterbuck.

# Chapter 14

When I reentered the spa, Jason was chatting with a youngish female customer who was twirling a tendril of blond hair around one finger, her hip cocked to one side. Her efforts at flirting wouldn't pay off. During his interview, Jason said he was gay and asked if that would be a problem.

*As if,* I'd replied. In my group of students during the stint in Tibet, there were a few that were gay, lesbian, or nonbinary—persons who preferred the pronouns *they/them.* Who cared? When not meditating, we found we had a lot in common. We all loved books. We adored the smell of strawberries and cinnamon. We cherished the sound of the sea as well as the sound of silence. Big deal if we had different sexual preferences. To this day, we chatted every few months on Zoom.

Jason cleared his throat, brushed a thatch of his dark hair off his forehead, and let the young woman down gently. Crestfallen, she looked appeased after he presented her with a discount coupon.

An hour before closing, I phoned my grandmother and asked if I could make her dinner.

"To pick my brain?" she joshed.

"Absolutely."

"You're on."

When I got home, Vivi was at the door. The instant I entered, she flew across the living room, crouched beneath the sofa, and peered out at me.

"Oho," I said. "Are you getting ready to attack my ankles?" I knelt down and drummed the hardwood floor with my fingertips. "Come out, come out, wherever you are."

She ran into me headlong.

I nabbed her. "Gotcha." I kissed her nose. "I don't have time to play right now. Nana Lissa is coming to dinner."

Vivi purred her approval. She adored my grandmother.

"Come with me." I plunked her on the floor, and she padded after me to the kitchen.

I fixed her a meal of salmon, then pulled two mahi-mahi steaks from the freezer. Yes, I knew it was best to take them out twenty-four hours earlier to defrost, but so be it. After preheating the oven to four hundred degrees, I set the steaks on a plate, covered them with a paper towel, and inserted the plate into the microwave. While they defrosted on low for one minute, I pulled out parchment paper. My favorite way to cook mahi was to put a dab of butter and mustard on the parchment paper, place the fish on top, sprinkle it with Old Bay seasoning, fold the parchment paper, and twist the ends to trap the steam inside while the fish was cooking.

When the oven was ready, I slid the parchment-wrapped mahi steaks onto a baking tray and slipped it into the oven, set a timer for fifteen minutes, poured two glasses of chardonnay, and tossed a salad with dressing I'd made using one of Nana Lissa's recipes. She was a good baker. She was a great chef. She was the one who had mentored Sierra and had encouraged her to go into the culinary field.

Next, I went to the bedroom and switched out of my top. I

threw on a lightweight aqua tunic, spritzed myself with vanilla fragrance, retied my hair in a knot, and zipped to the kitchen.

Vivi was already done with her meal and requested more. I gave her the side-eye. She knew I wouldn't indulge her, but she always tried.

I clicked on a Henry Mancini playlist from my cell phone. Nana loved the award-winning composer's music. The strains of *Charade* funneled through the Bluetooth speaker on the counter. Hearing the song made me laugh. Talk about a movie plot with secrets!

I then arranged place mats and silverware on the table and began mulling over the theories I'd considered this afternoon regarding Hugh, Quinlyn, Ava, and now Naomi. I fetched two Royal Doulton Pacific Splash plates—Nana had supplied each of the units with china that went well with the decor—and was setting them on the counter when the doorbell rang.

I greeted my grandmother with a hug. "Dinner in a few in the kitchen."

"Why don't we eat in the yard? It's such a lovely evening."

"Great idea."

Nana carried our wineglasses outside, and I took the tableware.

The kitchen timer chimed. I said, "Be right back."

Once we settled at the table to eat, Vivi decided to explore, but she wasn't investigating as she usually did, looking for lizards and bugs. She was peeking upward at the undersides of flowers and bushes, as if searching for something else. Out of the blue, she batted a leaf.

"Vivi," I called. "What's going on?"

"Don't mind her," Nana Lissa said. "She's made a fairy friend."

"A fairy . . ." I pressed my lips together. "My cat can see a fairy, and I can't?"

"Most animals can. They're tuned in to nature much more than we humans."

I watched Vivi scamper after something—invisible to me—and

sighed. Was the fairy the imaginary ball my cat had been toying with on the comforter this morning?

My grandmother chuckled. "Emma, stop staring. Fairies don't glow like lightning bugs. Be patient."

Normally, I prided myself on my patience, but not being in tune enough to see a fairy was infuriating. I mean, I was dialed into the universe. I was attentive to my spirit as well as to other people's spirits. Why in heck couldn't I see a danged fairy?

*Breathe, Emma. Semi-cursing will get you nowhere.*

Nana Lissa took a bite of her fish and hummed her appreciation. "Lovely flavor."

The texture was a bit tough, but she didn't mention it.

"Now"—she set her fork down—"what do you need from me?"

I reiterated the story about running into Palmer and Indy at Percolate.

"You told me."

"Yes, but I didn't tell you that when I was leaving, they were whispering, and I got the feeling they were conspiring."

"Well, they are on the same tennis team," she said.

"Indy plays tennis?"

"She might not look it, but she's quick as lightning. For all you know, they were scheming how to beat their opponents. The summer season is in full throttle."

"I suppose that could explain why Olivia was staring daggers at her mother. Palmer was ignoring her."

"Poor girl," my grandmother said. "Palmer doesn't dote on her the way she did Olivia's older sister. But let's be frank. Olivia is not the reason we're discussing Palmer and Indy, is she?"

I smiled slyly. "You are intuitive."

She couldn't curb her laughter.

"Do you know Naomi Clutterbuck?" I asked.

Nana Lissa sobered. "She's a charming woman. She reads historical romance and is quite insightful in discussions at the library. She's a language arts teacher, and I hear she's a good one."

"Is she married? Does she have family?"

"Her husband is an international attorney in San Francisco and is always on the road, splitting his time between there and here. He helped her and her mother and sisters out of a bad situation. That was how they met. And, no, they don't have children. Why do you ask?"

"Why would she be friends with Palmer and Indy? She's years younger."

"Friends? Oh, that's right. We saw them together Tuesday at the café." My grandmother took a sip of her wine and mulled over the question until light dawned in her eyes. "I think Naomi takes art lessons somewhere in town. She could know Palmer from those. Palmer enrolls in lots of classes in all sorts of media."

How frustrating it must be for Palmer to have a dream that might never be fulfilled. Was her obsession with art, tennis, and bake sales—activities that prevented her from having time or energy to devote to the family—the real reason her older daughter left?

Mothers and daughters. I sighed. Did they ever see eye to eye? I thought about the chat with Kate. Her big reveal. How we'd bonded because of her pain. Did that mean we would honor and appreciate one another going forward? Ha! Not on a bet.

"What's tickled your funny bone?" Nana speared a bite of lettuce and cucumber with her fork. "Do you have another of Meryl's jokes to share?"

"Nope." I was never any good at telling jokes, let alone remembering punchlines. "I have a theory . . ." I told her how I'd wondered whether Indy had slipped the threatening postcards under Willow's and my doors to appease Palmer, but had ruled out that theory. On the other hand, because Indy and Palmer had alibis for the night Willow was killed, perhaps they'd convinced Naomi to help them with the next phase. "She was dining with them at the café that night. She'd acted embarrassed by their heated exchange, but what if she hadn't been? What if she had a bone to pick with Willow, too?"

My grandmother pressed a hand to her chest. "I can't imagine Naomi doing any such thing. Conspire with them to kill someone? No. The way Willow was murdered required strength and pure unadulterated hatred." She shook her head. "Naomi is slight, and, believe me, lashing out is not her nature."

Vivi leaped into the air, nearly doing a somersault.

My grandmother applauded. "You almost caught her, little one."

"Do you recognize the fairy?" I asked.

"As a matter of fact, I do. She's a nurturer."

"What does a nurturer do?"

"Exactly what it sounds like. She nourishes the soul. She calms. She provides sustenance, if necessary. She cultivates the earth. She can charm plants and flowers." My grandmother rotated a hand. "This fairy, in particular, adores playing with cats."

For the rest of dinner, I kept an eye on Vivi, hoping to see the fairy, but, alas, I didn't.

On Saturday morning, I awoke feeling as if I'd been mired in a dream for six straight hours. In it, I was jogging along a bridge, avoiding being struck by speeding cars and looking for a doorway that wouldn't appear. I had the address written on a card in peacock-blue ink, but it kept vanishing.

"I'm going for a walk on the beach," I said to Vivi after brushing my teeth. "Want to come?"

Vivi was nestled at the end of the bed. She sprang to the floor and followed me. I slipped into running shorts, an aqua-blue tank top, and FitFlop sandals, then drank a big glass of water, inserted Vivi in a cat carrier with a bubble-view window, and strapped her to my chest. It gave me joy to feel her purring. It meant she was content.

Like yesterday, I took the route along Ocean Avenue to the beach. The repetitive crashing of the waves grew louder, and the intoxicating aroma of the salty water intensified as I neared the iconic cypress tree at the entrance to the strand. A slight woman in short-

shorts and a tank top, carrying a backpack, sped past me on a bicycle, kicked off it, and, trustworthy soul, laid it on its side, unchained to anything. In a rush, she dashed down the hill toward the water. I recognized her: it was Naomi Clutterbuck. Her backpack bounced with each stride.

Nearby, an older woman said to a woman of similar age, "Always in a hurry, these young ones."

"She'll wish she'd covered up," her companion replied. "The sun is going to be brutal today."

I wondered what they'd say about my getup. At least I'd put on sunblock. I removed my sandals and proceeded down the incline, slipping in the soft sand. Singles like me as well as couples and groups were walking parallel to the water. Farther along, a group of artists facing canvases on easels were capturing images of the bay. Among them I saw Naomi eagerly pulling a canvas and acrylic paints from her backpack.

Seeing the class made me think of my conversation with my grandmother last night. She said Palmer enrolled in art classes. Was this the one where Naomi and Palmer had met? I also recalled Nana saying Palmer took classes in a variety of mediums. The only works of hers I'd seen were watercolors. Was she learning other methods in hope of discovering her breakout style? If she was, perhaps the avant-garde art on the postcard I'd received had been hers, after all.

*No, Emma. Stop going there. It would be idiotic of her to use her own artwork to taunt you and Willow.*

Half an hour later, I returned to the cottage with Vivi, fed her, gave her a catnip toy, and put a homemade protein bar I'd made using one of Sierra's recipes in my purse. Next, I switched into one of my most feminine outfits, cotton slacks embroidered with flowers and a cream-colored Boho blouse with tie-front neckline. On my way to the spa, I ate my breakfast. It was gooey and soft, more like a brownie than the crisp bars I purchased at the store, but it would do the trick.

When I reached the courtyard, I was surprised to see Floyd Marblemaw again. He must have heard me coming because he swung around. My clogs were anything but quiet.

"Got a few minutes now?" He whisked the fedora off his head with two hands and ran the brim between his fingers. He was wearing the same rumpled suit he'd worn the other day. Was he homeless or just strapped for cash?

"No, sir," I said, making my impatience known. "I have a full day ahead."

"Was Willow dating anyone?"

"Not as far I know." And it was none of his business.

"Do you know who she dated last?"

"No."

"Is her mother alive?" he asked.

"Yes, but what does that have to do with—"

"Did she have siblings?"

"One. A half sister. Why do you want to know? You said you were writing an article about women entrepreneurs."

"I am. But her murder has put a whole new spin on my viewpoint. I heard you're a suspect."

"I didn't kill her."

"Did she have enemies?" he asked.

"I have no clue. She could be curt. She might have ruffled a few feathers."

"Do you suspect anyone?"

I tilted my head. Was he, like me, trying to solve Willow's murder? Did he think that would get him a front-page headline? "Honestly, sir, you should talk to the police—"

"I tried. They won't tell me a darned thing!" He scrunched up his face.

When I was six, my grandmother took me on a day trip to San Jose to see the movie *Pollyanna* in a retro-style theater, saying it had been one of her favorite movies as a girl and that she absolutely had to share the experience with me. Now, looking at Mr. Marblemaw, I was reminded of the sick, tart woman in that movie, Mrs. Snow. Pollyanna had brightened that woman's life. What would it take to bring this man joy?

"Sir," I began again, my voice appeasing. "I'm sorry, but I am busy. Let's talk Tuesday. Does that work for you? I'll set aside a full hour."

"Yeah, yeah," he muttered, and stomped down the steps.

Why was he blaming me for being short on information? It wasn't like Willow had been the most forthcoming of women. Like I said to Ginnie, she had secrets. I stared after him, wondering why he was adamant about getting this story. Would he lose his job if he didn't? Another thought came to mind: What if he'd killed Willow and was trying to determine whether anyone suspected him? What would his motive have been? Jilted lover? Was that why he'd asked whether Willow was dating? She'd preferred going out with mature men, but he was older than the professor she'd been seeing—*way* older.

Making a U-turn, I went into the spa and stopped when I saw Jason, Sierra, and Meryl in a huddle, laughing hysterically. I rushed forward, finger wagging. "You guys, *shh*. People are trying to relax here."

Jason covered his mouth and nose to get control of himself. "Sorry, but Meryl told us a good joke."

Sierra was snickering so hard she sounded like she was sneezing. She pulled a tissue from the pocket of her striped apron and dabbed her nose.

I frowned at Meryl. "Another one?"

Looking mortified, she smoothed the front of her salon jacket. "Bad habit, I know, but I'm always working on material."

"I understand that you think the goings-on at the spa are perfect fodder for your routine, but for now, would you keep your jokes to a minimum?"

"Sure, boss, but Jason goaded me—"

"Uh-uh, girlfriend." He moved his head side to side. "I did not beg you to tell jokes. You came waltzing in here saying you simply had to share."

Meryl checked her watch and *eek*ed. "I have a pedicure in ten. Gotta prepare the room."

Sierra slung an arm through mine. "You're prickly. What's up?"

I told her about my testy exchange with Mr. Marblemaw.

"Reporters are pains in the you-know-what," she teased. "How about a cup of calming chamomile?"

"No tea, thanks. Only water. I need to cleanse." I poured myself a glass of cucumber water from the pitcher on the beverage cart and rounded the counter to check appointments.

"Everything is up to date," Jason said. "Not an empty slot for the rest of the afternoon, and tomorrow, as planned, you're free."

For now, we would close on Sundays. I figured everyone needed a day off, and in Carmel, most tourists were out sightseeing if it was their last day in town. On Sunday afternoon, a cleaning crew would come in and give the spa a good scrub-down, and we could begin anew on Monday.

"FYI, those coupons are a hit," Jason added. "You booked ten massages next week because of them."

"Sweet."

"Also, your grandmother phoned to confirm that you're going hiking with her tomorrow. She said she'll show you a fairy hollow."

"A hollow?"

"That's what she said." He rolled his eyes. "Fairies. Sheesh. Give me a break."

"Lots of people see them."

He harrumphed. "I haven't, have you?"

"No, but one has to believe."

"I'll believe it when I see it," he carped. "Oh, heads-up. Yelp reviews for Aroma Wellness are piling up. In a good way. I went through all of them. They're legit. And the café is killing it with favorable evaluations. Killing. It."

His emphasis on those two words made my insides snarl. Willow's murder needed to be solved. She deserved justice. That prompted me to ask, "Have the police reached out with any new leads?"

"Why would they call here?"

Good question. They wouldn't.

# Chapter 15

At the end of the day, after I'd performed a sound bath for two new customers, my grandmother strolled into the spa clad in the sunniest outfit I'd ever seen her wear. Usually, she preferred simple but elegant patterns. Today she was dressed in floral capris and a bright—I mean superbright—pink blouse, gold dangly earrings, and gold sandals.

"Wow!" I said. "You look amazing. Going somewhere special?"

"Hardly." She scoffed. "I thought I'd take you and Sierra wine tasting."

"Did we have that on the schedule?"

"No, but I could do with a glass of something yummy and a long walk. I need to unwind before tonight's poetry reading."

"We're going to the fairy hollow tomorrow. That should be relaxing."

She smiled indulgently. "Yes, we are. Tomorrow. But tonight is tonight, and there was a big upset at the library today. A nasty, horrible patron who shall remain nameless—"

"Mrs. Snow," I inserted, referring to the *Pollyanna* curmudgeon.

"Mrs. Snow. Perfect." She nodded. "Yes, Mrs. Snow chastised me for the way books were categorized on the shelves."

"Why you? You're not in charge of the Dewey decimal system."

"Exactly, but she simply could not tolerate how some titles were mixed in with fiction when they were clearly *genre*." She stressed the word and added air quotes. "Suffice it to say, I need a moment to breathe."

"You don't have to ask me twice. I'm down for a glass of wine."

Minutes later, Sierra, Nana, and I entered Take Flight, a coffee place by day and wine bar by night. It was as charming as any café in Carmel-by-the-Sea, with a European-style exterior featuring traditional ornamental detail. The interior was equally rich in flavor. Prior to Take Flight's assuming ownership, the coffee-wine bar had been an English pub with dartboards and raucous customers. Now patrons sat on high stools at tall tables and chatted softly.

A singer was sitting beside the stone fireplace—no fire was lit on this warm night—his feet resting on the lower rung of a ladderback chair. His guitar was strapped over one shoulder and perched on his thigh.

"Handsome guy, Emma," Sierra said, waggling her eyebrows. "Exactly your type."

I elbowed her.

"A date wouldn't hurt you," she added.

"Why don't you make yourself available?" I gibed. "Could it be you're not on the market because your pastry chef dreamboat broke your heart and ruined your plans for a happily ever after, or are you waiting for him to waltz back into your life—"

"Stop!" My cousin held up a hand. "Do not remind me." The day her boyfriend at the Culinary Institute graduated, he moved to New York to pursue his passion. He'd hoped to land a Michelin star–worthy restaurant. The last I'd heard, he was making scones and muffins at a diner. He never even asked Sierra if she might want to go with him, the louse.

"Girls." Nana Lissa signaled us to follow her. She sauntered to the dark mahogany bar at the far end of the room, where a perky blond sommelier was pouring flights of white wine. "Three of those, please."

The sommelier set stemless glasses on three paddles, each paddle carved with circular cutouts to hold the glasses in place, and pushed them toward us. As she poured the wine into our glasses, she described them. The sauvignon blanc was pineapple forward with a tang at the end. The pinot grigio, made from grapes that were a mutant clone of pinot noir grapes, was the type of wine that ran anywhere from deep yellow to light pink. The one she was offering happened to be in the yellow family and would taste spicy with a hint of mango. When she finished describing each of our choices, we carried our flights to a table and perched on the stools.

The sauvignon blanc was crisp but made my tongue tingle. I set it down and tried the pinot grigio. Hints of melon, not mango, filled my mouth, but what did I know? I wasn't a wine connoisseur.

"I like this one," I said, tapping the pinot grigio glass.

Sierra swapped her pinot for my sauvignon blanc, and said, "À votre santé!"

"Show-off," I teased. I spoke English and broken Spanish. She could speak five languages.

For the next hour, the three of us talked about the spa, the activity at the café, and how well the items at the shop were selling. The conversation was light and sometimes silly.

Sierra said, "You should see some of the characters that venture into the café. Most wouldn't know a healthy diet if you served them the right food three hundred and sixty-five days a year."

"That's where you would excel." I grinned. "Creating specialty diets for each person in Carmel."

"Uh-uh, no way. I will never be a personal chef."

Nana tweaked Sierra's cheek. "Think how much each of your customers would appreciate seeing your cheery face in the morning."

Sierra snorted. "Yeah, not happening. I'm going to focus on our café customers and inspire them to great heights."

"Right on." I clinked my glass to hers and changed the subject to Nana Lissa's fundraiser project. "Did you land on a theme?"

She beamed. "We did. Board game night."

"Everyone loves board games," I said. "Parcheesi, Monopoly, Risk."

"Scrabble, Stratego," Sierra cut in. "And Clue. We can't forget Clue."

Nana said, "Speaking of clues, I've been thinking."

"About the murder?" Sierra asked.

"Yes."

"Have you learned something new?"

"No. I feel like I'm missing something."

"What about you, Emma?" Sierra eyed me.

I recapped the conversations I'd had with our grandmother about Indy and Palmer's tête-à-tête at Percolate.

"You and your caffeine habit." Sierra wrinkled her nose.

"I drink it sometimes. Sue me." I sipped my wine. "Both of the women had alibis for the night of the murder. However, I was wondering about Naomi Clutterbuck." I explained to my cousin who she was. "Anyway, this morning . . ." I told them about my walk on the beach and seeing Naomi fly up on her bike, and how she joined an art class, and how that triggered a new theory. "Nana, you said Palmer dabbles in all sorts of art media."

"Mm-hmm."

"Could she possibly have painted something using an avant-garde or abstract expressionist style?"

Her forehead puckered. "Why?"

"I can't help wondering who created the threatening postcard found under the spa's gift shop door. You saw it. All swirls and splatters, like Jackson Pollock or Willem de Kooning's work." I'd taken an art history class in college. The curriculum had covered twentieth-century artists.

Sierra said, "I've seen postcards like that all over town."

*Not at Shabby Chic Nook*, I mused. "I was wondering, too, whether it was possible Palmer slipped it under the door on behalf of her BFF Indy"—I explained why Indy might have held a grudge against Willow—"but decided against it."

Nana Lissa said, "The incident regarding Indy's ex-boyfriend involved Willow, not you."

Sierra agreed. "I think the postcards were a prank. Maybe someone who'd had a bad spa experience lashed out."

I hadn't considered that. Why not threaten Tish, too? "Nana, you have the inside scoop on everyone in Carmel. What's Palmer's story?"

"She grew up in a rigid family from Connecticut."

"How rigid?"

"College was a must. Finding a good husband while there was her aim. Church was not to be missed on any given Sunday, and if she was going to play tennis, she was expected to become a winner, though her parents refused to let her become a professional. That would be unladylike."

"She's that good?" I asked surprised.

"She wins tournaments."

"What does her husband do?"

"He's in insurance."

"Boring." Sierra pretended to yawn.

Nana Lissa laughed. "When he's not working, he's golfing."

"He doesn't play tennis like her?" Sierra asked.

"No. That was one of Palmer's requirements when falling for a man."

"Honestly?" Sierra made a wickedly funny face.

"That doesn't make sense," I said. "Didn't she want to have a companion to play with?"

"She didn't want the competition." Nana Lissa smiled.

"How long have they been married?" I took another sip of wine.

"Over twenty years. They met in college and married the summer they graduated. He neglected to tell her until after their honeymoon that, being from California, he planned to move home. Palmer didn't put up a fuss. She'd heard wonderful things about Carmel. It wasn't until she'd spent a few months here that she realized she hated living near the ocean. The occasional foggy gloom really affects her."

"Do they have children?" Sierra asked.

"Yes. Two daughters, Olivia and Alexandra, and they own a modest home on Dolores, not too far from where you two live."

I said, "Tell me about the older daughter."

"Alexandra left Carmel a year ago. She was nineteen. Her relationship with her mother was acrimonious. Palmer could be quite controlling."

"No, really?" I said facetiously.

"I heard through the grapevine that Palmer's husband accused Palmer of driving the girl away by poisoning her against Carmel. Palmer was always comparing Carmel to Connecticut." Nana Lissa ran a finger around the rim of her wineglass. "According to her, they had better schools there. Less traffic. It was close to New York, the cultural hub, yada-yada. And going to college in the East should be Alexandra's goal, Palmer contended. But Alexandra had no interest in attending college. She was a bit of a wild child who blew with the wind."

That surprised me. "Her younger sister paints a saintly portrait of her."

"Alexandra was good with Olivia, but she was restless to see the world. And she was daring. She hitchhiked everywhere, much to her parents' dismay."

Dread slithered down my spine. "She didn't meet with disaster, did she?"

"No. Palmer assures me the girl is fine, just stubborn." She finished her glass of wine.

"She strikes me as a very unhappy person," I said.

"I think you're right on that point," Nana replied. "You rarely see her and her husband together, and when you do, one or the other is scowling. She can be quite critical. She pulls no punches when she says living with an insurance statistician can be boring."

"Insurance statistician? What's that?" Sierra asked.

"It's like an actuarial," our grandmother explained. "They're responsible for the analysis of future risk probabilities. They help determine policy premiums and rates."

*No, no, no* clanged in my head as a worrisome notion occurred to me. My mother had not hooked up with Palmer's husband, had she? They could have met after Kate took up golf a couple of years ago. A man who worked as a statistician might know all about people opening new concerns and believe, given the stats, that they would fail. He might feasibly offer his two cents about the sanity of opening a new spa, too.

"Ready?" Nana rose to her feet. "I need to walk."

"Yes!" I said a tad loudly.

My cousin and grandmother stared at me.

I didn't want them to ask what was cycling through my fraught brain, so I covered my mouth dramatically and forced a giggle. "Sorry. That's enough wine for me."

The sun was waning as we exited. Lots of people were taking a stroll.

"What a gorgeous night," Nana Lissa said. "It's like someone has painted the heavens."

Wisps of clouds dotted the sky, each a different shade of orange.

"No wonder artists come to Carmel," I said.

After the devastating 1906 earthquake in San Francisco, Carmel became a haven for artists, actors, and authors who'd wanted a colony where they could thrive as creative people. Nowadays, art galleries peppered the landscape of our fair town. In addition, the Carmel Arts and Crafts Club held exhibitions and lectures and produced plays and music recitals at numerous locations.

We strolled along Dolores Street, pausing outside Flair Gallery—

located in the same courtyard as Courtney Kelly's shop, Open Your Imagination—then continued on, peeking in the windows of other places.

"Isn't Carmel special?" our grandmother asked. "We're blessed to have talented artists and such a wealth of beauty."

I thought about how some artists, like Palmer, never sold a thing. That had to be frustrating. Did her dissatisfaction drive her daughter away? Was Palmer, with her laser focus on her own pursuits, pushing her husband into the arms of another woman? Had she put the postcard with the word *die* on it under the spa's gift shop door, thinking I would show it to my mother, and Kate would take a hint and stop the affair?

No, the message on the postcard was exactly the same as the one Willow had received. She and I were the targets of someone's wrath, not my mother.

"Emma, did you hear what I said?" Sierra asked.

I felt my cheeks flush with embarrassment.

She looped her hand around my elbow. "I asked if you want to step into Shabby Chic Nook." She gestured to the shop, which was a half block west on Ocean Avenue.

I hadn't realized we were close. "No." But the theory I'd dreamed up after giving the facials to Quinlyn and Ava returned. Had they conspired to kill Willow? Had Palmer and Indy and possibly Naomi cooked up a scheme to get rid of her? Were the police considering either of these angles?

"Emma," Nana Lissa said, sensing my anxiety, "put the murder investigation out of your mind tonight. Detective Summers is not breathing down your neck."

"But he will if I don't prove—"

My grandmother shushed me as if I were a child. "You're innocent, sweet girl. He knows it. Trust me. Now, I'm escorting you two home, and then I'm off to the library for that poetry reading. Don't forget, Emma, tomorrow morning, I'm taking you fairy hunting."

As we neared 4th Avenue, I heard something making a *bounce-bang* kind of sound.

"Who is causing that racket?" Sierra asked.

"Hold up," Nana Lissa said, blocking us with her arm. She was staring at a house to the left where a woman was hitting a tennis ball against the garage door of a two-story Spanish hacienda-style home. "That's Palmer," she whispered.

"Darn it, you idiot, focus!" Palmer shrieked as she whacked the ball again. *Bounce-bang.*

"Oh, my," Nana said. "She confided to me that she doesn't like to practice at the tennis facility where she competes because she doesn't want competitors watching. I had no idea she worked out at home."

Seeing the way Palmer was exerting herself, I wondered if I should take up tennis to release some of my anxiety but decided no. Meditation was the way to go.

Palmer swiped and missed. The ball veered into a tree and skittered to the right. "Crap!" She hurled her racket on the pavement. It bounced.

Nana whispered, "Go, Sierra, Emma. Skedaddle! Before she sees us and is mortified."

When we were safely out of sight, I said, "Well, that was illuminating."

"Why?" Sierra asked.

"Because Palmer has a vile temper, and if she could swing a candlestick the way she wields that tennis racket, she could have easily killed Willow."

Nana Lissa tsked. "Having a temper doesn't make someone a murderer."

# Chapter 16

Vivi was thrilled to see me, but I wasn't content to stay home. I was too wound up. I appeased her with an extra-large helping of salmon and texted Sierra to see if she wanted to grab a light meal at Bibi's Bistro on 8th east of Dolores. She did. Like me, she was agitated. Seeing Palmer that angry had disturbed her. My cousin could take the heat in the kitchen, but sensitive soul that she was, other people swearing and throwing fits made her uneasy.

As we were entering the bistro, I caught sight of Hugh Ashbluff down the street. He was punching in a code on a building. He squinted in my direction. Something about the way he studied me was unnerving. I ducked out of sight and followed Sierra to our table.

Bibi's, a charming red-and-white–checkered place with a limited menu, was filled with patrons, but the waitstaff was quick to serve. We ate spinach-and-ham quiche and drank ice water, seeing as both of us had imbibed enough wine at Take Flight. As we ate, Sierra asked why I'd felt edgy near Shabby Chic Nook. I told her about Ava's and Quinlyn's conflicting stories and my theory that they could have teamed up to kill Willow.

Sierra said, "You're working yourself into a frenzy over this."

"The snapping of handcuffs and the slamming of a jail cell haunt my dreams."

"Have you spoken to the police about your suspicions?"

"Nana said not to. I have nothing concrete to share."

She tapped the back of my hand. "Your crystal reading said you are powerful. Intuitive."

"It said I *would* be. Future tense."

She knuckled my arm.

We passed on dessert, and I paid the bill.

When we left the bistro, we veered right in the direction of Mission, thinking we'd window-shop before heading home. As we passed Yarn Diva and drew near to San Carlos Street, my gaze fixed on the sign in the leftmost group of office units—*Ashbluff Associates*. I hadn't noticed Hugh's business on previous strolls. A keypad was fitted into the exterior wall. This must have been the place I'd seen him entering a code.

The display window of the business was plastered with *For Sale* advertisements. One for a house on Casanova. Another for a home on San Antonio, perhaps the one he'd been showing the lady on the beach. The ad for the house on 10th Avenue read: *Charming Cottage, Perfect for One . . . or Two.*

The lights were on inside. Through the window, I spotted Hugh standing behind a cluttered oak desk, a telephone wedged between his chin and shoulder. His mouth was moving. I didn't see anyone else.

"It's late," I said. "Why is he burning the midnight oil?"

"Maybe he needs more clients, and he's cold-calling them."

I wondered again, despite my grandmother's claim to the contrary, whether Hugh was short on cash and killed Willow because she, by withholding funds, had threatened his financial status quo. Ava told Quinlyn he was struggling.

Hugh stopped what he was doing and stared at us. How I wished I could vanish into thin air. Where was an invisibility cloak when I needed one? He hung up the phone and beckoned us inside.

Sierra nudged me. "Go in."

"To the lions' den," I muttered.

"You don't know he's a killer. Besides, I'm with you. There's safety in numbers. Pretend you want to buy property."

I snorted. "As if I have the cash to purchase anything."

"He doesn't know that. He's sort of cute. I like his cowlick." She twirled a finger above her head. "It makes him look, you know, frisky. Is he single? Maybe you could ask him out for a date."

I whacked her shoulder. "Will you get off that train? I'm not in the market to date anyone, and certainly not someone who looks like an adult Dennis the Menace and is old enough to be my father."

"He can't be more than forty-five."

"Old." My quip made me pause. Willow had liked dating mature men. Had she and Hugh dated? Was it possible that when I'd seen them arguing, they were actually having a lovers' spat, and, seeing me approach, switched gears?

"C'mon." Sierra prodded me. "Question him. Find out his alibi."

Resigned, knowing she wouldn't stop badgering me until I agreed, I opened the door.

Hugh ended his call. "Welcome. You're Lissa's granddaughters, aren't you? You're cousins. Wait. Don't tell me. She mentioned your names." He snapped his fingers. "Emma and Sierra. You two opened the day spa."

"Emma's in charge of the spa and gift shop," Sierra said. "I run the café."

"I appreciate when someone is specific," he said. "Why were you staring at me?"

"Staring?" Sierra repeated. "We weren't staring."

The corkboard behind Hugh was covered with ads for homes or

apartment complexes for sale as well as units to rent. To his right, there were two plaques announcing he'd been an all-star athlete at Carmel High School. To the right of those hung a Padres shirt emblazoned with the number 9. Beyond that was a Louisville Slugger on wall mounts. I shivered and thought again of Hugh's prowess as a baseball player.

Hugh said, "Is it the lipstick mark on the bat that's caught your attention, Emma?"

I saw what he was referring to. An impression of bright red lips adorned the fattest tip of the bat. "It is," I lied. I'd been imagining him swinging a candlestick.

"My girlfriend was proud of me that day. We won the tournament, and we were going to the state championship. I was afraid if I washed it off, we'd lose."

"Is she the woman you married?"

"Nope. We parted ways. And I'm not married any longer."

Sierra elbowed me and waggled her eyebrows. I glowered at her. Was she nuts? I was not interested in dating a possible killer.

"Sir," Sierra began.

"Call me Hugh."

She smiled as sweetly as a Jane Austen heroine. "Hugh, you knew Willow Shafer pretty well, didn't you? She was your tenant."

"She was. It's a shame what happened. I heard the spa was such a disaster after—" He screwed up his mouth. "The police said cleanup was nearly impossible. I'll need to hire a specialty crew to redo it."

That answered the question I'd considered regarding Ginnie's responsibilities. She was off the hook.

Sierra gave a sympathetic look. "Did you know the police think Emma killed her?"

My stomach did a flip-flop. I hadn't expected her to be blunt and threw up my hands. "I didn't."

Hugh eyed me. "If Dylan Summers had concrete evidence, he would've put you in the slammer by now."

"You're friends with the detective," I said, thankful for the opening. "You were dining with him the night . . ." My throat went dry. "The night Willow was killed."

"He and I play golf together occasionally." Hugh busied himself with papers on his messy desk. Stacking. Restacking. Not making eye contact. What was swirling inside his brain?

I peeked at the papers. Upside down, I could see they were leases and bank statements, but I couldn't tell if Hugh was in arrears.

"Did Detective Summers inquire why you quarreled with Willow earlier that day?" I asked.

Hugh jerked upright, his eyes flickering with irritation. "Who said we did?"

"I saw you, as did Ava Daft. She owns—"

"I know perfectly well who Ms. Daft is. She wants to let Willow's space."

Oho. She'd reached out to him as Quinlyn had said she would. So much for sticking to her guns about not being interested in a location where someone was murdered.

"For your information, Willow and I weren't arguing," he went on. "We were negotiating. I held no grudge against her. She would pay on her lease eventually. I warned her, but I'd pressed her before."

Alas, only Willow would be able to corroborate that.

"Also, I have an alibi for that night," he said, "since I can see you want me to be on the police's short list of suspects."

"Care to share?" Sierra asked sassily.

He didn't respond.

"Did you and Detective Summers hang out after dinner?" I asked.

"No. I had a date."

"With?"

"None of your business."

I gulped as yet another notion flitted through my mind. He hadn't gone out with my mother, had he? No. Of course not. She said she'd been seeing a married man. Hugh was single.

"Sir," I went on, "you were spotted with binoculars outside Mystic Waters days before the murder."

He screwed up his mouth and lasered me with a hard look. "I was searching for rodent nests. Willow had complained about hearing noises." He lifted a set of file folders and fiddled with them to align the edges. "If you ask me, Ava Daft is the one the police should look into. She had it in for Willow. Why, every two months, she's been asking when I'd boot Willow out of her lease. That woman has business expansion on the brain." He dropped the stack of folders on the desk with a thud. "Now, if you don't mind, I've got business to attend to. Good night, girls."

*Girls? Honestly?* My grandmother could call us girls, but not him. I wanted to say, *Good night, old man,* but restrained myself.

Sierra and I hustled home, chatting about Hugh's nebulous alibi. If I told Detective Summers about the argument between him and Willow, would he dig deeper or dismiss it because they were friends?

At the foot of the fourplex, I said good night to Sierra, and she trotted upstairs to her unit.

As I was pulling the front-door key from my purse, my pulse kicked up a notch. The door was ajar about an inch. I hadn't left it open. I'd specifically locked it, as I always did. It didn't look as if it had been jimmied. No splintered wood lay on the doormat. Was someone inside? I nudged the door with my toe. It squeaked open a few more inches.

Vivi bolted out and leaped into my arms. Her heart was chugging like a motorboat.

I stroked her neck and kissed her ears. "You're all right. Is someone—"

She yowled, scrambled from my arms, and sprinted into the unit. She wouldn't have gone in if someone was still there, would she?

Plucking the kinetic dual flower spinner from one of the potted plants to use as a weapon—some weapon, but the shepherd's hook in the other pot was unwieldy—I rushed through the door, screaming like a banshee. There was no one inside. However, what I saw made me judder. My favorite Jane Austen plate was on the foyer floor in pieces, the display stand lying on top.

Vivi mewed from the kitchen. Fearing she was in danger, I tore in and instantly burst into tears. Not for Vivi. She was fine and perched on the kitchen counter. But, like me, she was staring at the shards of my giclée book covers that were lying on the floor. The magnets that once clung to the refrigerator lay there, as well, along with the postcards they'd held in place. The teensy art of Jane Austen books balanced upon a teapot was in pieces by the hutch.

"Oh, oh, oh," escaped my lips, and kept popping out like a car backfiring. Throughout my life, I'd tried not to attach myself to things. The spirit was what mattered. But seeing my treasures destroyed hurt deeply.

Vivi jumped off the counter and raced into the living room. She pawed the door leading to the yard.

"What is it, little one?" I peered out the beveled window into the dark. I didn't see movement or anyone lurking in the bushes. Cautiously, I opened the door and glanced to the right. The rear door to my studio was ajar, which triggered a queasy feeling at the pit of my stomach.

I told Vivi to stay put, dashed to the unit, and peeked through the window. Dozens of vials of essential oils had been hurled to the ground. *"No-o-o!"* I mewled under my breath. All that work and product down the drain. I pulled the door shut and locked it and yelled, "Sierra!" at the top of my lungs.

She didn't respond. I could hear Bob Marley crooning "Get Up, Stand Up," in her unit. Knowing my cousin, she was singing along.

I sprinted to my kitchen, collected Vivi in my arms, and texted Sierra, begging her to come downstairs at once. Next, I dialed 911 and informed the dispatch agent of the situation. I wasn't hurt, I told her. The EMTs did not need to be sent.

Sierra showed up in seconds and eeked. "Geez, Emma, OMG! Who do you think did it?"

My first thought was Hugh, but that would've been impossible. Even though he'd glowered at me earlier as I was entering the bistro, he couldn't have guessed, prior to our chat in his office, that I suspected him of murder. But someone surveilling me, knowing I was out of the house dining at Bibi's Bistro, could have sneaked inside. Who? Was this the killer's way of warning me to keep my nose out of the investigation?

"Emma?" Sierra rested a hand on my shoulder. "Are you—"

"Ava Daft!" exploded out of me. I explained how I'd questioned her and Quinlyn about their alibis.

"But how would they know where you live?"

"Good question. I'd used a credit card at Shabby Chic Nook. They hadn't asked me for an address."

"I suppose they could've followed you home from work. Whoever did this . . . it seems personal." Sierra motioned to the room. "Your poor keepsakes."

"Also the vials in my studio."

"Oh, no. I'll help you clean up."

"No, don't touch a thing. The police . . ." I sighed. "They'll need to document it."

I didn't have much else to trash. I set Vivi on her faux-fur pillow on the bistro dining chair, but she didn't settle down for a snooze. She sat on her haunches and stared at me like a sphinx.

Minutes later, Officer Rodriguez arrived. Unsure if I realized we'd met when Summers first questioned me about Willow's death, she reintroduced herself and added that she was the younger sister of the woman who owned Seize the Clay.

"Detective Summers's friend," I said.

"Fiancée. Her name's Renee. She used to be a cop, but she gave it up. It has always been my calling."

I didn't know how to respond.

For a brief time, she asked me basic questions. When did I get home? Was the door opened or closed? Then she called in the situation. Within seconds, she learned from someone at the precinct that I was a person of interest in Willow Shafer's murder. While she was taking pictures, lifting a few fingerprints, and bagging the evidence, I made tea. I needed something to calm my nerves.

A short while later, Detective Summers, dressed casually in a polo shirt and jeans, showed up. He and Officer Rodriguez toured both of my units in less than five minutes, then explored the rear yard and returned to me and my cousin. Summers said the way the intruder got into my unit and didn't damage the door was by using an air wedge.

"A what?" I asked.

He explained how it worked. "Your other unit didn't show signs of forced entry, either."

"We found this in the bushes in the backyard." Rodriguez raised a keychain that held my spare keys.

"Those are my backup set." Usually the keys hung on a hook in the foyer. I hadn't noticed them missing.

Rodriguez continued. "Perhaps that's how the intruder escaped."

"They wouldn't need keys to exit," Summers said dismissively.

"Maybe the intruder threw them there as a diversion," Rodriguez suggested.

Summers regarded me. "Who did you make angry?"

"Not fair!" I swung an arm. "This is not my fault."

"I didn't say it was." His voice was flat, unemotional. "But it feels personal, like the intruder was irked with you."

"Does this prove someone else killed Willow?"

"No." His forehead creased. "Why would you come to that conclusion?"

"Because whoever did this lashed out in rage. The kind of rage that was unleashed on Willow, given the way she was killed."

He mulled that over.

Sierra said, "Emma, what if the killer knows you're snooping around?"

I gawked at her. She instantly realized her faux pas and had the decency to look sheepish.

"You've been snooping, Ms. Brennan?" Summers asked, his tone stern.

Rodriguez stiffened. Sierra shifted feet.

"No," I said. "I don't snoop. I am a curious person. I like to be informed. I'm not nosy." My throat grew thick, as if I'd swallowed a walnut whole. I lifted my mug of tea and took a small sip. Too hot. I started over. "But, to answer your question, yes, I've been asking around. On my own behalf. To clear myself."

Sierra said, "She has every right."

"No, she does not," Summers snapped. "This is police business."

Sierra squared her shoulders. "She didn't kill her friend."

Summers folded his arms. "Ms. Brennan, have I arrested you?"

"No, sir."

"Who have you been questioning?"

"A few people. Not many. And not directly."

"Stop digging into things."

"Do you have suspects other than me?" I asked, hating the plaintive tone in my voice. "For example, do you know that your friend Hugh Ashbluff—"

"Stop!" Summers held up his right hand. His palm was rough, probably from golfing without wearing a glove. My mother had developed a few calluses over time. "We are studying all angles. We're checking into Ms. Shafer's dealings. She and you had many of the same customers and suppliers."

"Did you question her accountant? That's who she dined with the night she died."

"Yes. He has no idea who wanted her dead. He has an alibi. A clear-cut alibi. He was with his wife, their two children, and the children's nanny. I've also questioned Tish Waterman to see if there was any crossover of employees or clientele with her business. There is not."

"I know she didn't receive a postcard," I said. "She said no one threatened her."

"Tell him what you learned about Indy Hendriks," Sierra prompted.

I relayed the information Zinnia had shared about Indy losing her boyfriend and blaming Willow. Summers listened but didn't comment.

"However, our grandmother verified Indy Hendriks's alibi," Sierra added.

Summers's mouth quirked up on the right in a sinister way. "Why did she feel the need to?"

I said, "Because she thought it was highly coincidental that Indy saw me outside Mystic Waters, not to mention she was the first person to find Willow dead."

"I've questioned Ms. Hendriks," he said.

"Because you suspected her?"

"Because, as a rule, I ask witnesses their whereabouts. No stone goes unturned."

Sierra said, "Emma's kicked up a few pebbles of her own. Tell him about Ava."

"Ava Daft?" Summers said, lifting one eyebrow.

"Yes." Quickly, I recapped how Ava wanted to lease Willow's retail site and, in fact, she'd already discussed that possibility with Hugh. "Her alibi is sketchy for the night of the murder. She was doing inventory."

"Alone?" he asked.

"Her business partner, Quinlyn, claims she was with her, but I don't believe her. What if they . . ." I didn't finish the sentence. The theory that they'd conspired together seemed far-fetched.

"Tell him about Hugh," Sierra prompted.

"Hugh and Willow had an altercation." I summarized the set-to. "He wanted Willow to pay up on her lease. Pronto. She'd been late in the past. Why the immediacy?" I folded my arms.

He didn't reply.

"What if Hugh owes somebody money?" I continued. "Due yesterday. And that's why he was adamant."

"Killing her wouldn't solve that problem," Summers said.

"Don't forget to tell him about Palmer." Sierra poked me.

"Palmer Pilsner didn't like Willow, and she is Indy's best friend,"

I stated. "What if she killed Willow on behalf of Indy? You know, as her proxy? Her alibi is pretty flimsy." I told him what it was.

Rodriguez chewed on her lower lip. Did she expect Summers to bite my head off?

He didn't. In fact, telling by his expression, he looked amused. Was he mentally comparing my cousin and me to Cagney and Lacey . . . or, more likely, to Curly and Larry of the Three Stooges?

"Oh, there's one more suspect!" The words popped out of me as I recalled how strangely Floyd Marblemaw had been acting.

"There is?" Sierra asked.

I bobbed my head.

A nervous laugh burbled out of Rodriguez. She covered her mouth with her hand.

"He's a reporter, and he's been nosing around." I told Summers his name. "I'm not sure where he fits into the scenario with Willow, but isn't it curious that he showed up the week she died?"

"Curious," Summers echoed. "Nothing more."

"Sir," Rodriguez said, "is it possible Willow was simply robbed, and she caught the thief in the act?"

Summers shot her a curt look. She mashed her lips together.

"She could be right," I said. I'd wondered the same thing and had meant to tell the detective, but it had slipped my mind. "When I went to visit her that night, I saw her tallying receipts. What if someone caught sight of her doing that? What if he or she sneaked in after I left?"

"We're considering all angles," Summers replied.

"Why would Emma kill Willow, Detective?" Sierra asked. "They were friends."

"People overheard your cousin and Ms. Shafer quibbling." He studied my face. "Apparently, she chided you about opening a competitive business. Isn't that true, Ms. Brennan?"

My cheeks flushed with heat.

"Admit it," he went on, "she rubbed you the wrong way, didn't she?"

"What do you mean?"

"She insulted you. She was critical."

I raised my chin defiantly. "I rub you the wrong way, sir, but you wouldn't kill me."

Summers's right eye started to twitch. "Listen up, young lady. Simply because I'm friends with your grandmother does not give you a free pass to be cheeky with me. Understood?"

"Sir, yes, sir."

# Chapter 17

A half hour later, after Summers and Rodriguez went upstairs to see if anything untoward had occurred at Ursula's unit—nothing had—Summers came downstairs and said to me, "We'll be patrolling the area. We'll look in the database for fingerprint matches but doubt we'll find anything but yours."

I doubted it, too.

"Keep your doors locked," he added.

"You can bet on it."

After they left, I noticed something sparkly whiz by. My heart skipped a beat. Was it a fairy? I peered into the darkness and saw nothing more.

"Sierra," I said, "did you see that?"

"What? A stranger? Is someone out there?" She rotated her head right and left.

"No, nothing like that. It was . . ." I shook my head. "Forget it."

Vivi wasn't around. She couldn't confirm the sighting for me with a *meow* or a whoosh of a paw. Shoot.

"Why don't you sleep at my place?" Sierra clasped my elbow.

"I've got too much to clean up."

"You can hire someone tomorrow. C'mon. Upstairs."

"No. I'm fine." Though I was scared, I had to be proactive. I needed to scrub floors and take account of what I needed to replace. "Don't worry. The intruder wouldn't be stupid enough to return. Not with the police making the rounds." I said it with confidence even though I was trembling. "See you in the morning."

After she went upstairs, a shiver coursed through me. Was I safe? Did I need to install a security system? Hire a twenty-four-hour guard? Adopt a German shepherd?

Vivi appeared and mewed.

"Yes, you're sweet, cat," I cooed, "but you're no watchdog."

Quickly, I locked the front door. Luckily, the air-wedge way of breaking in hadn't damaged the mechanism. Next, I positioned a chair in front of the door. After that, I went online and filled out an appointment request for an estimate with the main security company for Carmel and selected a date for them to come by to give me their pitch. Thursday was the earliest they could make it.

Resigned, I lifted my cat and nuzzled her nose. "The disaster in the kitchen can wait. Let's assess the damage in the studio." I grabbed a broom, a dustpan, a slew of rags, and a wet mop, and with Vivi in tow, peered through the rear window to scope out whether anyone was lying in wait in the backyard. Seeing no one, I stepped outside, locked up, and rounded the patio to the studio's rear door. After unlocking it, I entered, switched on the lights, and relocked the door. The unit was more of a mess than I'd realized.

To protect Vivi's paws, I set her in the cat bed in the nook of the end table in the living room. She peered at me from within, too strung out to snooze.

First, using fingers, I plucked the glass that was embedded in the essential oil. I used the broom and dustpan for any that was separate from the goo. It would take me a few days to remake the twenty-plus essential oils that had been destroyed. I mopped up the slop. It was maddening. Even soap, followed by a rinse of vinegar, wasn't doing the trick.

"Swell," I muttered when I realized I'd have to hire a professional cleaner to get it really spotless, maybe even a cleaner with a super vac that could suck out oil that had seeped into the seams of the hardwood floors. "Money, money, money."

Over the next hour, as I continued to intermittently clean and jot down items I needed to purchase—more vials, for instance—I thought about Willow's murder and this break-in. Were they connected? Had the killer figured out I was investigating and lashed out at me to make me stop?

My cat mewed.

"Yes, Vivi," I said, "you're right. No more thinking about murder. Not tonight. I need to clear my mind."

When I was certain I couldn't do a better cleanup job, I locked up the studio, returned with Vivi to my place, secured the rear door, and put all the rags I'd used in the washing machine. Then I set about fixing what I could of the kitchen chaos. I couldn't do anything to repair the Jane Austen teapot and books or the giclée art, but singing along with the Taylor Swift playlist I'd queued up—I rocked "You Need to Calm Down"—and thanks to a few sips from a glass of wine, I was able to keep my wits together and, calmly, with the help of a glue gun, mend most of the magnets.

Task complete, I assessed the damage to the Jane Austen plate that had stood in the foyer and determined that if I took it to a professional china repair shop, it could be salvaged. *Phew.*

"A half hour more, little one," I said to Vivi, who was sitting on the countertop, watching with fascination as I reorganized my father's postcards on the refrigerator. He'd sent them from numerous places—India, Thailand, Guatemala, Chile. Wherever he was needed, that's where he landed. For a nanosecond, I wondered why he was out of communication for a week, but decided not to worry. He'd tell me when we next spoke.

The last postcard I secured was an image of a Bali water temple. *BEAUTIFUL BALI,* my father wrote in block letters. *HOME TO THE BALI STARLING, A MEDIUM-SIZED MYNAH, ALSO KNOWN AS THE JALAK BALI. TRIVIA FOR FOUR HUNDRED, KEN.* In deference to our *Jeopardy!* bond, he always included an unusual tidbit in his notes, as if imparting information would continue to link us, distance be darned. As it so happened, I knew a lot about the starling because I'd recently read a witty mystery, *Cheap Trills,* in which a quirky travel agent takes on a ring of songbird smugglers. I told my father about it when we spoke a week after receiving his postcard. He promised he would read it.

"Dad," I whispered fondly. "Wish you were here to help me solve this craziness."

I awoke Sunday to the sound of church bells and a pounding headache. Before going out with my grandmother for the day, I stuffed the rags into the dryer. Vivi positioned herself in front of the appliance and stared at the items going around and around. I dressed in cargo shorts, a tank top, and a sunhat; slathered on sunblock; and bid her goodbye, knowing she would be occupied for a long time, if not rendered comatose given the way her head was bobbing in rhythm to the spin.

When I arrived at my grandmother's house, she pulled me into a hug, nearly yanking my arm out of its socket. "Why didn't you call me last night? I had to hear via a text from Sierra this morning?"

"I didn't want to worry you."

"A break-in?"

I nodded.

"I'm furious."

"With me?"

"No, sweet girl, not with you. With whoever did that to you. Who would dare . . ." She squeezed me harder, then pushed apart and held me at arm's length. "We are going to schedule an appointment with a security company pronto and—"

"I already did. They're coming Thursday."

"Not until then?"

"It's the soonest they could do it."

She mulled that over. "At least you did your due diligence. Now it's time to do some serious fairy hunting. You need a sighting."

"I think I saw one fly past my door last night."

"Really?"

"I'm not sure. It was sparkly, but not like a firefly."

"Keep your eyes peeled," she said, not quelling my hope this time as she had the other day. "Have you eaten?" Fondly, she tucked a loose lock of hair behind my ear.

"No, my stomach is still in knots."

"With good reason. Who could eat after what happened?"

"I could go for a cup of coffee."

She pulled a thermos from the backpack she'd set by the front door and handed it to me.

"With caffeine?" I asked.

She grinned. "Don't tell your cousin."

We drove to Garland Ranch Regional Park, which had fifty miles of hiking and riding trails. We crossed the willow-covered banks of the Carmel River, passed the visitors' center, and took the Lupine Loop toward the Waterfall Trail. In the summer, the park was lush with grasses, and the aroma of wildflowers was heady.

About an hour into our walk, after stopping often to take photos of the gorgeously blue sky and a number of birds, Nana Lissa told me to veer left past a coast live oak.

"Is the fairy hollow this way?" I asked. "I mean, I've hiked here before, but I've never seen it."

"You've got to have keen eyes. If we're lucky, we might even see a fairy portal."

"Really?"

I knew what a portal was, in theory—a spot through which

fairies could pass to enter the human world. I remembered my grandmother describing the first one she'd encountered. Sierra and I were six and seven at the time. Nana said the portal had been barely visible, hidden in a glen, and resembled a twist of gnarled trees embedded with grass . . . until it started glowing, and a fairy emerged. I'd thought the story was whimsical. Fantastical. But I believed her now. She was steadfast about the existence of fairies. How I wished one could tell me who had broken into my place and scared my cat and killed Willow.

Poor Willow. She didn't deserve to die.

"Emma, don't move a muscle," my grandmother whispered, blocking me with a hand. "There's a frollick of fairies up ahead."

"A what?"

"A frollick. A gathering. F-r-o-l-l-i-c-k. That's the fairy way of spelling it." She put a finger to her lips. "Do you see them? In front of the portal."

"What portal? All I see is a convergence of branches creating a circle."

"Look closer. There's a round shape reflected in the leaves. See it?"

"No." I didn't see squat. I was ready to scold her for teasing me when, suddenly, sunlight streamed from above and washed over me, and out of nowhere, I felt everything was going to be okay. I meant *everything*. I'd be safe. I'd find solutions. I whispered, "Nana."

She was beaming with vibrant energy. "Yes?"

"Did a fairy sprinkle you and me with magical dust or something?"

She clasped my hand. Hers was warm and vibrating.

"Because I feel . . . I can't explain it. I feel calmer."

"Did you see anything specific?"

"Bright sunlight."

"No fairies?"

I frowned. "No. Were they here?"

"They were. They've passed through."

"Are they gone? It's over?"

"Yes, but not forever. Perhaps next time."

I felt like crying but stemmed the tears. I was an adult. Not a child. I could handle disappointment.

We rested on a bench beneath a cypress tree, and Nana Lissa laid out the lunch she'd prepared—iced tea, crustless sandwiches, and fresh fruit. We talked about the library and the poetry reading. I noticed we were avoiding any conversation about Willow's murder. The lunch—the day—felt normal and restorative.

Until we were ready to head home. That was when reality hit me full force. I knew, even if I did encounter a fairy, that she wasn't going to solve my problem. I had to drum up the identity of the killer because Summers wasn't working fast enough.

Though it was our day off, I'd promised to teach Yoly how to conduct a sound bath after the cleaning crew left. I met her at the spa at three, and the two of us convened in the meditation room. The skirt of her floral frock fluted up as she spun in a circle to take in the multiple bowls on the shelves. She didn't look like a deer in the headlights, but I could see she was slightly overwhelmed.

I assured her if she could give a good massage, she could do this. "Think of it as a discipline in concentration, not only for your clients but for you, as well."

For a half hour, I taught her how to swirl the rod around the bowls, moving from one bowl to another, making each emit its unique tone. "Rotate the rod slowly. Consistently. Feel the energy surging through your arms into the vessel."

When she was ready for a practice run, I dimmed the lights in the room and nestled in one of the recliner chairs.

"Did you review what I gave you to recite?" I asked.

"Yes."

"A typical session will last forty-five minutes, but let's go for a half hour today," I said. "Fair warning, your right arm might get tired. If necessary, switch hands."

Lowering her voice, she intoned the words I used when orchestrating a sound bath. "Let the sounds wash over you. Let them guide you to a place of deep relaxation. Focus on the sensations you're feeling. Don't let your mind wander. Stay attentive to the sounds."

What seemed like minutes later, she said, "You're waking now. Waking. You're returning to the present." She undimmed the lights. "How do you feel, Emma?"

"That was too short."

She smiled. "Nope. It was exactly a half hour. You went out after I told you to let emotions wash over you."

"Excellent!" I rose to my feet and gave her a hug. "You're a natural. I knew you would be." How nice it was to have a backup to provide this form of life-energizing treatment. "We'll have you do a few more practice sessions with friends to make sure you're comfortable. I'll oversee them. On my feet," I added, "so I don't zonk out."

She laughed.

"After that, we'll start scheduling you." She didn't need to be certified as she did for giving massages, but I wanted her to be as ready as possible.

She hugged and thanked me, and I went home feeling centered and focused.

Vivi was eager to play when I arrived. She crouched in the foyer, ready to pounce. I picked her up and kissed her nose. "No break-ins, my sweet cat?"

She mewed.

How I wish I knew who'd smashed my things. It had to have been Willow's killer, because I'd been investigating, as Sierra said. Honestly, why else would someone sabotage my living space and studio? The timing was too coincidental.

I needed to clear my mind. I wouldn't be able to sleep if I didn't. I thawed some jumbo shrimp and threw together a light green salad with a vinaigrette dressing. Then I filled Vivi's bowl, grabbed the Agatha Christie mystery I'd been reading, poured myself a glass of ice water, and carried it all to the courtyard.

Vivi devoured her meal and romped off to play in the herb garden.

I ate a couple of bites of my dinner—I wasn't really hungry—and read three more chapters of *The Body in the Library*. Miss Marple's comment, that people were far too trusting for this wicked world, stopped me cold. Was I naive? Did I have blinders on? Was there a suspect I'd overlooked? I thought of Willow's mother, Ginnie. Would she have had any reason to want Willow dead? If Willow had been low on funds, I doubted she'd had much of an estate to bequeath. On the other hand, what if she hadn't been struggling? What if her set-to with Hugh had all been an act, and she'd been flush? What if Ginnie had seen Willow's will and knew what she stood to inherit?

*No, Emma. Ginnie is innocent.*

By nine, my eyes drooped to half-mast, and I slogged to bed. To ensure I slept well, I performed a mini-meditation my aunt had taught me. Eyes closed, I concentrated on my toes and imagined they were becoming so light that they drifted upward and hovered above my body. I moved on to my ankles and calves, willing each part to float and relax. I didn't remember reaching my neck.

Monday morning, after donning shorts and a T-shirt, I ambled outside to pluck dead leaves from the front garden and hunt for snails. I attended to the chore once a month to stay on top of things. Task complete, I stood and stretched. At the same time, a woman on a bicycle whizzed past my place heading toward Ocean Avenue, and I drew in a sharp breath. It was Naomi Clutterbuck. She was wearing shorts and a tank top again, but this time she'd added a floppy hat. Was she on her way to the beach? I reasoned that she might live nearby and that riding a bicycle was her form of exercise. A chill coursed through me, however, as I considered another possibility . . . that she was the one who'd broken in and destroyed my things. Why would she have? She didn't know me. Had Indy or Palmer put her up to it?

*You're grasping at straws*, I told myself, and shook off the concern. It had to be a coincidence that the fourplex was on her route.

I fed the cat, dressed for work, and hurried to the Courtyard of Peace. I went to the café to check on Sierra. It wasn't open yet. There weren't any customers. I sauntered into the modest kitchen where I knew she'd be busily preparing for the day. The small space was fitted with a Vulcan six-burner stove, griddle, and a number of sinks. Staples and bowls were arranged on shelving above the sinks. The shelves below held all the cookware. Sierra was standing at the prep table, dicing vegetables.

"Hello, cuz!" I said.

Sierra swung around. Flour dusted her nose. I mimed it with a finger. She used a towel to wipe it off and tossed the towel into a hamper.

"Where were you last night?" I asked. The lights in her unit had been out when I was eating dinner in the backyard. "Did you go on a date?"

"I was with a friend. We went out for wine and tapas."

"Do I know this friend?" I gave her a sly look.

"No, and you won't. She's anti-touchy-feely anything."

"Really? Why are people so closed down?"

"She was abused as a girl."

My insides snarled. "I'm sorry. That was heartless of me."

"You didn't know. She's very nice and unassuming. She's a pet groomer." She washed her hands, wiped them on her apron, and resumed dicing vegetables.

"What do I smell?" I asked.

"Green-tea soup with noodles. Want a cup? It's made with bok choy, spring onions, and ginger. It's very good for the immune system."

"Sure, I'll give it a try."

She served up a bowl, set it on the counter, and nudged a stool with her toe. "Sit."

I did and inhaled the soup. The aroma was heavenly.

"How was fairy hunting yesterday?" she asked.

"I didn't see any."

"Big surprise."

"I believe Nana," I said.

"Aw. You're cute when you're gullible."

I ate a bite of noodles. "Delish."

"I've been thinking. You should talk to Ursula," Sierra said. "Ask if she heard or saw anything suspicious Saturday."

"She's out of town."

"No, she's back. I saw her milling about when I got home last night."

"Summers and Rodriguez went to her unit," I said. "It wasn't trashed."

"That doesn't mean she hasn't noticed anything unusual since then."

# Chapter 18

I checked in with Jason at reception. He wasn't feeling well. I told him to go home immediately. I didn't want a sick employee working at the spa and interacting with customers. He thanked me, apologized profusely, and slogged away.

Meryl waltzed into the area, a cup of steaming tea in her hand. "I told him you'd tell him to leave, but he was adamant that he stay and show you how sick he was." She made a goofy face. "Writers. They're a weird lot of insecure sluggards, prone to procrastinating."

I begged to differ. All the writers I'd met were industrious and clever. Sure, they might struggle with plotlines and characters, and sometimes they had to work hard to fashion a story, but their brains were always in overdrive. I tilted my head. "Why are you anti-writers?" I asked. "Let me guess. You dated one."

"Ha! More than one." She groaned. "It's sickening how drawn I am to creative types, and don't get me started about dating actors or comedians. They're even worse than writers. How's this for a come-on line from a writer at a bar? This actually happened." Modulating her voice to a lower pitch, she said, "'Well, yeah, bae, like, the people and their stories around here, like, never fail to captivate me.'"

I happened to know *bae* was a slang term for "babe." It originated from hip-hop music.

"'Like, I draw inspiration from their lives,'" she continued. "'Wanna come to my place and be my muse?' Puh-lease." She poked a finger into her mouth and fake gagged.

We both laughed.

"Got any fun dating stories?" she asked.

"Nope." In truth, I had a few, but I wouldn't share them. My relationship flops should stay buried. "Can you man the reception desk for an hour? I have an errand to run."

"For your information, I can man anything better than a man." Meryl cackled at her cleverness.

I thanked her and hurried to the fourplex. Ursula typically didn't see clients until the afternoon and well into the evening. If she was home, I hoped she would be awake. Dramatic orchestral music was playing in her apartment, which was a good sign. She had a thing for Rachmaninoff. I rapped on her door and heard the padding of bare feet, which buoyed me.

She opened the door wide without peering out the peephole. She claimed she had no fear of strangers because she always knew who was visiting her. "Hallo, Emma," she said in a Serbian accent. Exotic didn't come close to describing her. She had dark, expressive eyes and the fullest mouth I'd ever seen. For clients, she invariably wore glamorous dresses, like the silk one she had on. She'd wrapped a long scarf stylishly around her head. Her long brown tresses spilled from beneath. "Long time no see." She embraced me and held me at arm's length. "Did you sense I am now back in town? You are becoming psychic perhaps? Or you heard my music?"

"Sierra told me."

"Ha!" She released me.

"Are you on your way out?"

"No. No. A client will come in one hour. Enter, please." She led me by the hand into her dramatically decked-out unit and closed the door. The aroma of patchouli incense pervaded the space. Colorful pillows abounded. Paintings of shining orbs and winged angels adorned the walls.

"Follow me to the kitchen. I make tea." She wandered inside, humming to the music. "Is herbal tea okay?"

"Yes, thanks."

Around her kitchen were pictures of a pretty Siamese cat. "Do you have a cat?" I asked. I'd never seen it.

"Not any longer. It was not right of me to travel and leave my kitty alone. My sister took her."

I remembered my mother saying, in addition to her allergies, her long hours at work were another reason we couldn't have a pet. That was why, in high school, I'd lent my time at the shelter, to get my fill of holding cats, dogs, and bunnies.

"Something bothers you, yes?" Ursula asked, setting two mugs of tea on the table. "Sit."

I did and, pulling my mug close, told her about the break-in.

Her eyes widened. "I am sorry. I did not divine anything."

"It's all right."

"I did not arrive home until last night."

"Yes, I know. The police said you didn't answer your door, but your place hadn't been broken into, as far as they could see."

"Everything was intact." She sipped her tea. "Did you suffer damage?"

"Many of my essential oils were smashed and some of my collectibles."

"Oh, no. Those are precious to you."

I'd invited her over for a glass of wine the week I moved in and had given her a tour of both units.

"I have two Ring home security cameras," she said. "You know of what I speak?"

"Yes."

"Do you have these?"

"No." I added purchasing them to my security to-do list.

"They are positioned at the front door and back door. I trust everyone who is my friend, but there are those I do not trust. For example, my clients I trust. They come to the front door. And I trust the delivery guys. They are gems, always bringing me exactly what I need."

*What you order*, I thought wryly.

"However . . ." She rolled the R theatrically and paused. "However, there are some people who are nefarious. They are the ones who appear at the back door."

Was she speaking metaphorically or had people come to her place to do her harm? The notion made me shiver. I hadn't paid attention to all of Ursula's activities. Maybe I should.

"Would you like to see my Ring feed?" she asked. "Maybe we can determine who broke into your studio."

"Yes!" I nearly shouted the word.

She opened the Ring app on her cell phone, logged in, and tapped on History.

"There is no one visiting my house between five and nine Saturday at the front door. You can see the police officer here, at ten." She selected a Snapshot and Live View opened. "I cannot make out your door because of the angle of the staircase."

"How about the rear door?" I suggested. The stairs in the back didn't curve. They went straight out.

She studied another Snapshot. "Yes. Here is the view from that camera. *Aha.*" She bobbed her head. "I see you crossing the patio at eight minutes past nine. You are in a hurry."

That must have been when I'd dashed to the studio and peeked in the window.

"You don't see anyone other than me?" I asked.

"I am afraid not. Whoever did this damage must have entered your studio through the front door."

Meaning the perpetrator must have thrown the keychain with my spare keys out the back to confuse the police or baffle me, as Officer Rodriguez had speculated.

Another thought occurred to me. "Ursula, in the Ring app history, is there a view of me last Tuesday night exiting the rear door and going to my studio?" Soon after I got home from giving Willow her gift basket, I went to the studio with Vivi to work on the essential oils. "It would have been around eight twenty or eight twenty-five."

"I am sorry. The Ring was not working that night. There was a glitch with my Internet service."

Foiled again. I mustered a smile, thanked her, and returned to the spa.

Meryl was at reception entertaining Sierra. "Did you hear about the time Bob Marley went to the hairdressers? He was dreading it."

"Ha-ha. He has dreadlocks. I get it," Sierra said. "Who told you he's my favorite musical artist?"

"I've got ESP." Meryl sniggered and pushed a notepad toward me. "Emma, that reporter was here, but I told him to return tomorrow because you're booked for the afternoon. You have a mindful meditation at three with Zinnia Walker, and"—she glanced at her watch—"I'm outta here. I've got a manicure in five." She whisked her hair over her shoulder and hustled to her therapy room.

Sierra handed me a smoothie in a pretty fountain-style glass. "I thought you could use this. It's coconut and turmeric. It'll boost your immune system. You've been dealing with a lot of stress."

I took a sip and smiled. "Love the raspberries."

"I added extra just for you. Now, what did Ursula have to say? Was she there?"

I told her our findings, or lack thereof. "Also, her Internet wasn't functioning on the night of Willow's murder. Seeing me after eight fifteen wasn't possible."

"Rats. What good is the Internet if it doesn't do its job?" Sierra groused.

I elbowed her. "It's amazing it works at all."

A few minutes before three, I asked Yoly to watch the reception desk. She hung the *Back in a Few* sign in the door of the gift shop and arrived right as Zinnia Walker showed up.

"Emma, it is such a delight to be here." Zinnia was wearing glitzy jewelry, plus a floral T-shirt over slim-fit pants and sparkly sandals. "In case you didn't realize, I am the person who bought the Brazilian amethyst cathedral."

"For a pretty penny," I said.

"Tosh! One should spend money if one has it. It's good for the economy." Her cheeks tinged pink. "I'm not flaunting my wealth, mind you. I'm simply excited to own the crystal. Ever since purchasing it, I've felt . . ." She flicked her fingers in the air. "I've felt mentally alive." Her expression grew grim. "However, I feel my chest is quite tight." She drew a line across her upper body indicating where. "I am perfectly healthy. No issues. My old ticker is in good shape. Hence, the need for a meditative session. Courtney Kelly raved about your talent."

I was thrilled to hear that. Word of mouth was essential to expanding the business.

For an hour, I put aside all thoughts of investigating and murder, and focused on helping Zinnia with her breathing. I assisted her in some light stretching exercises. When she left, she said she'd never had such a unique experience and couldn't wait to tell her friends.

The desk was empty when I resumed my post at the reception desk. "Yoly?" I called.

She didn't answer.

I peeked into the courtyard and saw her talking to a woman by the wishing well. Not just any woman. It was my neighbor Dottie, who lived in the fourplex next to mine, a dainty octogenarian who looked like the wind could blow her over. She was cuddling Cupcake, her aging Yorkie, and stroking the lock of the dog's hair that she'd secured with a bow.

Yoly beckoned me. "Emma, come here! You've got to hear this. Tell her, Dottie."

"Emma dear." Despite her diminutive size, Dottie's voice was full of vigor. Her cadence reminded me of someone else's, but I couldn't put my finger on whose. "I'm happy to see you. I've been out of the loop. I had no idea you needed my help."

I exchanged a look with Yoly, who rotated her hand, encouraging Dottie to continue.

"I'll be going to the police directly," Dottie said.

"Why?" I asked.

"Because I saw you Tuesday night. At work in your studio. Every few minutes starting at seven, Cupcake and I went outside."

"Poor thing had to pee repeatedly." Yoly clucked her tongue. "Bladder infection."

"She's fine now," Dottie said. "The vet prescribed some medication, but now that's upsetting her tummy." She cooed to the pup. "I must admit I don't listen to the news, and I don't get a newspaper. I had no idea your friend was murdered."

"Apparently, she doesn't talk to her son, either," Yoly said.

"Her son?" I raised an eyebrow.

"Dottie's last name is Summers. Her son is Detective Summers."

My mouth fell open.

Yoly stifled a snort. "You didn't know?"

"I had no clue." That was why her speaking rhythm sounded familiar. Like the detective, she had an assured way of presenting herself.

Dottie bobbed her head. "I simply can't fathom how Dylan could think you culpable. You were home, moving about in that studio of yours, one room to the next, from eight twenty on. I'll tell him. Rest assured."

I stared at Dottie, trying to make the connection. She didn't look like her son in the slightest. Their eyes were different as were their mouths and bone structure. Maybe he favored his father's features . . . or he was adopted.

Yoly said, "We were standing here by the well, and I was suggesting that she purchase a few essential oils for Cupcake when she asked how the spa was going and which massage she should consider."

"I'm a fan of massage," Dottie said. "And meditation, and all things spiritual. If we don't nurture ourselves, our bodies and minds will grow flaccid."

"I brought Dottie up to date," Yoly said. "Aren't you glad I did?"

"Absolutely." I felt like doing a happy jig. Exonerated. I was *exonerated*. Or I would be as soon as Dottie spoke to her son.

"It's very sad about Willow Shafer," Dottie went on. "I didn't know her, but it's simply tragic. What is this world coming to?"

"You know, Dottie," Yoly said, "a combo of basil and ginger might be a good concoction for Cupcake. It soothes the tummy."

"You'd like that, wouldn't you, Cup-cup?" she cooed to her dog. "Yes, you would."

"I'll fetch it for you." Yoly hurried to the shop.

"It's on the house," I said to Dottie.

She thanked me. "Emma, I heard about the break-in at your place. Neighbors talk. How are you faring in that regard?"

"I'm upset, of course, and a lot of my things are broken, but I'm alive and so is Vivi. I'm having a security company come out and give me an estimate this week."

"That's a good idea."

"And I'm getting the Ring app, as well."

"Dylan is always saying I should do that."

I still couldn't wrap my head around Dottie and him being related.

"Just so you know," Dottie said, lowering her voice, "because of the break-in, a few of my friends and I are going to keep a lookout for any suspicious goings-on. Hattie Hopewell, she's the woman who heads up the Happy Diggers garden club, of which I am a member—"

"I met her." At my grandmother's book club.

"Hattie is very proactive about neighborhood watch programs. She doesn't live far from us."

I thought of Willow telling me how intrusive Indy was when it came to neighborhood watch efforts. I hoped Hattie wasn't that gung-ho.

"A few of us are going to patrol," Dottie continued. "It won't look like we are. We all walk our dogs regularly. We'll report back."

"Thank you. That is very kind. But don't take any risks."

"Never! Also, I thought you should know that Hattie saw someone spying on your place Friday."

"Spying? Like using binoculars? Was it a man?" I thought of Hugh.

"No binoculars. And no, it wasn't a man. It was a pretty Japanese woman with chin-length black hair. She was taking pictures with her camera."

Whoa! Naomi Clutterbuck had been outside my place the day before the break-in? The same person who happened to ride by on her bike this morning? Why was she checking up on me?

"Hattie said she looked harmless, and she supposed the woman could have been taking pictures of the unit next to yours. There is a *To Let* sign in the front, after all." Dottie narrowed her gaze. "However, in Hattie's opinion, the woman was focused on your front door."

# Chapter 19

When I returned, Meryl was at the reception desk, the phone pressed to one ear. "Hold on," she said into the receiver. "Emma, you've got a last-minute request. I know it's not your regular day for sound baths, but Quinlyn is on the line asking if you have time right now to do a private one."

"Tell her to come on down. I'm primed to bring joy to anyone."

After Meryl ended the call, I told her how Dottie had exonerated me.

She clasped my hands and twirled me in a circle. "That's bussin'."

"I agree. It's great news." I also shared that Dottie and the Happy Diggers would be taking turns patrolling my neighborhood.

"What nice ladies. Hey, did you hear? There was a robbery at the local hair salon. The police are combing the area."

"*Combing.*" I groaned-chuckled. "You've got to come up with better material."

"But you laughed. That's what I'm going for." She aimed a fingernail at me, and I noticed the tattoo of the name *Dante* on the back of her hand.

"New?" I asked, gesturing to the ink.

"Yep. It's for my son. I figure if I can't see him, I can think about him often, and mindful meditation will mend our relationship." She moved her head to work out some kinks. "I'm cray-cray, right?"

"No nuttier than the rest of us."

"Oh! I almost forgot. This came in the mail for you."

She handed me a padded envelope with Aunt Sophie's return address on it. I tore it open and pulled out the translucent smoky quartz and fluorite stones Sophie had used in my virtual crystal reading. As instructed, I slipped them into the inside front pocket of my yoga pants, pulled down my black T-shirt, and instantly felt cleansed of negative energy.

Less than fifteen minutes later, Quinlyn strode into the spa. "Hello!" She was struggling with the strap of her purse while straightening the high collar of her boxy taupe dress. She apologized for arriving early. I assured her it was fine and said we could get started. I prepared the room right after Meryl had booked the appointment.

After asking her to lock her tote in one of the spa's safes, I guided her into the meditation room. She seemed a bit nervous. She was wringing her hands, and her cheeks were blooming red. I assured her this was going to be an enjoyable meditative journey and advised her to sit in one of the recliners.

As I dimmed the lights and picked up a rod, prepared to bring the first bowl to life, Quinlyn said, "Emma, I . . . oh!" A sob erupted from her mouth. "I'm sorry. I lied." She bounded to her feet. "I'm not here for meditation. I came because I'm worried about Ava."

"Why?"

"She . . . she . . ." Quinlyn licked tears off her lips and swiped her face with the backs of both hands to clear the rest. "She's not herself lately."

"Tell me your concerns." I wasn't a therapist in the psychological sense, but I figured the best way to handle this was to act like one. Keep the questions brief and let the patient—in this case client—come to her own conclusions. "Sit, please."

She did.

"Start at the beginning."

"She's been acting furtively, and she's messing up at work."

"Messing up how exactly?"

"The books. Our finances. They don't look right. Plus, she mumbles as she does things. All the time. When she's counting stock. When she's rearranging displays. Something is bothering her. I've asked her what's wrong, but she won't talk to me."

I couldn't help wondering whether Ava had, indeed, killed Willow, and a guilty conscience was finally breaking her spirit.

"I caught her on the phone a week ago making a call," Quinlyn said.

"To whom?"

"I don't know. She hung up right away, like she didn't want me to hear the conversation."

"Is your birthday coming up? She could be trying to surprise you."

"No." She sniffed and wiped her nose with the knuckle of a finger. "I caught her doing it before. About two weeks ago. The day before that, I spied her in the stockroom making a recording."

"A recording of . . ."

"Ghost sounds."

Omigosh. Ava was the one who'd been pranking Willow?

"The other day when you mentioned that someone had been taunting Willow, I hadn't even considered Ava was the one responsible. She loves Halloween. We decorate to the hilt in the shop. I thought she was preparing some spookiness way in advance. However, to be sure, I asked her about what I'd witnessed. She said I was hearing and seeing things." Quinlyn lifted a thumb to her mouth and began to gnaw the cuticle. Restless, she gripped that hand with the other and set both on her lap. Her toe started to tap. "That's not the only thing she lied about. She went out the night Willow was killed. Alone. I don't know where. She didn't kill her. I know she didn't."

How could she be certain, or was she merely holding out hope?

"I wanted to follow her because she's been acting strangely, but I chickened out. If she caught me tailing her, she'd end it between us. You see, her husband . . . her dead husband . . . always told her he didn't trust her as far as he could throw her. Not that she ever gave him reason to doubt her. But he was a slug. I didn't know him. Never met him. But that's what she said. Two years after he died, when we met and fell in love, she made me promise to always trust her. I said I would. And I do. But I'm worried about how she's acting." Tears trickled down her face again. She swiped them with her fingertips. "I'm sorry to bring all this negativity in here."

I pressed my palm against the stones in my pocket, willing them to keep the negativity away from my psyche.

"I didn't know who to turn to," Quinlyn said. "I can't get Ava to go to couples therapy."

It occurred to me that Ava had an awful lot of power in this relationship. Perhaps Quinlyn could benefit from taking a positive-thinking course or she could go to therapy on her own.

"I was hoping a sound bath would clear my mind and tell me what to do." She surveyed the room.

"The bath isn't magical. The sounds don't give answers. They help steady your mind. Why don't we give it a try?"

The door to the meditation room flew open. "Emma!" Ava stormed in. "Stop this at once." Something gleamed in her hand. Something long and sharp.

*Aw, heck, no.* She had a knife! My stomach lurched. "Ava, don't come any closer," I ordered, aiming the sound bath rod at her. It would be useless against the knife, but it was all I had.

"On your feet, Quinlyn," Ava ordered.

"Don't bully me," her partner mewled.

"Bully you? I would never . . ." She whirled on me, brandishing the knife. "What have you told her?"

I was so stunned I couldn't form a response.

"You sure have been nosy," Ava said.

*Man, I hate that word.*

"You pushed and shoved until you made Quinlyn lie about her whereabouts for last Tuesday," she went on, her voice venomous. "Is that why she's here? Do you want to squeeze more lies out of her?"

Quinlyn stifled a sob.

I didn't look in her direction. I couldn't take my eyes off of Ava. I wished I had a cell phone and could call for help, but I never brought one into a session. It was too distracting. I made a mental note that if I got out of here alive, I'd install silent alarm buttons in all the therapy rooms and always pack a phone with the notifications switched off.

"Ava, calm down. Quinlyn came in for a sound bath," I said, surprised by how matter-of-fact I sounded. "She needs to chill."

"Chill?" Ava arched an eyebrow.

"Why don't you go to the café, have a cup of tea, and we can discuss this after her session?" I deliberately didn't acknowledge the knife with my gaze or my words.

"Don't handle me, Emma. Do. Not." She jutted the knife. "If you try, I'll destroy every bowl in this place."

I gawked at her. "Like you made a mess of my apartment?"

"What are you talking about?"

"Someone broke into my place and smashed my collectibles and an array of essential oils. Was it you?"

"No."

"Were you angry because you let slip that you wanted Willow's retail space?"

"What? No!" Ava's jaw started to quiver. "I came because you told me Quinlyn said she was doing inventory with me Tuesday night when . . . when she wasn't. She lied. I came because I want to know where she was. I want her to say it out loud, and I want a witness."

"Did you kill Willow, Ava?" I asked.

Ava gasped.

Yes, the question was blunt, but I couldn't help myself. My body was shivering with fear and rage. How dare this woman enter an inner sanctum at the spa and disturb me and my customer!

"Kill Willow?" Ava spit out the words. "Are you crazy? How could I beat her with a candlestick with these nails?" She wiggled the fingers of her left hand.

"I've seen you do workarounds. Picking up coins off the ground. Flicking light switches with your knuckles." I indicated with the rod. "You're gripping a knife."

"And ruining my palm in the process." She moved the weapon to her left hand and showed me her right. Blood oozed from where her nails had cut into her flesh. "If I'd wielded the candlestick, I'd have gashes to show for it."

"Ava," I said, trying to believe her, "why don't you give me the knife and take a seat? You need to cool down. Join Quinlyn in the sound bath. It'll soothe both of you. Afterward, we can talk about what's really upsetting you."

"I didn't kill Willow," Ava said in a voice a toddler would use. "I didn't. I was—"

Quinlyn said, "Who were you calling all those nights and hanging up on? Your lover?"

"My lover? You're my lover."

"Why were you making eerie recordings this past month?" Quinlyn demanded.

Ava swallowed hard. I held out my hand for the knife. She shook her head once, unwilling to relinquish it.

"You were the one scaring Willow, Ava," I said, "with hang-up phone calls and ghostly sounds."

She didn't deny it.

"You wanted to frighten her to make her cancel her lease."

She remained mute.

"When you couldn't get her to do that, you killed her."

"No! I . . . No."

"You went out that night," Quinlyn said. "You didn't go to the shop to do inventory. I know because I went there to pick up scarves for a customer who wanted home delivery. Where were you?"

"I . . . I went to San Carlos Cemetery."

"You *what*?" Quinlyn squealed.

"I couldn't tell you"—Ava spoke directly to Quinlyn—"because you wouldn't understand."

"Try me now." Quinlyn looked brittle and ready to snap.

"I went to the cemetery to talk to my husband."

"Her dead husband," Quinlyn explained to me.

"It upsets Quinlyn when I go there," Ava said, also to me. "She doesn't understand why I want to communicate with him."

"He belittled you." Quinlyn jutted a hand at her partner. "He made you feel small every single day of your marriage. Why would you go there?"

"Ava," I said, "tell Quinlyn the truth."

"Don't bother. I've heard it all before." Quinlyn folded her arms.

"Then tell me," I whispered, and edged to one of the sound bowls. I started stirring with the rod. A peaceful hum filled the air.

Ava perched on the edge of a recliner and laid the knife across her lap. "He died in a car accident. He . . . we fought. He stormed out of the house and got behind the wheel of his Honda. He was speeding down a windy road and missed the curve. His car somersaulted."

"What did you fight about?" I asked, moving to another bowl.

"I'd made a mess of the business's books. Again."

I swirled the rod. A higher-pitched sound than the hum from the previous bowl resonated around the room. I could feel the warmth of the reverberation radiating through me.

"I miss him," Ava said.

Quinlyn hissed her disdain.

"I don't miss him in that way," Ava said hurriedly. "Not sexually or even emotionally. I won't ever be with a man again. But I miss him because he had a head for numbers. He helped me start Shabby Chic Nook."

"He demeaned you," Quinlyn said. "He called you sloppy and scatterbrained. And you're neither. You have a mind for math. That's what impressed your grandfather."

Ava sucked back a sob.

"A ghost can't give you what you need," Quinlyn added.

"No, it can't. Only you can. I love you, Quinlyn. You're wonderful, but you don't ground me like he did. To make the business thrive, I think we . . . we need . . . we need someone with his vision."

"We'll hire a marketing guru."

The two were silent for a long moment.

Finally Quinlyn said, "Why did you lie to me?"

"I was afraid if I told you where I'd gone . . ." Ava hesitated. "I was afraid you might leave me for being weak."

"Did the police question you?" I asked softly. "Did you lie to them?"

"No!" Ava raised the knife. Light flickered on the blade.

Quinlyn gasped. I held my breath.

At the same time, the door whipped open. Nana Lissa rushed into the room with Detective Summers at her heels. "Emma! Meryl contacted us. She said—"

"Drop it!" Summers bellowed.

Ava sprang to her feet and released the knife. It fell to the floor. She wrapped her arms around herself and started to moan.

"Ava, breathe," I said. "It's all right, Detective. She's not going to hurt anyone."

He retrieved the knife.

I flicked on the lights, crossed to Ava, and touched her shoulder. "That's it. Inhale." She did. "Hold it . . . exhale. Good. You're going to be fine. Quinlyn, come take her hand. Tell her you love her."

Quinlyn did as I said, and I quickly recapped for my grandmother and Summers what had gone down. Ava. The knife. Her alibi of going to the cemetery Tuesday night.

"She's not lying," Nana Lissa said. "I saw her."

"What were you doing there?" I asked.

"Visiting Papa's grave."

I'd visited my grandfather's gravesite twice since his passing.

"Ava, you were wearing a black floppy hat, black coat, and boots, is that correct?" Nana gestured to her head.

"Yes," Ava replied. "But how could you know it was me?"

"I didn't know at the time, and your back was to me, but your hourglass figure is hard to match, young lady. I also happened to notice your long nails. They were sparkly that night, weren't they?"

She nodded.

"I'll swear it was you."

Summers crossed to Ava. "I'm afraid I'll have to take you in for aggravated assault."

"Wait, Detective," I said. "I'm not pressing charges."

"You're not?" His expression was grim.

"She wasn't going to harm us. She was distraught. She needs to talk to a professional."

"Dylan," Nana Lissa said, "Emma's right. Ava needs to see a doctor, not the inside of a jail cell."

Summers said, "It's a good thing my mother corroborated your whereabouts last Tuesday, Ms. Brennan."

I wanted to cheer. Dottie had contacted him.

After informing Quinlyn that he planned to take Ava to a hospital, he glowered at me. "Going forward, stay out of this investigation—"

"Or what? You'll arrest me?" I pressed my lips together, shocked by what I'd uttered. Was Merryweather Rose of Song sprinkling me with smart-alecky dust?

Summers frowned. His right cheek ticked. After a long moment, he guided Quinlyn and Ava from the room.

At the doorway, Quinlyn glanced over her shoulder. The curious look she gave me made me shudder. Had she come to the spa for a sound bath to uncover Ava's truth or to bolster her own lie?

# Chapter 20

Meryl was upset when I emerged from the meditation room. She was pouring a cup of tea while chastising herself under her breath.

"It's fine." I slung an arm around her shoulders. "No one got hurt. Be good to yourself."

"I saw her come in. I didn't see a weapon, but she was so wired and uptight that I dialed nine-one-one. I should have . . . I should have wrestled her to the ground."

"You did the right thing by calling for help," I assured her.

"But . . ."

"Breathe. All's well—"

"That ends well," she finished. "Are the police hauling her off to jail?"

I shook my head. "They're taking her to the hospital to sedate her, and Quinlyn is going to seek the help of a therapist for her."

"Therapy is good. When it works, it works."

I arrived home a half hour later, edgier than ever. Yes, Ava's incursion at the spa and Quinlyn's parting glance had unsettled me, but I also couldn't erase the images of last night's home invasion from my mind. Who, if not Ava, had broken in and destroyed my things?

Vivi mewed, begging for attention.

I lifted her and crooned the most well-known line of Bob Marley's hit song, "Everything's Gonna Be Alright."

But was it? Could a bubbly tune put the bounce back in my step? I stroked my affectionate cat for a solid ten minutes, drinking in her good vibes until she nudged my arm.

"Yes." I grinned. "I'll feed you."

I wasn't hungry but I needed something to calm me. After filling Vivi's bowl, I poured myself a glass of sauvignon blanc. As I took a sip, I spotted the postcards that I'd reaffixed to the refrigerator with the magnets. I plucked the one my father had sent while I was studying in Tibet and flipped it over. The stamp was Australian and featured Mount Warning. On it, he'd written in block letters: *I'M PROUD OF YOU. I'LL VISIT SOON. P.S. MOUNT WARNING WAS FORMED FROM A VOLCANIC PLUG OF THE TWEED VOLCANO, WHICH DOESN'T EXIST ANYMORE. TRIVIA FOR TWO HUNDRED, KEN.* I pressed the card fondly to my chest and mentally wished him a good day wherever he was. Then I returned the postcard to its spot and headed to bed.

Sleep was fitful. I woke up drenched in sweat, having dreamed about a volcano that scorched the trees outside my building, its lava reducing them to mere stubs.

"Thanks a ton, Dad," I muttered.

Vivi looked as ragged as I felt. I pulled out her comb and brush from the side table and gave her a good grooming. Next, I headed to the shower. After doing my ablutions, I threw on leggings and a cute Carmel T-shirt and downed a peach smoothie. I didn't add all the goodies Sierra did, but I figured the protein powder I'd included would carry me through the morning.

As I was preparing to leave, someone knocked on the front door. I flinched and hated myself for it. I didn't want to be afraid of neighbors needing a cup of sugar. "For Pete's sake, Emma," I chided under my breath, "get a grip. It's morning. No one is going to attack you now." I peeked through the peephole and saw Ursula. I opened the door. "Hello."

To my surprise, she wasn't dressed for the day. She was wearing a fluffy pink bathrobe and furry slippers—not at all the dramatic kind of leisure wear I would have expected.

"You need to advertise," she said matter-of-factly. "I had a vision, and this is what you must do to make your business thrive." She flourished a hand. "I know you dream of success."

I'd asked her for a reading a few months ago. Wanting my business to prosper had weighed heavily on my mind.

"You must ask the newspaper to do a story on you, as well."

"Now that I'm not a suspect in a murder, I suppose I could, but what would the angle be?"

"Opening your spa."

"There's nothing unusual about that."

"Perhaps explain why going to a spa for massage or meditation is good for the soul. There. I have said my piece. I leave you now." Yawning, Ursula climbed the stairs to her unit.

When I arrived at the spa, the front door was wide open. Jason was sitting at reception.

"Get any writing done on your vacay?" I asked.

"Very funny. I was sick for real. You saw me. The porcelain throne was my nearest and dearest friend."

"Flu?" I asked, worried that he had come back too soon and could infect all of us.

"No, I think it was something I ate. A tainted shrimp taco from a food truck most likely," he added. "Newbie move."

While organizing the desk, I said, "My neighbor suggested I advertise in the newspaper to boost business and also ask the newspaper to interview me."

"That's a great idea!" Meryl said, striding in, the tassels of her fringe jacket swinging to and fro.

"Nice getup," I said. "Farmers market steal?"

"How well you know me." She grinned. "Hey, what kind of marketing does Dracula do?"

Jason and I exchanged a look.

"A-count based marketing," Meryl continued.

"Keep your day job," Jason said.

She stuck her tongue out at him and shrugged out of her jacket to reveal a madras print blouse. Another farmers market coup, I supposed.

"Boss," Jason said, "speaking of advertising and, might I suggest, expanding, you ought to hire another masseuse. I had to turn down a few appointments this morning because we don't have enough staff."

If only Yoly was ready to get on board. "Noted. But having too many customers is good news." I high-fived him and Meryl.

For three hours, customers came and went. Each, when leaving, seemed more relaxed. I thanked them for their business, gave them discount coupons, and directed them to check out the shop and café.

At noon, my grandmother stopped into the spa. She was carrying two café bento boxes. "I grabbed some lunch for us," she said. "Want to join me on the patio?"

I smiled slyly. "If you'll go to *Carmel Pine Cone* with me afterward. I'd like to set up some advertising." I quickly told her Ursula's suggestion.

"That's a great idea, but most of the paper's employees work from home. Management prefers if you contact each employee by email or telephone."

"Really? What happened to doing business face-to-face?"

"You're a dinosaur, Emma, but a cute one. Like a baby T-Rex." She strolled to the patio, choosing to sit at a table for four.

I perched on a chair opposite her and checked out the customers dining at other tables. Two were women to whom I'd presented coupons, meaning they'd hung around. Yay! The babble of the waterfall was soothing, and the heady aroma of gardenias enticing. I opened my bento box and eyed the tortilla wrap within. "Avocado–crab meat?"

"Your favorite."

Nana Lissa dialed a number on her cell phone, said hello to whomever answered, added quickly that she wanted the person to speak with me, and handed the phone over. "This is the woman in charge of classified ads, Emma. She's a lovely human being and a regular at the library. Talk."

I pressed the phone to my ear. After a brief introduction, I asked the woman how to go about advertising. What did she need? Did she have preferred artwork sizes? I wasn't much of a digital artist, I told her. She said that wouldn't be a problem. She would help me design content for the ad as well as the artwork, and we agreed on a price for a two-week ad. All she needed was an email with the basics of what I wanted to achieve.

After she provided her contact numbers, I said, "Is there someone I can talk to about being interviewed by the *Pine Cone*? I was thinking the angle would be something along the lines of why going to a spa is good for the soul."

"Or we could do a perspective on female entrepreneurs," she suggested.

The notion gave me pause. "That's the angle your reporter Floyd Marblemaw is going for with his piece. He seems quite eager to pin down the story. I've been putting him off. Will he lose his job if he doesn't get it?"

"I don't know anyone named Floyd Marblemaw."

"How about Flo or Florence or—"

"No, nor any variation of the name."

"That's odd. He specifically said he was writing the article for your paper. Are there freelancers that you aren't familiar with?"

"I know everyone," she said. "He's lying."

As if fate were intervening, when I ended the call, Floyd appeared at the top of the stairs, smiling brightly. Were his ears burning? I whispered to my grandmother, "Speak of the devil. That's him. That's Floyd."

He strode toward me as he smoothed the tie beneath his rumpled jacket. "Well, well, Emma Brennan." He attempted to stand taller, to no avail. "It's Tuesday and it seems the perfect time for that interview, don't you think? Good day, madam." He nodded politely to my grandmother, then brazenly sat in one of the empty chairs, removed his fedora from his head, and pulled his leather notepad from his pocket.

"Sir, you were not invited to sit." Nana Lissa scowled.

He started to rise.

I gripped his wrist, holding him in place. "You lied to me, Floyd."

"Wh-what?" He faltered and settled back down.

"You're not a reporter for the *Pine Cone.*"

"I'm a freelancer." He pulled the pen from the notepad's attached loop.

"No, sir. The woman I spoke to at the paper does not know you."

"I'm doing it on spec," he replied quickly. "I haven't gotten the gig yet, true, but I intend to. I'm a handyman by day, but this story could propel my career."

What dream world was he living in? One article did not build a career.

"Look at what I've written so far," he said, flipping open the notepad's leather cover and turning the pad in my direction.

I began to read the opening paragraph, and my breath caught in my chest. The scrawl on the pad matched the writing I'd seen on the ecru card in Willow's file named *Self.* I eyeballed his pen, realizing it wasn't a regular pen. "What color ink is in your fountain pen?" I asked.

"Blue."

"What color blue?"

"I don't know."

"I'm guessing it's peacock blue," I stated. "Why are you really looking into Willow's death?"

"Huh?"

"You knew her. You wrote her a card. On it, you scrawled, *When will we meet?*"

"I had nothing to do with her death!" he blurted.

"I didn't ask if you did, but now that you mention it, what's your alibi for last Tuesday night?"

"I . . ." His voice caught. He cleared it. "I was chasing down another story."

"You're not a reporter," my grandmother said acidly. "We determined that a minute ago."

"No, ma'am. I'm not a paid reporter—yet," he stressed. "But I am trying to drum up stories. A local historical fiction author has a new book coming out. Her name is Eudora Cash. Perhaps you know her." He aimed the pen at her and quickly retracted it.

"Yes, I know her," Nana Lissa said. "She's a good friend."

"Lucky you. She's really excellent. I've read all her novels. What she's written this time is hush-hush," he went on. "Getting a scoop on what it's about could really help me."

I'd read one of Eudora Cash's books. My grandmother had assigned it as a book club selection. I wasn't a historical novel buff but I'd enjoyed it.

Floyd glanced from her to me. "To answer your question, where was I? I was hanging outside Ms. Cash's house last Tuesday night from seven until at least two a.m. I was on a stakeout of sorts, hanging out in my old Ford Escort, eating too many Twinkies for my own good, waiting for her to appear. She didn't. It turned out she was out of town."

I would've laughed at how ridiculous his story sounded if this wasn't such a serious conversation.

"Twinkies?" My grandmother arched an eyebrow.

"I've been hooked since I was a kid." Floyd's veiny face tinged red. "I know they'll be the death of me, and I've tried to stop, but, oh, the cream inside is addictive."

*Huh. It's not a lack of sugar that is making you a sour dude,* I mused. Maybe, if he proved to be innocent, I could entice him to come to the spa and let me realign his chakras, and Sierra could give him some nutritional counseling.

"Someone must have seen me. Check out my alibi. You'll see I'm not lying." Hat in hand, he rose to his feet and scuttled away, vowing he'd return to get the interview once I realized he was innocent.

My grandmother and I finished our lunch in silence.

When she was tossing our garbage, she said, "I have an hour before a library event. Why don't we canvass Eudora's neighborhood? We'll ask a few neighbors if they saw Mr. Marblemaw."

"Why don't we tell the police about him instead?"

"Emma, if he's telling the truth, then he's not a suspect, and the police will have gone there for naught. We don't want to burden them with unnecessary investigations, do we?"

"No, but you heard Detective Summers. He told me to bug off. Let's put him in charge of following up on Floyd."

She tilted her head, waiting patiently for me to change my mind.

"Fine. I'll go with you." I swung around and froze. "Hold on," I said under my breath. "Do you see him?"

"Who?"

"Inside the gift shop. Hugh Ashbluff. What's he doing here?"

"Hopefully buying something." She clasped my elbow. "C'mon, I'll drive."

I freed myself and strode into the shop. With a huff, my grandmother followed. Yoly was tending to Hugh, who had set a number of items on the sales counter—a lilac-colored protection mala necklace, a bottle of lavender essential oil, and a gorgeous reed diffuser.

"Good choice on your purchases, Mr. Ashbluff," I said.

He glanced over his shoulder, his gaze placid. "Hello, Emma. Lissa."

"The reeds naturally absorb the oil in the small glass vase," I went on, "drawing the scent to the top of the reeds and allowing the fragrance to be released into the air. Is it a gift for yourself?"

"I was sorry to hear your home was raided," he said, an odd conversation pivot.

Was he baiting me? No, he couldn't have instigated the incursion. As I'd explained to Sierra, the timing would have been off.

He eyed my grandmother. "Lissa, I think we need to get the city council involved in the darkness that is starting to pervade our beautiful city, don't you?"

"Indeed."

Hugh handed Yoly his credit card and said to me, "Be careful, Emma. From my experience, if someone has invaded a home once, it's more than likely they'll do so again."

# Chapter 21

Despite the veiled threat inherent in Hugh's words, Nana Lissa wouldn't be deterred. She was determined to check out Floyd's alibi.

Eudora Chase lived on Lincoln Street near Third Avenue. At this time of day, there were some neighbors in their gardens. One elderly woman in a sunhat, a long sleeved T-shirt, and jeans was on her hands and knees, pulling weeds from beneath a bed of roses.

Nana Lissa said, "Miriam! Hello!"

The woman twisted her torso without rising. "Lissa. Lovely day."

"Miriam is a teacher," my grandmother said to me. "But she adores gardening and she enters her roses in competitions." Smiling at her friend, she said, "I was wondering if you might have seen anyone skulking about last Tuesday evening."

"Can't say as I did, but I had a lot of homework to grade that night. I was in bed asleep by nine. I'll be by the library soon. I need you to acquire a few more books on rose gardening."

"I look forward to it."

We moved on and stopped by a cottage in need of repairs. A youngish man in overalls, his San Francisco Giants baseball cap turned backward, was giving the house's gray siding a facelift.

"Thomas!" she called. "Hello."

The man swung around and set down his paintbrush. He was in his thirties but appeared older because his face, neck, and forearms were weathered from exposure to the elements. "Lissa!"

"Thomas is an artist," she explained. "Trees are his main focus. You should see some of the work he's done. To make ends meet, he does lots of home makeovers."

Thomas loped to us with an easy gait. "Nice day for a stroll. What can I do for you?" He slid his hands into the pockets of his overalls.

As she had with the previous neighbor, Nana explained our mission. "We're on the hunt for anyone who might have seen an old Ford Escort or a scraggly-haired older man in the neighborhood last Tuesday evening." She added, "He's a person of interest in Willow Shafer's death."

That wasn't exactly true, but using that term could carry more weight and make someone like Thomas think harder.

"Nope," he said, "but I was finished here around six and left to see my girl in a summer play. She's eleven and has Hollywood in her sights." He grinned. "We all aspire to greatness, don't we? Sorry I can't be of help, Lissa. It's not good if a murderer gets off scot-free."

"No, it's not," she agreed, and nudged my arm. "Oh, there's Brady! In front of Eudora's house." She pointed to a home that sported the name Azalea Cottage. Many of the homes in Carmel had names. It was a quaint tradition.

"Isn't it a charmer?" my grandmother exclaimed.

"It's lovely."

"It was refurbished a decade ago, but it retains the character of a quintessential Carmel home, with its pitched roof, cobblestone rock-work, gorgeous gardens, and white picket fence. Considering Eudora's stature and wealth, it's understated, yet it suits her perfectly. She's extremely down-to-earth." Nana raised her hand a second time. "Brady!" To me she said, "You know Brady, don't you, Emma? He's Eudora's son."

"He's the owner of the Hideaway Café."

"Exactly. He's also a fabulous chef. He and Courtney are an item."

"Lissa," Brady said as he drew near. I could see Courtney and him together, she with her warm demeanor and him with his easy smile.

"We're looking for your mother," Nana Lissa said.

"She's not in town. She's got meetings with her publisher in New York. Dad went with her. I'm watching the place for them. Want me to give her a message?"

"Heavens no. I can text or call. My granddaughter Emma and I were merely doing some sleuthing."

He chortled. "Don't tell me. Courtney and her fairy roped you into it."

"They have nothing to do with this," my grandmother said. "You might have heard Emma was a person of interest in Willow Shafer's death."

Brady regarded me. "I heard you were cleared."

I was always amazed at how fast news traveled around Carmel-by-the-Sea. "Yes," I said, "but Willow was my friend. I'd like to find closure for her and her family." Quickly, I recapped Floyd Marblemaw's account, that he'd been staking out Eudora's house last Tuesday. I added that we hadn't found anyone who'd seen him.

"We've been asking neighbors," my grandmother explained. "His car is an old Ford Escort. I imagine he was hunkered low eating his silly Twinkies."

"Twinkies?" Brady's mouth quirked up to the right. "Huh. I found a couple of Twinkies wrappers the other day. In the bushes. I got rid of them fast. Mom hates when trash uglifies her garden. I thought a couple of the neighbors' kids tossed them in, but unless you can catch them in the act, they pull the whole 'It wasn't me' excuse."

"Do you remember when you found them?" I asked.

Brady scratched his chin. "Yeah, it was Wednesday morning. Mom and Dad left for the East Coast the day before."

Brady's statement didn't completely exonerate Floyd. After all, Floyd had lied about working at the *Pine Cone,* and he could have tossed the Twinkie wrappers into the garden to establish a phony alibi; however, it had the ring of truth.

"Thank you, Brady," Nana Lissa said. "Bless you."

She and I walked back to the library, kissed goodbye, and I continued on to the spa.

After checking in with Jason, I went to my office to clean up some of the bookwork I'd been neglecting. When I spotted the color-coded three-by-five cards pinned to the corkboard, I got an idea. I flipped them all over, added a couple of pink and orange cards, and began to jot down my thoughts about who murdered Willow.

*Ava Daft, on the pink cards—Motive:* to get rid of competition and lease the retail space. Not exactly a strong reason. But mentally unstable. Tried to spook Willow. *Alibi:* at cemetery. Exonerated. Seen by Nana Lissa.

*Quinlyn Obermeyer, on the yellow cards—Motive:* to be supportive of her lover, Ava, with same outcome as above. *Alibi:* iffy now that Ava's is confirmed. Should have asked who she delivered the scarves to.

*Hugh Ashbluff, on the purple cards—Motive:* did he want to free up the retail space to rent it? To sell it? Does he need money?

*Nana says no. Hugh is flush. Former baseball player. Could easily have wielded the candlestick. Alibi: won't say where he was or with whom but swears he has an alibi. I asked if he was dating a married woman. He didn't reply. Why did he show up at the gift shop today?*

*Indy Hendriks, on the orange cards—Motive: lost boyfriend and blamed Willow. Did Willow steal him? Zinnia said water under the bridge. Did Indy put threatening post-cards under Willow's and my doors? Under Willow's to warn her but beneath mine so the police would think some kid was pranking us? Alibi: playing bridge. Verified by police and a friend of Nana Lissa's. Question: Did she ask Palmer to act on her behalf?*

*Palmer Pilsner, on the green cards—Motive: angry because Indy lost ex-boyfriend. Acted as proxy? Question: Why was she so upset that Willow meditated? Why did she hate anything New Agey, although Willow's spa was not that? She has had massages. Bad spa experience? Strong tennis player. Good baker. Not a very attentive mother, but a do-gooder with her causes. Alibi: watching Jeopardy! reruns. Weak.*

*Floyd Marblemaw, on the blue cards—Motive: lied about writing an article on female entrepreneurs. Was he upset with Willow because she didn't grant the interview? Or because she didn't want to be involved with him? He didn't admit to writing the note on the ecru card, but he didn't deny it, either. Alibi: was staking out Eudora's house. He and his car weren't seen by anyone, but Twinkies wrappers were found. Did he plant them?*

I stepped away to examine my handiwork. Was Summers doing the same thing I was? Jotting down ideas? Trying to come up with alternate scenarios? Who was he interviewing? What evidence did he have? Fingerprints? Phone records? Witness statements?

Referring to the business card Summers gave me, I sent him a quick text about what I'd learned regarding Floyd. I didn't have the courage to call him. I didn't expect him to respond but thought my willingness to help might earn me brownie points.

Next, I added some white cards to the board and jotted down what I thought were clues.

- *The ecru notecard was inscribed with peacock-blue ink. Why did Willow keep it in her Self file? She liked older men. Was she having an affair with Floyd?*
- *The postcards under the doors. Were they Palmer's art? Put there by Palmer or Indy or their friend Naomi Clutterbuck? Or a prankster?*
- *When I saw Palmer and Indy chatting at Percolate, they looked like they were conspiring. About what? Tennis? Murder?*
- *Naomi seen in my neighborhood spying on me. She passed by again on her bike. Why?*
- *The large amounts of money in Willow's*

*ledgers coded 7000. Who was receiving it? Payoff or something else? Had she been in debt? Or did she have savings?*

"Yoo-hoo," Sierra said, entering the office briskly. "I have an afternoon treat for you to try. Oatmeal-raisin cookies made with natural honey and chocolate chips."

"Ooh, chocolate?"

"Dark chocolate. Not a lot of sugar."

After thinking nonstop about Twinkies, having a goodie sounded like a gift from heaven. I bit into one and hummed my appreciation. "Chewy yummy delicious."

"I used pecans. I know how much you love them. Where did you and Nana go?"

"Sleuthing," I said, using my grandmother's term.

"Sleuthing what?" She crossed to the corkboard and studied what I'd written on the cards.

"Floyd Marblemaw. He gave us his alibi. Nana wanted to check it out."

"What did the note on the ecru card say?" Sierra asked, tapping Floyd's blue card.

" 'When will we meet?' " I ate half of a second cookie.

"*Oho!* It sounds like Floyd was her lover, but you don't buy that." She gestured to the note I'd written under the clue.

"Willow dated older guys, but no one that old."

*Why hadn't he signed the card?* I wondered.

Sierra tapped a purple card. "Hugh came to the gift shop? That's sort of weird. Do you think, after our chat in his office, he figured you were investigating him and wanted to intimidate you?"

"Emma!" My mother stormed into the office. Her face was pinched with fury. She'd be appalled if I told her that rage made her look a good ten years older.

*"Shh,* Mother. Please respect the spa and its customers. They need quiet."

"I will not hush. Why did it take a full day before I heard about the break-in in your apartment?" she asked, her tone still sharp and loud.

"Honestly, keep it down." I used mollifying gestures. "Not all of the walls are soundproof."

She wrestled with the admonition but finally lowered her voice. "A student of mine said the intruder smashed your collectibles. Why didn't you call me?"

"Because I'm a grown woman. I can take care of myself. I contacted the police. They arrived in short order. Where did the student get the info?"

"I don't have a clue. A text. A social media post. Who knows in this day and age where anyone gets their news?"

I doubted my cousin had posted anything. Had Ursula? Or a neighbor?

"How can you be working at a time like this?" she went on. "You need to rest."

"Work is the best thing for me. It takes my mind off things."

"What about your cat? Is she stressed out?"

"You don't give a hoot about my cat, but she's fine." Though, to be sure, perhaps I ought to have Vivi meet with a cat therapist. A friend of mine swore by the one her Siamese consulted. If Vivi was feeling jittery but was hiding it from me, bringing her to work might be a solution.

"You've got to give it up," my mother said.

"My cat?"

She glowered at me. "You know to what I'm referring."

*To what I'm referring?* Sheesh, sometimes she could ruin the flow of the English language. "If you mean the spa, not happening?" I said tartly.

"I'm talking about this snooping you're doing."

"Snooping? I'm not snooping. I don't snoop."

"I've heard what you're up to. People's tongues are wagging." She jutted her right hand. "You went with Willow's mother to Mystic Waters."

"She asked me to help her sort through Willow's things."

"You've got to stop, Emma."

"Aunt Kate, she can't," Sierra said. "She has to clear her name."

"But you're . . . innocent," my mother sputtered. She never sputtered. "I heard . . . people said . . . you're not a suspect any longer."

"For now," I said, "but the police haven't arrested the killer yet, and let's face it, until they do, they could always put me back in their sights."

"I think Hugh Ashbluff is the best suspect," Sierra said. Her gaze flicked toward the corkboard.

My mother glanced in that direction and scowled. "What is that?" She rounded my desk and stood arms akimbo.

Uh-oh. I was in for it now.

"Is this what I think it is? Have you created, what do they call it on TV . . ." She ran a palm along her jaw. "Is this a murder board?"

"Not exactly." On TV and in the movies, the police would've added photos and arrows and all sorts of doodads to provide a visual roadmap for their murder boards. "It's a way for me to summarize my thoughts. See how organized it is? Color coding has come in handy."

"Darling, you're not the police."

"That doesn't mean I can't try to figure out a few things." I pointed at the note cards. "As you can see, some people have verifiable alibis. Others have iffy ones."

"Like Hugh." Sierra indicated his purple card again.

"And Ava Daft," I said. "Nana Lissa corroborated her alibi, although Hugh believes she is the likeliest suspect because she wanted to take over Willow's lease."

My mother motioned to a white clue card. "Naomi Clutterbuck. Why is her name written down?"

"She isn't a suspect," I said, unless she was a co-conspirator, of course. "But she was with Indy and Palmer the night they verbally attacked Willow at Hideaway Café."

"Naomi had no part in Willow's murder. I know her very well."

"Hattie Hopewell saw her spying on our fourplex," Sierra said. "The day before Emma's place was trashed."

"You can't possibly think she had a hand in that!" my mother exclaimed. "For heaven's sakes, Emma, Naomi is the kindest . . ." Kate studied the cards again and said over her shoulder, "Naomi escaped a harrowing experience in Japan that set her on her life's course to do no harm in this world. Do. No. Harm." She smacked one hand against the other.

I said, "Nana told me a little about that. Could you elaborate?"

"Her father was a vile doctor. He did despicable things. Her family suffered great shame. Her husband was able to obtain safe passage for her and her mother and sisters to America. She owes him everything." She flourished a hand. "Mark her off your list. I'm right about this. Now, who is this Floyd person?"

"A man who claims he's a reporter," I replied. "He's sort of sketchy. He said he planned to do a story on women entrepreneurs and wanted to interview me and Willow." I paused when I realized he'd never asked me anything about my business. His questions were always focused on Willow. Her life. Her career. What had he wanted from her? Why reach out to me?

"Emma, I'm still thinking about Hugh," Sierra said. "Remember that baseball bat in his office?"

"What bat?" My mother looked between us, her gaze filled with confusion. "When were you two in his office?"

I said, "On Saturday, after dinner, we were passing by, and he saw us and invited us inside."

Kate tsked. "You are taking way too many liberties, young lady."

"And what about Palmer?" Sierra asked, continuing her line of questioning. "Her profile is on the green cards, Aunt Kate," she added, cagily drawing my mother into our analysis.

"Her motive is anemic," I said. "Big deal if she didn't like Willow's business or the practice of meditation."

"Lots of people are wary of New Age techniques until they try them," Sierra replied.

"They don't kill someone over it."

Kate blew a raspberry. "Palmer's alibi is as insipid as light beer. She was watching *Jeopardy*! Who told you that, Emma?"

"She did when I ran into her and Indy at Percolate."

My mother hummed. Then sniffed. Then clicked her tongue. It was her way of implying she'd alighted on something important. Had she? Had Palmer given me her alibi to throw me off the scent?

I said, "You know, her daughter Olivia was at Percolate that day, and she—"

"Olivia. I'm quite fond of her," Kate cut in. "She's one of my students."

"She's in college? She doesn't look old enough."

"She skipped a grade or two. She's very bright. She loves reading gothic stories like *Frankenstein*, *Dr. Jekyll and Mr. Hyde*, and *Dracula*. However, I can't convince her to pick up anything written by Jane Austen. I mentioned the resistance to gentle literature to her father, suggesting she might want to expand her interests, but he—"

"You know him?" I bleated. She actually knew Olivia's father, the insurance statistician? Meaning he could be the guy she'd been dating? Gack. I swallowed hard. "Um, Mother . . ." *Tread lightly, Emma.* "Was Mr. Pilsner the, you know . . . the man you . . ." I let the sentence hang.

"Pete?" A peal of laughter gushed out of Kate. "Is he the married man I was dating?"

Sierra gawked at me. I hadn't told her about my mother's affair.

"Heavens no," Kate went on. "He's merely a friend. I see him occasionally on the golf course. He has a regular foursome that plays ahead of mine." She flapped a hand. "He's widely read, that's all. I suggested to him that Palmer take an interest in Olivia's pursuits, but he said Palmer neglects their daughter. For Palmer, life purely hinges on her art, tennis, and charity events. Which also speaks to motive. I can't see her allowing herself to be bothered by Willow in any way. Certainly not enough to murder her."

Sierra said, "Aunt Kate, you don't know the whole of it." She explained why Indy might hold a grudge against Willow. "As Emma stated, Palmer could've been acting on Indy's behalf. BFFs go to great lengths to protect BFFs."

"She lost a boyfriend? Big whoop," Kate said. "If you ask me, she's well rid of him and should thank Willow. Indy has a very successful business. As for Palmer—"

"You haven't seen Palmer wield a tennis racket." Sierra mimed the movement. "She's powerful."

I agreed. Palmer might or might not be a murderer, but she was a devoted friend, she had a temper, and she sure could whack a tennis ball.

# Chapter 22

Once again when I arrived home, I was so tense I looked as if I was wearing my shoulders as earrings. I needed to take a walk. Vivi seemed more than happy to accompany me. Perhaps she was picking up on my inner turmoil or she was, as my mother suggested, stressed out and needed fresh air as much as I did.

I inserted her into the cat carrier, strapped it on, filled my reusable beverage bottle with cold water, and off we went. The sun was setting. The air was misty, not foggy, and the temperature was mild. We strolled to Carmel Bay. Within minutes, I found myself breathing in rhythm with the waves as they lapped the shore. A few people were out. One woman, who was luring a colony of seagulls to her with potato chips, reminded me of the bird lady in *Mary Poppins* who fed pigeons outside the cathedral.

Vivi purred contentedly against my chest, and by the time we returned home, I was feeling centered. I sat in the backyard to eat my light dinner of grilled cod and asparagus and gazed at the rear door of my studio. I knew I had to make a new batch of essential oils but didn't feel up to it. Vivi was playing in the flowers, romping as she had the other night. Did she truly have a fairy friend? I was dubious. She stopped and, peering hard at me, swished her tail. Had she picked up on my mental musings? Was her fairy talking to her about me?

*Uh-uh. I'm not paranoid. No way.*

Laughing, I beckoned her and told her to come inside. I would read until I fell asleep.

Wednesday morning, I decided to take my frisky Birman with me to work. I settled her in the office, slung the empty cat carrier over the arm of a chair, told her she could drink from my water glass, and promised her I'd return for a cuddle soon.

At five to nine, Quinlyn walked through the spa door. She'd dressed differently than she had on previous occasions. Today's outfit was still shapeless, but it was bright red instead of a drab color.

"You don't have an appointment," I said.

"No. I came to give you this." She pulled a gift box from her oversized tote. She handed it to me and swept her braid over her shoulder. "I want to thank you."

"For . . ."

"For coaxing Ava into telling the truth. It meant the world to me. It's a load off my shoulders. I'd been feeling weighed down by my suspicions. You're probably . . ." Her eyelids fluttered rapidly. "You're probably wondering what my real alibi is for that night."

"You were delivering scarves to a customer."

"Yes, that much was true, but I . . ." She squared her shoulders. "Following that, I consulted an attorney after hours. I needed advice in case I had to break up with Ava and dissolve our business partnership."

Meryl dashed into reception. Before she spoke, I motioned for her to stay back. Quietly, she eased into the hall.

"Go on, Quinlyn," I said. "Why might you need to dissolve the partnership?"

"She'd been acting strangely with the ghost noises and weird phone calls. I didn't think she was a killer, but, well, I wasn't sure. She's calmer now, but she was so upset about threatening us with that knife, she asked to go to a mental-health rehab facility. They have her on medication that is helping. The doctor says she'll be fine. In the meantime, I've hired an assistant at the shop."

"You should tell the police what you told me."

"I have," she replied. "And my lawyer has confirmed I was with her. We spoke and drew up papers for nearly two hours. I came here to tell you because you were so brave to face Ava like that. When I was leaving, I was so shaken. I should have hugged you or thanked you or done something, but I didn't."

That was the look she'd thrown in my direction? Wow, I'd missed that completely. "I'm glad you have an alibi," I said, "and I'm happy to hear Ava's in treatment."

Impulsively, Quinlyn threw her arms around me. "Thank you."

When she left, I opened the gift she'd brought. It was a beautiful silk scarf with a Carmel setting. Apparently, she had been able to switch out the Monterey-themed stock they'd received.

Jason ambled around the corner, a glass mug of steaming tea in hand. "Full day ahead. Which reminds me, I need tomorrow morning off."

"To write?" I asked, putting the scarf in a drawer beneath the computer.

"Very funny." He grimaced. "No, I have to go to a doctor's appointment that I can't cancel."

"Are you all right?"

"I am, but it's my mom. She can't drive herself home after the procedure."

"Gotcha."

Meryl sauntered in, checking her watch. "Coast clear?"

I nodded.

"Did my customer call?" she asked. "She's late for a mani-pedi."

I checked the appointment schedule. "Your first is at ten."

"Really? Are you sure?"

"Positive."

"Sheesh." She palm-slapped her forehead. "I've got to get a better memory."

"Don't you log your appointments in a calendar?"

"Are you kidding? I can't tell you how many times I've messed that up. Besides, I have the memory of an elephant."

"Except for now," Jason said.

Meryl scowled at him, then grinned. "Hey, why do elephants have trunks?" She paused. "Because they'd look funny with a suitcase."

Jason groaned. "Please tell me you're not using that in your routine."

"No. Duh. I'm not an idiot. But I do love corny jokes. There's this one comedienne who does animal impressions. You should see her. She makes funny faces and sounds. She's a riot. Whenever she acts like a goose"—Meryl honked like one—"I literally lose it."

Jason was staring at her like she was an alien. I was, as well. Some humor—like silly kid jokes—didn't appeal to everyone.

"Excuse me." Olivia Pilsner rapped on the door and stepped into the spa. Her low-cut *No Justice* punk T-shirt clung to her lithe frame. For adornment, she'd added a velvet scarlet-cross choker and had switched out the hoop nose ring she'd sported at Percolate for a fire-black opal stud. "When will the gift shop open?"

Meryl sobered. "Oh, Emma, I forgot to tell you. Yoly had an emergency with her sister. She'll be here by ten."

"I'll help you," I said to Olivia, grabbing the keys to the shop. "This way." I motioned to the door and guided her across the courtyard. "What are you looking for?"

"Crystals, Ms. Brennan. Thank you."

"You can call me Emma."

"Um, sure."

I opened the shop's door and stepped inside. I didn't turn over the *Back in a Few* sign. I wasn't ready to help a slew of customers should the need arise. I guided Olivia past the bookshelves and bonsai trees to the glass display case that held the geodes and crystals.

"Is that jasmine I smell?" Olivia asked.

"It is." The scent was emanating from the reed diffuser on the sales counter.

"Gramma Beatrice loved that smell."

"Its aroma is known to help alleviate anxiety and stress." I didn't add that in some cultures, jasmine was considered an aphrodisiac, meaning it could heighten sexual desire. Information was important. Too much information could be detrimental. "Are you looking for any particular crystal?"

"I'm feeling lonely," she said softly. The vulnerability in her voice broke my heart.

"Because you miss your sister?"

"Uh-huh."

"Well, mookaite, which is also known as Australian jasper, is a great stone for loneliness. It helps you remember to be kind to others as well as to yourself." I fetched a pyramid-shaped stone. "See the fiery fusion of red and yellow? It fosters an invigorating frequency of strength and vitality." I offered it to her.

Tentatively, she allowed me to place it in her left-hand palm. She wrapped her fingers around it and closed her eyes.

"Where is Alexandra?" I asked. "In Connecticut?"

Her eyes snapped open. "Oh, no. She'd never go there. That's where our mother is from."

That reinforced my suspicion that Alexandra and Palmer were at odds.

"To be truthful, Emma, I'm not sure where she is." Olivia's face pinched with sadness. "She doesn't call. She doesn't write."

The lack of communication surprised me, considering the way Olivia had described their close relationship: going on hikes and rock climbing and bird-watching.

"Mother says she's in Timbuktu."

Palmer had probably uttered that facetiously.

Olivia lifted the stone overhead and examined it in the light. "I think our mother knows where she is but she's too upset to tell me."

I wondered if Palmer was refusing to share Alexandra's whereabouts because she was worried that Olivia might follow the same path—whatever that path was—and leave home for good.

"What's that green stone?" The teen pointed to a tray.

"That's malachite. It personifies the deep healing green of nature. Notice the flow and energy of its lines and swirls." I pointed them out. "Many think of it as a stone of transformation. It can help the possessor change her situation and enhance spiritual growth."

"May I hold it also?"

I fetched an oval stone with a semi-depression, good for caressing with one's thumb, and set it in her right hand. Automatically, she began to stroke it.

"Mother would be mad that I'm here," she murmured. "She doesn't like what you do."

"I don't get it. She goes to A Peaceful Solution for massages."

"It's the other stuff, like sound baths and aromatherapy. They're, you know, unconventional."

That was in keeping with what Willow had implied.

"I'd like to buy one of the stones, but . . ." Olivia worked her lip between her teeth. "No, I can't."

"They're not too expensive." I'd give her a discount.

"It's not the money. It's, well, they're taboo in my house."

"But you said you have tarot cards."

"They're a secret. My sister gave them to me."

I mimed twisting a lock in front of my lips.

"That woman who died," Olivia went on, her voice barely a whisper.

"Willow Shafer."

"I haven't told anyone, not even my dad, but I saw a creepy guy hanging around her spa two weeks ago."

My ears pricked up. Was this the reason Olivia had really come to the shop? To share something that might help solve the murder?

"He was, like, staring for a long time at the front of the place." She rubbed the stone more firmly, as though she were agitated.

"What made him creepy?" I asked, wondering if the guy was on the police's radar.

"He looked sort of homeless, you know? His clothes were messy, and his face was really . . ." She gestured but couldn't convey what she wanted to describe. "His hair was scraggly and he had sort of a hunched back, like Riff Raff in *The Rocky Horror Picture Show*. And he was super-old."

The description sounded a lot like Floyd. To someone her age, "super-old" could be anyone over fifty.

Something buzzed. Olivia pulled her cell phone from her teensy purse and gasped. "It's Mom. I'd better go." She set the stones on the counter. "I'll come back another time."

"Wait." I gave her the stones for free. Her face lit up. I asked her to refer friends to the shop. "They'll have to pay, of course."

"Yeah, sure."

"And, Olivia, hold out hope that your sister will contact you soon. Sometimes people need to explore the world before coming home to roost," I said, paraphrasing my grandmother's wise words after my boyfriend left town.

"Thanks." She hurried out.

At 11:00 a.m., I did a mindful meditation for Zinnia's friend, Violet Vickers, who was over the moon with the result.

"Lovely," she said repeatedly on the way to reception. "Just lovely. I feel ready to conquer the world."

As she was paying, I said, "Violet, the other day you and Zinnia had dinner at Hideaway Café."

"One of our favorite places. Comfort food is the best, isn't it?"

"Yes. You overheard the fracas between Willow and Palmer and Indy."

She tsked. "Indeed. Poor Willow."

"Zinnia hinted that there was more to the story. When I asked her, she said Willow was the reason Indy lost her boyfriend and added that it was 'water under the bridge.' She intimated Willow stole Indy's boyfriend."

"Oh, no, dear, she didn't steal him. Indy lost him on her own."

"Because . . ."

She hesitated. "Because the poor thing went into Mystic Waters for a scalp treatment a year ago. For some reason, she had a horrible reaction, and all her hair fell out. The next day the boyfriend—a shallow louse, to be sure—up and left her. It was crushing for Indy. After a brutal divorce, she had finally opened her heart and fallen head over heels for someone."

"Oh, my. Indy is a solo act because of a bad scalp treatment?"

"She got over it."

"Did she?"

"Her hair grew back. Her business is thriving."

I wasn't sure a prosperous venture filled the void of a broken heart. "Why didn't Nana Lissa know about the botched scalp treatment and boyfriend fiasco? It sounds like something she should've heard, being as tuned in as she is to the happenings in Carmel."

"Zinnia and I only learned because we were in Indy's shop one day when she and Palmer were discussing their outrage. Indy was trying on wigs."

"You never mentioned the incident to the police?"

She frowned. "Until this very minute, I'd never considered one of them might've killed Willow over it. As I said, her business—"

"Turned out to be successful. Got it."

As Violet left, I passed another customer in the hall who confided she was moving from a massage room to the facial room for a cellular renewal facial. "It should help with my cradle face, don't you think?" she kidded.

"Yes." Cradle face was what happened after a client lay facedown on a massage table. Despite the wrinkles, she looked radiant. "Enjoy," I murmured.

Minutes later, Sierra swanned in with a platter full of food from the café. "Goodies," she announced.

Jason nabbed one of the smoothies, Meryl took a veggie pita pocket, and I opted for a repeat of yesterday's lunch—an avocado–crab meat tortilla wrap.

"Spill the tea," Sierra said to me. "Any updates?"

"I was just about to text you." I hitched my chin. "Outside."

We went to the patio. I chose the table closest to the fountain, and quietly, so that nearby guests wouldn't overhear, I told her what I'd learned from Violet.

She whistled. "You've got to tell Detective Summers."

"But Indy has a solid alibi."

*"Hmm.* Unless, like you said the other day, she killed Willow, changed into fresh clothes at her shop, and hustled to her bridge game."

I told her what I'd learned from Olivia.

"Wow. Do you really think the man she was describing was Floyd?" she asked. "You said his alibi wasn't verifiable. You have to tell the police that, too."

"I sent a message to Detective Summers when I was creating the suspect board. Texting again might earn me an outright threat of incarceration for interfering."

"He has to know what you've learned, Emma. Has to!"

A man cleared his throat. I turned and spotted Floyd Marblemaw making his way toward me. My insides turned to jelly. "It's him," I whispered. "The reporter."

Sierra swiveled in her seat. "Are you scared?"

"No. Sort of. I don't know."

"I'm sticking to you like glue."

"Floyd, this is my cousin, Sierra."

"How do you do?" He removed his fedora and tipped his head in a gentlemanly fashion. "Ms. Brennan, I told you I'd return for that interview. I'm assuming since I wasn't arrested that you realized I was telling the truth about being outside Eudora Cash's house."

He could assume all he wanted. I remained tight-lipped.

"Let's get to it." He pulled the leather notepad from his pocket and flipped it open.

A small photograph fluttered from a slot inside the cover and fell to the ground. Floyd hurried to retrieve it, but I reached it first.

"Give me that," he demanded.

I examined the photo. It was of a man holding a raven-haired toddler in a cream-colored tutu. The photo was old, the edges frayed. Going by the hound-dog sad eyes, I'd say the man was Floyd. He had dark black hair and ruddy cheeks back then. I peered harder at the girl, zeroing in on her eyes. Then I refocused on Floyd's younger face and suddenly I knew why he reminded me of someone. His eyes had the same downturned shape as Willow's.

"Is this Willow in the picture?" I rasped. "You're her father?"

He licked his lips but didn't deny it.

"You walked out when she was a girl. You never contacted her again." My father may have left my mother, but he didn't abandon me. If anything, distance had made our love stronger, thanks to his postcards, text messages, and phone calls. "It broke Willow's heart," I went on. "Why did you do that?"

"Because . . ." His voice cracked. "Because Ginnie told me to leave. I had a vile temper. Nothing satisfied me. I was hostile. And manic. I went from job to job. Ginnie said I was dragging them both down. She said they'd be better off without me. She was right." He studied the toes of his shoes before raising his gaze. "I've been in treatment. I'm on meds, and they help." He paused. "I've been following Willow over the years. I know how well she did in high school. I know she attended Cal Poly. I know she majored in accounting, but she didn't pursue that career because she wanted something more spiritually fulfilling."

"Did Willow guess who you were?" I asked.

"No. I kept it a secret. Floyd Marblemaw was my best friend's name. He passed on."

An alias. Yes, that made sense. And I doubted Willow would

have guessed his identity by sight, because Ginnie had probably destroyed pictures of Floyd.

"You were seen hanging outside the spa a couple of weeks ago," I said.

"That's when I first got to town. I didn't introduce myself right away. I couldn't muster up the courage to do so. When I landed on the idea of being a reporter, I approached her."

"You made up this cockamamie story about interviewing women entrepreneurs to get close to her?"

"Yes."

Sierra sniffed her displeasure.

"She answered my questions," he continued. "She told me how proud she was, being an owner of a spa where people could relax. When I asked about her family, she said she didn't blame her father for leaving. She said that didn't crush her. She ended up where she was supposed to."

Did adversity make one stronger? Had Indy, after the scalp fiasco and loss of her boyfriend, toughened up, too? Was it possible she didn't bear a grudge?

"She said that my abandonment of the family is what made her set out to find herself," Floyd continued. "It helped her discover her purpose in life. She vowed never to disappoint her own family, if she ever had one, the way I'd disappointed her and her mother. She said going to a retreat last year in Arizona saved her."

I recalled seeing the black-and-white picture of a sanctuary above the foyer table in her house. Was that where she'd gone on her sabbatical? Or had she visited one of the many other retreats that I'd seen in photos at the spa?

"She said she came out revitalized," he went on, "and convinced she had chosen the right path in moving to Carmel." He worried the brim of his hat in his hands. "I didn't want anything from her. I just wanted to get to know her." His tone was mournful. "When you went into her house with Ginnie, I wanted to come forward. To tell you the truth. To reconcile with Ginnie as best I could. But I didn't have the courage."

"You saw us?"

He bobbed his head. "I was at the corner."

Of course. He was the person I'd thought was a UPS delivery guy.

He held out his hand for the photo. "Please believe me. I didn't kill her."

# Chapter 23

Close to three, when I was saying goodbye to a contented customer who'd come in for a deep tissue massage—the best she'd ever had, she confided—Indy sauntered in. I was astonished to see her after the hard time she'd given me at Percolate. She was wearing a stylish Moroccan-style top, similar to the one she'd worn the other day, over leggings and sparkly sandals. I wondered if the top was a piece from her fashion line. If so, I'd bet she had plenty of sales. She spun in a circle, assessing the place.

"Nice skylight," she said.

"Thank you." I smiled. "How can I help you?"

She handed me a business card. "I'm offering discounts at my shop. Ten percent off. It's marked on the backside of the card."

"You're going door to door to drum up business?"

"Entrepreneurs need to do so with regularity. Be well advised."

She was counseling me? Gee, how nice of her. "Can I book you an appointment?" I eyed her nails, which weren't chewed raw but were definitely neglected. "How about a mani-pedi? Our technicians are very skilled."

"I never get a manicure. It would be a waste of money. Working with pins and needles, day in and day out, rips my hands to shreds."

"A facial, then." I offered her one of our brochures. She didn't accept it.

"Hugh Ashbluff," she said—a total non sequitur.

"I found out why he was peering through binoculars. He was searching for rodent nests."

"He's borrowing a lot of money," she said, not interested in the explanation. "Not here in town. In San Jose." She used her hands to tell the story. "I was at the fabric wholesaler, which is located in a building next to Wells Fargo, and, lo and behold, as I was leaving, I saw Hugh sitting inside at a lender's desk. They seemed to be having a heated conversation. Wondering what was up, I sneaked in and eavesdropped."

I wasn't sure where she was going with this. I remained mum.

"He was asking for a loan of ten million dollars."

*Ten million. Yipes!*

"Which made me think about the argument Palmer heard between Willow and Hugh," she added.

"She never said what they argued about."

"She told me it sounded private, but it was finance related. Willow said, 'Now I know how you're paying for that trip you took to Antarctica, Hugh.' To which he replied snidely, 'You don't know dirt.' Willow countered, 'You won't get away with it, mister. It's not clean money. You're building a house of cards.'"

*A house of cards?* What did that mean?

"Palmer didn't understand any of it—financial matters are not her forte—but I understood once I saw him in the bank. Hugh buys and flips houses. I figure his contractors are doing subpar electrical or plumbing work or they're ignoring flimsy structural issues because he's low on cash. Willow had proof, and he killed her to shut her up."

"Have you told the police?"

"No. I thought I'd float the theory by you first. What do you think? Did he kill Willow? You've been snooping around."

"I haven't been snooping." How I hated that darned word.

"Palmer said Willow was too curious for her own good. Maybe you are, too."

I shivered. Was that a threat?

"What have you uncovered?" she asked.

"Me? Nothing." Nothing that Summers considered important, anyway. I had suspects. I had motives. I didn't have any proof, which was why I hadn't texted him, even though Sierra had prodded me mercilessly to do so.

"Nothing? Not a thing? As in *nada*?"

Was she fishing on Palmer's behalf or her own?

"Actually, I heard through the grapevine"—I wasn't going to give up Zinnia and Violet's names, but why not be bold?—"that you had a less than satisfactory scalp treatment from Willow, and as a result, your boyfriend left you. That had to have incensed you."

"Hold it right there. Yes, I hated her, but I didn't kill her. I realized my boyfriend was a good-for-nothing and I moved on. I have my shop, my career. I'm content. End of story. Good day, Emma. Don't even think of patronizing my boutique." She added under her breath, "Snoop," and strode out of the building.

After the door closed, I wheezed with exhaustion.

Despite my misgivings about the truthfulness of her revelation, I thought again of Hugh Ashbluff showing up at the gift shop, and I had to admit, learning he had been attempting to obtain a loan piqued my interest.

Summoning courage, I messaged Summers again and, for good measure, tossed in the bit I'd learned about Indy, despite her protestation. If he didn't respond by dinnertime, I would find the pluck to phone him.

Oh, if only there were a fairy who could instill me with confidence.

To find my center, I went to the office to spend a little one-on-one time with my cat.

Midafternoon, my mother traipsed into the spa, accompanied by none other than Naomi Clutterbuck. Naomi's high-necked dress with a fluttery skirt gave her a baby-doll appearance. It wasn't a style I could pull off on the best of days. She would have rocked it if she didn't look as if she'd been crying. Her eyes were red-rimmed.

"Kate, what're you doing here?" I doubted she had brought Naomi in for a treatment. Their names weren't on the books.

"We . . ." Kate gestured to Naomi. "We wanted to chat with you. Got a sec?"

"Sure."

"After seeing you yesterday, I asked Naomi about her friendship with Indy and Palmer."

Naomi lowered her chin and dropped her arms to her sides as if I were the school principal and this meeting couldn't have been more daunting.

"In the course of our conversation, I mentioned your . . ." Kate struggled for a word. "Your idea board and the variety of suspects on it."

Naomi raised her chin. Her eyes were flooded with moisture. I pulled a tissue from the box by the computer and handed it to her. She blotted her eyes.

"After hearing her name invoked," Kate went on, "Naomi said she had to confess something. As it turns out, she is having an affair with Hugh Ashbluff and says they were together the night Willow died."

I cocked my head. He was actually seeing a married woman? He'd remained tight-lipped about her identity because he had a modicum of decency? Wow.

"There's no way Hugh could be a suspect," Naomi said. Her voice had a tinge of a Japanese accent.

I said, "He had dinner with Detective Summers. You dined with Indy and Palmer."

"We met after."

Kate said, "When she confessed to me about the affair, I suggested she come talk to you."

*How the tables have turned,* I mused. My mother, advice giver extraordinaire, was now champion of the underdog after confessing her own affair.

"I don't want to go to the police," Naomi said. "If I do, my husband will find out about me and Hugh, and he'll leave me."

"Do you want to save your marriage?" I asked.

"No. I don't. I want a divorce." She fanned the air. "Please don't get me wrong. My husband is a good man. He has helped my family in ways you cannot imagine. But I do not love him. I know it is wrong of me, but I am in love with Hugh. If my husband walks out, I will end up with nothing other than my salary. In order to negotiate, I need him to believe it is my wish to dissolve the marriage for reasons of incompatibility and not because I have fallen in love with another man."

What a complicated scenario.

In a surprise show of warmth, Kate caressed Naomi's shoulder. "She and Hugh met in an art class. On the beach."

"I saw you join a class the other day," I said. "Hugh wasn't taking part."

"He is a terrible artist," Naomi said, "but he wanted to give it a go. He is open to trying many new things." Her mouth curved up coyly. "Because we first met on the beach, we often meet up there now. I dress incognito. That way no one can report to my husband."

"Incognito?" Kate asked.

"I cover up from head to toe and even wear big hats, face masks, and sunglasses. It is Hugh's and my little joke."

Aha. She was the one on the beach the other day that he'd kissed pristinely . . . on the mask.

"Hugh is everything I have ever wanted," Naomi continued. "He is smart. He listens. My husband . . . he is much older. He is set in his ways. He did me a kindness by helping my family, but he does not truly love me. He knows we are not soulmates."

"She hasn't been prepared to leave her husband because Hugh is struggling financially," Kate said.

"Struggling how?"

"He is in debt," Naomi said. "But after the divorce, following a settlement, I will be able to help him."

Was my grandmother wrong about Hugh being flush? Was Indy telling the truth about him taking out a loan? Was she right about the context of Willow and Hugh's argument? Did he kill Willow to cover up nefarious business dealings?

No. If Hugh really had been with Naomi that night, he couldn't have done so.

"Can you prove you were together?" I asked.

Naomi could and did. They'd gone to Post Ranch Inn in Big Sur and had a staff member take pictures of them in the meditation pool that overlooked the Pacific. The photo was time-stamped at 9:00 p.m. Tuesday night. It took at least forty minutes to drive to Big Sur. If they'd ended their respective meals at the Hideaway Café around seven thirty and left immediately, they would have arrived at the hotel at around eight fifteen to eight thirty. Time would have passed while they checked in and changed into swim clothes. Therefore, there was no possibility that Hugh could have killed Willow after I left Mystic Waters.

Unless . . . they took the photo to ensure others saw Hugh, after which he zipped back to Carmel, killed Willow, and returned to the inn.

"Naomi, I have one question. Why were you peering at my fourplex the other day?"

"Your fourplex?"

"On San Carlos southeast of Fourth."

A gentle smile graced her lips. "My youngest sister is looking to rent her own place. She is tired of living with our mother. There is a unit to let there. You live there, too?"

"Next door. The Spanish-style building."

"Ah, yes." She nodded. "I was staring at your place. I was admiring your garden."

The explanation satisfied me, and she and my mother left.

I didn't text Summers. I didn't call him, either. I asked Sierra to accompany me to Hugh Ashbluff's office, but she was supremely busy at the café. I messaged my grandmother and explained my plan. She had time. No library events were scheduled until later. She took the reins and made an appointment with Hugh. We arrived at four.

"Welcome." Hugh spread his arms wide as he ushered us into the office. He repositioned two chairs that abutted the wall in front of his desk. "Sit, please."

My grandmother remained standing. I did, too. I noticed her taking in the photos, the diplomas, and the Louisville slugger on the wall.

"Lissa says you've changed your mind, Emma." Hugh rounded his desk but also remained standing. "You're ready to invest."

"Mr. Ashbluff—"

"Hugh." He adjusted his paisley bowtie.

"Sir, I had a chat with Naomi Clutterbuck today."

His face went ashen. He sank into the chair. It squeaked beneath his weight.

"She said you were with her on the night Willow was killed."

"You're not here to look at properties?"

I shook my head. "Don't worry. I'm not going to tell her husband, but I imagine the police will if what I heard from Indy Hendriks about your finances proves to be true. She said you took out a sizable loan at a Wells Fargo bank in San Jose."

His eyes widened. "How would she—"

"She was there. On business. She heard you. Is there something weird going on with all the houses you flip? Subpar contractors and the like?"

He groaned. "It has nothing to do with the houses. They're in good shape. I haven't cut corners. In fact, that's the problem. I've made sure each project is the best of the best. Carmel and the surrounding areas deserve quality construction. I go the extra mile."

My grandmother said softly, "Meaning you've gone into debt." She perched on one of the chairs.

"Yes."

I said, "Did you siphon off money from one project, hoping to pay off the other with the proceeds, but you couldn't get square by month's end?"

"Yes." He rolled his eyes. "Borrowing from Peter to pay Paul, they call it. The loan from Wells Fargo is a bridge loan, but even with that, I'll be short." He pushed a stack of folders out of the way, dramatically propped his arms on the desk, and held his head with both hands.

"Willow knew," I said. "She was going to tell the authorities."

He released his head and peered at me, his eyes brimming with tears. "She threatened to, but she wouldn't have. She wasn't a vindictive woman. She was passionate and altruistic, but not vindictive. You have to believe me, I didn't kill her. I was with Naomi that night. We've been keeping our relationship on the down-low. I need time to figure out how to support her in the way to which she is accustomed. Her husband went out of town last Tuesday, giving us time to take an overnight trip. We went to Post Ranch Inn. It's located up the coast. We drove up after our respective dinners."

"When did you arrive?"

"Around eight thirty. We spent the next twenty-four hours talking seriously about our relationship. She said she wanted to tell her husband about us and suffer the consequences. I told her she shouldn't. She said we could live cheaply. I begged her to give me more time to get my act together. It's a matter of pride." He picked up his cell phone and swiped through photos. He displayed the phone screen to us. "These are pictures of us. In the meditation pool. Dining in Sierra

Mar. The food was some of the best I'd ever eaten. And here we are later on taking a private yoga class." He offered me the phone.

I checked each of the photos, which, like Naomi's, were time-stamped. The first was of them in the meditation pool—9:00 p.m. The second, in the restaurant—9:27. The third, both dressed in exercise clothing—10:15. If the coroner was right and Willow was killed between eight and ten, there was no way Hugh would have been able to drive to town to murder her and do all these things. He wasn't guilty.

My grandmother rose, moved to him, and rested her hand on his shoulder. "Talk to your father, Hugh. He will help you."

"He wants nothing to do with me. I'm a loser in his eyes."

"He's one of my best patrons. I happen to know how much he loves you. Bury your pride and call him."

# Chapter 24

Ursula was sitting in an armchair in the spa's reception area when I entered. She was dressed in a spa robe and slippers and flipping through a magazine. A cup of steaming herbal tea sat on the table beside her chair.

"Give me a sec," I said. I'd seen her name on the appointment book earlier. She'd scheduled an aromatherapy session, but with the hoopla about Hugh, I'd nearly forgotten. I went to my office, dumped my purse, kissed Vivi on the nose, and returned.

Jason said to me sotto voce, "Meryl prepared the room for you."

Bless her. I had to give her a raise. "This way," I said to Ursula. "I'm glad you could come in."

"I cannot wait."

I settled her in the room and began my spiel. "What brings you in today? Are there any specific things you'd like to address through aromatherapy?"

"I have heard it is good to try every kind of treatment. This is one I have not experienced."

"I appreciate your open mind."

"Did you arrange for advertising like I advised?"

"It's in the works. Now let's focus on you."

For the next few minutes, I asked whether she had any medical conditions or allergies I needed to be aware of. She didn't.

"I am not a slave to medicine," she said flatly.

I didn't consider medicine a bad thing, but those who didn't believe in it could be adamantly against it. "Do you have any scents you like a lot?"

"As you know, patchouli."

"Patchouli is wonderful," I said. "It relaxes the mind and boosts your libido."

"What is this libido?"

"A psychic drive or energy."

"Ah, yes. It does boost that." She beamed.

"Is there anything that worries you right now?" I asked. "Any mental concerns? Perhaps we could address those in this session."

"My business struggles. I do not have as many clients as I need."

"You should advertise," I joked.

"Ha-ha. No, really, I am concerned. People are becoming wary of truth telling. There are lies everywhere. It is difficult to make my clients trust me. Because of this, my confidence is waning."

I invited her to lie on the massage table and switched on the vaporizer. During the session, I would introduce her to the self-confidence essential oils blend I'd created using the scents of orange, bergamot, cedarwood, and coriander. Orange because it was uplifting, bergamot because it was emotionally fortifying, cedarwood because it helped calm the nerves, and coriander because it stimulated cognitive abilities.

"Inhale the scent," I said as I moved to her head. I rubbed a drop of the oil on her forehead and massaged it in. "You are amazing. You have more potential than you realize."

A few minutes passed, and I sidled to her right hand, where I repeated the oil-massage routine. "Remember to recognize your achievements, no matter how small."

I rounded the table to her left hand. "You own your destiny. You can create the future you dream of."

By the time I reached her feet, forty-five minutes had elapsed. I rubbed oil into the tops of her feet as well as the soles. "You are resilient and capable and deserve all the happiness this world can offer you."

She sighed.

I said, "How do you feel?"

"At peace."

"Excellent. You may sit up now."

Ursula did and swung her legs over the side of the table. "Emma, that was the best therapy I have ever had. I feel refreshed and powerful. I must do this regularly. Before I forget, the Happy Diggers say hello. Do you know them?"

"A few. Our neighbor Dottie, of course. And I met Hattie at a book club."

"They are wonderful ladies. Hattie is one of my clients. She is, how do you say, a hoot." Ursula slid off the table and ruffled her hair with her fingertips. "It is good they are patrolling the area around us. I hear from another fortune teller that there is an evil spirit lingering."

"Literally?" A shiver shimmied down my spine.

"If you believe in such things."

After Ursula paid for her treatment, Jason beckoned me. "She's in the café waiting for you."

"She who?"

"Ginnie Sperling, Willow's mom. I thought you had a date."

I shook my head.

"Huh," Jason said. "I've got to get better at reading people."

The café wasn't very busy. We didn't serve dinner. One table held two people sipping tea. At another, a single person was drinking a smoothie and reading a book. A server was wiping down the counter. I caught sight of Sierra through the pass-through window. She waved. I made a beeline for Ginnie, who was seated at the far end of the café.

"Hello," I said.

"Hi, Emma." She was dressed in black. Her demeanor was somber. On the table in front of her was a cup of green tea and a black-bound book.

"This is a surprise." I sat in the chair opposite her. "What's up?"

"I found this." She nudged the book toward me with one finger. "Or I should say the movers did. Between the mattresses of Willow's bed. It's a diary. Read it."

I opened to the first page. In elegant italics it said: *This book belongs to Willow Shafer.*

Ginnie motioned. "Turn to the blue Post-it flag."

I did.

*Day 2: I've never been so at peace. The air is crisp. The scenery stunning. I love Arizona. The way the sun graces the mountains in the mornings and the evenings is breathtaking. Namaste Retreat is everything it claimed it would be.*

"This must have been written when she went on sabbatical," I said.

"Her writing explains a lot," Ginnie replied. "Read on"—she pointed—"yellow flag."

I turned to that page.

*Day 3: We sleep on a mat in an empty room with 10 other women. We have gym lockers where we stow our mats, a blanket, 2 robes, and a shawl.*

*Each morning we awaken at 4 a.m. and spend 4 hours meditating. The rest of the day we are in classes studying ancient literature or we are working the chore rotation. Sometimes we and the other sisters travel to serve and prepare meals for the underprivileged or homeless.*

"Sounds like she was enjoying a life of service," I said.

Ginnie frowned. "It's always *we* this and *we* that. Who is the *we*?"

"Perhaps it's the communal way of addressing themselves."

"Turn to the lavender flag."

I did.

*Day 8: The sisters say we are part of the New Age. The awakening to mysticism and holism. Our favorite time is when we make the honey. It is an integrated approach to train the sisters to care for bees using intuitive beekeeping practices while fine-tuning our own intuitive natures. We open hives. We cultivate the colonies and understand their needs. It's mind-blowing. All of our devotional practices are to honor the Great Mother and the Divine Feminine.*

"And now the green flag."

I obeyed.

*Day 10: Today we allowed the sister superior to guide us in a meditation and chakra alignment. I found great solace in it.*

I closed the book and gazed at Ginnie.

"It was a cult," she murmured. "It had to be."

"I disagree. I think it was a place run by women to empower women."

"Chakra alignment!" Ginnie spanked the table. "What is that?"

Her vehemence surprised me and a few others in the café, who stared.

Gently, I said, "It's a meditational way to unblock the energy of the body to allow it to flow freely through you."

"Is this the reason my daughter lived a spartan life?" She tapped the book. "Is this why there was a lack of worldly goods at her house?"

"Ginnie, calm down. She didn't stay in that world. She didn't devote herself to the retreat for life," I assured her. "Willow returned to Carmel to attend to her business." I recalled Willow saying that she wouldn't come to me for a chakra cleansing or gemstone reading because she'd had enough. It wasn't *her thing* anymore. The glowing reports in the diary were just moments in time. Views changed. People moved on.

"I'm wondering if this retreat is where her money was going," Ginnie said. "You remember those entries coded with seven thousand in her accounting books? What if this . . . group . . . made her sign some kind of contract when she got there and demanded she pay them, month to month, even after she left?"

"The payments weren't identical. They varied. I don't think they were for rent."

"What about blackmail?"

"For staying at a retreat?" I waved a hand. "No. I can't see it, and most likely blackmail would be a consistent rate." At least that was my guess. Who knew? If only I could find out more about Namaste Retreat. "Hold on," I said, as a notion occurred to me. "Do you remember a picture of Willow and another woman on her desk at Mystic Waters? Both were dressed in beekeeper outfits."

"I do."

"What if the woman is the other half of *we*? If I can track her down, I could get more of the story. Have you read the entire diary?"

"No."

"She might be mentioned by name. Let me peruse it." I raised it, retaining possession.

"No, please. I need it back. I can't . . ." She sighed. "I can't part with it."

"I understand." I handed her the book. "I'll find her somehow. I'll even go to the retreat if I have to." I was certainly no Philip Marlowe, but over the course of the past few days, I was learning how to ask questions and dig deeper. "You know, when we were in college, Willow wrote down names and dates on the backs of photos."

"She got that from me. I'm obsessive about it."

"Maybe she did the same on that one. Did the movers pack up the spa yet?"

"No. Just the items in her house. I plan to tackle the spa tomorrow. I have to decide what to keep and what to sell. I'd do it tonight, but my husband and daughter have driven down. We're going to dinner to process it all." She sounded exhausted.

"How about I go to the spa on your behalf?"

"You would do that?"

"Sure."

"That would be kind of you. If I never had to enter the building again, I'd be relieved." She pulled the keys from her purse and handed them to me. "Here."

"By the way, your . . ." I hesitated, weighing whether it was wise to tell her about Floyd, but I felt I owed her the truth. "Your ex-husband is in town, or he was."

She wheezed. Her face went pale.

"He has been using an alias—Floyd Marblemaw."

"That was his best friend's name."

"He asked to interview Willow and me for an article he was writing, and he sought us out. He didn't reveal to either of us who he was. I think, by spending time with Willow, he hoped to get to know her better. I figured out his cover story, though. When I confronted him, he was very ashamed. He said he was sorry he'd abandoned you. He claims he has been in treatment."

Her gaze narrowed.

"Willow confided to him, not knowing his identity, that he was the reason she went searching for herself," I went on. "She didn't want to disappoint her family, should she have one, the way he had."

"Should she have one." Ginnie began to cry. "Now she never will."

At the end of the day, I found the courage to go to the precinct. Not alone. I wasn't that daring. I asked my grandmother to join me. She was a respected elder of the community and on a par with Detective Summers.

I'd never walked inside the precinct. The modern cream-colored building was located on Junipero Street at 4th Avenue. Nana Lissa was waiting for me in the foyer. "Merryweather Rose of Song has accompanied me," she whispered. "She'll give you courage."

I hoped she was right.

My grandmother hugged me, then held me at arm's length. "You look lovely. Formidable."

Dressed in yoga pants and an otter-themed T-shirt, my tawny hair swept into a clip, I knew I looked anything but formidable, but I had slipped the stones Aunt Sophie sent me into the interior pocket of my pants, and Merryweather was supposedly nearby, so I stepped forward with confidence and addressed the reception clerk through the bulletproof window.

"Is Detective Summers in? I'm Emma Brennan, and this is—"

"Lissa Reade," the clerk said. "Nice to see you."

"You, too, dear."

"I really enjoyed the poetry reading two weeks ago."

"It was lovely, wasn't it?"

The clerk nodded. "Do you have an appointment?"

"We do not," Nana replied. "It's about the Shafer murder. We have information."

The clerk pressed a button and spoke to Detective Summers. He asked her to bring us to his office.

It looked as I had expected. Plain and utilitarian with a few framed commendations on the wall. Summers appeared unofficial as always in a polo shirt and tan slacks. I wondered if he ever donned a uniform or even a sport jacket.

"Good evening, ladies. Lissa, I intend to pick up those books I have on hold at the library. Is that why you're here?"

My grandmother laughed in a warm yet sassy way. "You know it's not."

Summers genuinely smiled. "Sit." He gestured to two chairs opposite his orderly desk. "What've you got?" He sat in his chair and folded his arms on the desk, fingers tented.

I told him about Hugh having a verifiable alibi.

"He was never on my radar," Summers said. "What else?"

I explained that a reporter who was using an alias, Floyd Marblemaw, was Willow's father, which I'd figured out because of the photograph that fell from his notepad holder. "He has an alibi, as well. He claims he was staking out Eudora Cash's house, hoping to get a scoop on her new book."

My grandmother said, "He told us he discarded some Twinkie wrappers, and Brady did find a few. He is house-sitting while his parents are in New York. However, none of the neighbors could corroborate seeing Mr. Marblemaw."

"No, Lissa, say it ain't so." Summers worked his tongue inside his cheek. "You're not in on this investigating gig with her, are you?"

I bristled. "My name is Emma."

"I know full well what your name is, Ms. Brennan." His gaze

grew steely. "What would the motive be for this person who calls himself Floyd Marblemaw, if, indeed, he didn't have someone who could place him elsewhere?"

"At first, I thought he wanted the scoop on Willow, and she turned him down, and if that had cost him his job at the *Pine Cone*, he'd held a grudge. But that reasoning felt weak. And then it turned out he didn't even have a job there. He lied."

Summers listened attentively.

"Then I theorized that he might have hit on her and she rejected him, which angered him. However, when I learned he was her father, I was convinced that all he wanted to do was get to know her. Being a long-suffering man, he didn't have the gumption to tell her the truth."

"What other leads do you have?"

Nana Lissa said, "Do you really want to hear, Dylan, or are you appeasing us?"

"I would never think to appease you, Lissa, and to be frank"—he leaned back in his chair and heaved a sigh—"my team and I have been running into a brick wall."

My grandmother said, "Go on, Emma."

"Well, we've ruled out Hugh and Floyd, and we've eliminated Ava Daft, after Nana confirmed her alibi. For a moment, I'd wondered if her partner—"

"I've spoken with Ms. Obermeyer," Summers cut in. "She met with an attorney on the night in question, and I've confirmed her alibi."

"Good," I said. "I'm glad." I liked Quinlyn. "That leaves us with Indy Hendriks and Palmer Pilsner. I'm presuming you received the text message I sent about Indy's scalp treatment incident and the fallout from that?" *Literally, the fallout,* I thought, trying not to snicker at the unintended pun.

He shook his head. "Honestly, Ms. Brennan?"

"Emma, Dylan," Nana Lissa said. "Call her Emma."

He squinted one eye. "Emma, you know very well Ms. Hendriks has an alibi."

"Yes, but what if she killed Willow, quickly changed clothes at her shop, and raced to the bridge game to establish it? Or what if she and Palmer planned the murder together? What if Indy was staking out the place and alerted Palmer when I left? Palmer says she was home watching TV, but she can't prove it."

He noted that on a pad on his desk.

"Do you suspect anyone?" I asked. "Have you checked with others who wanted to lease the Mystic Waters space?"

"We've interviewed many of them. They all have alibis."

"What about an ex-boyfriend named Bruno Bonzini? He goes by Bonzo."

"He's in Europe touring with a band."

Wow. Europe? Touring? He'd actually made a career with his music? I pushed thoughts of him aside. "There was a computer geek Willow dated, about forty years old, from Silicon Valley."

"Deceased earlier this year. Heart attack. We've reached out to everyone in Ms. Shafer's contacts app."

"You've been thorough, Dylan," Nana Lissa said.

"I always am."

I said, "Willow has some entries in her accounting books that are questionable."

"Our team is on it. Thank you for your theories." The detective rose to his feet and started for the door. "Now, please leave, and don't worry your—"

"OMG, Dylan!" Nana Lissa popped to her feet. "You weren't going to say what I think you were going to say, were you?"

I tamped down a nervous giggle. Had my grandmother actually said *OMG* out loud?

"What did you think I was going to say?" he asked.

"Don't worry your pretty little head."

Summers looked sheepish. "No, ma'am. I would never."

*Oh, yes, he would,* I mused.

He splayed his hands. "I was going to say . . ."

My grandmother folded her arms and leveled him with a stern gaze.

He puffed out air. "C'mon, Lissa. You know me. Tell your granddaughter that's not the kind of man I am. I work with women. I've even consulted a non-pro like Courtney Kelly, if necessary. Forgive me."

She grinned. "You're forgiven. For now."

I stood up and said sweetly, "And, sir, don't *you* worry your . . ." I let the rest of the sentence hang in the air as I exited the room.

When my grandmother and I stepped outside the building, she cradled me in a warm hug. "You were superb. Your closing line was spot-on. You can thank Merryweather."

"Why?"

"She sprinkled you with a confidence potion."

I touched my hair to see if I might feel the potion. I didn't. Oh, well, at least Detective Summers knew I wasn't a pushover. That was something.

# Chapter 25

I thanked my grandmother for her support and thanked Merryweather, as well, if she was still hovering around, and then paused at the corner, pondering my next move. I needed to return to the spa to fetch Vivi, but the question Ginnie had asked preyed on my mind: Who was the *we* Willow had referred to in her diary? Should I have mentioned her to Detective Summers?

Before it became too dark, I decided to go to Mystic Waters to look for answers. On my way, I consulted an online directory and found the telephone number for Namaste Retreat in Arizona. I dialed it and reached a recording that the sisters were meditating. I left a message and asked one of the sisters to return my call.

Mystic Waters wasn't lit when I arrived. The blackout paper had been removed from the windows, but the interior was dark. A *To Let* sign hung in the window. How many interested tenants had contacted Hugh by now? I twisted the key in the lock, stepped inside, and flicked a switch on the wall. In the soft lighting, even with a room full of furniture, the place felt eerily empty. I didn't detect the scent of the white sage smudge candle, and there was no ambient noise. I noticed the photographs of the retreats on the walls and wondered if one might be Namaste. None had captions identifying them.

I strode to the office, switched on the lights, checked the photos of retreats that hung on those walls, and came up with the same result—no captions. I crossed to the desk and pulled the photo of Willow and the other woman in beekeeper outfits from its frame. I peeked at the back. As I'd hoped, Willow had written *B and me,* with a date from last year, when Willow had been on sabbatical. I flipped the photo over and studied the faces. Even through the uniform's veil, the woman—*B*—looked blissful. Her smile was beatific, and her eyes were a luminescent silver-gray, as if she had no melanin in her irises. Sadly, those attributes didn't give me a clue as to her identity. I was reinserting the photo into the frame when I heard a *clack*. I spun around. Was someone else in the spa?

With my heart butting my rib cage, I raced to the office door, frame in hand, and peered out. I didn't see anyone. No shadowy figure ducked behind the reception desk.

Something went *clack* again. To my left. In the office. I peeked behind the door and started to giggle. A room air conditioner had kicked on. I was surprised to see it. Carmel had such a moderate climate, nobody installed them.

I exited the spa, closed and locked the front door, and hurried to Aroma Wellness wondering whether I would ever find closure for Willow.

As I was entering, Meryl strolled into the reception area, escorting a mature Asian woman. "Hi, Emma," Meryl said. "I'd like you to meet my mother." Like Meryl, her mother had tattoos on her upper extremities and blue ombré hair. "Mom is a comedienne, too. In Los Angeles. She's way more popular than I am. She rocks it at the Comedy Store. Her sense of humor is like a ray of sunshine on a cloudy day."

"I paid her to say that," her mother quipped.

"No, really, I dream of being her one day." Meryl blew her mother a kiss.

"It's nice to meet you, ma'am," I said.

"I'm not *ma'am* to anyone." She fanned the air. "Call me Mah."

"That's really her name," Meryl explained. "Mah."

"Mah," I said. "You're welcome anytime."

Meryl grinned. "Emma, we're heading out. Need anything before we go?"

"Yes. Where's Jason?"

"Oh, him!" She blew a raspberry. "He quit. He got hired to write the true-crime story of a murderer in some town near San Jose."

"No word of warning? No two weeks' notice?" I asked.

"Receptionists. They're a dime a dozen."

"Wrong. Finding the ideal person is a challenge." I loathed the idea of another search.

Meryl tilted her head. "Your breathing is ragged. Are you okay?"

"Yes," I lied. I wasn't.

"What's that thing in your hand?"

I showed her the picture. "It's of Willow and a friend. I couldn't fit the frame into my purse."

Impishly, she said, "Hey, how do you know the painting was innocent?" She waited a beat. "It was framed."

I groaned.

Her mother punched her in the arm.

"Ow, Mom!" She grinned at me. "Admit it, Emma, you're probably going to tell that joke to two friends." She flapped both hands. "Don't worry. No more corny jokes. Mom and I are off to catch my friend's gig. She's doing a bit on self-awareness."

"To know yourself, you must sacrifice the illusion that you already do," Mah said.

"Gee, Mom, who knew you were so deep?"

"I didn't come up with that. A Ukrainian poet did."

"You and your quotes." Meryl rolled her eyes. "Back to my

friend. I hope she's funny. It's her first time onstage. She's so nervous."

"Nerves are necessary and positive," her mother said. "Tension is a sign that you're doing something that you're passionate about."

"I think you mixed up that quote," Meryl said.

"Maybe," her mother said, guiding Meryl out the exit. "It's the thought that counts."

I retreated to the office. Vivi was purring contentedly when I picked her up, as if she'd truly enjoyed her day at the spa. I wondered if it was the gentle music or the aromas of lavender and rosemary that had appealed to her. I deposited her into her carrier and wedged the photograph into the side pocket.

As we were crossing the patio to take the stairs to the street, I spotted Yoly in the gift shop. She was talking to Sierra, who was clad in a cute outfit, as if she were ready to go on a date. I joined them.

"Why are you still here, Yoly?" I asked. "Is your sister okay?"

"She's fine. She blew a tire." She motioned to a pile of boxes. "I'm staying a little longer because we got a shipment of crystals. I wanted to rearrange the display cases while it was quiet."

"And I came in," Sierra said, "because I want a crystal that will boost my self-esteem."

Yoly turned to me. "You're the expert. Advise her."

"Aunt Sophie is the expert," I said.

"Mom is off the grid." Sierra pushed her long hair over her shoulders. "I can't get hold of her."

"Why do you need to boost your self-esteem? You're beautiful. Your café is a hit."

"I'm plagued by thoughts of self-doubt and the fear of failure."

I studied her. "Are you channeling me?"

"Ha! As if. You are my idol."

I gestured at her date-night getup. "Are your emotions running amok because of the guy you're seeing? Is he making you feel 'less than'?" I mimed air quotes around the term.

She shook her head, but the shaking morphed into bobbing.

"Drop him," Yoly ordered.

"I agree," I said.

"C'mon," Sierra pleaded. "Help me out."

"Okay." I reached into the display case and produced two stones. "Tiger's eye engages the crown chakra, which enhances mental clarity. Carnelian is one of the most effective crystals for confidence. It interacts with the root, sacral, and heart chakras."

I set the stones on a velvet mat on the counter. As Sierra deliberated between the two, I caught sight of postcards we'd made depicting the courtyard. We didn't sell them. We offered them free to customers. Seeing them, however, made me think of the postcard with the word *die* on it that someone had shoved beneath the shop's door, and I wondered aloud, for the umpteenth time, who had delivered them. "If it was Palmer—"

Sierra cut in. "On your suspect board, in the office—"

"What suspect board?" Yoly asked.

I explained.

*"Ooh."* Yoly silently clapped her hands. "Courtney does the same thing. She writes down everything on a dry erase board. You should talk to her. She's really smart when it comes to sorting through ideas."

I hoped I was equally wise.

"On the board," Sierra continued, "you noted that Palmer was a strong tennis player."

"She sure can swing a tennis racket," I said.

"Being strong doesn't make someone a killer," Yoly countered.

"Nana Lissa said having a temper doesn't make someone a murderer, either, but . . ." I thought about Indy coming in to tell me about Hugh's financial issues, which had proved a non-starter. Had she confided in me to roil the waters? To divert suspicion from her or her good friend Palmer? Were they a team, as I'd theorized? I remembered shivering when she said: *Palmer said Willow was too curious for her own good. Maybe you are, too.*

"What is Palmer's alibi?" Yoly asked.

"She was watching reruns of *Jeopardy!*" Sierra said, raising the stone into the air the same way Olivia had earlier, and a thought scudded through my mind.

"The television!" I cried.

"What about it?" Sierra asked.

"When I ran into Indy and Palmer at Percolate, Olivia was carping at her mother because the television and computer weren't working. A few minutes later, when Palmer offered up her alibi, the searing look Olivia gave her could have scorched fields. At the time, I didn't make the connection."

Yoly's eyes widened.

Sierra shook her head. "I'm sure the Pilsners own more than one television. Olivia had to have been upset about something else. Or she needs glasses, and you mistook a searing look for squinting."

I pictured Olivia's eyes and another thought came to me. They were nothing like the beekeeper *B*'s eyes, but they were similar enough that it made me wonder whether the woman in the photograph could be Olivia's sister, Alexandra. I explained my theory to my friends.

"What picture are you referring to?" Sierra asked.

I pulled it from the cat carrier and removed the photo from the frame. "See this woman's eyes? Olivia's are soft gray."

Sierra inspected it. "Willow wrote *B and me* on the back, not *A and me*."

"Right. Olivia told me her gramma's name was Beatrice," I said. "What if Alexandra received the middle name Beatrice, in honor of their grandmother, and now she goes by the initial B." Another idea sparked. "Willow and this woman, who I'd bet is Alexandra, were at a retreat. What if Alexandra stayed even though Willow left? What if Palmer blamed Willow for introducing her daughter to an ascetic life"—abounding with meditation, I mused—"that would keep her away forever?"

"You're grasping at straws," Sierra countered.

"I want to go to Palmer's. Now."

"Why?"

"I want to see a picture of Alexandra and compare it to this one."

"Let's be reasonable and look for her online instead." Sierra tugged her cell phone from her pocket and typed in Alexandra's name. Nothing came up. She tried spelling the girl's name a different way with two Xs . . . two Ns . . . two Ds. Nothing.

"Add a B as the middle initial," Yoly suggested. "For Beatrice."

Sierra complied. "Zilch. Crud." She snapped her fingers. "High school yearbook." She typed in Carmel High School graduating class pictures and landed on an Ancestry.com site, which required that she create an account. Giving up, she said, "Let's call the police."

"The police don't want to hear my theories," I said. "Trust me."

# Chapter 26

Yoly begged off going with us to Palmer's house. She lived with her sister, cousins, and grandparents, and it was her turn to make dinner. Thankfully, Sierra bowed out of her date and joined me. A half hour later, after dropping Vivi off at the fourplex, we approached Palmer's two-story home.

"What if she's not here?" Sierra asked.

"I see silhouettes of people upstairs and downstairs."

Through gauzy curtains, in a room to the far right on the second floor, I could make out the profile of a lithe female dancing. Olivia, I determined. Downstairs, another person—female, telling by the silhouette—was sitting idly in what had to be the living room. The linen drapes made it impossible to see through the plate-glass window and determine who it was, but I presumed it was Palmer.

"What do you plan to say?" Sierra whispered. "We're going off half-cocked, and you know me. I don't do anything unprepared."

"Yes, you do. You cook without using a recipe."

She gave me the side-eye.

An idea came to me. "I know what I'll do. I'll tell Palmer what went down with Hugh today. After all, Indy came to me with the tidbit about his finances. They're besties. I might as well loop in Palmer as to the outcome."

Sierra clucked her tongue. "You're a lousy liar."

"Can you think of something better?"

"At least tell her you tried to reach Indy first, but she didn't answer her phone."

"Good idea." I rang the doorbell. It bonged loudly. I flinched.

"All smiles," Sierra prompted. "We're not accusing anyone of anything." She smoothed her hair which had tangled on our walk.

"Coming!" yelled Olivia—I recognized her voice. She ran down the staircase, her footsteps making her sound as big as an elephant. She peeked through the peephole. "Mom, Emma and somebody are here for you!" Telling by the pounding feet, she was already sprinting back up the stairs to her room.

I frowned. So much for answering the door and politely saying, "Hi."

After what seemed like an eon, Palmer opened the door. She was dressed in tennis togs, her hair secured off her face with hair clips. In her hand, she held a pair of scissors. "What's up?"

"May we come in?" I asked. "This is my cousin Sierra."

"I know who she is," Palmer said. "The health food nut. What do you want?"

"Indy came to the spa today with a tip about Hugh Ashbluff. I followed up, and after learning some juicy details, I went to the police. I thought you'd like to know since I couldn't reach Indy."

She motioned for us to enter. "Is Hugh the one who killed Willow?"

"No, he's not guilty. He's got a solid alibi."

"Poor Willow," she said. "Will she have no justice?"

She guided Sierra and me into the living room, an expansive

space filled with a stylish sofa and a variety of overstuffed chairs and ottomans, all arranged for maximum conversation opportunities. A beautiful Persian carpet adorned the hardwood floor. Expensive art hung on every wall. A grand piano stood to the right by the plate-glass window. I didn't realize an insurance statistician made such good money. I supposed he or Palmer could have come from wealth. Nana Lissa hadn't mentioned it.

"Your art is impressive," I said.

"Thank you."

"Are any of them your work?"

"No."

Shelves flanked the fireplace. The leftmost shelves were lined with books. A number of golf trophies and framed photographs were displayed on the rightmost ones. An opened rolltop desk stood at the far end of the room, its ladder-back chair pushed away as if we'd disturbed Palmer while she was doing a bit of business.

"Is that a Jackson Pollock?" I asked, motioning to the piece above the mantel.

"It is."

"I love the Miró over the desk," Sierra said.

"It's a lithograph," Palmer countered, as if apologizing for it.

"Your husband must be quite the golf enthusiast." I gestured to the antique umbrella-stand container that stood to the left of the desk. It was filled with golf clubs, and they didn't look typical. "What kinds of clubs are those?"

"Pete collects old ones. He's got cleeks and mashies and spoons. One's a Simon Cossar putter, circa the late seventeen hundreds."

"Wow," I said, as if I knew who that was. "May I inspect?" Before she could say no, I strode past her, hoping to glimpse the photographs on my way to the clubs. "My mother plays with your husband occasionally."

"Oh," Palmer said. No jealousy. No interest. She regarded her watch. "I have a tennis match in a half hour. You should go."

"Palmer's an artist," I said to Sierra, ignoring the time factor.

"I've seen some of her work at plein-air festivals. She's quite good." It dawned on me that if Sierra could lure Palmer out of the room, I might do my reconnaissance undeterred. I signaled Sierra with a discreet hitch of my chin. "Your studio is in a room behind your garage, isn't it?"

Sierra picked up on the prompt. "You have a studio? I love to paint but can never find the time. To have my own studio would be a dream. Give me a tour."

"I never show my unfinished work." Palmer folded her arms.

Rats. That idea tanked. "Palmer is quite the cook, Sierra. I bet she rivals you."

My cousin threw me a look, but quickly I saw realization dawn in her eyes.

"Care to discuss recipes?" Sierra asked sweetly. "If you share one of yours, I'll share one of mine."

"What could I possibly want to eat that you make?" Palmer asked snottily. "A kale smoothie? Heaven forbid."

"How about lasagna alla Massimo Bottura? Massimo is a good friend of my mother's, and a—"

"Three-star Michelin chef," Palmer exclaimed, for the first time showing interest. "We went to his restaurant in Moderna two years ago. Come this way."

Sierra peeked at me over her shoulder with a look of triumph as Palmer guided her out of the room.

Quickly, I scrutinized the photographs on the bookshelves and saw a picture of what I guessed was Olivia and her older sister, Alexandra, who was, indeed, the woman in the beekeeper's outfit. There was no mistaking those luminescent eyes.

I heard Sierra laughing hysterically. What a ham. She was probably doing her best to make Palmer feel witty.

My gaze drifted to the right and paused on an array of postcards that were strewn on the rolltop desk. I inched closer. Each was a depiction of a different piece of art. Some were impressionistic while others were—a gasp escaped my lips—avant-garde splatter.

"Holy moly," I whispered. I'd ruled out Palmer or Indy having slipped the threatening postcards under the spa doors because neither would have wanted to implicate Palmer. Was I ever wrong. Palmer must have been so enraged with Willow that it had made her careless.

Something beyond the postcards caught my eye, and my pulse kicked up a notch. The door to the cubby in the center of the desk was slightly ajar, and the stamped end of an envelope was jutting from within. The stamp was an image of the Grand Canyon in Arizona and, other than the vibrant colors, identical to a picture hanging in Willow's house. When I'd rung the doorbell, Palmer must have tried to close the cubby door in haste and failed.

I listened to see how Sierra and Palmer were faring. They were still in the kitchen. Discussing herbs. Telling by the feet pounding the floor above me, Olivia was in her bedroom dancing to rowdy music. Quietly, I opened the cubby's door. There were more stamped envelopes. I eased the one with the Grand Canyon stamp out. It was addressed to Olivia and postmarked about ten days ago. There was no return address, but a single letter, *B*, in a fancy scrawl adorned the upper left corner. It was slit open. There wasn't anything inside. I glanced at the trash can beside the desk and saw a crumpled piece of stationery. I retrieved it and read:

*Dear O,*

*Me again. Wish you'd write. I love it here at Namaste. I've found myself. You should visit. I'll show you around.*

*In peace, B.*

Upon closer inspection, I realized that all the envelopes had been addressed to Olivia and all had been opened. Alexandra—*B*—had written her sister repeatedly. Had Palmer kept the letters from Olivia, fearful of what she might do? Palmer had been holding scissors when she'd answered the door. Had she decided it was time to shred each of the letters, but we'd interrupted her?

"What the blazes do you think you're doing!" Palmer ran at me with the scissors.

I *eeked* and seized one of her husband's prized golf clubs. It had a wooden shaft and a knobby bronze head. "Sierra!" I yelled. She didn't answer.

"I knew I couldn't trust you." Palmer closed in on me. "I knew you'd come here on a hunting expedition."

I wielded my defense weapon, which looked nothing like today's golf clubs, and skirted the end table, hoping to put the sofa between Palmer and me. "Sierra!"

Palmer's lips curled into a snarl. "Your cousin is indisposed."

Oh, no. Had she hurt Sierra? I would never forgive myself if something had happened to her. Suddenly, I heard what sounded like a person moaning. It had to be Sierra. She was alive.

I said, "Palmer—"

"Shut up!" She tossed the scissors on the rolltop desk and, like me, snatched one of the clubs. A putter. It looked way more lethal than my piddly weapon.

Palmer rounded the end table waggling the putter like a baseball player warming up at the plate. The light in the room reflected off the flat-edged blade. "You think you're clever. Spying on me."

"Spying?"

"I saw you, your cousin, and your grandmother outside my house Saturday night. You were trying to get dirt on me, weren't you? Admit it."

Aha. She had caught sight of us. Which incited her to retaliate. "That made you so angry, you broke into my place and destroyed things."

"Your cat isn't a very good watchdog. I'd ask your landlord to replace those locks with better ones."

"When did you learn how to use an air wedge?"

"I was a crafty teenager who liked to slip out at night."

As she continued to stalk me, a way to halt her progress came to mind. I yelled, "Alexandra Beatrice Pilsner! That's your daughter's full name, isn't it?"

"How dare you." She swung at me.

I blocked the attack with my club and retreated, bumping into the piano bench. It made a horrid scratching noise on the hardwood floor. I kicked it aside. It toppled and impaired Palmer's forward movement. She cursed.

I said, "B, as she likes to be called now, is at a retreat in Arizona living a life of service."

Palmer scoffed. "Being a slave in a convent isn't service."

"She's staying forever."

"Not if I have anything to do with it."

"Alexandra and you aren't close." I snaked between the piano and the sofa and rounded the other end table. "You have mother-daughter issues like many of us do. When Willow befriended her, you went ballistic."

"Willow." Palmer uttered a *Halloween*-worthy laugh and cut around the bench.

"How did they meet?" I asked, but in an instant, it dawned on me. "Wait, I know. Willow spoke at a high school forum, the one where they invited local women entrepreneurs to describe their success to students." I was in Tibet at the time when Nana sent the article about Willow. "I'm guessing Alexandra introduced herself, and Willow took her under her wing. Mentor-mentee or sister to sister."

"Sister? Are you crazy? She wanted to be my daughter's mother!" Palmer yelled. "She wanted to replace me!"

I heard a toilet flush. Was it Sierra? Was she okay?

"When Willow told your daughter she was going to a retreat," I continued, "Alexandra decided to join her, but she didn't loop you in. She simply left. I imagine she wrote you and your husband a note saying goodbye. Otherwise you would have had the police turning the country upside down looking for her. You didn't have a clue where she went until a letter came for Olivia. You recognized Alexandra's handwriting, saw the *B* in the return address corner, and you opened it. What you read inside incensed you."

Tears pooled in Palmer's eyes. "She said she loved living there. She'd found her path. It broke my heart."

*And your spirit.*

I said, "You didn't tell your husband."

"After she left, he grew cold. He hated me and berated me."

"You blamed Willow for not only influencing your daughter but for ruining your marriage."

"Stop. Talking." Palmer swung the club. It *whooshed.*

"Emma!" Sierra called. She appeared in the archway and screamed.

The music and dancing overhead stopped. Footsteps pounded the floor above.

I could see Sierra out of the corner of my eye, but I didn't dare take my focus off Palmer, who swung again and connected with a very expensive-looking lamp. It shattered and fell to the floor.

"Mom!" Olivia sprinted down the staircase. "Mom, what's going on? Are you all right?" She cut around Sierra and skidded to a stop. "Emma, why are you—"

"Do not call her Emma," Palmer ordered. "You do not know her that well."

"Yes, I do." In her skull-adorned crop top and gym shorts, Olivia looked about twelve years old, but she held herself as proudly as an Amazon warrior goddess. "I went to the shop at Aroma Wellness. Emma taught me about crystals."

"You *what*?" Palmer whirled on her daughter.

The distraction gave me precisely enough time to release my golf club and grab the one Palmer was holding. I wrenched it to the right, forcing her to back into one of the overstuffed chairs. The collision made her lose her footing. She toppled onto the ottoman and pitched head over heels onto the Persian carpet.

"Mom!" Olivia hurried to help her.

Sierra yelled at the top of her lungs, "Palmer! Olivia! Stay put. I called nine-one-one. The police are on their way." She raised her cell phone to show the connection and resumed talking to dispatch, giving Palmer's address.

Palmer began to weep. "Oh, Alexandra. Alexandra. My baby girl."

Olivia tried to cradle her mother, but Palmer pushed her away. Olivia turned to me for an answer.

I fetched the envelopes and crumpled piece of stationery from the rolltop desk.

# Chapter 27

I handed the letters to Olivia and began to tell her the story.

"She's lying," Palmer said, trying to drown me out. "Don't believe a word of it. Alexandra is not in Arizona. She's not living with a bunch of nuns. It's nonsense."

Someone pounded on the front door. "Police!"

Sierra sprinted to let them in.

Detective Summers and Officer Rodriguez trailed Sierra into the room. Rodriguez went to attend to Palmer.

Summers, dressed in black and reminding me of a villain in a spaghetti Western, threw me a lethal look. "Well?"

"Let me explain." I recapped what I'd learned from Willow's diary, which Willow's mother, Ginnie, had in her possession. "It chronicles Willow's time at Namaste Retreat in Arizona. Ginnie was disturbed by the constant use of the word *we* in the diary." I summarized how I'd gone to Mystic Waters to view the photograph of Willow and the woman in beekeeper garb. "On the back of the photo were the words *Me and B.* I guessed she was Palmer's daughter, Alexandra, thinking she might have been given her grandmother Beatrice's name as her middle name and had adopted using the initial. I came here to confirm it, and that's when I saw B's letters to her sister—all had been opened—each sent from Arizona. I believe, after the set-to with Willow at Hideaway Café on Tuesday night, Palmer found a new one from her daughter when she arrived home. The crumpled one Olivia is holding." I motioned to the rolltop desk. "The envelope was postmarked around ten days ago. Palmer opened it, and what she read angered her so much, she couldn't stand it any longer. Seething, she went to Mystic Waters to accuse Willow of coercing her daughter to leave Carmel and start a new life."

"She's lying, Detective." Palmer struggled to her feet and pushed past Rodriguez. "Yes, I went to Mystic Waters to talk to her, but Willow was in no listening mood. In fact, she . . . she came on to me. She backed me into a corner, and she . . . she . . ." Fake tears pooled in Palmer's eyes. "She touched me. I didn't want her to. I told her no, but . . ." Finally, the waterworks began. "I reached behind me for something to defend myself. That's when I grabbed the candlestick."

"Detective Summers," I said, giving him my best *Don't believe her* look. "Willow would never have made a play for Palmer. She liked men."

"She made a pass at my daughter."

"I doubt that," I said. "Willow was an educator. She wanted others to understand and embrace the power of meditation. Your daughter gravitated to that and took Willow's advice." I motioned to the golf club on the floor. "Sir, Palmer attacked me after I found the collection of letters in the desk and confronted her with the truth. I was able to disarm her."

"Ladies, I've heard enough." Summers held up both hands. "Officer Rodriguez, cuff Ms. Pilsner and read her her rights—"

The front door burst open. Nana Lissa entered breathlessly. "What is going on?"

"Lissa," Summers said, "remain outside."

"No, Dylan, I will not. My granddaughters are in here." She eyed me and Sierra. "Yoly texted me about what you two were up to. What were you thinking?"

"Nana," Sierra began.

"Silence, everyone!" Summers barked. "Lissa, please go outside. You"—he aimed a finger at Sierra—"stay put. I'll get to you. As for you, Ms. Brennan . . ." He motioned me to the far side of the room. In a low voice, he warned, "If you ever interfere with one of my investigations again—"

"Sir, pardon me, but in your office, you said you work with women. You even said that you willingly consult a non-pro like Courtney Kelly, if necessary. Did you say that to appease my grandmother?" I watched her retreating figure.

He glowered. "No."

I smiled. "Glad to hear it. She would be disappointed if that were the case. For the record, I doubt I'll ever become involved in another investigation, but if I do, consider me a non-pro who believes in justice. May I be excused? I'd like to comfort my cousin."

"I have more questions."

"I won't leave."

Summers directed his attention to Rodriguez and Palmer, and I rushed to Sierra.

She threw her arms around me. "I'm sorry." She squeezed hard before releasing me.

"What happened to you?" I asked.

"Palmer offered me some coffee, and to be polite, I drank it even though I'm allergic to caffeine. I knew you wanted me to keep her busy."

"You're allergic?"

"Big-time. In a matter of seconds, I was one with the porcelain bowl."

"No wonder you don't want me drinking caffeine."

She knuckled my arm. "If it doesn't bother you, have at it, although it's still bad for your health."

"I hear you."

"But far be it from me to tell you how you should live your life." She clutched her stomach dramatically and moaned. "Wait until we fill Nana Lissa in on all this. She will be proud of you for figuring it out."

"I'm not so sure. Did you see her face? That was not pride. It was . . ." I searched for a word but couldn't come up with one. "She reminded me of my mother."

Sierra blanched and held up two fingers in the sign of the cross. "Do not utter her name."

Laughing, I batted her hand away. "Kate is not a vampire."

"She will suck you dry if you let her."

"Give it a rest. She loves me." I glanced at Olivia, who was nestled in one of the chairs, legs tucked under her rump. She was reading the letters from her sister. Tears—real ones—were trickling down her face. I moved to her and put a hand on her shoulder. "You and your father should visit her."

# Chapter 28

A few days later, Ginnie held a memorial service for Willow at Church of the Wayfarer. Afterward, she asked everyone to convene in the Aroma Wellness courtyard for a reception. All of the employees of Mystic Spa were in attendance. So were Yoly, Meryl, and Mah. My mother and grandmother and a few of her friends came, too. When I asked the receptionist from Willow's spa about Willow's other friends, she said she didn't have any. She'd lived a private life. Willow's birth father, known to me only as Floyd Marblemaw, was in the mix. I also saw Olivia and her father lingering to one side. Palmer's attorney had filed a motion to have her evaluated for competency following the arrest. She'd pleaded not guilty by reason of insanity and was immediately remanded to a mental facility. Olivia had confided to me at the memorial that she'd been in contact with Alexandra, and she and her father were going to visit her next week.

My grandmother sidled to me and slung an arm around my waist. "The array of food is lovely."

Sierra had made a wealth of treats, including a few honey-laced sweets. She was moving among the crowd alongside her waitstaff ensuring glasses were filled and appetites satisfied.

"How are you holding up?" Nana Lissa whispered, giving me a squeeze before releasing me.

"I'm fine. But I'm worried about Willow's mother."

Ginnie was standing beside the well with her husband and their daughter. She was clenching a tissue in one fist and looked bereft. When she spotted me glancing her way, she crossed to me. To give us space, my grandmother joined her friends.

"Thank you for all you have done," Ginnie said. "Willow couldn't have had a better friend."

Despite her reassurance, and although I knew I couldn't have foreseen Palmer's plan, guilt continued to eat at me for not having spent more time with Willow.

"My husband and I ascertained that the money with the seven thousand code in Willow's account was sent to Namaste Retreat to cover Alexandra's expenses. It varied because the expenses weren't constant." She attempted a smile. "To honor Willow's memory, we've decided that whatever is left in her estate will go to the retreat as a grant, even though in her will she stated that everything she had was to go into a college fund for Sissy."

"How gracious of you."

"That won't be necessary," a man said.

We both turned to see Palmer's husband approaching. In a somber black suit and white shirt with dark tie, he looked as dour as a mortician. He jutted a hand and introduced himself to Ginnie. "I will be taking care of Alexandra's needs as pertains to the retreat going forward. It's the least I can do. My child is happy, thanks to your daughter." He hooked a thumb. "Your youngest will flourish with a good education. It's what Willow and Alexandra would have wanted."

Overwhelmed with emotions, Ginnie pressed a hand to her mouth.

After a moment, she spoke through split fingers. "That is very"—her voice caught—"kind."

"I'm sorry for your loss. If only I'd known." He didn't wait for a response. He pivoted, collected Olivia, and left the courtyard.

"Emma!" Meryl tapped my arm. "Am I interrupting?"

Ginnie shook her head, thanked me again, and made her way to her family.

"Mom is thinking of moving here." Meryl arched an eyebrow. "I told her that's fine. However, she can't move in with me. Boundaries." She held up two hands. "Also, no way may she steal my gigs."

I wasn't sure lighthearted humor was appropriate at a memorial, but the gleam in Meryl's eyes made it all right.

"She might want the receptionist job," she added.

"Really?"

"Yep."

"We'll talk. Now, if you'll excuse me, I have to mingle."

Floyd was standing near the gift shop entrance, working the brim of his hat through his fingers.

I moseyed over to him and said, "Take the chance. Say hello to Ginnie."

"I . . ." His gaze focused on his feet. "She hates me."

"No. She's moved on." I gave him a small nudge. "Give her your condolences. She's mourning your daughter."

Like a shy kid at a dance, he shuffled toward her. After a long moment, he found the courage to say something. Ginnie registered his face and burst into tears. He embraced her and, as she sobbed, he exchanged a look with Ginnie's second husband, who nodded compassionately and led Sissy away, leaving the two grieving parents to have their moment.

"Well, this worked out nicely," Kate said, joining me. Dressed in a gray suit, she appeared appropriately grim. "Who knew the courtyard would make the perfect spot for a memorial reception?"

"Or a party," I countered. "We'll be having plenty of parties here in the future."

"It's sobering, isn't it? Death?"

I didn't know how to answer.

"I still don't like the idea of you operating this spa," Kate continued. "It could have been you that Palmer went after."

"Mother, it wasn't the spa business that angered her. It was Willow's relationship with Alexandra. Palmer was jealous. She wanted to be revered. She wanted to be her daughter's adviser and best friend. Sadly, she failed."

"Like me."

I snorted. "Yeah, just like you. *Not.* I love you. You did not fail. We're good. But be honest, you do not want to be my best friend and hear all my secrets, do you?"

"Heavens no!" She laughed.

My grandmother joined us and guided my mother to the buffet table. Over her shoulder she said, "Dinner tonight, Emma. Your place. Sierra's cooking."

"Am I invited?" my mother asked.

Nana Lissa didn't respond.

To my surprise, my grandmother did invite my mother, and to my bigger surprise, Kate showed up with a housewarming gift for me. I figured that was my grandmother's doing. Kate hadn't wanted me to move into the fourplex in the first place. She'd wanted me to move in with her. *As if.*

I opened the gift and found a set of beautiful blue-rimmed Wedgwood china.

"Jane Austen had Wedgwood china," Kate said. "I thought you'd like to own some yourself."

"Thank you."

"Also, if you'll tell me which of your art pieces were broken, I'll be glad to replace them."

I gawked at her, amazed by her largesse. "I'll make a list."

While Sierra plated our dinners, I poured everyone a glass of wine and mentally made a note that I needed proper crystal to go with my new china plates for future get-togethers.

"This way, everyone," Sierra said, leading us outside. She'd installed a couple of tiki torches and lit a number of candles on the table.

"It looks magical," I exclaimed.

"Glad you like it."

Sierra didn't skimp on the meal. She made mushroom risotto, grilled chicken in a luscious lemon vinaigrette, and roasted broccoli. Everything was cooked to perfection. We could cut the chicken with a fork.

"What in the devil is your cat doing?" Kate asked.

Vivi was scampering under and around the daylilies and herbs.

Nana Lissa said, "Why, Kate, she's playing with a fairy."

"Oh, cut it out, Mother," Kate said, and turned to me. "Does Vivi always cavort like she's on catnip?"

"When she's playing with a fairy," I teased.

"Emma and Sierra, my sweet girls"—Nana Lissa raised her glass—"this has been quite an eventful week. I'm proud of both of you for holding it together and pleasing your customers while also negotiating roiling waters. Here's to both of you."

We clinked glasses.

"I didn't have to do much," Sierra said, sipping her wine. "Emma did all the heavy lifting."

Vivi crouched beside an evergreen bush, as if preparing to pounce.

I stared in that direction, and my breath caught in my chest because something was glimmering. Like gossamer. It wasn't a leaf or something that had caught the reflection from the tiki torches' flames. No, it was alive and bigger than a firefly. Bigger than a butterfly, too. Whatever I'd seen ducked out of sight beneath the bush. Seconds later, it burst into the air.

Vivi reared up on her hind legs, trying to swat it.

"Nana!" I exclaimed. "See that?"

The fairy—it had to be a fairy—whizzed away and began giggling. Yes, giggling. She stopped in midair and hovered, wings flapping. She had lily-white skin. She wore a flower bud upside down on her honey-blond hair as a hat. Her yellow-and-green dress matched the colors of her lacy wings, and she sported the most adorable striped stockings . . . but no shoes.

I glanced at my grandmother, and she grinned. It wasn't until Nana Lissa was leaving that I learned the fairy's name was Dewberry, and that she was a nurturer fairy.

Exactly what I needed.

# Epilogue

The last entry from Willow's diary.

*Day 90: time to return to the real world. I am not meant to be a nun. I miss fine food. I miss my friends. I miss going on an occasional date, though I'm going to wait before jumping into the dating pool. Most importantly, I miss helping my clients find peace and serenity while facing real-world issues. That is my purpose. That is who I am. I'll be sad to leave here, but I have learned what I want in life, and that knowledge is beyond amazing. I can't wait to become my best self. Of course, I'll have to watch my acid tongue. The retreat didn't knock that out of me.*

# RECIPES

## Brioche Bread

### Gluten-free Version

*From Sierra:*

*Let me say right off the bat, this is not a seven-grain anything. It's brioche bread and it's simply delicious. It's gluten-free, and for some reason, this is the one bread recipe that I've found that really works with gluten-free flours and still winds up light and fluffy. Enjoy.*

(Yield: 1 loaf, approx. 10 slices)

1 tablespoon dry active yeast
5 tablespoons sugar, divided
¼ cup warm, not hot, water
⅔ cup superfine brown rice flour
1 cup tapioca flour
2 teaspoons xanthan gum
¾ teaspoon kosher salt
4 large eggs, divided 3 for bread, 1 for brushing on dough
9 tablespoons unsalted butter, room temperature, divided

Combine the yeast, 1 tablespoon of sugar, and warm water in a small mixing bowl. Whisk to combine. Let stand until it's foamy, 5–6 minutes.

In the bowl of a mixer, whisk together the brown rice flour, tapioca flour, remaining 4 tablespoons of sugar, xanthan gum, and salt. Make a well in the center and add the yeast mixture.

Put the bowl in the mixer and mix on low speed to combine. Add 3 of the eggs, one at a time, mixing each egg in thoroughly. Add 8 tablespoons of butter, one at a time, mixing after each addition.

Increase the speed to medium and beat for 1–2 more minutes until the dough is smooth.

Scrape the dough into a clean mixing bowl and cover with a tea towel. Let sit in a warm, draft-free place until doubled in size, about 2 hours. *It might not double. That's all right for now. If it looks "more" than doubled, hurray!

Butter a loaf pan with the remaining tablespoon of butter. Make sure you coat it well. Scrape the batter into the pan and smooth evenly using a wet spatula. Cover with the tea towel and let rise again, for 45 minutes. You *may* do a cool rise in the refrigerator. This means letting it rise in the refrigerator for 2–24 hours.

When ready to bake, uncover the pan and let it come to room temperature, about 15 minutes, while the oven preheats.

Preheat oven to 350° F and place the rack of the oven in the lower third.

Meanwhile, cut a slit about ¼ inch deep in the center of the loaf with a wet, sharp knife. Mix the remaining 1 egg with 1 tablespoon water. Whisk. Brush the egg mixture onto the top of the loaf. Let sit 5 minutes.

Brush the loaf again with the egg wash. Bake 40–45 minutes, until the bread is a deep golden brown and it sounds sort of hollow when tapped.

Cool in pan 15–20 minutes. Turn out onto a rack to cool further.

Bread may be sliced and wrapped individually in airtight saran wrap to freeze. Keeps well in the fridge for about 1 week.

## Honey Banana Muffins with Coconut Flour

*From Sierra:*

*I love muffins any time of the day. They're my one weakness. As long as I make them with honey and not sugar, I feel better about eating one. Customers at the café love the mini-muffins because they don't feel guilty eating one.*

(Yield: 10–12 muffins or 20–24 mini muffins)

3 very ripe bananas
⅓ cup honey
¼ cup canola oil
1 large egg
1 teaspoon vanilla extract
1½ cups coconut flour
1 teaspoon baking soda
¼ teaspoon salt

Preheat the oven to 375° F. Set 12 muffin liners (or 24 mini-muffin liners) in a cupcake tin. Set aside.

In a large bowl, mash the bananas with the honey, oil, egg, and vanilla. Add the flour, baking soda, and salt. Stir until well combined.

Divide the batter among 10–12 paper-lined muffin cups, filling them almost full, and bake for 18–20 minutes or until they are golden and springy to the touch. *If making mini-muffins, bake for 16–18 minutes.

Remove from oven and lift the muffins out of the cupcake tin. Set on a wire rack and let cool completely.

May be frosted with a simple drizzle or cream cheese icing.

## Kale-Banana Protein Smoothie

*From Emma:*

*I love this smoothie. Kale isn't for everyone, particularly because it creates a "green" drink and also because it's quite bitter, but in this mix, you don't taste any bitterness. This smoothie keeps me going all day long.*

(Yield: 1 drink)

½ cup chopped ice
2 cups kale, chopped, no stems
¾ cups milk
1 medium-sized banana, chopped
¼ cup plain nonfat Greek yogurt
¼ cup pineapple chunks
1 teaspoon honey
1 tablespoon protein powder (coconut protein powder is great!)
1 tablespoon creamy peanut butter, if desired

Place all the ingredients in a blender and blend until smooth. Easy peasy.

*FYI, I have a Ninja blender, which is the perfect size for making single smoothies. It's powerful and easy to clean.

## Lemon Butter Cookies

*From Lissa:*

*I have a sweet tooth. It's why I'm a good baker. I like to test recipes often. Emma and Sierra's grandfather loved cookies better than any treat, so I made them for him often, rest his soul. The lemon in this cookie is delightful.*

(Yield: 12–16 cookies)

***For the cookie:***
1 stick unsalted butter, softened
½ cup confectioners' sugar
½ tablespoon lemon zest
¾ tablespoons lemon juice, freshly squeezed
1 cup flour
¼ teaspoon salt

***For the glaze:***
¼ cup confectioners' sugar
½ tablespoon lemon juice
½ tablespoon unsalted butter, softened
Finely grated lemon zest for garnish

Preheat the oven to 350° F.

In a large bowl of a mixer, whisk the butter with the confectioners' sugar until smooth. Beat in the lemon zest (finely grated) and the juice, then blend in the flour and salt.

Refrigerate the dough for 30 minutes.

Roll the dough into 1-inch balls. Line a baking sheet with parchment paper and arrange the balls on it. Using your fingers, flatten each cookie to about ¼-inch thickness. These will s-p-r-e-a-d.

Bake for 12–14 minutes, until the cookies are lightly browned and firm.

Let the cookies cool on the baking sheet for 2 minutes. Transfer to a rack to cool.

Meanwhile, make the glaze. In a small bowl, whisk the confectioners' sugar with the lemon juice and softened butter until smooth.

Ice the cooled cookies with the glaze and dust with lemon zest. Let stand until the glaze is set.

These can be stored in an airtight container for 2–3 days. The dough can also be frozen, if desired, and thawed before baking.

## Oatmeal Honey Chocolate Cookies

*From Emma:*

*My grandmother loves to make cookies. As a girl, I loved to help her. And Papa loved eating them. I remember him roaming the kitchen, hovering around the oven until the timer went off. He'd even turn on the light in the oven to watch the cookies bake. How he made me laugh.*

(Yield: 24 cookies)

4 tablespoons butter, melted
1¼ cups quick-cooking oats
1 cup white flour
1½ teaspoons baking powder
1½ teaspoons cinnamon powder
½ teaspoon salt
¼ cup applesauce, no sugar added
1 large egg
1 teaspoon vanilla extract
½ cup honey
⅓ cup dark chocolate chips or carob chips
¼ cup golden raisins

In a small bowl, melt the butter in the microwave, about 30 seconds, and set aside. If you do not have a microwave, put the butter in a small saucepan and melt on low heat. This might take a minute to do.

In a large bowl, whisk together the oats, flour, baking powder, cinnamon, and salt. Set aside.

In a medium bowl, combine the applesauce, cooled butter, egg, vanilla, and honey. Whisk until blended. Pour the liquid mixture into the flour mixture and stir until combined. This is going to be a very wet and sticky dough.

Fold in the chocolate chips (or carob chips) and raisins. Place mixture in the refrigerator and chill for at least an hour and up to 3 days.

When ready to bake, preheat the oven to 350° F. Line a large baking sheet with parchment paper. Remove the dough from the refrigerator and, using a cookie scoop or spoon, drop the dough on the baking sheet. They don't spread so it's all right to have 12 cookies per sheet. If you want, slightly flatten the cookie, but it's not necessary.

Bake the cookies 10–11 minutes, until they are golden around the edges. Cool the cookies for about 3–4 minutes, then transfer to a rack to cool completely.

## Oatmeal Honey Chocolate Cookies

### Gluten-free Version

(Yield: 24 cookies)

4 tablespoons butter, melted
1¼ cups quick-cooking oats, gluten-free if necessary
½ cup sweet rice flour
½ cup tapioca flour
1 tablespoon whey powder
½ teaspoon xanthan gum
1½ teaspoons baking powder
1½ teaspoons cinnamon powder
½ teaspoon salt
¼ cup applesauce, no sugar added
1 large egg
1 teaspoon vanilla extract
½ cup honey
⅓ cup dark chocolate chips or carob chips
¼ cup golden raisins

In a small bowl, melt the butter in the microwave, about 30 seconds, and set aside. If you do not have a microwave, put the butter in a small saucepan and melt on low heat. This might take a minute to do.

In a large bowl, whisk together the oats, gluten-free flours, whey powder, xanthan gum, baking powder, cinnamon, and salt. Set aside.

In a medium bowl, combine the applesauce, cooled butter, egg, vanilla, and honey. Whisk until blended. Pour the liquid mixture into the flour mixture and stir until well combined. This is going to be a very wet and sticky dough.

Fold in the chocolate chips (or carob chips) and raisins. Place the mixture in the refrigerator and chill for at least an hour and up to 3 days.

When ready to bake, preheat the oven to 350° F. Line a large baking sheet with parchment paper. Remove the dough from the refrigerator and, using a cookie scoop or spoon, drop the dough on the baking sheet. They don't spread, so it's all right to have 12 cookies per sheet. If you want, slightly flatten the cookie, but it's not necessary.

Bake 10–11 minutes, until the cookies are golden around the edges. Cool the cookies for 3–4 minutes, then transfer to a rack to cool completely.

## Peanut Butter Maple Protein Bars

*From Emma:*

*There's nothing quite like a protein bar to fill one's appetite. It's like breakfast all in one serving. The added protein powder makes it the kind of treat that will carry me through the morning and long into the afternoon. Sierra is my hero for coming up with this chewy goodness. FYI, these are more like a brownie in texture and not like store-bought bars.*

(Yield: 9–12 bars)

½ cup milk, lactose-free is fine
1 cup peanut butter (chunky is best)
½ cup maple syrup or honey (I prefer syrup)
1 cup whey protein powder, unflavored or vanilla
2 cups whole rolled oats, uncooked *if necessary, the gluten-free kind
1 teaspoon cinnamon powder
½ cup dark chocolate chips
½ cup golden raisins

In a saucepan, combine the milk, peanut butter, and syrup over a low heat. Stir until melted and heated through, 3–4 minutes. Remove from the heat.

Add the protein powder, oats, cinnamon, chocolate, and raisins. Stir to combine. If the mixture is too thick, add 1 teaspoon of milk at a time, but only until it's stirrable. This should be thick, not thin.

Line an 8-by-8-inch pan with parchment paper. Press the mixture evenly into the pan. Allow the bars to cool completely. Once cool, cut into squares. Wrap in an airtight container and store at moderate room temp for several days, or chilled in fridge for a week. These may be frozen if wrapped tightly in saran.

***Alternates:***

May use sunflower butter instead of peanut butter

May use dried cranberries or other small dried fruits instead of raisins.

May omit all add-ins.

## Raspberry-Turmeric Smoothie

*From Sierra:*

*Turmeric is a very healthful and, therefore, helpful spice. Curcumin, the most active ingredient in turmeric, is a strong anti-oxidant and has powerful anti-inflammatory effects. Now, not everyone loves the flavor of turmeric. It can have a very strong currylike flavor. So be delicate as you use it. I like a half teaspoon in my recipe. Some of my customers demand a full teaspoon. Some might prefer a quarter teaspoon. Play with the recipe and decide.*

(Yield: 1 12-ounce drink)

2 tablespoons coconut collagen protein★ (see below)
1 tablespoon MCT oil
2 tablespoons acacia fiber
1 cup milk or almond milk
½ teaspoon turmeric maca powder
¼ cup fresh raspberries
½ cup crushed ice

Place all ingredients in a high-speed blender and blend to the desired consistency.

★I use a coconut collagen protein that is keto certified and paleo friendly. No gluten, refined sugar, dairy, whey, or soy ingredients. Good for your hair, skin, and nails.

★What is MCT oil? It is a flavorless oil made from coconut and provides medium-chain triglycerides.

★Turmeric powder helps boost immunity. The blend I used had Lakadong turmeric, ginger, cardamom, fennel, cumin, coriander, Ceylon cinnamon, black pepper, and cloves.

## Avocado Face Mask

*From Emma:*

*This is the simple face mask that I use and will teach at my first class. It will spoil in a day. Whoever makes it must use it soon.*

1 ripe avocado (about 1 cup, skin removed)
⅓ cup plain yogurt
2 teaspoons honey
1 tablespoon lemon juice

In a blender, mix the avocado, yogurt, honey, and lemon juice until smooth.

Use immediately.

***How to use:***

Wash your face with a light cleanser and pat dry. Apply the mask to your face, but not your eyes or eyelids, and, if desired, apply to your neck. Lie back and let the mask rest on your face for 20 minutes.

Wash the mask off with warm water and then moisturize your face. I like a simple coconut cream moisturizer.

# Acknowledgments

Whenever I write the acknowledgments, it's a challenge, because I don't want to forget a soul. There are so many who have helped me on this journey.

Thank you to my family and friends for all your encouragement. You have cheered me on, through the loss of my sweet husband, the joy of bringing new little ones into the world, and the ups and downs of the publishing business. What a roller-coaster ride, right?

Thank you to my dearest friend, Jori Mangers, for always being there. For listening to me. For "getting" me. You are precious in my life. Yes, English matters!

Thank you to my talented author friend, Hannah Dennison, for your words of wisdom and encouragement. I wish you supreme success in all your endeavors. Thank you to my PlotHatcher pals: Krista Davis, Janet (Ginger Bolton), Kaye George, Marilyn Levinson (Allison Brook), Peg Cochran (Margaret Loudon), and Janet Koch (Laura Alden; Laurie Cass). You are a wonderful pool of talent and a terrific wealth of ideas, jokes, stories, and fun! I adore you. Thanks to my Delicious Mystery author pals, Roberta Isleib (Lucy Burdette) and, yes, Krista Davis. Are you seeing a trend? Krista, you have been a mainstay during my journey. I attribute my choice of writing cozy mysteries to you. You are an inspiration, my friend.

Thank you to my early readers and reviewers. I treasure your insight and your support. Thank you to all the bloggers who enjoy reviewing cozies and sharing my books with your readers. Thanks to Lori Caswell for leading the charge when it comes to blog tours. You are the best.

Thanks to those who have helped make the first book in the

Aroma Wellness mysteries come to fruition: my publisher, Kensington Books; my editor, Elizabeth Trout; copy editor, David Koral; my agent, Jill Marsal; and cover artist, Kristine Mills. Thanks also to Madeira James for maintaining constant quality on my website. Thanks to my virtual assistant, Christina Higgins, for your clever ideas. And many thanks to my stalwart supporter Kimberley Greene. Love you tons.

Special thanks to Kathleen Kaminski not only for being a first reader but for your wonderful and insightful help regarding crystal readings and other spiritual enlightenment pursuits. You are a gem. Also many thanks to Diane Schiller, a masseuse and spiritually enlightened woman, who gives of her heart and soul daily.

Thanks to my adorable dog, Sparky, for sharing your life with me. Also thanks for allowing me to share you on social media and in memes. For being my emotional support. For giving me unconditional love . . . as long as I feed you and take you on walks.

Last but not least, thank you, librarians, teachers, bookstore owners, and readers for sharing the fragrant world of an enlightened entrepreneur in Carmel-by-the-Sea with your friends. I hope you enjoy the magical world I've created. May you encounter a fairy one or more times in your life.